FIRST GLADIATOR OF ROME

THE STORY OF MARCUS ATTILIUS

The Gladiator oath of servitude

Uri, vincri, veberari, ferroque
I will endure to be burned,
to be bound, to be beaten,
to be killed by the sword

DEDICATION

For Lee and Jan

B1 29041952
Cover Art by coverart
Published 2018 Kindle Hardcover
Ebook March 2018

I hold that one is braver at the very moment of death than when one is approaching death. For death, when it stands near us, gives even to inexperienced men the courage not to seek to avoid the inevitable.

So, the gladiator, who throughout the fight has been no matter how fainthearted, offers his throat to his opponent and directs the wavering blade to the vital spot. But, an end that is near at hand, and is bound to come, calls for tenacious courage of soul; this is a rarer thing, and none but the wise man can manifest it.

(Seneca. Epistles, 30.8)

PROLOGUE

CHAPTER 1

Early Augustus 83AD

The Emperor of Rome, Flavius Vespasian, lay resplendent in his purple toga, reclining on a comfortable lounge with his head and shoulders raised at one end on a pillow. As he lay there, he ruminated on an old saying that reverberated in his mind on that calm evening in the palatial villa of the richest man in Rome, Cassius Laurentius.

'*Optimum est pati quod emendare non possis*' kept repeating in his mind as he sipped wine through his thin lips, slightly marked from his days in the legion on campaign and most of it in the hot sun. He wiped his hand across his balding pate, waiting for the dancers to finish.

'It is best to endure what you cannot change' It was true of course, but nevertheless unpleasant. He glanced over his finely crafted cup with his eyes fixed firmly on one of the two dancers who gyrated close to him on the floor. She was a rare beauty and lissom, with those long, muscular legs all the dancers seemed to possess.

He had seen a thousand dancers in his life and in reflection, they all appeared much the same. Long legs and undeniable beauty with supple bodies. His mind shifted from the movement on the floor to the reasons he decided to request the company of the men who sat, fattened and sated, on their seats around him.

The night held important decisions to be made and the three senators that sat across from him, happily residing on their individual lounges, namely, Caius, Sulla and Gratian held the political *gravitas*, to assist him in his quest. On the lounge closest to his sat, ever upright, Cassius Laurentius with his eyes constantly surveying the guests before him.

His mind held a vision that had come to him as he stood outside his tent on the brown sands of Judea with the legion at his back and the scroll that held astonishing news in his hand

His thoughts were broken by a single dancer who moved past him as he

—

4

caught the scent of her perfumed skin. Her eyes were shaded by a thin, red veil but he knew they were not looking directly at him because he had forbidden it and only the God of the underworld, Vulcan, would dare to contradict that decree.

That is, unless he changed his mind and then, he supposed, he would meet the queen of the underworld. In his life, he had very nearly met *Mania* in her shining, black opalescence, several times.

He smiled at Cassius Laurentius who sat on a couch opposite him and he nodded politely back at him. The opulence of his surroundings and the seductiveness of the dancers before him on the terrazzo marbled floor, made persuasive territory for his quest.

His guests were arranged around him on lounges, each speaking their business and political manoeuvrings in lowered tones to each other and eating like horses. But, like all senators and influential businessmen in Rome, they knew the power sat on top of the legs of the couch on which he lay. It was an unassailable power base unless you had a few legions and a liking for bloodshed.

He eyed the men cautiously while keeping a thin smile on his face; a common practice in the great state of Rome and one in which he never forgot the saying his tutor told him, all those years before. It resounded in his mind each day he spent on the hill in the senate and when he rode at the front of the army. '*Imperium in imperio*'.

To be ultimately successful and to gain the highest power one must create an *empire within an empire*. It was his mother, a daughter of an equestrian family who saw his potential. A poor childhood, a career in the army, a little luck and the rest came from the ability to grasp the opportunity of power.

A slave brought an opulent jug across to him to refill his wine as he looked at her admiring her elegance. She was clearly of Nubian birth and the darkest skin on a person he could remember since he was back from the war in the East. He admired her youth without great desire and that, of course, was one of the penalties of growing old and tired.

He thought back briefly. How long was it since that rogue Seneca had been forced to commit suicide at the behest of Nero? Now, that lay a scant year later when that same fat, bulbous, insane emperor set fire to Rome, only to blame it on the Christians.

The awful fire, once committed, was made worse by the news that Nero played the fiddle from the palace whilst watching half of Suburia burn to the ground. Only the Gods might have known what was going through his idiot head at the time. Then, some four years ago, the supposedly safe states of Spain and Gaul rebelled against the utterly insane emperor Nero, and Nero then decided to suicide, rather than fall into their hands. Rumour had it that he wanted his favourite gladiator, Spiculus, to do the job but no one could find him so the poor bastard did it himself.

The reports he heard, albeit second hand, whispered with seeming knowledge that Nero chose that option rather than staying in Rome to be murdered while he slept. Rome burns and then he suicides! By the Gods he was a stupid and insane man and that never constituted a good mix.

Then to make matters worse the butcher of Spain, the governor Galba, decides to make his bid for power and pronounced himself the new Emperor. Vespasian would rather have had Nero at the helm of the sinking trireme of Rome, rather than the man who tried to take it over.

At least Nero was manageable; albeit a little insane. That son of a jackal, Galba was about as worthy an emperor as Nero but Vespasian played his sycophantic part as he waited patiently for some sort of outcome.

The truth of politics, he reflected throwing a large grape into his mouth, was to support those in power with love and relish and then work out how to be rid of them. Politics was never about the greater good. It is simply about power and how to gain it and then how to keep it. The masses, the great Plebeian state, never understood as long as they had grain and circuses.

He sniffed the scented air with his long aquiline nose. The broad countenance of his face and wide spaced eyes looked at ease as he lay back on the pillow behind his head. He looked up at the ceiling, noting a mural he could not remember.

Insanity and politics seemed to go hand-in-hand in Rome and at least he held a stable mind and unerring devotion to his state of Italia, even if his memory for unimportant things remained hazy.

He sighed as he reflected on it. A year after the butcher of Spain made his push for the top job, it changed again. Galba viciously and thankfully murdered by the Praetorian guard mainly because they were not getting paid enough. Then, to make matters worse, the general of the German legions, Vitellius, marched into the country to claim not just the empire but himself as supreme ruler and this happened in the space of four years, which in retrospect, seemed to go by with a blur.

—

6

It was almost as if anyone with a legion behind them could make a claim for the role of emperor. But, he reflected with just a hint of irony, he was no different.

He sighed deeply and retrained his eye onto one of the dancers. In truth, he would rather the night by himself. Unlike many of the political vanguard that held seats in the senate, Flavian Vespasian did not come from royalty or great money or as a child of rich parents but he clearly understood the lessons of his early life.

He was a man of humble beginnings; very humble beginnings and a man who understood the need to keep as close as possible to his enemies which held the specific reason for the meal on this very night. He was taught early, by his dominant and strict mother, that power was only worthwhile if it could be managed and manipulated.

Stationed in the Mount of Olives garrison outside Jerusalem under the relentless heat of that God forsaken country, he remembered sitting inside his command tent, at his cluttered desk, when the scroll was passed to him by a messenger directly from Rome.

He recalled the tent, which suited his humble beginnings, remaining one of the few pleasant memories he held of the shithole known as Judea. He did not like the people, the women were small and stunted, the food almost inedible and everything in the place stank of mistaken, religious superiority.

Save the fact that they held three legions on bivouac and awaiting orders he would have pulled up the tent with his army and headed back to Rome. The legions were dissatisfied and unhappy with their time and the intended siege of Jerusalem, which dragged on and on.

The men were restless and wanting a change and he recalled the heat of the sun as he walked outside the tent on the burning desert sand on that day to read the message. He was astonished and worried when he contemplated the news it held. He remembered his hands shaking with anger when he read the contents of the parchment.

That bastard, Vitellius, had assumed control of Italy and was in the process of proclaiming himself the new man of Rome. If it were not true, it was almost laughable. He had no more chance of managing the Roman empire than Flavian had of climbing one of the high walls of Jerusalem

There was not one sinew in his body that could allow the charade to continue, allowing someone like the pumped-up imposter Vitellius, to

—

take over the reins of Rome. He rolled the parchment up in his hand and spent time shuffling his feet in the hard sun as he thought about the future and consequences he realised he must take. He decided there, on the sands, to take action.

He immediately placed his favoured son, Titus in charge of the siege of Jerusalem and packing up two legions he set out to secure Egypt and a long and torturous trip it was, as well.

He consulted his generals, including Primus, by written scroll, who claimed a part of the empire for themselves as reward for their support and he sent orders to mobilise his legions with the intent to march on Rome whilst he stayed in Egypt to keep it under his control.

He ensured that each and every centurion understood that the march and subsequent battle lay in the best interests of Rome and when they fought they were to remember that their city and their very country was at stake.

He acted quickly and ruthlessly, moving to take control of any emerging factions from Egypt. Primus and Mucianus led his forces against Vitellius and the rest was written in history.

In that year of sixty-nine, Vitellus was soundly defeated at the second battle of Bedriacum through Cremona. His men later murdered Vitellius in as an act of revenge. At the time, Vespasian could not have been happier. After the murder took place, what else could the senate do? Well, they declared him emperor, of course, but then he was the only choice with the legions at his beckoning and encamped near the city.

The past can be viewed many ways, he decided thoughtfully as he took another long sip of wine. The hard-forced march and battle at Cremona by the available legions, held under the ample experience of Antonius, was one of those offers of fortune that happen so rarely in life.

The win only occurred through a fortunate incident that ensued victory that day and it made his smile, even laugh out loud, when he recalled the ridiculousness of it.

The scribes wrote that Antonius gained the advantage against the Vitellius legions. The next day when dawn broke Antonius's men, the third Gallica, who had served prior in Syria for some years had, whilst stationed there, adopted a local and somewhat strange custom.

As the sun rose on that next day before the battle began, they all turned to the East to salute it and the stupid bastards on the other side, under

Vitellius, thought that they were saluting reinforcements in the distance and started to lay down their swords.

Vespasian stifled a laugh as he thought about it. The Vitellian forces were then driven back to their camp under the onslaught of the saluting legions and then they attacked Cremona and it was burnt to the ground by the troops.

The weather on the march proved beneficial and Vitellius did not hold either the experience or intelligence to win a battle against someone as experienced as himself. After his command in Judea and Egypt he held a breadth of experience very few could possibly match and he had made sure he held the best generals in the army.

He defeated the 'new man' resoundingly and took the prize, which he thought briefly, he should have taken after Nero took his own worthless life. But, he thought pragmatically, power was very much about timing.

The Vespasian dynasty annexed their power in Rome with unnerving speed. Flavian Vespasian and his son, Titus, held insurmountable power. He pushed his second son, Domitian out to the Legions to try and gain the experience he had awarded Titus.

That *annus horribilis*, which was to become known as the year of the four emperors meant that his job was to grasp the very centre of power whilst ensuring that the year of four did not become five. His ability to act decisively held the future for his son.

But, despite it all, he covered a fear, held deep inside, and it was his personal, though not spoken, acknowledgement that he was born a man, ill-equipped for politics.

After all, his parentage lay devoid of political favour and had come from an equestrian dynasty. The destiny provided by the Gods had thrust him into the position he now held as emperor of Rome and as ill-equipped as he was to manoeuvre and postulate the moves of politics, he knew he held one outstanding feature.

If he needed to, he moved quickly and ruthlessly to rid his life of dangerous opponents. Politics provided the arena of power and ruthless division and the gladiatorial arena was nothing in comparison to life in the senate of Rome. The thought broke his concentration and he sat up with an urgent thought.

Cassius Laurentius and esteemed senators!' He said, rising from his

—

couch 'Come, let me show you something wonderful.'

With a smile, Cassius Laurentius hefted himself off the couch, averting his gaze from the exiting dancers. As he rose, the other four moved with him. The three senators all wore white togas with a rim of pink dyed lapels over their sizable bodies.

Vespasian and Laurentius were the only ones who stood straight and slim. Both arrived from humble farm beginnings and learnt in early life to eat sparingly. Both were taught by life that a fat body indicated a failing mind. Laurentius was the only one in casual dress, albeit he wore a very expensive garment and with his prodigious wealth, he could afford anything.

He motioned to the others to walk with him into a side room and to stand around a table with a large cloth over it. As they stood around, making jokes about the cloth and sipping wine, Vespasian pulled the cloth gingerly from the table.

'The last time I did this I took the table with it!' He said with a modest smile. He lifted the cloth from a large-scale model which sat prodigiously in the middle of the table reaching almost to shoulder height of the men. It was finely and beautifully crafted with admirable accuracy, highlighting the colours from the wood used to create the model.

'Behold' He said with a familiar flourish of his hand. The same mannerism he used in the senate when offering advice or proposing a new idea. 'The new Forum!'

The four men moved in for a closer look 'Magnificent' Said one

'Perfect.' Said another

Cassius was the only one to raise his head with a question. 'Flavius, this is a magnificent building but were we not discussing the financial issues in Rome just yesterday. How does Rome afford it?'

'Ah, Cassius, hold your questions, there is more to come. I have commissioned a new building for all of Rome on the site of the old stadium and gardens of Nero as well. Come across here and let me show you all'

The next table held a large cloth as well and he lifted it with a flourish. The flames from the oil lamps reflected off the round walls and features of the yet to be built structure. It rose prominently from the table

---

displaying its five storey, structure and massive interior arena. With extreme care Vespasian moved half of the model away to show the interior and sub-floor. 'This my friends, will be the new Flavian amphitheatre.' He said with a slight bow of his head. 'It is magnificent is it not? It will be the dominant structure on the Rome skyline and, of course, visible from the Forum.'

He looked briefly at the intent faces of the senators next to him and continued. 'Because of its size it will be the greatest structure in all of Rome and the world. It will span a large area and stand five stories high with cages and an underbelly which will allow the greatest spectacles in the world. Think about it; multiple Bestiarii, Gladiators, large circuses for all and in a place built for the purpose. The citizens of Rome will love us for it and it will last for a hundred years, long after we have enjoyed our last indulgence.'

There were guffaws all around the scale model before them on the table. One of the men clasped his hands at the sight. 'Now this is a building!' He exclaimed with a delighted smile.

'This building will be east of the Forum and as you know constructed over the gardens of one of our esteemed past emperors. Of course, I am referring to Nero.'

'What about the gardens though, they are a favourite of Suburia.'

Vespasian looked at Senator Caius with a fleeting look and furrowed eyebrows. 'Perhaps I am not making myself clear; Nero built those gardens for himself. I will build the Flavian amphitheatre for the citizens of Rome to enjoy themselves. Could there be a more popular building in all of Rome? We build one for our political advantage and one for the masses.'

Senator Caius, lost in thought, circled the model once again and put down his cup. 'The Flavius amphitheatre is a fine name and it will appease the great citizens of Rome. What say you gentlemen?'

Senator Sulla moved around the model with an appreciative eye. 'Yes, a good name.'

Vespasian smiled at the excellent fawning of the successful senator before him. 'That statue of Nero remains in the gardens, correct?'

'It does, emperor'

11

Vespasian slapped the table with his hand as an angry look crossed his face. 'Well it will be going to be pulled down with the gardens and pushed into the obscurity the area deserves. Those gardens will be transformed into the colossus you see before you. Plebeians and noblemen and women will flock to the Flavian Amphitheatre for all the world to see.'

Cassius shifted his tunic and stood back to review the model. 'Yes, it is entirely magnificent and a worthy enterprise but again, Flavius, how does Rome afford it and how long will it take to build?'

Vespasian sipped his wine contemplatively and looked over his cup at the men before him. 'Ah, the sort of question I would expect from the richest man in Rome. The forum will be at the top of the hill and from there we can look down onto the Flavian Amphitheatre and the games inside the stadium will be heard all around Rome. Before we get to the money the question remains. Are they worth building?'

He looked around at the nodding faces with the understanding that they could do little else. There was a rule in politics that was taught to him by Nero, of all people. The rule was simple. Never, never, let anyone know what you are thinking. It worked for Nero until he grew madder than a wounded bear.

Only Cassius stood firm with his steady gaze meeting Vespasian's eyes as he turned to survey the faces of the others. The emperor disliked Laurentius and his ability to stand up against force and he did not trust him. But then, he reflected, he did not trust anyone save his son, Titus.

'Of course, Flavian.' Caius replied, as he rubbed his wide girth under the toga. It did no good to defy the emperor on his quest for immortality.

'Well, the answers are simple' Vespasian continued. 'To build them will take some four to five years, maybe six, according to my calculations engineers but they always underestimate the time and cost to be in my favour. Let us assume at least six years and as you are aware foundations for the Forum are in the process of being planned.'

There was a murmur of assent and acceptance around the group and Cassius Laurentius himself, a man used to the excesses that great wealth brought could only marvel at the audacity to build both massive structures at the same time.

The cost will be enormous, he thought briefly but then he did not care

---

about cost and he knew, even the citizens of Rome did not care about cost. Like all populace, they cared about themselves. This comprised a building for the people, one that they could attend to take their minds off the augurs of their everyday lives and relationships.

'What say you, good senators? Will you support me as we take this forward to our honourable friends at the Palatine hill, to gain a positive outcome?'

'Agreed' came the shout from one and a hand clap from another.

'I have an idea for the opening of the Flavian Amphitheatre; Let us also look to gain a champion of Rome for the arena when it opens. A man of the people! The people's gladiator! This will be a colossus and perhaps that is the other name for this magnificent building. The colosseum, something that will dwell in the ordinary Romans mind. We will open it with the biggest circus the world has ever witnessed. Rome will be the centre of the world.

'It already is!' Caius quipped as he looked more closely at the model

'Just so, senator.' Vespasian countered. So, six years?' One of the senators said with a nod at Vespasian.

Vespasian shrugged 'That is in the future, dear friend. Only the Gods know the answer to that one but let us keep in mind that true quality takes time.'

'Six years' hence? Laurentius asked with a wave of his arm. 'That is a while to wait.'

Vespasian moved forward a step to carefully replace the removed model part to its original position. 'It is Cassius; However, as we discuss almost every day of our fortunate lives; our job is to stay in power and ensure these monuments are built in good order and time and in answer to your concern about finances the solution is simple.'

Vespasian looked at the keen interest on their faces. 'We have taken a large fortune from Judea when we sacked Jerusalem and there is the option to raise taxes which I humbly suggest we start as soon as possible.'

The five of them returned to their couches. They lay down to engage in banter and self-reflection. Vespasian watched them as he waited for his wine to be filled. The three senators were harmless enough and might easily eat themselves to death before the buildings were finished but

---

13

Cassius, however, was another issue altogether. Charming, intelligent and ambitious. No military experience which was a blessing but the eyes of a snake, and beset by ambition, as his burning companion.

Vespasian lay his head back again and listened to them speak about the buildings. There was an old saying in Rome that came to mind; *orvus oculum corvi non eruit.*

'A crow will not pull out the eye of another crow', which worked everywhere, except for men in power. It was crow, eat crow and that was the point, he mused, looking at his political allies back on the couches around him. Trust no one, move forward with stealth and kill those who got in the way. Good Roman tradition.

He left his guests to make his way to the latrine. Once he relieved himself he crossed the floor of the next room towards his office. A centurion came quickly to attention as he approached. He walked through the door, closing it behind him, and sat down at his desk.

Across from him on another chair sat an elderly gentleman who nodded as he sat down. 'Hail, Elder Pliny, how does the writing go?' Vespasian smiled.

The man looked up at Vespasian in distaste and shook his head. 'It will be the death of me Flavius, but I enjoy the surroundings and I thank you once again for the use of the room.'

Vespasian waved the compliment away with his hand. 'Perhaps a mention at the front of *Naturalis Historian* might help. You are a respected man, Pliny and a foremost citizen of Rome. How could we not assist with your work?'

Pliny nodded and returned his attention to the board he was reading. Vespasian fussed through the papers on his desk until he found what he was looking for which comprised of a small note on the left of his enormous desk. He held it up and read the contents.

'You see, Pliny! The work of the emperor never rests. These are the costs for the Flavius Amphitheatre to be built over the next six years. But what is the cost of glory?'

He turned to leave as Pliny the elder put his pen down and looked up from his writing. 'Flavius, the world does not relish change but, as you and I know, change of any sort is inevitable.

14

'Of course, Pliny, you are correct but change also meets with resistance and the only way to reduce that resistance is to challenge it and eradicate it if necessary.'

Pliny smiled showing his almost toothless mouth. 'Be careful, Flavius Vespasian. '*auribus teneo lupum*.'

Vespasian nodded with a wry smile on his face. 'Pliny, I hold more than one wolf by its ears. I will leave you to your work and I will return to the wolf pack, that eagerly await my presence. My job, before I leave this city and cross the black waters of the River Styx, is to build the Forum and the Flavian Amphitheatre as well as take care of the great state of Rome.

'Anything else?' Pliny offered with a mildly sarcastic tone.

Flavian stopped and turned to face the elderly man in the corner. 'One, hundred-days of games, Pliny senior. When the Flavian Amphitheatre is completed it will be for all Romans to attend. Think of it! Fifty thousand spectators and on the first day I want a contest between champions, gladiators of Rome, to crown the First Gladiator of Rome.'

CHAPTER 2

North of Rome –Late 69AD

The dull echo of wood on wood rebounded off the side of the barn wall as Marcus and his brother, Manilus, played against each other in an aggressive but mock fight with heavy wooden swords.

Manilus, the smaller of the two at the age of fifteen held his brother at bay by mixing forward strikes combined with a backhanded slice that made his bigger brother move backwards.

'Parry, thrust, parry, thrust.' Manilus shouted as Marcus moved in with his sword that looked like a bad replica of a Gladius, the favoured sword of the Roman army.

Their father, Valerius, made them a basic copy of a sword he held in the farmhouse in case there was ever a problem with the vagrants and thieves that roamed the countryside. The bone handled, hand forged Gladius, handed down by their grandfather remained a prized possession of the house.

Over the years the boys, like most boys their age, waited until their father had left the house to pick up the heavy, slightly rusted sword.

They carefully peeled off the oilcloth that swaddled its handle and blade and attempted to use it like they did with the wooden replicas, but it was too heavy to wield. Only in the last year with the continued work on the farm did they gain the strength in one arm to pick it up and hold it with the sword tip upwards.

Their father forbade them to use it and like all teenagers who found boredom a constant companion they sighed and found other ways to spend their time and the constant supply of energy that was the envy of those much older.

'Now, go overhead. Good. Parry! Thrust and forwards.' Manilus looked at his slightly older brother who was taller with wide shoulders and a body, thin of fat and made of muscle and sinew.

Manilus knew that he had inherited his mother's side so he was wider in the shoulders but shorter and not as strongly defined and he lacked the black hair and blue eyes of his brother.

Manilus already carried a slight paunch and had nowhere near the energy of his older brother. Marcus was limited with a spear but far superior with a dagger as well as a sword and his undeniable strength and speed was impossible to keep up with.

Marcus stopped and leant against the whitened wood planks of the barn. He breathed heavily as he leant the wooden sword against the wheel of a cart and sat down. 'It is hot today and we still have work to do.'

Manilus looked down at him nudging his shoulder as he did so. 'Had we kept going we would have had it done by now. You are the one that wanted to stop.'

'I wanted to give Dessus a break. He looked as tired as you do brother.'

'Well if I am that tired perhaps you should do this yourself' Manilus said with a smile. 'C'mon let's get it done. If we keep playing, father will be down on us and I can do without that on this hot day.'

'Once more' Marcus said picking up his wooden sword.

Manilus picked up his pitted and forlorn looking sword and crouched in front of his brother. 'First to a point on the body is the winner.' How much, do you want to wager?' Marcus said with as he crouched in unison with his younger brother.

'Why do we have to bet, Marcus, let us do it just for the fun.'

'Ha! There is no fun unless we gamble you fool. Come on, pick a prize.'
'Alright then, the loser feeds the chickens first thing in the morning and milks as well.'

Marcus worked a quick calculation in his mind. If he won it would give him at least a while longer in bed before the sun embraced the horizon at dawn and the thought of his brother doing the chores made the bet all the more worthwhile.

'You are on' Marcus said with a laugh. 'Make sure you feed the chickens well when you get to them and as mother has always told you; use a light hand on the cow. Otherwise it will get sore udders from your ham-fisted paw.'
The dull, thudding, sound of the wooden swords could be heard by their

---

father who sat inside the barn over a hard, circular stone that he used to gain an edge on the farm implements that sat like old and comforting friends, against the wall.

He let the sound go on for a while but with his temper rising he wondered why they had not given him the plough head earlier that morning. He knew his son's well and he knew that his elder son, Marcus was blessed with a strong body but little aptitude for farm work.

He was too busy fighting with the boys from the other farms and lazing around while his brother, Manilus had probably done most of the work. Marcus was a lazy boy but well protected by his mother.

'Your break is more than over. Get back to work' Valerius shouted out. In the background the sound of hard wood against another continued.

'*Cacare*' He muttered under his breath. Shit.

He peddled the lever below with his sandal clad foot and the stone wheel turned slowly around. He splashed a little water on the top of the worn stone as it revolved, laying the hoe against the abrasive surface until the rusty blade edge reformed from its blunt and dented shape. He flexed his left hand again against the pain that grew from his knuckles. The pain was worse in winter and mostly from the cold winter winds that flew down from the Tuscan hills, far away.

The high hills lay in the far distance from the farm. Now, it seemed that any weather brought the pain in is joints. He massaged the joints with his right hand and wrapped his hand in a cloth.

He thought about the farm as the seductive sound of the wheel stone continued to grind the hoe edge. The soil around the farm was productive but his lot held many stones and larger rocks.

When tilling new ground, the work was doubled as they stooped to pick up the small stones and lever out the larger ones. There seemed to be an inexhaustible supply of rock given the fields were alternatively hoed each year with some left without crops to renew the soil in alternate seasons.

There was an upside, Valerius thought, as he honed the edge of the hoe wetting it to inspect the edge with his thumb. All of the walls that adorned the farm perimeters and most of the farmhouse itself were made of the stones and rocks, held in place by a mixture of dung, mud and straw. Many had lasted since his grandfather's days on the farm and showed no sign of aging.

Many times, the hoe that dragged behind Dessus, their large and aging farm ox, hit a large rock and the Dessus, despite all his strength would stop in mid stride as the hoe snagged. They only had two options; go around the rock and leave it to be marked as a point where the seeds would not be sown or mark it and come back another day to bring it up and cart it somewhere else.

He was proud of the farm he had worked since he was a young boy. His father had handed it to him, as he had inherited it from his father, as well.

Farming held an enviable life and, in the country, farming was regarded very highly because the farming community supplied the increasingly large, city of Rome and its surrounds.

The farm stretched as far as the small hills in the distance where the boys went to play when they were younger and the responsibilities of work not as pressing. There was plenty of flat land and the soil held abundant growth of anything that was sown in the right season.

Valerius, taught by his father, believed in the need to allow soil to rest and so each year some of the fields were left fallow and the others tilled and then next year it was reversed.

The farm held eight tilled fields, situated between two creeks where the neighbour's properties adjoined his property. The gate at the entrance to the farm was a walk down from the farmhouse; a place where the boys would go and play when they were younger and down to the creek that swept lazily past the nearby barn.

Finally, he lost his patience and shouted out to the boys through the thin walls of the barn. 'Hey, get back to work you two and don't come back until the field is finished.' He listened with satisfaction as the clacking of wood on wood stopped and the boys sauntered off to the field closest to the farmhouse that sat with one whitewashed wall in the background.

Valerius went to the door of the barn holding the sharpened hoe blade. 'Hey' he called out to them as they walked off 'You will need this unless you want to finish it off by hand!' He waited until Marcus walked back and handed him the hoe. 'Make sure you take care of this. It is blunt because you have hit too many rocks. If you hit a rock, stop, remove it and then keep going.'

'You must be referring to Manilus. He would not stop Dessus for a lightning storm, let alone a rock.'

'I guess that is typical of you Marcus. You just don't take care.' His father said with a resigned sigh.

Marcus started to argue and thought better of it. He hefted the hoe blade with his left hand, putting a sackcloth on his shoulder before he picked it up and placed the hoe on top and walked off. His father looked at him with a mixture of admiration of his strength and youth and irritation at his insolence. The boy could never amount to anything.

He walked the longer way to his brother around the bottom path and towards the field stone wall. He jumped over the wall and walked up towards the middle of the field where the large, grey form of Dessus stood at the side of the field.

He found his brother sitting on an old stump on the other side of Dessus and looking out towards the hills.

The air was swirling with light dust as the winds picked up under a sky laid clear of clouds allowing the moon, in a barely washed white, to stare at them in the middle of the horizon. It was unusual to see the it in the middle of the day.

'What is that globe in the sky?' Manilus asked as Marcus neared him.

'That is the home of La Luna, you idiot. Everyone knows that'

Marcus dumped the hoe blade down beside him and took a little of the stump next to his brother to sit down glumly beside him. 'There must be more to life than this farm,' Marcus said gazing out with a heavy sigh.

It was early afternoon and they would not be able to finish until the field was fully hoed and the ox completely exhausted before it was led back to the farm to be fed. To do anything different would be to incur the wrath of their father.

The only desire Marcus held was to leave the farm and move to Rome. He suffered from wanderlust for as long as he could remember. He yearned to travel, to experience another side of life other than the farm that took his labour seven days of the week under the tutelage of a man who cared less about school work and only about the amount of work to be finished.

He looked over at this brother who sat chewing an old stalk of wheat in his mouth and looking pensively at the same hill that Marcus had studied. 'We used to have great fun up there, Marco. Do you remember the day we caught that wolf puppy and took it back home only to have our mother tell us to take it back as the she-wolf would come looking for it?'

Marcus smiled as the memory swirled in his thoughts. 'All I remember is mother telling me to take it back to the top to where we found it and you backing away as I took it back. I also remember you saying you were going to follow me.'

'Yes, well I may look dumb, but I am not that stupid. I wonder what ever happened to that pup?'

'Probably hunting our goats as we speak. Perhaps, we should have killed it but you never know. One day it might come back to help us.'

'Unlikely 'Manilus said with his gaze still on the hills in the distance. 'Come on, let's get this done.'

Together they reassembled the plough tip onto the wooden brace sitting its side on the ground next to the stump. They positioned it between the two holes that held the metal head in place on the wooden arms, reaffixed the bolts and then attached the leather straps to the side of the plough.

Once the plough was in position they fed the reins through to the harness that circled the neck of the ox. 'You want front or back?' Marcus asked as his brother picked the handles of the plough up and the reins around his shoulder.

'You pull Dessus for a while and then we can change later.'

Marcus shrugged as he put the reins through the brass ring on the nose of the great ox and started to pull him on the line of fallowed earth. Within minutes Dessus was labouring and slowing. Each time Marcus pulled gently on his nose ring to move him along.

The earth was hardened from the sun and wind and the work at the back of the hoe was difficult. Once the plough had started with Dessus in the lead, the metal head dug into the earth and turned the farrow. It took great strength to keep it in line and the momentum going as the plough hit harder earth and a variety of smaller stones and the occasional rock.

At each rock point, where the plough stopped, they changed ends with Marcus throwing the reins over his shoulders and grabbing the hoe handles and guiding it through the field.

Lines of churned the earth lay behind them as they pushed on. Some

---

21

hours later the field was finished at the corner nearest the hills and they stopped. Manilus sat down momentarily, exhausted but relieved the field was prepared.

They knew their father had the ability to use Dessus by himself and with urging and holding the reins around his shoulder he could continue for a morning before he stopped. Neither, Manilus or his brother could get Dessus to move by themselves but both knew they could plough faster with the two of them than with a single person.

After surveying their work, they turned the plough upside down and placed it on the back of Dessus and led him back towards the farmhouse as they dangled the reins on the side.

Dessus was a massive beast with a heavy neck and large brown eyes, which he fixed ruefully on whomever put the heavy yoke on his neck as the work began. Marcus gave him a hard pat on the top of his head and watched as the beast started to walk towards the barn.

They knew to stay away from the heavy feet of Dessus as he sauntered down the path. Dessus had once stepped on Manilus' foot as he tied him up for the night and it took him four days to rid himself of the bruising.

Dessus quickened his pace as he knew that hay awaited and a rest in his stall. The ox seemed pleased that the strenuous exercise had finally stopped and it moved steadily beside them as they strolled down the path to the farmhouse in the distance.

It had been a lucky day. Very few rocks and only one they could not get out and it had been marked with a stick for further reference.

They reached the farmhouse and Marcus walked Dessus to the barn to unravel the plough assembly and feed him. As he neared the door his father came out with a menacing look on his face.

'You should have finished earlier. You and your brother do nothing but laze around.'

Marcus dropped the plough assembly on the ground and turned to face his father. He towered over the man and he looked down at him with a sneer on his face. 'If you think you can do it quicker, then you do it.'

'You watch your mouth, boy. I have tilled those fields many, many times and I know how long it takes. The reason you got fed as you grew up is because of my work. Not because of yours.'

Marcus glared at him and continued to put the plough assembly away. He tethered Dessus and put out hay for him. He grabbed a hairbrush and roughly bushed the ox down and gave him a pat for good measure.

Going to Rome would get him away from his father. There was little doubt that they clashed and the man favoured his brother. He and Manilus got along fine but then they were similar and perhaps that was the issue. He could not remember a time he and his father agreed on anything and the older he got the more he realized it was not going to change.

Closing the barn doors, he walked towards the farmhouse only to change his mind and direction and headed towards the stream at the bottom of the farm. He sat on a fallen log at the junction where the stream changed its course and he looked down at the slow-moving water beneath him.

He knew the time was coming that he would leave the farm either with, or without their permission. Running away was the only option he thought, as he sat, tired and a little sore in shoulders. He finally slumped on the fresh grass near the stream bank.

His father irritated him and he knew the reverse was true as well. His mother had always been the calming influence in his life an over his young years he had come to realize that he was like her in many ways, including his temperament, which was calm unless prodded and then the aggression surfaced.

He turned seventeen in the next month of Aprilis and that was his desired time to leave and find his fortune somewhere else. He knew that Manilus would stay on the farm and carry on the tradition and somewhere in the back of his mind it gave him comfort to believe that his brother would be there to work and support his parents; or at least his mother who was his primary worry. His father could visit the underworld permanently as far as he was concerned.

Absent in his thoughts, he threw a broad leaf into the clear water of the stream watching it flutter down onto the water. It finally moved through the currents, coming to rest on a small log in the middle of the stream.

The sight of an apple thrust in front of his face broke his reverie. He looked to find Manilus beside him. He passed him the apple as he bit into his own until only the core remained and finally threw the bedraggled core into the stream. It sank to the bottom and was dragged along the sand by the swirling water.

'Father again, huh?'

———

23

Marcus nodded glumly and bit hard into his apple. 'He favours you and criticizes me and I get very sick of it.'

'That is not quite true but you don't handle him well, Marcus. You should do what I do.'

'Which is?'

'I ignore him' Manilus said with a laugh.' If he asks me to do anything I agree and then I go and do what I was always going to do in the first place.'

'I can't do that.'

'You can, older brother, you just don't want to. Think about it; we have a good life on a fine farm. We have plenty to eat and the ability to work hard when we need to and a great place to live when we don't. It could be a lot worse and with the exception that there are very few girls around it is a good life. Be happy, Marcus Attilius'

Marcus put his arm around the shoulders of his younger brother as he threw his wasted apple into the water and leant towards him. 'You are my brother and I care for you but this is not for me, Manilus. I want to go and experience other things and there is a big city out there in Rome and that is where I want to be.

'You really want to leave?'

Marcus nodded. 'It gives me comfort that you will be here to take care of our mother and work the farm. The truth is that the harder we work the less work father does around the farm and that is a fact.'

Manilus nodded in agreement 'True but his hands hurt and his back is bad from all the work he did when he was younger. He can be difficult, but as I said just ignore him.'

'No' Marcus replied firmly 'I have to leave and I want to go in Aprilis and I will speak to mother about it. It will upset her but I need your support and if I make my fortune outside the farm I will make sure you get some of it.'
'What happens if you go broke?' Manilus said with a stupid look on his face.

'Then you can share in that as well.' Marcus replied with a similar look and they both burst out laughing as they stood to walk back to the farmhouse and the familiar smell of their mothers cooking.

*

The earliest, thin red light of dawn held the horizon when Marcus rose to feed the chickens and milk the cow. He had lost the bet the day before on the sword fight by the narrowest of margins.

He pulled his work tunic on, tied his sandals and as he left the room he heard his brother turn over on his bed. 'Be nice to the cow, Marcus, it only has four teats.' Manilus called out sleepily. Marcus smiled as he left the room. He would sorely miss his brother when he finally left the farm.

He walked down towards the barn and the chicken coop with the scraps bucket in his hand whistling a tune he had heard at a communal dance several weeks before.

Manilus, for all of his placating of his father's moods, was correct. The farm is a good life. It is safe, he reflected, and there is plenty of food unless the droughts arrived and even then, they had survived well in the past.

Marcus liked excitement and danger and all of his young life he had been the same way. He was the one that picked fights and fought the boys from the other farms and it was he who pursued the young women of the district.

Marcus spread the scraps around the coop watching as the chickens fought and bickered over the food. He cleaned up the chook manure and placed it in a bucket for that purpose to be used on the vegetable patches that surrounded the farmhouse.

The vegetable patches remained the sole responsibility of his mother and as everything else in her life she treated them with reverence and love.

He placed the manure bucket on the path for the trip back and entered the barn to milk the only cow they had on the farm.

Inside the gloom he could hear the milk sloshing into a wooden bucket and he looked inside the stall to find his mother softly caressing and pulling the cows teats with her fingers to let the milk spray into the bucket beneath. The top finger and thumb started the pressure as the other fingers followed and the white liquid sprayed into the bucket at her feet.

'You should have told me' Marcus said with a grin. 'I could have stayed in bed!'

'Good morning, Marco' She said using the endearment she had always used to him and from as long back as he could remember. 'I could not sleep with your father snoring, so I decided to take an early walk and ended up here.'

She smiled in that soothing way she had when addressing him and his brother. Her brown hair, going slightly grey at the temples was piled on her head and her smock held the spray stains of the milk. Her hands, like his father showed the ingrained lines of farm work and the effects of the unrelenting sun.

'That's my job, but if you want to do it who am I to try and stop you.' He said with mock indignation. He sat on a three-legged, stool on the opposite side of the cow who, stood munching on hay and looking back at him for a moment before turning her undivided attention to the hay in the stall.

He stooped down low beneath the cow's belly and looked up at his mother who smiled benignly at him 'There is always the goat in the other stall, Marco. Your father is starting to lay down cheese so that needs to be completed as well.'

Marcus sighed and got up taking the stool with him to tether the goat and start the milking.

'Remember to push up the udder first and then use the first three fingers' She said as the sound of milk squirting came from her stall. 'It has been a time since we have talked, you and I. Are you happy about your upcoming birthday?'

Marcus shrugged. 'Yes, but I am getting old. Almost seventeen.'

His mother laughed out loud. 'Dear Marco; you are so young. You know nothing of the world and of life. I hear from Manilus that you want to travel and live in Rome?'

Marcus winced but thought better of lying. 'I want to leave the farm and live in a city. If I can get a job in Rome I could get paid and live there for a while.'

'It is not as simple as that Marco.' His mother cautioned. 'The upside of living on a farm is we grow our own food and live in our own house as free people. You have no skill to take to Rome, or anywhere else, to gain employment.'

'I can read and write.'

'That is true, Marco, but so can many others and many of those better than you. I am not trying to make it difficult for you, but you must be realistic.'

'Then I shall go to Rome and try my luck.'

'But you don't know anyone in Rome, Marco, and Rome is a large city with very many citizens living there. It is not like a farm, young man, it is a large and difficult place to live if you are not wealthy.'

Marcus grimaced as he milked the goat that stood patiently while he completed the task. 'I know but I want to try something different. It is the dream of father and of Manilus to live and work on this farm but it is not mine and I have been thinking about this for some time.'

'I know you have Marco as I have watched your restlessness for some time but as long as you know your father will be very against this and you will leave him only with Manilus to assist in the planting and harvesting season. How long do you plan to go for?'

Marcus shrugged his shoulders, which she could not see but could feel the resignation coming from him. 'I can't answer that because I don't know. But if I continue to stay on the farm my father and I will come to blows. He does not like me and he has no patience.'

'Nothing could be further from the truth, Marco. Your father is a difficult man and yes, he had a difficult father. He has worked hard on this farm to feed us all and to leave something for you and Manilus when we leave this world. Try not to be too harsh on him.'

'This is not where I want to be mother. I want to be out there.' He said with a flourish of his hand that his mother could not see.

'You really want this?'

'More than anything' he replied.

He could hear his mother sigh "Leave it with me, I will see what I can do.'

'How?' he replied as he saw the dawn light spreading across the fields for the first time since he arrived in the dark. The light of the morning sun competed with the candles, finally winning as they finished the milking. 'I will speak to your father. You also have an uncle; Tactius, who lives and works in a nobleman's house and estate in Rome. I will contact him to see if he can assist but it will take time. I will need to send him a message.'

'I have an uncle? How come I never heard of him?'

'It's a long story, Marco and not one I want to go into. Your father doesn't like him.'

'Now there's a surprise.' Marcus said with a desultory laugh.

His mother continued with her milking. Finally, she stood up with her hand on her lower back and stretched. You did meet him once but a long time ago so I am not surprised that you don't remember him. Just remember that your father will be very unhappy about this change but if it is what you really want, I will see what I can do.'

'Thank you.' Marcus murmured. He adjusted the pail and finished milking the goat.

CHAPTER 3

The month passed quickly with the final work before the sowing began and tilling completed. It was time to sow for the second crop of the year, with the boys under instructions from their father, as if they had never done it before.

Manilus and Marcus took in turns to walk along the furrows with a long stick and each half step they pushed the stick into the soil to make a hole and as the one behind passed they dropped a seed into the hole and covered it with one motion.

A single field took a full day to sow with Valerius walking around most afternoons to ensure the job was completed and that they sowed the seeds in the right measure. There was little else to do once the fields had been seeded but to wait for the rains to fertilize the fields and support the growth of the crops.

At the end of each day they met at the shrine at the back of the farmhouse and gave blessings to Ceres, the Goddess of earth. Flowers and small parcels of food were left as a daily ritual at the shrine in the hope of early rains. Every evening the boys could hear their father mumbling at the shrine.

Each day they sowed the fields, chased away the birds and inspected the droppings around the fields for the type of animal visiting the fields at night. The worst were the deer who could vault the stone fences in one leap and start feeding on the seedlings with a field made barren, in one night.

Each day, in the morning they would look skyward for signs of the clouds that might harbour the coming of rains but by the middle of that month the skies remained clear and unwelcoming of the low, dark clouds, that heralded the rain.

The streams were low for the time of year and as each day progressed the waiting became frustrating and each evening before night fell they continued to lay offerings to the Goddess.

The month turned into the next and Aprilis arrived and with it the rains they wanted. Ceres released the rains, clearly sated, their father told them, by the prayers and food that adorned his shrine. Late of that month Marcus turned his seventeenth birthday.

Fully grown, he towered over his father and brother and his physical ability at running and wrestling with his brother turned into a no-contest the year before and now it was hopeless for Manilus to even try. Blessed with agility and strength he continued to fight with the neighbouring boys but now the fights were harder and fists the choice of the contest.

The night of his birthday arrived and like all Roman birth days there were no gifts but a small feast marked the special day. Marcus sat at the table for the meal his mother had arranged for him with the added personage of their closest neighbours from the farm to the North of their land.

Ortho, the only friend that Marcus thought his father had, sat at the other side of the table devouring the last of the meat which he cut from the severely depleted leg of lamb in front of him. His vast girth slumped over his legs as he reflectively chewed the last morsel.

His hair was silvery grey and his dark complexion gave him the look of a man contented with his life. He burped which was considered acceptable, if not a required response, after a delicious meal.

'Well, Valerius, we cannot complain about the rain or the low winds this year. If it weren't for those damn foxes taking the lambs my life would be near perfect. However, in saying that, I run my farm with an exacting eye and nothing escapes my attention. The bees are not producing as well as previous years. Perhaps, but only perhaps, that means the rains will change.'

'Same problem and maybe the winds are to blame.' Valerius replied curtly as if the information they were sharing was only understood by men of their background and stature. Farmers conversed with farmers in a language only they understood.

His wife stood to assist Aurelia with the dishes. 'Don't believe him, Valerius. He does nothing but complain about the prices at the market, the lack of assistance on the farm and he is constantly at our daughter who works hard around the house. And since she is still only fourteen you might think he would leave her alone.'

Aurelia, the taller of the two women stood with her hair down and combed for the occasion. Her dark Italian looks shone in the light of the oil lamps.

30

Her wide face held large brown eyes and high eyebrows. She nodded as she prepared the dishes for washing. 'Sounds familiar to me.' She said with a laugh and looked over at her glaring husband.

'They don't work like they did in my day' came the expected reply. 'When my father was alive we worked hard and much harder than the youth of today, let me tell you that.' Valerius stated, with a sneak look at the honey cakes that were placed on the table.

Ortho moved his considerable bulk in the chair and chortled. 'As long as they work Valerius, just as long as they work! So, Marcus, your father tells me you want to leave the farm and live in the great city of Rome! Are you sure about that decision? I mean, it is a hard, cruel world out there whilst her you have the best of everything here. Let me tell you boy, I have been to Rome on a number of occasions and it is not that pretty. Lots of people, cramped quarters, hard to move in the streets and filth everywhere. You want that?'

Marcus shrugged and looked at Ortho who sat resplendent on the kitchen chair with gravy stains down his tunic. 'I am bored.'

'Ah, yes, the boredom of youth; well, young Marcus, you can easily get rid of that boredom by working harder for your father on the farm. Soon the harvest will arrive and perhaps it is time to find a girl to take as your bride.'

'Perhaps, Marcus replied with a sideways glance at his mother. 'I would like to experience the world first, Ortho, and then look at settling down. The farm is in good hands and besides there are very few girls around here, if you hadn't noticed.'

'Well, Valerius 'Ortho said with a wink. 'Aliana is now only a year or two off marrying her marrying age. What a great match eh?'

Varlerius nodded in response 'You know, Ortho, I had never thought of that.'

Marcus shuddered inwardly at the thought. The girl was ugly, fat and pimples all over her face.

'Perhaps, after I return from my travels.'
'That is not your decision to make, Marcus.' His father said glaring directly at him.

Aurelia intervened. 'Now, this is your birthday Marcus, so I made you

---

my special honey cakes.' She took the cotton cloth off the plate and placed them in the centre of the table. As she did she gave Blasius a steely look.

Marcus, bored with the conversation, stood up and went over to his mother and put his hand around her shoulders. 'Great feast, thank you, Ma.'

She smiled at him and returned his embrace. 'Can you fetch the water?'

Marcus nodded and moved outside to the well situated at the back of the house. Manilus was sitting on the small wall that surrounded the farmhouse, looking up at the star-studded sky stretching across the horizon.

The silhouette of the hills in the distance complemented the sparking sky and the full Aprilis moon shone brightly casting light as if it was day. The night was warmer than the previous months and there remained a stillness in the air.

Marcus filled the bucket, took it inside to his mother and returned to where his brother was sitting. He passed a honey cake that he had taken off the table to his brother who smiled and shoved the entire cake in his mouth.

'Perhaps I could come with you.' Manilus said as he chomped on the cake whilst picking off the crumbs from his tunic.

'You are too young and besides father needs at least one of us here.'

'Then you stay and I will go.'

Marcus laughed and then sat on the wall with him. 'I think our paths are different, Mani; But if I do make a success of it you can come and join me.'

Manilus went silent momentarily. 'Will you not miss beautiful nights like this, from the comfort of the farm?'

'There are beautiful nights everywhere, brother; the secret is to enjoy them other places than this. I will miss you and our mother but I will not miss the rest of it including the miserable mule inside the house.'

Aurelia came outside the house and called Manilus inside. He got up as Marcus patted him on the shoulder and a minute later his mother joined him on the wall. She sat softly beside him and took his hand. 'I have good news for you Marco.' She said with that soothing voice of hers. 'I have got a message back from Rome and your uncle can get you a position as a gardener on the estate. There is not much pay in this for you but apparently, you get fed, a warm bed and enough to live.'

Marcus looked at his mother in surprise. He grabbed her and hugged her shoulders.

'Thank you' he said excitedly 'Father?'

'I told him this morning which will account for his bad humour today. He will get over it soon, I hope. So, you need to finish the new hen coop with your brother and the wall near the barn. Once you have done those it will be time to go.'

'I need to tell Manilus.'

'He knows and that is why he is so glum. He loves you Marco, so you must be kind to him until you leave. It is not easy to lose a brother.'

'He is not losing me! 'Marcus exclaimed. 'I am just going for a while.'

Aurelia smiled thinly and held the face of her firstborn in her hand. 'Marco, because of the way you are, you may not be back for a very long time. You must always remember we love you and the farm is yours as well.

'I will…'

She interrupted him 'Whatever happens, make time to come back. That is the most important thing. So, get your work done and then we will work out the next step of your road to Rome. I must get back to our guests, Marco, don't discuss this with your father for a while at least.'

Marcus nodded and bent his head in relief at the news. He was finally on his way. His brother returned and sat down with another honey cake for the two of them in his hands.

They chewed the cakes without speaking but knowing that in a short while they would part and as close brothers there was little they could say but enjoy the companionship under the blanket of stars.

The offerings to Ceres which continued after the rains fell caused the Goddess to take notice and as the plentiful rains continue the crops showed early signs of growing well. Barley was a hardy crop but unless early rains happened the root systems were weak but in this particular year the month of Aprilis had offered the farm a prospect of a robust crop. Valerius, as was his custom, walked the fields each day to check the crop growth and any issues that may have happened. He found part of a bridle on one of the fields and cursed Marcus as he stood to throw it in his sack.

That next night, after they had washed themselves and eaten a huge meal of lamb, vegetables and the wheat porridge they both loved they sat at the table with a peculiar silence around the table. Aurelia had taken the time to bake several loaves of bread and this was placed on the table as well.

Since there was little conversation at the table. Aurelia tried to start the subject of how well the hen house and wall had come along until Valerius got up from the table after making a remark about laziness and left to go down the well-worn path to the barn. Aurelia winked at the boys and brought out some honey they could use to finish off the first loaf of bread.

'He will get over it, Marco. He is a hard man as was his father and he does not understand your need to get away. I do.' She said candidly.

After a small discussion about the road he must take to Rome and what to do when he got there they discussed the farm and the coming season and then they went to bed.

Early the next morning Marcus was up and preparing for the long walk to Rome. He eagerly packed some of his clothing, food that his mother had prepared and a stoppered hide of water, which he filled from the well.

By the time he had finished, Aurelia and Manilus were up and the three walked outside and down towards the gates. His father was nowhere to be seen, but then he did not expect to meet him that morning.

Valerius' bad humour was compounded by the knowledge that his first son, a sizable and immensely strong workhorse was leaving for Rome and that meant he personally would need to double his work to ensure the farm was in good order.

He could not afford a worker unless he could find the services of an old slave and they were hard to come by and probably would not work hard anyway. The last thing he needed was to oversee a slave that was intent on avoiding work.

The injury he received all those years ago from a vicious horse kick

---

made his walking more difficult each year and he was nearing his forty fifth year. Any desire to work harder was decreasing as each season went past.

It felt as if the seasons were getting longer and he could feel his increasing tiredness with each passing year.

He had taken Marcus aside one early morning and explained to him that it was the normal course of things, of life and of Roman families, for the son to take over from the father when the time was right. That time, he noted to him, was drawing nearer but Marcus had stubbornly refused.

Whilst he and his son were freeman which allowed for a life well above that of a slave, he had not afforded Marcus either a strong education or training to build himself a life above that in which he was born.

Aurelia had spent the hours teaching both of the boys to read and write and to take care of themselves. She was an excellent mother but too weak for the likes of Marcus.

The boy did not understand that farming was an honourable profession and perhaps the most honourable of all of them and certainly in the country it was the most important. Who could continue their life without food?

The farm he looked out to from the door of the barn on that day, the day his son was leaving, gave Valerius an intense feeling of pride. He had dedicated his life to its earth and its needs to ensure it provided and nurtured it so it would re-generate as each passing season aged its soils. As did his father and his father before him.

It perplexed him as to why his son turned his head away from a good life with honest work.

He walked outside the open door of the barn that held feed and shelter for some of the more important animals when the weather turned viciously cold. He looked out towards the farmhouse and watched his wife walk towards him. She had the look he knew only too well and he knew what she was going to say to him.

She stood before him, hands on hips, her beautiful brown eyes holding his gaze. 'Valerius, you must give him time. He is young and full of energy and he reminded me so much of you at the same age when we first met.'

Valerius grunted and started to turn away before she grabbed him by the arm to pull his attention back. 'He is eager and ambitious and I admire that. Your life's work may be this farm but for him the world awaits and I believe he must go and test himself and then, maybe then, if he fails, he will return.'

Valerius gave a grim smile and gestured with his hand.' And who takes care of this! It is not so easy, day-to-day.'

His wife with a similar flourish of her hand scoffed at him. 'You and I, Valerius, we will and if we can't we will find a way. The farm is in good condition and Marcus has worked tirelessly to make it that way before he leaves.

'Ha!' Valerius retorted.

'Allow our parting to be of good spirit not one that is riddled by scorn and anger. Go after him; he is just down at the gate and say goodbye.'

Valerius looked away angrily. 'We have no control over him. None' Aurelius looked at him with an of irritated countenance on her face. She turned to walk away. 'Have it your way Valerius, but the cost will be your relationship, with your first-born son. Think about that before you start worrying about your precious pigs and sheep.'

'Who will sow the wheat?' He said angrily as he walked into the barn. 'You?'

The audible sigh from his wife was all he heard as the moved hay away from the stack at the side to the animal pens. Now he realised he was faced with paying for labour on the farm with good for nothing slaves who ate like horses and worked hard when they were in the farmer's gaze and did nothing if left alone.

The farm would soon endure the long hot months of a Roman summer and work would increase. He had pleaded with his son to leave later, after the harvest, but like all young men he was determined to do what he wanted even at a cost to his family.

He blamed Aurelia, his wife, for this course of events. She had contacted her brother, Tactius, without his permission to see if he could get Marcus a job in Rome and by the Gods he did. Miracles did happen, he mused as he pushed the hay around, but not to him. Someone else created a miracle and he paid.

How she even contacted Tactius was a mystery. The woman had no way of sending a message to Rome and it was more than he could do. How did someone contact a brother all the way in city of Rome and get a young man, sight unseen a job in a noble household?

He stabbed at the hay with the three-pointed tool heaving it over into one of the stalls. His wife was a resourceful woman but a difficult one. Marcus had inherited her stubbornness which he had witnessed, first hand, almost every day.

He peered out of the barn window towards the farm gate where the two boys stood talking. Perhaps the farm would survive and at least he would be rid of an ungrateful elder son who stood firm and argued almost everything like his mother.

He finished the hay and cleaned the troughs and then walked outside the barn and peered down the path as Aurelia walked down to where her son was standing next to the gate post. She was holding a small parcel.

'What is this?' Marcus said with a smile.

'Honey cakes. I left several for Manilus and your father can go hungry.'

Marcus embraced her as he waited for Manilus to return to the gate. He was anxious to be on his way.

Manilus had ducked off towards the barn and finally arrived back to where Marcus and his mother were laughing together. 'What were you talking about? Manilus asked out of curiosity.

Aurelia stood back still smiling. 'I said to Marco that he should stay and I would go to Rome.'

Manilus laughed as well at the thought of he and his brother alone with their father on the farm. 'Here brother, I made this for you.'

Marcus grasped the shaped staff with his hand and held it up 'You think I am a cripple? He said to Manilus with a smile on his face when he grasped it with his other hand to hit one of the gate posts. 'By the Gods it is tough.'

'I know you are a cripple in the mind!' Manilus laughed.
Marcus looked at them both and hugged his mother and brother and passed through the gates and on his way. As he left his mother she pressed a small pouch inside his tunic and gave him a broad smile. 'For food' she said. 'It is not much but it is all the Denarii I have.'

As he walked down the road away from the farm that morning he could see his mother crying and his brother waving and in the far distance, he watched his father in his usual bad humour, walking across from the barn to the fruit trees in the orchard.

Marcus walked happily down the dusty road that led from the farm, through a copse of trees that lined the road and towards the hill in the distance. He finally quickened his pace and looked at the narrow road ahead with a mixture of anticipation and exhilaration.

Above him on the peak of the hill his father paused to look down the road that led from the farm through to the hills beyond but there was no one there. Marcus had disappeared into his new life.

CHAPTER 4

With the hand-made staff from his brother in his hand and a hefty pack on his young shoulders, Marcus set off from the farm in high spirits and happy to be on his way.

He followed the narrow dusty track leading from the farm that rose sharply through the hills which he reached by mid-morning. Now and then he saw parts of the countryside that he and Manilus ran through when they were younger and more adventurous and the duties of the farm not as heavy.

As the sun reached half way on its journey through the cloudless sky, Marcus stopped by a stream that sat just off the road. He refilled his water, bathed his feet in the water after taking off his sandals and looked around at his surroundings.

In the dense forest around him he could see the movements of animals that sat near the stream waiting for prey. In the distance, further down, he saw two goats grazing on the grass that seemed plentiful around the path of the stream.

He pulled out a piece of hard cheese and a lump of bread from his pack that his mother had given him and munched contentedly watching the animals wander off down the line of the water flow.

He rose and started the walk up the hills once again and when he finally reached the top he stopped to turn around and take the time to look out at the view. He was captivated by the grandeur of the scene and the view of the farmlands across the valley beneath. It was not a view that he had seen before.

With the exception of their travels to the market, which was in the opposite direction this was the furthest he had travelled from his home.

He surveyed the vast plain in the distance looking for his farm and finally located it as a group of fields dotted by trees and the stone walls that were so familiar as they criss-crossed the property.

He could see the faint outline of the track that led all the way back to the farm as well as the furrowed tracks that cast off to different roads in the area. It was a tapestry of interlinking, oblong fields of green and brown with the occasional burst of trees and streams. There were no boundaries save the hardly visible stone fences that tracked across the landscape through the boundaries of the farms.

In front of him the vista was different. The hills he walked over that day gave way to mountains in the distance that rose majestically into the sky. The path was changing to a wider road and it tracked away from the mountains and to a valley far below and he thought that might be the place to end up for the coming night.

The air held warmth and an abundance of light so he set a point in the distance and walked towards it. As he travelled his mother's words rebounded in his eyes. 'Uncle Tacitus, said to take the path towards the hills and then follow it until the road begins. At that point, there is a fork in the road so take the left turn and that will eventually lead you to Rome. Once you get there you need to ask directions to the household of the nobleman Laurentius and get introduced.'

In the distance, he could see high, voluminous, dark clouds taking up a large part of the sky but they seemed to be moving away from his direction. He kept walking for the last part of the afternoon ignoring the heat and insects that seemed to multiply the further he walked.

He walked until the sun dipped beneath the horizon and shadows left the road. Spotting a clearing amongst of trees up the hill to his left he headed up to the flat area at the top.

Sitting down heavily on the soft grass he let out a sigh of relief. The night was cooling from the loss of heat as the day closed and night beckoned.

Marcus checked his surroundings and started to look for twigs and branches, as well as the dry grass that catches easily alight to start a fire.

He paused to look at the vista before him from his position on the hill. There was a very different broad plain below with long, brown grasses covering it through to the hills in clear view in the distance. They held a deep blue haze in the fading light and around him the forest started to come to life.

From his bag, he pulled out an implement that looked like a horseshoe folded on itself. He held the steel of the horseshoe shaped metal down towards the tinder, striking it with a piece of obsidian, which created a spark each time it hit the metal. Finally, the tinder caught a spark and he built up a small fire by adding increasingly larger pieces of dry wood.

The remaining dead grass he gathered was put around the bottom of the tree to cushion his sleep, and he finally lay by the fire. He watched the flames and the sparks that rose into the sky. Around him the flickering light illuminated the trees, causing ghostly shadows to dance around the foliage. At least once he heard a growl from the undergrowth.

Now and then he would see the flickering green eyes of an animal in the woods beyond the light cast by the fire. The howls of wolves started to fill the air from the hills in the distance as they came in search of prey but they sounded far off so he lay back in repose against the light cast from the flames.

Marcus stoked the fire with thick logs, burying down in his cloak while keeping his hand on his staff, as he enjoyed the warmth on his side. The noises of the night, so familiar on the farm lulled him to rest. The warmth and familiar crackle of the firewood carried him into a deep sleep.

The next sound pulled him out of his sleep as a startling crack of thunder echoed through the deep canopy of the forest. As each thunderous sound from the heavens erupted, another bolt from above could be seen in the distance, as it laced the hills, lighting them for a brief moment.

The sound from the sky was deafening and startled by the deep booming of thunder he was instantly awake clutching his staff and pack under his cloak. In the next moment, the heavens opened up and heavy rain began to fall.

It started with drops on the leaves and finally a torrent of water. The fire went out and Marcus hunched himself under the trees with his pack beneath his legs and his cloak around his body. He sat there, soaked and miserable and waiting for the rain to stop.

In the distance through the curtain of rain he saw the gleaming eyes of an animal, probably soaked and as miserable as he was. With that in mind, he grabbed his staff holding it close as the rain continued to flood the area. As he pulled his belongings closer to him the eyes disappeared, replaced by an even heavier downfall.

He dosed on and off as the rain came and went. He awoke past dawn feeling stiff and sore from his cramped positon under the tree canopy and he hastily got to his feet and trudged through the sodden grass out of the clearing and down towards the path.

The fleeting thought of his comfortable bed in his home flashed across his mind as he continued his walk through the forest. The rain eased, replaced by a cold misty light which filtered through the forest, creating shafts of brilliance inside the gloomy copse of trees as he picked his way through.

He walked steadily through the forest where he found a fast-flowing stream and around the banks he could see the hoof and paw prints of animals who had drunk from the same point. He filled his flask, replaced it in his sodden pack and started on the path a little while later.

The morning proved uneventful, and disappointment joined him as he expected the road his mother had described to be around each bend, but it was not. He was impatient but enjoying the adventure and the sun had burned off the heavy cloud by late of the morning. Blue skies, beckoned once again in the distance.

The scent of blossoms filled his senses as he moved carefully down one steep slope. He stopped to peer into the forest beyond to a field of lilies, carpeting the trees in the clearing.

He stopped to drink from his flask sitting on a large rock at the side of the path and as he rose to start again he saw a farmer leading a cow down the hill towards the wide path that Marcus was walking.

The man stopped as Marcus came near. 'Salute.' Marcus said as he dropped his pack momentarily.

The farmer stopped pulling on the rope that held the cow.

'Salute, to you citizen. You look to be a long way from home. Where do you travel?'

'To Rome, is this the right way to the road?'

The farmer nodded and sat down on the rock next to him. 'It is, young man but you have a long way to go, young'un. It is many days walk from here. Much more than a week. That is, if you travel by foot. Do you have a horse or mule?'

Marcus shook his head as the man stood up to pull a package out of the bag he had slung over the cow's shoulders. He released the stopper and took a drink. He smiled a toothless grin. 'Where do you come from?'

'Almost two day's walking behind me.'
'So, you are on the right path. The Gods are on your side. What is your name?'

Marcus Attilius.'

'The son of Valerius?'

Marcus nodded as the farmer looked at him in amazement. 'By the Gods I have not seen you since you were a child and I have not seen Valerius for as long as I can almost remember. Do you remember me?' Marcus shook his head. 'We used to see each other at the market but he stopped coming. I remember back in those days you were about this high.' He noted the height with his hand and laughed. "Now, you have grown, boy, into a man. So, citizen, why do you venture to Rome?" He offered the bottle.

Marcus took it and a long swig and handed it back. 'Anywhere will be better than the farm.' He replied sullenly.

'Don't be so sure of that until you have been to Rome and maybe after you get there you will want to return.'

'Maybe' He replied, with the unwarranted confidence of youth and continued on his way.

'Farewell, boy and give my regards to your father!' The farmer shouted out. Marcus turned, waved and went on his way.

CHAPTER 5

Marcus stopped at the fork where the roads interlaced. Across the paved road, lay the sign with 'Roma' on it and a wide sculptured arrow pointing to the South.

The road was wide enough for two carts and it led directly North and South and another, not as used and rougher, towards the West and the grassy plain he watched as he walked down the wide track, the previous afternoon.

He inspected the signs that sat on stonework on the main road noticing that well ahead of him two men ambled along the side of the road but in the opposite direction to his intended travel. He expected more on the road and was disappointed to find it was bare of travellers besides himself and the men he saw as he reached the crossroads.

The stones on the road were worn down from use with holes made from dislodged rocks thrown by heavy carts and draft horses that used the road. Many of those rocks, thrown by angry travellers who had slipped on them or had broken a wooden wheel, lay in neglect on the side of the road like orphans, with grass growing around them.

The road stretched along a wide plain in front of him and with a deep breath he turned left in direction of the 'Roma' sign and started his journey in earnest.

That night he slept not far from the road under the stars with not a rain cloud in sight. In the distant hills, he saw the flickering of another fire as strangers lay down for the night and above him the stars shined with the occasional howl from the wolves that inhabited the surrounding hills.

The moon was full and shining in the firmament surrounded by a blanket of stars and as he sat down by the fire and looked up at the stars in wonderment.

The fire, he had lit some time before, continued to blaze solidly as he ate more of the bread and cheese his mother had packed tightly into his pack.

He found the remains of a maize pancake at the bottom of the pack which was sodden, but he was hungry enough not to care. He dozed as he sat against the tree, half dreaming of the farm and the effect his leaving would have on his mother and brother. He gave thought, once again, as to whether his decision had been the right one or not and finally pushed it out of his mind.

The next two days were uneventful and he made his bed off the road as usual and slept soundly. With dawn breaking the horizon on his fifth day he doused the fire with earth and rose to start the day's journey.

He tried counting paces and setting goals for his distance each day but as he got to the places he set himself, it seemed the road went on for eternity. As each passing stranger met him on the road he would stop and ask them 'Roma.'

Some laughed, others pointing in the direction in which he walked and some stopped for a break and a drink of water. 'Many days' came the reply. 'Where are you from? How goes your journey?' It was an instant camaraderie of sorts when travellers met. There was much to discuss. The weather, the road, the pitfalls and the need for food.

Marcus checked his pack that morning and he was running low. The more he walked the hungrier he got and he realized he has eaten his way through a week of food in less than five days.

He stopped on the side of the road late that afternoon and rested his sore feet. He hobbled to a well that had been excavated next to the junction point of two roads and quenched his thirst and thought about staying the night.

He pulled off his sandals and rubbed them trying to work the soreness out of them. He had a cloth around his right ankle to lessen the pressure after he had stumbled on a rock on the road that morning.

He tried walking without sandals, but it made the journey impossible on the road. As he rested a man walked past with his son leading a pack horse that seemed tired and ill tempered. They stopped at the junction where Marcus rested and looked around.

'Hail, citizen' Marcus called out

'Hail, traveller? Where do you go?'

Marcus looked at his feet and his bound ankle. 'Not very far at this stage due to sore feet but eventually to Rome; do you know how far it is?'

'I am taking my young boy home from Rome. From here it as least another five days of walking. I suggest you be careful from here on as we were accosted by a gang of young thieves only a day ago. They came up asking for food and as I was assisting one, the others tried to take the packs off my mule.'

'Did they succeed?' Marcus asked

'No, they picked the wrong one' He said motioning to the Gladius that hung at his side. 'I know how to handle young men like that. I should have run one of them through to teach the rest a lesson but my boy stopped me. Lucky for them!'

Marcus nodded glancing at the sword handle which was ornate and embossed with brass. 'That is a fine, looking sword, friend, it must have cost a fortune.'

"Cost?' the man said in surprise. 'No, this was a gift young man, from the emperor himself; however, it was quite some time ago and they don't mention his name much these days.'

Marcus looked at him quizzically. 'Who?'

'You really want to know?'

Marcus nodded and smiled as he waited.

The man smiled slightly 'The Emperor Nero; He is no longer with us as he has taken flight to the underworld. Dragged there by the will of his enemies and Cerberus in assist, I guess.'

Marcus shrugged. 'You have me at a disadvantage. I grew up on a farm which I have just left to travel to Rome so I don't know much about the political side of Rome. Was he a great man?'

The large, muscular man before him shook his head slowly and a smile creased his face for the first time 'No, he was a fool and I was the champion of the fool. Have you tried the water?' He said motioning to the well near him.

The well was level with the ground with large rocks around it and a wooden structure above to allow a bucket to be lowered for water and raised once full. Marcus nodded. 'Yes, the water is fine.'

The man motioned to his son who moved to the well. 'Then you should be very happy, boy; politics is for politicians and best left alone. They are all jackals anyway, picking over the spoils of Rome. All they do is line their own pockets while the rest of us do the hard work. Do you stop for the night? We are about to make camp. If you care to join us we can forage and my son will make a fire?'

Marcus felt his sore feet again and nodded in assent. 'Where did you have in mind?'

The man stroked his stubbly beard growth and looked around. 'Hmm, there is a well here and some trees for shelter from this wind so let's take this area. Suit you as well?

Marcus nodded and followed the man over to the thick set of trees near the drinking well. The earth was not soft but there was a plentiful supply of wild grass to make a comfortable mattress.

'This is my boy, Aru, he turns fifteen this month.' The boy gave Marcus a shy smile and set about pulling the packs from the wide girth of the mule.

'My name is Britanicus.' The man replied with a deep accent.

'Marcus' came the reply and they nodded to each other as new acquaintances do after they have met formally. He looked for the first time at the size of the man before him and guessed him to be a centurion at the very least.

His large head held short curly hair, with just the slightest grey at the temples. His hair showed small areas where it was worn away from the heavy burden of a helmet. His muscular body and large arms foretold his profession of holding heavy shields and spears and his countenance remained direct and professional.

Marcus pulled a knife from his pack and checked the sharpness. He watched as Britanicus pulled a bow and arrows from the mule pack and retied the bow string that held the ends together and created the energy to fire the arrows he held in his hand.

'Are you a good shot with an arrow?' Hillarius asked casually, as he inspected the fire pit his son was in the process of creating.

'I have had much practice but my favourite is the dagger. My brother and I used to practice a lot as there was not much else to do on the farm other than work and one can get sick of that quickly.'

Britanicus laughed as he picked up a dagger and placed it in his belt. 'You are still young and by the Gods, you sound as if you believe you are old. Come let's see what we can gain before the light fades, and Ceres welcomes her victims.'

They walked off in the direction of the forest that lay on the other side of the road. They started to roam through the forest in which Marcus had spent most of his nights.

Moving slowly and as quietly as possible, they watched for prey movements in the trees beyond. They had circled the area for some time without sighting anything.

'The animals must have left for Rome' Britanicus said with a smirk.

The sun started to fade. They trekked carefully and as quietly as possible through the undergrowth, looking for smaller animals as there were no tracks or spoors from larger ones in the area they moved.

They picked their way through the fallen leaves of the forest, stopping momentarily to watch and listen. As dusk approached, they found their prey of two rabbits standing pensively near a burrow. Marcus saw them first and touched the big man on the shoulder pointing in the direction.

Britanicus placed an arrow across the shaft, and with his right hand he drew back the gut string of the bow which groaned under the stress. He took careful aim through the line of the bow and let fly. The arrow sailed across the clearing collecting the hare and pinning it to the ground.

The other took flight across the clearing towards them and Marcus taking aim with his dagger let fly, catching it in the hind quarter as it dashed past.

'Good shot, Marcus' Britanicus said clapping him on the back 'It looks like a feast tonight.'

They tied the legs of the rabbits together with a leather thong and strung across the bow they walked back to the camp. Britanicus questioned Marcus about his trip and his reasons for wanting to go to Rome.

'You are a freeman, Marcus, and that gives you a great deal of opportunities that slaves like myself never have and you must use those wisely.'

Marcus listened attentively and told him about the position his mother

———

48

found for him at the Laurentius household. Britanicus whistled when he heard the name 'Ye Gods, boy, you have found the richest man in Rome to work for. What do you work as?'

'A gardener. It wasn't my doing, it was arranged.' Britanicus shrugged as he dropped the rabbits near the fire. Marcus moved to gut and skin them but he was stopped. 'Let Aru do it. He is the best cook I know outside of my wife and he likes to be left alone to do it which is fine by me. He is a good boy but does not resemble me in any way. His mother is a fine lady too, but in my profession, I don't see her much'

'Where is your farm?'

'Less than a day's walk from here. It will be nice to be home for a change and to be able to relax a little. My wife is a good woman and she has raised the boy and done a fine job but there is isn't much resemblance is there?'

'A little I think' Marcus replied, with good manners. He moved across to the fire to throw larger logs on it for the night ahead. 'I can't offer much tonight but I have a small flask of wine at the bottom of my pack I can share.'

Britanicus pulled off his heavy tunic, stretched his arms and with a wince he massaged his knotted left shoulder.

He walked over to the bucket of water next to the fire and washed himself with a rag that lay beside it 'That is just fine. We have food and wine and no women to bother us. How can we ask for anything more!' He laughed at his own joke and returned to the fire.

Marcus produced the wine and poured a half cup each and filled the rest with water from the well. The sky was clear of clouds and the stars were starting to shine. The smell of freshly cooked meat, wafted in the early evening air.

Aru laid out plates of wheat porridge, olives and apple pieces he cut from the remaining fruit they held in their mule bags. Patiently, he turned the spit on which the two gutted rabbits cooked over the fire, spitting fat into the glowing coals below.

The conversation increased as they spoke about the road to Rome and the issues they had all encountered. Finally, a pause occurred and Marcus moved his attention to Britanicus who was sitting back on one of the bags sipping his wine and looking up at the darkening sky.

When Marcus took a moment to look closely at the man across from him, he was astonished at the number of scars that adorned the man's body. Mostly on the torso and arms, with several long welts on his upper legs as well.

One particularly livid scar travelled from his shoulder across his chest. It was prominent enough to shine in the firelight. The man possessed huge shoulders but there was an air of nonchalance about him, as if he did not care what the Gods or anyone else thought of him.

'That is some scar' Marcus said pointing to the one on his chest.

'Yes, it is. I was lucky that day and to my credit I moved quick enough not to be run through by that devil. I ended up killing him which is not the best result, but sometimes inevitable.'

'Was it a brawl?' Marcus asked tentatively.

'No, young man, I am a gladiator in Rome. My life is dedicated to fighting and winning. That is what I train for each and every day.'

Aru moved over to where they were sitting with plates.' Come, father, eat while it's hot.'

Britanicus shifted his position and took the plate with a smile. He graciously gave thanks to his son, who went to retrieve his plate to sit with them.

Marcus took his and started to eat with relish. The rabbit was perfectly cooked with just a hint of rosemary and garlic. He nodded at Aru and then at Britanicus as he wolfed down the plate.

'You are hungry, boy?' Britanicus said looking at his son. 'Aru, is there any left?

'What about tomorrow?' Came the plaintive reply.

'By tomorrow you will be home on the farm and a while later I can return to Rome. Come on, dish it out.' The three of them finished the meal and sat back on their packs to watch the star's glow brightly above the evening air.

Britanicus picked his teeth thoughtfully with a piece of bone. 'So, you return to Rome?' Marcus asked, as he poured the last of the wine.

'When you are a slave or a freeman for that matter, and you become a gladiator under a manager called a Lanista, you are attached and live within a training school. You become their property. You sleep, eat, train and fight as a gladiator, every day of every year.'

'Then how do you get to travel from Rome?' Marcus asked quietly as if the trees could hear.

'You fight hard and successfully, and sometimes you are given limited freedom, like this moment, as I have to take my boy home.

'Are you famous?'

'The women think so but you did not hear that did you, Aru?'

The boy smiled and finished his plate.

Britanicus smiled. 'If you are going to Rome you will find out if you ever go to the stadium to watch the gladiator contests. Make sure you have a look, it is very popular.' Marcus nodded, making a mental note to find a way to attend a contest.

Now it is time for us to turn in because we have a long way to go tomorrow.' He stretched his large frame, replaced the tunic and sat back to watch the fire as Marcus pulled his cloak, and started to make a bed on the other side of the fire.

'Understand, young man,' Britanicus said pensively and in a different tone to his usual composure 'We are all here for a short period of time and we must do what we can to get ahead. It is said that the Gods on Mount Olympus ordained this life for me, and I am sure that is true but I will not do this forever. It is said I will be offered the Rudis and that will give me freedom and then I see what the future holds. At the moment, my wife and Aru have a beautiful farm and enough to live a comfortable life, so that makes it worthwhile.'

Aru picked up the plates and took them to the well to wash. Britanicus followed him as did Marcus and in short time the wash was completed and the plates and cups returned to the pack. As they put more logs on the fire and Britanicus moved to the well to get a final drink before his bed, his son came over to Marcus and sat down beside him.

'They say my dad is the best in Rome by a long way.'

Marcus looked at the size of the man and remembered the scars on his body. 'I don't doubt it.' He replied 'Does he go back to fight?'

The boy looked down at the ground 'Unfortunately yes; but he intends to stop soon enough and I hope very soon. We miss him on the farm.'

'Why were you in Rome?' Marcus asked. The boy sat beside him momentarily with his eyes downcast.

'I wanted to see him. I ran away because my mother would not allow me to go and see him; so, I took off and went anyway.'

Marcus laughed and clapped the boy on the shoulder. 'You sound like me, but younger!'

Aru sat for a while and then rose as Britanicus came back to the fire. He whispered as he got to his feet. 'He is taking me back, and now I have to face my mother.'

Marcus smiled knowingly as the three positioned themselves and bedded down for the night. From the hills, Marcus could hear the now familiar sound of wolves as they moved through the night, circling and looking at the fire light with apprehension.

He laid another log on the fire and pulled his cape around him, using his pack for a pillow. Close to him Britanicus snored softly as if the world of fighting was many stars filled nights away.

In the morning, the cloudless, blue sky gave the promise of heat and no rain.

Marcus and Aru quelled the fire and laid rocks around the fire pit for good measure. Britanicus started to pack his bad-tempered horse. Each time as he moved to place the packs it jittered away and reared every time he raised the packs to place them on its back.

Losing his patience Britanicus smacked it across the snout with his fist. Stunned, it finally stopped moving away from him and the pack he was attempting to lay on its back. Marcus looked at the horse.
'You almost knocked him senseless.'

Britanicus looked over at Marcus and simply nodded. 'I should have knocked him out but I need him. I won him in a game of twelve. No wonder the loser was happy to get rid of him. If he doesn't improve he will end up as meat for the dogs.'

At the cross road, Britanicus indicated their intended direction as they were heading North in the opposite direction of Marcus. The intersection road which led to the West remained empty. They shook hands and bade each other good times and they turned their backs on each other to continue with their journey.

CHAPTER 6

Cassius Laurentius, walked with a limp favouring his right side, as he ambled through the gardens of his estate outside of Rome. The previous day, he had ridden his chariot from his villa on the second hill of Rome to inspect one of his grain ships that had lost a mast in a storm off the coast of Sicilia.

The ship was disabled and he cursed the captain for not taking better care and ordered a new mast to be installed from heavy oak. He fired the captain for good measure.

After a light meal at one of the cafes that surrounded the docks he rode the chariot back to the outskirts of the farm, leaving it with his servant to take it forward while he walked quickly the rest of the way to the estate, to keep his physique in some sort of shape. It also gave his servant the chance to let the household know the master was on his way.

His right hip pained him after the exercise and that night he ordered a hot bath and a rub down to ease it. He walked the next morning amongst the olive grove, inspecting the fruit. It was the same hip injury resulting from a collision between his chariot and another, on a rain-soaked day, near the *Via Tibuna* many years before.

His estate lay outside of Rome in the countryside near Tiburnia. He chose it because it held a slow, flowing tributary through the middle of it which finally fed, so the engineers told him, to the great Tiber river running through the city in the far, far distance.

The large and strong flowing stream, allowed water for the estate, including an extensive network of irrigation channels. The best irrigation that money could buy, and he held a great deal of wealth to purchase whatever he wanted.

The journey from his villa on one of the seven hills of Rome, to the country estate promised a long, two-day walk or a long day's ride in his chariot. He went often to be surrounded by the beauty of the estate and with time to himself the effort always proved worthwhile. In the very least it gave him time away from pursuing the crusty members of the Palatine hill and the rigors of business life.

The previous night he sat, as was his custom, on the second-floor balcony overlooking his estate and the wines grapes that stretched into the distance. His grape vines produced the finest wine in Rome. The afternoon light and fading heat of the afternoon gave him peace and allowed the quieting of the burning ambition that besieged his life. He used the time to reflect and to plan.

The crushing of the grapes was drawing near as the harvest season beckoned. It remained a popular event. Over the years, he had requested many of his political allies to make the trip to the estate to indulge in the foot pressing of the black grapes.

Plentiful food and fornicating with the whores he imported for the night time, remained a prerequisite for them to turn up to the event. There was not a woman in Rome who could equal an experienced whore, he mused with his favoured wine residing in the cup in his hand. He paid for the best so that when his allies arrived they enjoyed themselves, and of course, he expected and received favours in return. *Quid pro quo!*

The finest, of course remained the *Prostibulae*. Usually upper-class women who used prostitution as either a source of income or pleasure, or both, and who relished the chance of five days at a sought-after estate such as the one he owned.

They fucked themselves, and everyone else, silly and then left with their pouches full of Denarii. The senator's wives were supposedly chaste, but when the access to power was at stake, they used whatever it took to gain leverage including orgies, and full time illicit affairs.

Over the years he had been to many of those '*parties*' and many a full time *Meretrice*, a registered whore, played a subservient role to the ladies of power, and there were very few whores who could endure a night of fucking against the competition of the noble high and mighty.

He smiled to himself at the thought of senator's wives, who were prohibited from any form of prostitution but were amongst the worst offenders in Rome. But, he reflected, rules were made to be broken and in his business career, he had broken many.

He inspected the cup that lay in his hand, wondering momentarily why it felt so familiar. Fashioned from basic clay and glazed, it did not even bear a crest on the side as was the favoured disposition of cups and plates for the rich and famous of Roman society.

He held it lightly between his fingers, with the simple wonderment that the companionship of a basic cup might please him. Given his wealth and what he could command if he chose an ornate and expensive cup it was that simple cup that gave him pleasure.

Perhaps one in Venetian glass or the finest pottery thrown by an expert would be worth the investment but he rarely invested in anything that did not offer a substantial return and that included senators and their whore wives.

But, he reflected, like emperor Vespasian, he also held humble beginnings. He knew enough of his human brothers, to know that once the human sword was forged it remained that way, until broken by force or by death. Habits remained a friend for some and an enemy for those who did not understand the error of their ways.

The estate stretched as far as he could see from his perch above the front courtyard. It always reminded him of the work and perhaps, a little luck, that offered him the opportunity to sit on that chair, on that balcony, on his land, on that very evening. Wealth remained his constant companion but the burning ambition to be the best, the wealthiest and the most powerful burned in him as it had done the day he was born.

He had gained an advanced age, and enough wisdom, to know that there were only two gilded paths to power in Rome, albeit that both paths held nests of vipers.

The first and most obvious choice was the army. The current emperor, Vespasian, gained merited positions at the head of the Roman legions, finally using that power to take his position at the top of the political heap, getting rid of the newly appointed emperor, Vitellius in the process.

The second and no less challenging path remained wealth, and wealth, unless inherited, could only come from business. His father taught him early in his life that business requires influence and gaining associates required time and patience.

The one lesson he fully understood about business, related to those who might offer access and loans when the weather of business remained fine, but changed instantly when it started to rain. In the great state of Rome, business remained as cutthroat as the battlefield of any army.

The difference, he knew, was that death on the battlefield could be mercifully quick whereas in business, death was usually slow and painful. In the heat of battle there are those who fight with you but in business it remained a dark night with creatures circling. Once, many years before, he found himself in that dark forest. It held a lesson he could never forget.

Early in his life, and with the intent to follow his father's footstep as a businessman, he remembered sitting on a wharf near the ancient town of Capus and watching the cargo ships, come and go on the bay. It was the day of his birth day. He had just turned twenty and the lure of riches lay firmly in his thoughts.

As he sat on the heavy wood planks of the wharf, looking at the clear water of the ocean below, he could not comprehend why the grain carriers were so small.

Each time one came to the dock it unloaded grain which was transferred to drays for the trip to the Rome granaries, and the grain-supported regions. He noticed as each pulled away from the dock, yet another took its place and he counted on that hot afternoon, how long it took for them to be unloaded. After the second ship unloaded its cargo to barrows and to the cart he sauntered over to the side of the vessel.

There were no rowers on the sides of the boat. The top deck held two small sails on high rigging. Grain scattered the deck and the men sat on the side of rails with an exhausted look on their sunburnt faces.

'Hail captain' He said with his hands on the rails of the boat. 'How much do you carry on this craft?'

The captain moved over to where the young boy was standing and sat down. 'Why do you ask, young un?'

Cassius shrugged. 'Just wondered, that is all. Take no malice from my question it is just an interest.'

Perhaps twelve hundred Libra, give or take a few, to answer your question.' He replied with an easy manner.

Cassius nodded 'Why do you not take more?'

'You are obviously not a seafarer. We have a long trip to Sicilia and the port for Campagnia and then back to drop off the grain. The seas are unpredictable you know. If a big storm occurs and we are overloaded; well, down we go and let me tell you boy, many have. I have no desire to meet with any of the Gods including the great Trident on a stormy night.'

Cassius thanked him and headed back to the wharf side where he sat until the last of the grain carriers had docked and unloaded. He walked off

---

towards the town to find his father who met him on the way.

They walked back to the town while his father spoke about his deal for the cattle supply to his newly built abattoir near the edge of Suburia.

Cassius waited for his father to finish and then discussed his idea for a larger grain ship, to supply the increasing need of Rome and its states. The government of Rome, subsidised grain to its citizens and the need was growing day by day. He did not understand the logic of smaller ships which may have been faster but by their very size were clearly inefficient.

His father listened, impressed by the idea and promised to take it further. Some months later it remained on the table and had not progressed so the young Cassius took it in his own hands and started the project.

He found a marine architect, a man who designed the largest of the triremes of the Roman fleet and discussed the idea. The ship would need to be ten times larger than the current grain carriers, hold large sail capacity and the assistance of forty rowers to ensure stability and speed.

Once the plans were completed Cassius took them to all of his father's wealthier friends and all of them declined. The reasons were obvious, they told him. Too big, too much grain on one ship and too much risk. What if it went down? 'What you need to understand, young Cassius' One of the men said to him in a haughty manner. 'The reason we use many, smaller ships are that if one goes down in a storm we do not lose much. Do you not understand that?'

Finally, one contact liked the idea and the deal was set. The ship was built and Cassius owned half the enterprise. A new dock was built to hold the ship and in the space of eight short years the one ship turned into a fleet of ninety-three and he held the grain market in his hand.

For some years, he rode the ships to Sicilia and other regions to watch the unloading of the grain and how to improve the time. At the docks of Rome, he became an insidious figure, constantly around the docks looking for improvements and harassing anyone who did not work. He became hated and respected and he never yielded in the face of an argument or business change.

His ships were faster and held ten times the amount the smaller ships could hold. The larger ship unloaded in the same time as the smaller ones by using levers and ropes to pass the grain in large hessian bags to the carts waiting on the wharf.

One by one the smaller ships left the grain route unable to compete with the pricing that Cassius had negotiated in the grain lands of Sicilia and the lower Agean lands.

Cassius was young and rich and within another five years bought his partner out and started to import other goods that remained in high demand. Silks and spices, slaves and beasts. It did not matter if it created a profit.

He wondered, as he sat high on his balcony that evening, whether his future might have changed had he not visited the wharf that day and wondered about the cartage of grain.

The issue, he reluctantly admitted to himself that night, was his waning energy. Back on that dock, in his youth, he held the energy to change the world but today, despite all of his wealth he would give it all away to have that energy and the excitement it brought, once again.

That evening, with a bellyful of his own wine he arose from his seat and walked across to the stables. He held a herd of finely bred *Maramenno* mares, the finest in Rome, in a special enclosure. The horses were favoured amongst the rich and famous and he parted with them for either a large sum of a favour to be returned at a later date.

As he neared the enclosure he noticed one of the entrance logs was not in place and several of the mares were nosing to find a way out. He looked at it with anger rising in him. He saw the stable slave in the distance and turned angrily to him.

"Hey, you! Get over here.'

The slave looked at him with fear at the tone of his voice. He dropped his bucket and ran over to the gate where Cassius was standing.

'Who did this, boy?'

The slave, a small dark haired young man with bent shoulders stooped in front of him, eyes downcast and a frightened look on his face. 'I was returning in a moment with the bucket.'

'What is your name?'

Cassipur, sire. We have seen each other before.'

'That is not what I asked you, boy. What I asked you, is whether you left the fence in this state?'

The slave looked at him, speechless and shuffling his feet. Cassius reached over to one of the reins hanging on the side of the stable wall and started to flay the boy who fell before him, shouting.' Do you know how much these mares cost? Do you? You, worthless scum!'

He continued to flay him until the boy fell to the ground and then Cassius put his boot into his back. 'One mare, is worth your bloody life and the life of your wretched family you...' He stopped, breathless, dropping the reins to his side as he half listened to the boy crying on the ground.

A noise made him turn abruptly and he turned to find a girl behind him. 'It was my fault, sire, not his. I was brushing one of the mares and had gone to get a larger brush. I did not replace the log because I was one moment away.' She was pretty and he could not remember seeing her before. She held the dark eyes and broad chin of those around the district of the farm.

Cassius glared at her and at the sobbing boy at his feet. He backhanded her across the face and watched with satisfaction as she sprawled across the dusty enclosure.

He moved over to where she lay on the ground and grabbed her viciously by the hair. 'Next time, I will kill you.' He hissed and turned on his heels. As he passed the boy crying on the ground he shouted. 'Get up and get back to work or I will make you wish you had.' He threw the reins in the boy's face and stormed off.

He walked around the house several times trying to quell his vicious temper. What was it that drove him to such a rage? He walked slowly, noting there was not a slave in sight. Word had got around and no one would dare approach him until he told them.

It was those bloody buildings, he thought to himself, visualising them in the sand at his feet. Vespasian and his monuments to himself; the Forum and then to rub salt into the wound of all the people in Rome, the arrogantly named, Flavian Amphitheatre.

By the Gods, what insanity allowed this measure of benevolence of funds that were not even the ownership of the Vespasian'. They were the property of Rome.

Yes, Vespasian held some wealth but most of it would come from the plundering the lands of Judea and Egypt. Illegal, well covered and very well hidden. Who was going to question the emperor?

He had seen so many come and go. He barely knew Caligula, but Vespasian had done much to ingratiate himself to the madman in those days and much of his future success, of course. Anyone who could look Caligula in the eyes and still survive had balls and Vespasian was one of those who did not understand fear.

Then the stuttering fool of Claudius spent some years in the house on the hill before he was murdered by his niece of all people. Then to make matters much worse that idiot Nero becomes emperor. All of Rome still have memories of his great contribution in burning half the place down including some of the grounds of Cassius's own villa. By the Gods where did the world find these idiots?

When Vitellius was defeated and consequently put to the sword it was a dark day for Cassius. He held faith in Vitellius only because he realised the man could be easily bought. The first day he met him, he knew he held an alliance with someone of high position and easily influenced.

Vespasian was another matter; Strong, independent and untouchable. The man held his sons tightly to him and Titus, his eldest son, was clearly, a force in his own right.

Whilst Vespasian took off to Egypt to hold it he left Titus in Judea to scatter the Jews which he did with honourable purpose and brutality and no doubt the riches that paid for Vespasian's expensive equine hobby and his estates were underwritten by the spoils of those lands, alone. Cassius held wary of Titus and the seeds never fall far from the tree, he mused as he about faced, walking off towards the stables, to see if the wretched slaves had fixed the mares fence.

With his anger diminishing and the thought of a hot bath in front of him he gave thought to the buildings. It was a magnificent ploy by Vespasian, to put his name down in history through the buildings and the name of the stadium. It was genius and it seemed to him that the only one who understood Flavians' quest for immortality was Cassius himself. The others just primped and danced and took care of their own business.

However, it was not lost on Cassius that Vespasian was going to need large funding outside of the cache of spoils from Judea to finish the buildings and wealth were something that, he, Cassius Laurentius had in plenty.

Cassius knew instinctively, that name, influence and legacy journeyed

———

hand-in-hand through the political forest. He needed to make the name Laurentius more prominent and to be found in history at a later date. He had no son and no heir and by the Gods on the mount the world would remember his name well after his death.

His wife, who he could hardly bear to be near except for fucking which she did with excellence, bore him a useless daughter. Beautiful, like her mother and about as stupid. The Laurentius name would live through him, he reflected as he neared the stables.

The boy had disappeared and as he walked through the stables away from the mare enclosure he stopped to inspect the saddles and rein assemblies to see if they were in place. The main door of the feed area was open and he walked towards it in the fading light of the late afternoon. A faint red glow from the sunset settled across the wooden beams and in the back, he heard a noise.

He walked through to find the girl washing herself from a bucket of water on the side of the feed trough. She was naked from the waist up, heavy breasted and with her tunic tied at the waist. When she saw him she immediately grabbed for her tunic to pull it up.

'Sire, I ...' She mumbled dropping the sponge she was using into the bucket.

Cassius moved quickly over to her, grabbed her by the hair and turned her front to the bales of hay. He pulled his tunic tie open and entered her from behind. She started to scream and while he thrusted into her he held his hand over her mouth.

Her muffled screams and his grunting filled the small hay lot until he was finished. When he finally came, he felt almost disappointed. A little more fight from her might have made it more enjoyable.

Suddenly, he realized the act was finished and pulled himself out. Maybe she would give him a boy, he thought ruefully. Satisfied he pulled his tunic and left the way he came. There was nothing she could do. The law in Rome was very clear. In his position of power, he was untouchable.

Besides, he reflected as he slowly returned to the house, he owned her like he did everything else on the estate and in his business empire.

Sated, he walked slowly towards the estate villa and sat briefly on the stone wall near the entrance. He was tired from the day's events and a bellyful of wine did not help. It was on the wall that the thought entered his mind.

He held the wealth to fund the opening games and there was a chance that Vespasian would allow it given the huge cost. If so, he would move towards being bestowed a seat in the senate and if he underwrote the games cost, he would set the deal so he could advertise them in his family name and use the term; Colliseum. And on that Colliseum, that magnificent building, open to the world, for all to see, would be the inscribed name of Cassius Laurentius.

For the games, at least, no more Flavius Amphitheatre. The Colliseum would resound through Rome under the games held by Cassius Laurentius and he would provide the champion of Rome for the first day, not Vespasian.

The champion would be known from that day as the first gladiator of Rome at the behest of the sponsor; Cassius Laurentius. From his position on the wall he watched the dying sunset laced with vibrant magenta and orange across the far horizon. The bird calls were settling, and the oncoming night highlighted the olive groves towards the entrance to his estate.

For the first time, since that night with Vespasian, he felt at ease. The future would be created in his image.

CHAPTER 7

Early that evening, in the far distance, Marcus saw a light on the side of the road across a rolling hill and at the start of another long road climb. In the hope it was a tavern and a hot dinner he redoubled his steps towards the light.

As he neared the building, he noticed the four lamps at the front, lit early for the coming night and he breathed a sigh of relief. It was indeed a tavern and outside on the front of the building, under a wide, tiled area, patrons sat in the early evening, downing wine and speaking loudly to each other.

Marcus pulled his pack off and walked inside to the gloom of oil lamps and large, fat candles adorning most of the tables within the tavern.

A large overweight man walked over to him as Marcus slumped at the table. 'Welcome traveller, what will it be for you tonight?

Marcus shrugged 'What do you have for food?'

'Only the best in all of the country. Oven cooked chicken and rabbit with turnips and maize. A hearty meal if there ever was one. It comes, with a free watered wine.'

Marcus nodded and ordered the proffered meal. There were few inside so it was either a slow day or travellers were yet to come down the road and look for a rest site.

He left his pack at the table and walked over to the serving area which was made of timber and large stones to make a serving top. 'Do you have a room?

The man nodded his head. 'Yes, we have few rooms ready and you are welcome to use one for the night. The cost is eight As and does not include your meal.'

Marcus checked the coins in his pouch and nodded his head in agreement. In a short while, a wooden bowl was placed before him and the watered wine which, Marcus knew, would contain more water than wine, placed on the table as well.

He ate hungrily quickly and finishing the bowl and realising he could easily eat another. He pushed it away after wiping the rim of the bowl with bread supplied with the meal.

He ordered a carafe of wine with a jug of water and wearily sat back to watch the patrons who moved in and out of the tavern.

His mind turned to Britanicus, the gladiator he had met on the road and his young son. The size of the man's strong shoulders and strength with a bow made him wonder what life might be for a man of his skill. Did he fight every day and did he fear the fights he contested?

Marcus continued to sit at the table and disconsolately drank wine for much of the evening. He felt lonely for the first time amongst the tavern patrons and he smiled at a waitress who made a number of excuses to come over to his table, enquiring about where he was travelling to and from where he had come.

His thoughts returned to brother and mother and his decision to leave the farm. He could not have worked easily with his father and he kept that thought in his mind, determined to get on with his journey and his life.

Later that night, as he was about to retire to a comfortable bed for the first time in over a week, he heard a commotion at the far end of the tavern and his inquisitive nature got the better of him. He picked up his belongings and walked over with a cup of wine in his hand.

A small crowd was gathered around a table with three men playing a game with dice. Around the side of the table, bets adorned the small, coloured squares they sat within.

He watched for a while, trying to understand the game and how the betting worked. A clean, shaven man with a bald head that shone in the oil lamplight, whispered to Marcus to explain the game.

'Three players and each has a turn at the dice in succession and there are ten throws. At the end of the throws the person who has the highest score wins the tournament.' Marcus nodded as he listened to another dice throw onto the table which resulted in a seven.

'So;' the man whispered turning more towards Marcus so he could hear. 'The bets on the side are equal and if, for example, the man to the left wins he takes the pot from the other two players. All bets must be equal so the winner can't lay two Denarii in front of himself and it not be the same in front of the others. However, if one player does not want to put up the same pot as the others his pot can be added to by spectators who share in the win from the other two losing players if that player should win the total of the ten throws.'

'Seems easy' Marcus said as his interest started to rise. The sound of the shouts and excitement filled his ears and for the first time since he left the farm, he was starting to feel alive.

'It may seem easy, but you can lose easily' The man said rubbing his hand across his bald pate.

Marcus nodded, barely listening to the man as his eyes held their gaze on the action below. The man to the left of the table appeared to be winning as each time he threw his dice down they settled with a higher number.

'Do you know how dice work, young friend?' The man whispered to Marcus and took a drink from his wine cup. Marcus slowly brought his gaze from the table and shook his head at the question.

'Simple, my friend, very simple. The sides always add up to seven. So, opposite the six on the dice is a one and opposite the four is a three and so on.'

Marcus watched the dice fall again and he counted the numbers of the dice side up. This was a pure game of chance and the sort of game he loved.

'How do I get to play?'

The bald man, smiled at the impetuousness of youth. 'You wait, young man until someone gets up and you take your chance. It is a one Denari minimum bet if you can afford it.' The man smiled at him.

Marcus walked across to the tavern bar and ordered another wine. He returned the smile of the waitress who rushed over to serve him and he went back to the game.

Finally, the player closest to Marcus got up and stretched. 'That's it for me.' He said with a tired look on his face 'Anyone else want the seat?'

Marcus took his pouch out and stepped forward and he was allowed to sit down and start the game.

'Bets please' said one of the other players and Marcus took a Denari out of his pouch and put it on the side of the table.

'Stop the horses,' One said with a laugh 'We have a heavy gambler here!'

Marcus smiled as there was little else he could do as he sat, transfixed by the table and the mood of the gamblers.

The rest laughed in unison as the other two players laid a Denarii down. One of the other players turned to Marcus 'That is a low bet, boy, you won't lose much but you won't win much either. '

Marcus looked at him, fished another Denarii out of his purse and added it to the silver coin on the table. The two Denarii had almost emptied his pouch. The play began with Marcus throwing his first dice and the dice settled onto the table with a double six, the highest score possible.

A few sighs came from the onlookers and one low whistle from one of the other players.

Marcus studied the other two in front of him. Both appeared to be travellers and both were grimy from a day or more travel. Given there was a well at the side of the tavern, neither saw the need to wash. The one next to Marcus held the unpleasant smell of dirt and sweat together, and a dirty tunic as well.

The game continued through to the last throw with the lead ebbing and waning as each player threw the dice onto the table with their individual styles. On the final throw, Marcus threw a double six and payment was made on his single square.

He had made four Denarii. He made a mental calculation. A Denari was worth four Sestertii which equalled sixteen As. Since the meal in total cost six As, he had made a fortune, at least for a boy from the farm.

The bets were laid again and this time Marcus delved into his pouch and placed three Denarii on the marker square on the table. The dice were passed to his hand as he had won the previous bet.

The game continued with him winning on the last hand and he now had the total of ten Denarii in front of him.

'Might be time to up the bet from our young traveller.' One of the other players said with an expectant look. Marcus looked over to find the man with a dirty tunic giving him a competitive sneer.

This time, he laid four Denarii on the square, noticing the remaining two had met his bet total. Again, he won the game and now held four Denarii.

———

'Looks like the boy can't lose' Said one onlooker. 'Is everyone happy to increase the bet.'

In the next game, he laid down two Denarii in the square in the belief that he could not keep winning as he had conquered the last. One man to the side made the sound of a chicken and then the bald man, who had given Marcus the advice, held his hand up. 'By the Gods, he has the right to play what he wants, and if he does not believe he can win, he has the right to pull down his bets or leave the table. However, good manners might dictate that we get a chance to get out money back. Correct?'

There was murmuring around the table with voices rising as the atmosphere changed towards the win or loss of larger bets. Marcus pulled out four more Denarii and laid them on the table.

This seemed to satisfy the crowd and he threw his dice gaining three on the throw. By the end of the game they were locked in a tie and the last throw would be the decider.

The two men threw first, and Marcus on the third. The first threw an eight, followed by a ten and Marcus threw an eleven with the second dice spinning for quite a while before settling near the middle.

The place erupted with Marcus holding a pile of Denarii in front of him. He sat there stunned trying to work out what he had won in the space of a very short time. Marcus realized, with a shock, he had won thirty Denarii, was not only a small fortune but almost the earning of one month's produce from his father's farm.

Everyone stood around amazed at the result. There were heated discussions with the bald man walking aside to speak to another who bent his head in muted conversation.

'That is some winning streak.' The bald man said with an irritated and aggressive tone. 'One more game. So, we have a chance to gain our money back!'

Marcus cocked his head, feeling lightheaded from the wine that he consumed that night from very early that evening. 'I agree!'

'We raise the amount to forty Denarii'

'Agreed' Marcus said with his blood up and looking forward to the challenge 'However, I have travelled all day, as I assume have most of you and this is the last game win or lose.' There was murmur around the table and finally the bald man eyed the table players who sat opposite Marcus and after some discussion the answer was given back.

'Agreed.'

The play started with Marcus throwing the worst dice of that evening as the result was two single dots. By the sixth throw he was twenty behind and the other two players were starting to loosen up and laugh.

For the next five throws Marcus threw high numbers finally ending up with the last throw as the decider.

He was five dice points behind at the last throw and only a full twelve could be successful. He looked around enjoying the audience, noting that even the waitress was smiling and watching the action. He felt the familiar pump of his heart that he felt at the start of a fight or even a game he played with his brother for honey cakes.

In a slow, laconic manner he swirled the dice around the cup and finally let them slip across the table.

As they came to rest the was not a sound from the audience. The two dice, displayed the perfect score. Two sixes made a twelve and Marcus was the winner. He had made seventy Denarii, which comprised a considerable fortune.

Finally, the place erupted and Marcus rose from the table. He looked around at the unhappy patrons who were eyeing him from all sides of the table. The bald man was the first to speak as he came close to Marcus.

'Well done. Perhaps one more game?'

Marcus shook his head and as he collected the hefty winnings and placed them in his pack he looked around the room at the increasingly aggressive stares around the table. 'We agreed this was the last game.' He bade his audience goodnight.

As he moved from the table the waitress looked at him with a broad smile as she played with her hair 'You are the champion' She said looking up at him

'Tonight, anyway; Marcus responded with a smile.' What is your name?'

'Lydia' Came the warm reply.

He asked the man for the directions to the room and headed off into the cool night air to breathe before he returned to the room for the night. He was astonished at the number of coins that sloshed around in his pack. He returned to the tavern and walked up the creaking stairs to the lofts above, noting the number of eyes on him as he walked away.

In the space of a late evening he had won as much as his father might make in a season on a crop and for that he threw dice and watched them fall in his favour. He replayed the rounds in his mind knowing that he held the Goddess of Luck in his palm that night. However, he was winner on the night and that was gratification enough.

He opened the door and walked slowly into the room. He was tired and the thought of a soft bed and long nights' sleep was welcoming after a week on the road. Marcus dropped his pack and staff, threw off his cloak, washed his face and lay on the bed with a pronounced sigh and fell asleep immediately.

Some while later he awoke from a sound. He looked at the oil lamp and the flame flickered lower and he guessed it might be just before dawn. There was a knock at the door. He rose from the bed and as he moved towards the door he grabbed his staff for protection. He opened it slightly and he found the waitress at the door.

'Shh' She said 'The walls have ears.' Marcus stood there in surprise at her entrance. His heart started to calm down from what he thought was a threat and he dropped the staff to the floor. She looked up at him breathlessly. 'They intend to rob you on the road in the morning.'

Marcus sat wearily on the bed and nodded his head 'I thought as much.'

'I can show you a path through the trees at the back which will take you down a long way before you get to the road.'

Marcus lay down on the soft bed. 'No, I will face it in the morning if they are there. The Denarii are mine. I won.'

'They intend to get the coins and I am sure they don't care what happens to you. Perhaps you are better off to leave now.'

'How many will be waiting?'

'More than one. Do you remember the bald man you spoke to?'

Marcus nodded.' He is the ringleader' She continued 'He did not lose any

---

money but he will take a share if they get it from you.'

Marcus raised himself from the bed to a sitting position and thought for a moment. 'I don't run from fights, but I thank you for the advice.' The girl smiled at him and left quietly the way she had come.

He finally woke much later than the dawn that passed well before. He rose, dressed and walked downstairs. The tavern was deserted and the smell of the wine and human throng of the night before held heavy in the morning air.

He ordered pancakes and mead wine which he ate quickly with the intent to be on his way. He dropped four As, on the table, and made for the door and into the sunshine of the courtyard beyond.

Outside, he hefted his sack and took the track at the back of the tavern to the road.

As he turned the corner he was confronted by five men. In the front of the group stood the largest of them all who held a dagger in his right hand.

'Ah, young man, you have risen late and we have been waiting since before dawn for your arrival, and the repayment of our Denarii, of course.' The bald- headed man stepped from behind the giant. He was holding a club in his hand

'Your Denarii?' Marcus replied, slowly dropping his pack to the ground and his cloak quickly followed it.

'Our Denarii, young man. Perhaps you will be kind enough to pass them over so we don't have to kick your head in!'

Marcus gripped his staff with his right hand and looked carefully at the group. Clearly the bald man was the leader and beside him stood the greatest threat. He was a large, muscular man with a surly countenance and he remembered him from the previous night. The other three stood to the back which meant they were there for the threat but not necessarily the fight.

'My memory is that I won the Denarii in a fair contest against two other opponents and I threw the highest scores. Explain why you think they should be returned.' Marcus looked at each of the men noting how and where they stood and those that stood at the front.

71

'You cheated!'

'Cheated?' Marcus said with a laugh

'Loaded dice'

'But how would that be possible? We were all playing with the same dice.'

'You swapped them.' The surly giant next to the bald man intervened. 'We have seen it before'

'Have you? Where?'

'In Rome.'

'No doubt, you have' Marcus replied 'You, stupid oaf; but not from me. Since you are either stupid or dishonest, or both, how might it be possible to change the dice on all the games, in front

of two players and a group around the table?'

The bald man took control again as he raised his hand to silence the murmuring of the group. 'We do not want to hurt a traveller on this road to Rome but unless you return the Denarii we will be forced to take them'

Marcus tapped the point of his staff on a rock next to his foot and looked up at them with a smirk on his face. 'It appears that you are just sore losers, and you really know I did not cheat. You just want your Denarii back that you lost in a fair contest.'

'Something like that.' One of the men said at the back of the group.

Marcus was the first to move. He instantly picked up the rock that he had tapped with the staff a moment before to see if it was loose.

He threw it into the middle of the group and it hit one of them in the head and in an instant, he was down with blood gushing from a wound on his temple.

Marcus raised his staff moving quickly to his left and with a broad sweep he hit the big man to the right of the leader in the knees with a resounding whack and then followed up with the upper part of the staff into the man's face breaking his nose with a crunch that could be easily heard.

As the big man stumbled and started to fall, Marcus wielded the staff by grabbing the middle. He swung it as hard as he could into the midriff of the bald man who turned too late to parry the blow and he fell to one knee with the force of the strike.

Another blow across the side of the head and the man was down and then he applied the same fist to the giant who was trying to rise and he fell back under the weight of the blow.

One of the two men left standing, pulled his dagger and moved towards Marcus with a growl. He raised the blade to strike as Marcus moved into a crouch and brought the staff up under his chin, lifting him off the ground. He landing on his back unconscious on the road. The fifth man took off running in the opposite direction.

As he turned, the bald man was on his feet and had levelled his blade at Marcus's mid rift. With a scowl, he slashed his dagger through the air to put Marcus off balance. 'You want a fight, young one? Well, you have one.

One broad sweep of the blade, caught Marcus slightly on the shoulder and the flesh wound started to bleed, at the top of his arm. He wiped the blood away with his hand and with speed moved inside the bald man's knife arm and smashed a heavy fist into his face and watched him slump into the ground.

As the man rose he laid a hard fist into Marcus' ribs which left him breathless and as he turned the man slammed another fist into his jaw which sent Marcus staggering back on the dusty road.

As he tried to rise all he could see was the point of the knife heading for his throat. Instinctively, he grabbed his staff and slammed the point of the staff into the man's chest and within a moment he was up with the staff wedged into the man's throat. He stood above him, breathing heavily and leaning lightly on the staff to keep the pressure.

The bald man was groaning and with a well-aimed kick, he booted him in the groin and then gave him one in the head for good measure which almost broke his toes. He returned to his pack and pulled out a rag which he applied to the wound on his upper arm.

Behind him he heard another sound and he turned in alarm to face another attacker. It was the girl from the night before, almost breathless by the time she reached him. 'I did not know you had left' She said in short breaths 'I thought they were further down the road.'

73

Her wide eyes looked up at him and then she saw the wound. She grabbed the rag from him, refolded it and applied it expertly across the blade strike to stop the flow of blood and bound it again to hold it in place.

Marcus looked at her with admiration. 'My father is a soldier.' she said a little sheepishly. 'You understand wounds when you are in the army. Come back to the tavern and I will bind it properly.'

Marcus shook his head 'No, I must keep going. These are stupid men and they will not know when to stop. It is best, I be on my way.'

The girl stretched up and gave Marcus a long hug. As she did so Marcus heard the big man starting to get off the ground. He pushed her away and moved quickly to where the man was starting to rise.

He grabbed him by the hair and powered a full fist into his jaw. With that blow the big man's head snapped back and he fell back hard, onto the road surface.

Marcus grabbed his pack and cloak, took five Denarii out of his pack and put it in the girl's hand. She protested but he forced her fingers over the Denarii in her palm.

'You are the only one who has shown kindness so please accept part of my winnings. He nodded and smiled and he turned to leave. 'When they wake, tell them they were wrong. They were my Denarii and won in a fair contest.'

CHAPTER 8

Five days later, he finally arrived in the outskirts of Rome and entered the city to stop and look at a street sign; the first he had seen in his life. He followed Via Tiburtino towards the centre of the great city.

The city shimmered under the gaze of the seven hills that formed a natural barrier from the plains surrounding it and many of the large expensive villas, homes to families of wealth, looked down on the city, perched on expensive tracts of land.

On a number of occasions, he asked those he met for directions to the estate, and with the help of a single traveller he finally found the way to the Laurentius house, to meet with his uncle.

He arrived at the palatial villa that sat prominently on the second hill of Rome, looking down across the metropolis beneath. The house resided at the end of a long road and it stood, in all its grandeur, in the middle of a wide expanse of gardens and trees.

After the open space and untidiness of his farm he looked around, amazed at the opulence of the house and surrounding grounds. He walked up the long road to the house realising it was wide enough for at least two chariots abreast and paved with intricate care.

The space and quality of the villa was breath taking as he made his way to the front gated area. The difference between his farmhouse and the villa before him made him shake his head as he continued up the path to the palace.

The front of the villa was a deep yellow ochre colour, with large columns supporting the upper part of the building. The front, held a wide marbled area, leading to a gated wall with the windows adorned by shutters all affixed to all the windows.

The grounds looked extensive, with olive trees planted in perfect rows to one side and a manicured area on the other. The front of the villa, held strategically placed fruit trees amongst worn marble paving and edging that had yellowed slightly, over the years.

As Marcus looked around he considered the wealth required to upkeep such a property, as befitted a nobleman of Laurentius's reputation. His mother had forewarned him that the man who resided in the villa was as a leading businessman of Rome. He was a man of great influence.

At the front, he introduced himself to a slave who ushered him into the open area at the front and told him to stay put while she found the mistress of the house.

He stood inside the front entrance and looked down the long hall to the atrium. The walls were painted with colourful murals and the floors bedecked with the finest mosaic patterns. The slave returned quite some while later and brought him into what must have been the reception room and again he was told to sit and wait.

He looked out at a private courtyard area, elaborately decorated with mosaics, fountains and sculptures. As he studied the area around him, he could see doors that closed off the surrounding rooms.

He guessed they led to bedrooms or some entertaining areas. He realised with amazement that the courtyard and the two rooms he was ushered through, made up the same space as the farm house he grew up in.

The slave, a young woman who spoke very little and walked very slowly, motioned him to follow her as they walked to the back of the house. She paused briefly, noting the entertaining spaces and bedrooms in the front part of the home. She explained that the family baths and shrine were at the back and off limits to all except family members and trusted servants.

She indicated the servant's quarters were located underneath the back of the house and she stopped to show him the path that would take him there after his meeting with the mistress.

He finally arrived at the back of the house to find the matriarch of the villa sitting in the shade of a courtyard with her daughter in attendance.

The daughter was fair-haired, in contrast to her mother who sat with a mass of black hair which cascaded to frame her beautiful face. She was wearing makeup, to highlight her eyes. It was the first woman with makeup he had ever seen in his young life.

Lucia Laurentius eyed him coolly as he was motioned to sit down in front of them. Marcus looked at her intently noting the expense of her dress and the way in which she presented herself.

'*Salvete*' he said as introduction.

'*Salve*' she said curtly 'Please sit.' She motioned to a cushioned stool in front of both of them. 'So, Marcus Attilius, you are a farm boy and your uncle has found a job for you in our garden, I believe.'

Marcus nodded. 'He had been very kind, yes.'

'Hmm; it is not his kindness, it is ours' She replied with distaste in her voice 'I should introduce my daughter, Antonia. This is her fifteenth summer.'

Marcus nodded at the young beauty who held all of her mother's allure with the added bonus of youth on her flawless skin. A simple cotton dress adorned her body, with sandals and a tortoiseshell comb, holding her blond locks at the back.

Atonia smiled at him and blushed. Lucia continued watching Marcus intently. 'At all times you will do what you are asked. It should go without saying, but you must respect this household and its family.'

Marcus nodded, not sure of what to say.

Do you agree?'

'Of course, mistress' Marcus noted with his widest smile.

'If you are asked to do something, you must do it immediately, and that includes any instructions from your uncle. He has been with us for many, many years and he is very loyal to this household.'

Marcus nodded.

'Was there a large garden on the farm, Marcus'

'Very large. My mother tended the vegetables and my father as well as my brother and I tended the fruit orchards; as well as the field ploughing and sowing. I was brought up to respect the seasons, and to ensure the farm orchards and gardens were tended and made to prosper.'

'Where is the farm?'

'Several weeks walking to the North. Before the Tuscan hills.'

 Lucia nodded. 'You will be under the management of Tactius. I will keep in touch with him to make sure you are completing your duties. Are there any questions you may have, before I pass you to your uncle?'

Marcus shrugged. 'No, I don't think so mistress.'

'You will work all days, except for the public holidays of which we have so many.' She added with a desultory wave of her hand. 'We have several estates. Your work may include time on our land which, is two day's travel from here but we will let your uncle know.'

She rose from her stool with Atonia following her lead. 'We will meet again but you must be hungry. I will get you re-introduced to your uncle.'

She motioned to the slave who stood to the side. She walked over to Marcus and motioned for him to follow, which, he did with the unpleasant feeling someone was watching him as he left. He could only assume it was the mistress of the house.

He followed the slave, as they walked through the lower floor of the villa to the slave quarters, which were underneath. She kept walking until they reached a small hut at the back of the property. She pointed to a small hut and motioned him to go forward while she retreated to the house.

Tactius hugged him warmly when he arrived. Like all uncles, he noted surprise at how much Marcus had grown. When he looked at his uncle who he had met once, apparently, when he was a very small child he was surprised as to how physically similar they were.

Despite his uncles age, he had survived the rigors of time and labour well. He was tall, muscular and wiry like Marcus with a broad face and deep brown eyes. His face remained etched with the lines, that grew each year, from working under the hot Roman sun. He placed his pack and staff where his uncle indicated and joined him at a table near a brick enclosed cooking area.

He sat down, tired and jaded by the journey but interested to speak to his uncle for the first time. Immediately the warmth and interest from both was evident.

Tactius provided a meal of maize and mutton, which, was the first real meal Marcus had eaten in the last days. He ate hungrily, until he felt sated.

Over the course of the early evening they discussed his adventures on the road and leaving the farm. 'Tacitus, how long is it since you have seen my mother?'

Tacitus bowed his head and thought before giving an answer. 'A long,

---

78

long time ago. Too long, I guess, but she is a long way from Rome. I have duties here and a living to earn. Many time's I have thought about leaving Rome to visit her on the farm, but some part of life gets in the way. Is she well?'

'She is Uncle. She sends her love to you and thanks for assisting me.'

Tacitus nodded and started to clear the table. 'Let us get the dishes cleaned and then off to bed with you, Marco' He said using the same endearment as his mother. 'We share the room through there' he pointed to the only door in the area he lived 'And, you can have

the uncomfortable bed near the window.' He said with a smile. 'You are young and without the aches and pains of the elders such as me.'

He smiled as he downed the last dreg of wine from his cup. 'It is good to have you here, Marco, and I welcome the company. This is our area to live in and thankfully, we don't have to live with the rest of them under the house.'

Marcus got up and assisted with the final clean up. Gratefully, he laid down on the bed of which his uncle had not underestimated. He would replace the straw the next opportunity he had.

'Rest well' He called out softly.

The next morning, they arose at dawn and Tacitus walked him around the sizeable grounds of the villa Laurentius. He spent his time explaining the different part of the gardens, orchard and butchery.

It was like residing back at the farm, as the chores remained much the same. The only difference remained the absence of tilling and sowing, and there was a very welcome change away from his father's sullenness and negativity.

'For the next month or so you will be assigned to the orchard. The trees are neglected and there is need for new seedlings to replace those that are dying, so I will leave you to that area.' Tacitus said, motioning to him to follow him as he showed Marcus the tool shed and where the new seedlings were placed to grow in the shade and covered by light muslin cloth. 'Did the mistress explain our work requirements?'

Marcus nodded absently as he surveyed the orchard on their final inspection. There was much to do and that was exactly what he wanted. The work beckoned and he liked physical work. 'Do you need to inspect my work each day?'

'Apparently.' Tacitus smiled as he put his arm around Marcus's shoulder. 'But I won't. If you can't do this, then you should never have been on a farm. Come, it's time for lunch. Then, you can get your tools and start. The rest is up to you and you are young and strong so I don't see any areas of concern.'

As the days turned to weeks, Marcus worked the orchard to start new trees and to pare back the overgrown orchard area. He worked each day with a pick and shovel, which put muscle on his arms and chest and with each passing day he skin grew browner from the sun that beat down on the second hill of Rome.

Within several weeks, Tactius allowed him to venture into the city by himself to take part in the nightlife of Rome. He agreed to a return time that could be no later than when the moon rose to its highest position. On cloudy or rainy nights, Marcus held the perfect excuse to stay out.

Now and then, Tacitus would meet him in the orchard to talk about his work. He made suggestions and compliments but never laid criticism.

Respect steadily grew from Marcus towards his uncle and more frequently, he witnessed some of his mother in Tactius, and the fact that they held a sibling bond made him closer.

Each day he would complete his work and return the tools to the shed near where Tactius' hut was situated. Most nights, after a late evening meal he would dress and walk the long road down to Suburia.

Often, Tacitus would ask him what he did and he would reply that he drank and chased girls, which was true. The only secret he never confided in Tactius was his need to gamble. Marcus held his addiction close to him, hoping his uncle would never find out.

CHAPTER 9

It was the eve of *Matralia*, the night before a public holiday and a time for parents to lay flowers on the shine to the virgin goddess of the Dawn and matrons.

It also was a day that parents laid offerings for blessings on their children. The day had brought with it the signs of an early Roman summer, with clear skies and summer heat.

The noisy tavern held the happy disposition of citizens enjoying the prospect of the holiday before them. After the blessings in the early morning, the day offered the portent of good weather and the gladiatorial spectacle at the *Fortunis*, the following day.

Not that his father might ever lay an offering for him, Marcus mused as he downed yet another cup of wine. He now resided in Rome and a great distance from the farm with its rolling hills of wheat and grazing animals.

The noise from the table interrupted his thoughts as he brought his attention back to hot, smelly room and game before him. He looked around him at the crowd of sweating men and with the exception of one woman, a bored looking waitress still serving drinks, the rest were men of all shapes and sizes with one thought on their mind.

The small room was full of punters and Marcus knew from experience that all of Rome was a gambling haven. Despite the fact that it was prohibited, many games occurred in taverns each night and this gave testament to the fact that Romans liked to gamble. So much so, that Romans could not enjoy even a simple board game without gambling on the outcome.

The patron of the tavern stood near the door with an anxious look on his wizened face. Gambling was accepted but still it was illegal and the noise from the tavern would likely wake the Gods themselves on Olympus. It made good sense not to wake the reverie of the Marshalls, the Pretorian guard that strolled the city on a regular basis.

All he needed, was the urban *prefect* or his guards to come walking by and that would be the end of his business. There were two heavily armed men outside but he guessed they were with Vicinius.

He turned towards the back of the room trying without success to quiet the howls of excitement and anticipation that continued to cascade out of the small room as the bets mounted on the side of the table and between the players crowding the perimeter of the game.

Marcus threw the dice into the cup and swirled them around the bottom waiting until he was convinced they were in the right position. He let the cup tilt and watched the dice tumble out onto the game table.

The board game before him was his favourite. It was a deadly game when one player was losing. No amount of skill could change the outcome when loss was in the air. The game was known as the *'ludus duodecim scriptorum,* 'game of twelve,' which depended as much on luck as it did on skill. On this particular night Marcus knew he had the skill but as happened many times, the goddess had taken her leave of his side.

As the dice rolled out onto the table he stared, disbelieving at the numbers upwards on the dice. The dice displayed 2,4 and 6 and he had nowhere to move as his opponent's markers were on those slots.

He looked over at the one hundred and forty-two Denarii sitting on the side of the table next to his opponent's coins and with the knowledge that it was all he had left in the world he waited for his opponents throw.

'Not a good night, perhaps.' The voice whispered from above and he swivelled to look up at a young man with a grimace on his face. 'Did you bring a woman with you, to bring me luck?'

The young man smiled at him. 'No, not tonight'

'Then I have a worse problem. The Goddess Fortuna has deserted me again tonight and my luck has been down for weeks. Did you see my last throw?'

The young man nodded 'It seems you have another problem as well.'

'Which is?' Marcus replied

'You see that man over there, the short one with the man who looks like a very large, unshaven gorilla next to him.'

Marcus nodded blankly. 'Yes, I know him. Vicinius, the money collector'

'You owe?'

'I owe' Marcus paraphrased, with a distinct scowl.

'Much?'

'I have paid him but he keeps insisting that I still owe him because of the percentage paid on the debt.'

'How high is the percentage?' came the quick reply

Marcus nodded, with a quick glance at Vicinius, who stood watching him and the game. 'One hundred percent'

The man whistled slowly as he bent down to whisper. 'Well, good luck to you and if you have to run, take me with you. My name is Felix.'

'Marcus. You come to this tavern often?'

'Only to watch gambling. It is a tough game, friend.'

'Perhaps the Goddess will smile on this throw. I will be waiting at the door because your money collector may not be after you.'

'Oh?'

'I have been spending time with his beautiful daughter. Interesting, isn't it, that a man as ugly as that jackal, could have a daughter as beautiful as Luciana. By the way; you are sweating my friend.'

Marcus nodded. He wiped the sweat from his forehead and leant back against the wall behind him. The place was in an uproar as the game came to an end. In the crowd before him, many had placed bets on the opposing players, and as all games must come to an end this one was two dice throws, away.

Everyone moved closer to the table as the man across from Marcus moved the dice in the cup, in a fashion that made everyone hold their breath.

Marcus looked around at the swirling throng of men, all possessed with the same curse which for him started as a young boy on the farm, where he could remember playing games with other boys and his brother and wanting to play for something.

They stole figs and eggs from other farms. He would wager these to try and quell his need to take a risk. In reflection, he had lost more than he had won, but the thrill remained the same, every time he took a plunge no matter whether the bet was in his advantage or not.

This game before him, 'the 'game of twelve' had taken his interest the first time he saw it. There seemed to be some skill in it but it relied mainly on luck and luck, he knew, was a fleeting woman waiting to pull you up the mountain one day and drop you down the next.

But, he admitted to himself, that was the allure of spending hard won coins on a game that one could easily lose.

On the table before him there were three rows of twelve markings and pieces that fitted in each. Each player rolled three dice alternatively moving their pieces around until one player had no pieces on the table and they were the winner.

There were a number of rules including that fact that you could not land your piece on your opponents. If it was occupied you could not continue with your turn.

As Marcus watched the dice fall onto the table, Vicinius patted the giant beside him on the shoulder. 'Be ready, this boy is strong and fast and I want that Denarii of his on the table.

The giant beside him, grunted and shifted his feet. 'Let me tell you, this kid is no more capable of stopping gambling than defeating the God of War, in combat. But, we need him to keep gambling with us and losing, so don't kill him. Just pin him down.'

Vicinius shifted his tunic around his protruding girth and patted his stomach. He was full from the meal he had consumed across the street and the heat from the crowd in the gambling room was making him feel slightly ill.

Finding the young fool at the table, was a simple stroke of luck. As they passed the tavern an hour before he looked in and there was Marcus Attilius himself, looking at the board as he gambled and oblivious to anyone else in the room.

He looked around at the tavern; it was mostly empty tables with a bored and wandering attendant. The locals were clustered around the 'game of twelve' table as they gathered to bet on the winner of the game before him.

Most of them were drunken fools, he thought, as he continued to rub his stomach. Most of them, would likely lose tonight, but that was in his interest so he stood back and watched the play continue.

Rome had become a rough, hard environment and only the tough could survive in the low lands, of Rome city. Vicinius was approaching his fiftieth year and he had witnessed the past twenty years where Rome evolved from a peaceful city, to a cesspit of hoodlums and killers with many of them coming from the North, or from other lands.

It must be wonderful, he reflected, to live on the hill with servants and friends in politics, in big homes and with guards. For the rest of us, Vicinius reflected, life was a battle and he knew that those who lived on the hill cared not one As, for those embattled in the reclaimed swamp, beneath their carefully cleaned marble floors, and immaculate gardens.

The senate remained a standing joke and who could keep up with the emperors of Rome since they changed so quickly? The old Claudius at least had a stutter that made people laugh.

Gggood cit, citizens of Rrrome' Vicinius muttered the joke to himself, with a wry smile, as he thought of the speech he had seen Claudius make on the steps of the senate with people laughing at him.

Then, the stuttering idiot had not only adopted a boy by the name of Nero, he gave him the mantle of ruler, when he passed away. Nero who played his fiddle, killed his mother, set Rome alight and then took his own life. How could that ever be surpassed for arrogance, waste and stupidity?

By the fields of Mount Olympus, he thought to himself. Was it possible to have more idiots in charge of the nation of Rome, than the last twenty years? The new one, Vespasian, had yet to prove himself but at least he appeared sane which was saying something given the history he had witnessed.

However, his livelihood was gambling. In the form, of making money by lending to gamblers and charging a high, but fair one hundred percent for the risk. High perhaps; but then his business had many costs including enforcement and collection.

Vicinius understood enough of the game, to know that the money was made allowing fools, like the boy on the other side of the table, to gamble and lose and then follow them up for the debt. Romans, he knew by experience, were good at losing but bad at paying and the increasing cost of enforcement and protection made high interest and collection

———

inevitable.

As a funding provider, Vicinius looked constantly for degenerate gamblers, like Attilius who gambled compulsively and badly. When young men like Attilius were not fighting, they were gambling and as the losses increased, they needed a ready source of funds.

Vicinius always welcomed new customers with the tacit understanding that they needed to pay their debts and while they could not, the interest continued.

The secret of his business was not to allow them to pay back the entire debt. The idea was to keep them on a lead, so they could gain funds at any time, gamble and proceed back into debt and so the profitable cycle continued.

Gambling in the great city was outlawed but like all bad habits it flourished in the taverns and back rooms of Suburia. The larger the city grew, the more Romans wanted to play. It was rumoured that even the great fool Claudius, emperor of Rome, gambled his nights away whenever he returned from attempting to conquer some foreign land.

It was all very well to take the legions to fight a foreign war, but the real problem was here at home in Rome. Crime was increasing, due to the influx of foreigners and it got to a point where it was impossible to tell who was a native born Roman and who was not.

Still, he thought, the citizens of Rome gambled and fucked with abandon. So, the two areas of great improvement were the copiously presented brothels and bars with their backroom gambling dens, like the one he attended this very night.

The moral high ground of those on the rich hills of Rome, who sinned with greater alacrity than those on the low ground was always present. But, they held the power to do what they wished. He hated them, but then he hated everyone.

The dice finally came to rest on the table and with visible sweat coming off his brow Marcus glared at the result. All dice showed the single dot. It was a miracle as the man across from him looked in disbelief knowing he could not cast off the board, as the numbers did not allow it.

'It seems the Goddess smiles on you tonight and she has abandoned me' Marcus was too stunned to reply. He picked up the dice, returned them to the cup and swirled them around. He needed a 2,4 and 6 to cast off and even that was an impossible throw.

With a flourish, he sent the dice to the table and as they spun he looked over at Vicinius who was moving with his man towards him. The dice fell and the dice position of 2 and 4 settled and, as if commanded by its master, the third dice fell into the position of the six.

Marcus cast off with a whoop and moved to grab the side bets of the table. He was so astonished at winning, he waited a moment too long.

The man across from him was swearing and as Marcus started to rise from his cramped position at the table he felt the heavy hand of the giant on his shoulder. Vicinius moved into view placing his hand on the other side and looked benevolently down it.

'Ah, Attilius, you are not going to leave so fast, are you? My records show that you owe us a considerable sum and I look forward to receiving a down payment tonight. Pass the Denarii over, my boy, and let's discuss the rest outside.'

Marcus looked over at Felix who was motioning to the door. With a giant holding one shoulder and the protruding stomach of Vicinius next to him, it was difficult to move. 'I have been looking for you, young Marcus, and it is time for us to settle our debt. After all, a debt is a debt.'

Marcus smiled as he rose. 'Vicinius, there is no debt, you, big fat ass'

With that and feeling the giants hand loosening its grip, he ducked down and forward, spearheading himself through the crowd for the door. As he did so, he upended the table with the markers, dice and Denarii, that sat on the side of the table. They cascaded onto the floor, like thieves disappearing into the night. Vicinius immediately dropped to his knees to recover the Denarii

'Make way, make way' he said with a shout 'Those coins are mine.' He turned to the giant above him as he scrabbled, for the coins. 'Get him.'

The giant grunted, as he lost his hold, and Vicinius watched the back of Marcus disappear. Marcus took the ten Denarii that he held in his hand and passed them into his tunic.

As Marcus neared the door he found Felix grinning at the entrance. 'Quick departure, my friend'

'Follow me', Marcus replied, as he moved quickly out onto the street only to be confronted by two men with swords.

'Where are you heading, boy' one of them said as he raised his sword to face height of the two young men in front of him.

'Stop there and don't move a muscle. Who are you?' He said directly to Felix

'Just an innocent bystander' Felix replied more coolly that his face showed. 'But here to help, I guess'

'One more move and you will feel the end of the cold blade in my hand.' Marcus did not need a second invitation. He moved towards the man, with his eyes fixed firmly on the sword in front of him. He moved quickly to the side of the sword line, blocking the guards arm with his left hand and quickly landing a heavy blow into the man's stomach.

He moved forward to hit the man's arm with the side of his hand, forcing him to drop the sword and bellow in pain, as the sword clattered to the stones below. Marcus glanced over at Felix, who was grappling with the second guard and not succeeding as the man's size and strength overtook him.

Within a moment, the guard beside Marcus was up with the sword back in his hand. Marcus darted nimbly to avoid the sword slash in front of him. He grabbed his assailant by the head, sending a hard blow to his stomach. He finished off with a hard left to the man's jaw, watching as he fell heavily to the ground.

Felix howled with pain as he was hit. He turned and kicked at the man as he got to his feet, parrying another sword strike as he rose. He hit the guard hard in the midriff as he rose. The man merely grunted and started towards him again.

Marcus moved to assist Felix. At that moment, Vicinius exited the door with his man beside him and watched as Marcus grabbed the guard by his tunic, head butted him and followed up with a punch into the man's groin. With a loud groan, the guard sank to his knees, holding himself as he rolled over.

'Well, well. Hold fast, boys,' Vicinius said as he surveyed the scene. 'Young Attilius fights again. However, my boy, we need a further down payment on your debt as the coins on the tavern floor were not enough to even make a small distance into what you owe. Let us not fight about the debt, Marcus, let us make a repayment deal and get on with our lives.'

Vicinius folded his arms waiting for an answer and with no response from Marcus he continued 'So, if you hand over the Denarii in your pocket we can all be on our way. That is with the exception of my two soon to be ex-employees on the ground, who it appears cannot fight to save their miserable lives. Perhaps you might like to work for me Marcus, and you can pay your debt that way?'

Marcus stood up straight looking directly at Vicinius. 'Work for scum like you, Vicinius, I'd rather end up dead.'

Vicinius nodded to the man beside him. He looked bemused as he motioned with his hand to the giant, who was moving towards them.

'Ah, Marcus and you Felix, perhaps the heavy hand of authority might change your mind. You were never a good gambler, Attilius and the Gods did not gift you with much intelligence. Here I am offering you a job to save your miserable skin and what do I get back? Arrogance and your usual stupidity.'

Marcus and Felix stood together. 'Let's make a run for it' Felix said as he watched the size of the man moving towards them. Marcus studied the giant moving towards them with interest. He was huge but he appeared lumbering and slow.

Felix, realising they were out of time, grabbed Marcus by the shoulder. 'You go the front and I will get him from the back.'

Marcus looked at him with feigned surprise. 'Seems you have got the better part of the deal.' Felix smiled at him and moved forward to take on the man before him. The giant took one large step, planted a vicious punch into Felix's face before he could react and the effect was instantaneous, as Felix hit the ground unmoving.

The giant kicked Felix in the stomach for good measure and moved towards Marcus. Marcus looked at his companion who was vomiting on the ground, which meant he was hurt but still alive and then he fixed his gaze on the face of the giant. He bore the scars of previous combat and clearly most would have come off second best. This was not a man you could fight full on.

Vicinius, he noted, had deftly picked up the swords that lay on the ground next to the guards. Marcus did not have that aid and that left little course but to fight the man and beating a man of that size would not be easy.

'Cato is an ex Gladiator, Marcus; won four fights before he left the

---

arena.' Vicinius called out with a sneering laugh. 'Let's call it quits, Eh? You pass over the Denarii, come and work with me, to pay off your debt and you move on with your life. '

Marcus concentrated on Cato as he lumbered towards him. The man had a limp from his right leg. It was not obvious but it was there and that was a weakness. He looked up at Cato who towered above him.

'You, big hairy ape', Marcus said smiling, 'you may have been a gladiator but there was a reason why you quit. Want to know what that was? You, big stupid gorilla. You are too big and too slow. My old farm ox was smarter than you.'

Cato's eyes opened wide as he attempted to grab Marcus by the throat. Marcus moved sideways and viciously kicked the man's knee from the side. He looked at him with astonishment. He could not believe the man had not gone down. Anyone else would be lying on the ground in pain.

As he moved around the back of the giant, trying to get a hold, Cato let out a bellow and hit Marcus on the back of his head with his elbow and then hit him hard in the shoulder as he started to fall.

Instead of hitting the ground, he felt Cato grab him by the leg, lift him up with grunt and throw him towards Vicinius where he landed with a dull thud and a groan on the stone floor. He rolled over feeling his ribs.

Marcus lay there stunned.

'I told you' Vicinius said with a wry smile.

Marcus looked over at Felix, who was now in a sitting position, who looked back at Marcus with a shake of his head.' Give it up'

'I tell you one thing, Vicinius, this man hits like a bull but he is big and dumb and he will fall. And when he does you will be next.' Marcus looked into Vicinius's eyes with the satisfaction of seeing the slightest recognition of fear.

Vicinius gave him a steely look. 'It is time you learnt a lesson in manners. Cato will show you the meaning of respect. I hope you learn from it.'

Cato was upon him, lifting him bodily with his left hand while driving another punch into his stomach, and one to his nose, letting him fall to the ground. Marcus lay there bleeding profusely from his nose, winded and

---

trying to get his breath and clear his head.

As Cato reached down to deliver a final blow, Marcus moved with lightning speed as he drove a punch into the giant's groin and then moved to his left to drive another kick to the man's knee.

This time, the giant let out a scream as his knee collapsed. He landed a blow to the giant's head, which almost broke his hand and then he moved deftly to his left.

Cato bent over double from the force of the blows but stood shakily on both legs. Marcus landed two hard punches to the man's head and he sent another hard kick to Cato's damaged knee with another resulting scream of pain. The giant hit the ground with a thud, so loud, it reverberated off the outside walls of the tavern.

He then moved directly against Vicinius with a punch to the man's belly, landing a wide arcing elbow to his bloated face, which sent him to the ground as well. He picked up a sword that lay beside Vicinius and moved back to Cato, who lay groaning on the stony surface outside the tavern.

Marcus was breathing hard, as he put the point of the sword hard against the giant's neck so that he could see a trace of blood from the tip as it sat against the jugular vein.

Realising that Cato was not capable of rising he gave the giant a kick in the head as he passed over him and laid the sword with the bloodied point on Vicinius' arm.

'Vicinius, you piece of scum; our debt is settled and if you don't agree I will kill this poor, stupid son of a sow and then I will cut your balls off.'

He pushed the sword point across the debt collectors arm, until blood started to run and a cut appeared.

With some satisfaction, he saw Vicinius start to scream. He then let the sharp point of the sword travel down towards his belly and then he pushed it, against the fat man's groin.

'No' came a shout from the prostrate body of Vicinius who lay groaning on the ground. His head pounded with pain from the blow by Marcus. He looked over at Cato who lay holding his knee with his hands and tried feebly to shout.

'Your choice.' Marcus held his nose to staunch the bleeding. He spoke as if he had caught a fever. Vicinius looked helplessly at the ex-gladiator. 'Get up, you son of a dog' He snarled at Cato who lay doubled over. 'Get up, you, stupid oaf. What in name of the Gods do I pay you for?'

Marcus stood over him with blood still dripping from his nose where the giant had hit him several minutes before. He lifted the sword from his groin and placed it on the chest of the man beneath him.

'Vicinius, there is one difference between the man on the ground and you. He understands respect. He gives it and takes it but he understands it and you do not have the ability to understand that. Now make your choice; or as Mars is my witness, I will cut your balls off and feed them to the birds.'

'What choice.' Vicinius mumbled.

Marcus smiled. 'You have a short memory Vicinius. Your balls or we forget the debt.'

Vicinius nodded his assent as Marcus moved to lift Felix off the ground. Felix was groggy and disorientated but with assistance he started to move. As they passed Cato, who was trying to sit up, Marcus stopped and assisted the giant to his feet. 'Next time I will be wary of you Cato; you hit like an angry mule.' The giant nodded, looked at him and moved to a wall for support

Marcus assisted Felix down the road, pass the tavern. Behind him, Vicinius still lay on the ground holding his arm, as blood seeped slowly through his fingers.

One of the guards had made it uneasily to his feet while the other lay prone on the ground not moving. In the background, Marcus could hear Vicinius berating all of them and as he moved down the road, it was all he could hear.

'You are not a very good fighter, Felix' Marcus said, with a bloodied nose and mouth as he assisted his companion down the paved street.

'No, Felix replied,' not hand to hand but I have other talents and is precisely the reason I need friends like you. Come, my friend, I owe you a meal. Do you have a place to stay?'

'I currently have lodgings; in the stables of the nobleman where I work. The paterfamilia, Laurentius. I work as one of the gardeners.'

'Well, well, now I know a man who works for a very high-ranking nobleman. We call them assholes down here.'

They both laughed as Felix rubbed the side of his head. 'Am I bleeding? He asked

'No, you didn't get hit hard enough to bleed, Felix. Where are we?' Marcus asked as he started to look around the unfamiliar houses. He lightly rubbed his sore nose, noting the bleeding had stopped. He seemed to heal quickly.

'In Suburia, my friend. The home of every thief in Rome and many of them women and good looking.' Felix replied with a pained wink. 'Oh, my head hurts. Did you say you work as a gardener?'

Marcus smiled sheepishly. 'Yes, I know. It is not the worthiest of professions but it is all I know.'

'Where did you come from?'

'My father owned and worked a farm in the North and I decided that tending the farm was not for me so I decided to come to Rome and arrived some months ago.'

'How long have you worked at the villa?'

'About four months ago. I started in the middle of Maius. My uncle works for Laurentius and he arranged the job'

He is a freeman?'

'Why do ask that question?'

Felix shrugged as if it did not matter. 'No reason, really, it's just in Rome most menial tasks such as gardening is done by slaves. Unusual, for a freeman, that is all I meant.' Marcus continued walking slowly waiting for Felix to catch up. 'Nevertheless, he is a good man.'

'I am sure he is a good and upstanding citizen, Marcus, I meant no disrespect by the question.'

Marcus gazed up at the moon sitting half way up the horizon, highlighting the buildings around Rome with a faint glow. Faint whitewash, cascading from the full moon was broken only by the distant beacons of cooking fires, lit in the open on the hills, surrounding the city.

The heavens were shining and being late in the month, the air was warm and it beckoned a hotter season ahead. With the fight behind them they walked together down the stone road of Suburia.

He touched his nose as Felix and he walked slowly up another back street. Even with his bloodied nostrils, he could smell the garbage that appeared at the end of every almost every street in Rome.

Clearly, even the most intelligent Plebeian, in the Suburia did not have the capability to take garbage more than two steps from their door. Or, in a supreme effort, to any other area. He pitied those who lived closest to the end of the street or a junction, where the garbage was piled in large clumps.

He reflected, that in his travels to discover the city of Rome, the fine streets around the Forum did not see even a scrap of food on the Vicus Tuscus or the Argiletum. But then, it was the haunt and locale of the rich and famous.

However, despite the smell of the garbage, the night smelled more familiar than it had when he first arrived. Despite the pain from the fight, he was happy to have made a friend and he had forced the end of a debt. 'How did you learn to fight like that?'

Marcus shrugged, as they continued on. 'I really don't know. I was always good at it and I have the size to make an impression. When you gamble like I do, you get some serious practice at fighting.' He smiled ruefully at his remark and looked across at Felix who laughed.

'Does your uncle know you gamble?'

'Absolutely not.' Marcus replied, with a nasal twang from the congealing blood in his nose. 'He is a good man. He just believes I go out for women and song.'

They continued down the road and finally turned a corner with Felix limping beside Marcus as they made their way to the end of the street. 'There is a good tavern here. Well priced and good fare.'

They stopped at a table outside one of the tavern windows and a minute later the proprietor came out. He was bent at the middle with a vast stomach under his tunic and hair that came down to his lower back. He looked them over and smiled beneficently.

'You boys look like you came worse off in whatever fight you were in.'

Felix sat back heavily in his chair. 'I did but the man beside me was the champion of the night.' The proprietor smiled encouragingly and took the order. A wine jug and antipasto with bread.

'What about you Felix, what do you do with your life.'

'I am indentured, my friend, to a foundry not far from where I live. We make the finest Gladius in all of the Roman empire. It is hot, hard work and brutal in the hot months but turning out a fine sword is a long but rewarding process.'

'You make them yourself? Marcus asked.

'I do and my friend Blasius and I are indentured to the blacksmith. The owner, is a large brute of a man but fair in his dealings. We are not paid highly; but he provides lunch and it's only when we get a large order that we have to work hard. The rest of the time we turn out expensive swords, used by noblemen for show, because most of them would not know which end to grab!'

Felix laughed out loud at his own joke and was joined by Marcus who threw his head back and roared. 'You have a sense of humour, Felix, I give you that.' Are you a slave?

Felix looked at him with surprise. 'No. Ah, the name. Yes, it is more used as a slave name isn't it' He moved closer to whisper 'My full name is Publius Cornelius Felix. *Felix* means 'luck' does is not? As I grew up, my cognomen stuck and Felix is what they call me. I grew up there.' Felix gestured to the hill high above the city.

'Then why are you down here, in the hellhole? Marcus asked surprised.

'I have rich parents, who live on the hill of Rome and not far from where you work as a gardener.'

'Why work in a foundry of all places? From what I have seen at the villa of Laurentius, you would not need to work. A rich Daddy and a nice goose down bed to sleep on, seems better than this.'

Felix grimaced and lowered his head. 'My father and I do not get along. I see my mother occasionally but that is about it. I have a sister as well but she will not speak to me, so I leave them alone on the hill and I make my own way in world. A bit like you, Marcus.'

Marcus studied his new friend, briefly wondering why someone might give up a life of opulence and ease against the life he now led. He looked at his broad face and infectious smile.

He briefly recalled the last discussion he had with his mother, the day he left the farm. For a brief instant, he saw his mother at the gate and it made him smile.

'Why do you smile?' Marcus shifted uneasily for a moment. 'Just a memory, Felix.
Nothing more.'

Felix downed a black olive, savouring its taste and reached for the jug of wine and poured himself and Marcus another cup. 'Marcus, you are welcome to stay with me. I have poor but comfortable lodgings, not far from here and to cement our friendship, I will even pay for this meal.'
'That is kind of you, Felix. Maybe for the night. Part of the employment is that I have to live at the stables so I can start early and finish late.'

'But tomorrow is a holiday. The day of Matralia. How late do you normally work? Later than the middle of the day?'

'Usually' came the reply.

Felix smiled his broad toothy smile. 'Then, we have to find something else for you to do.'

'Like?'

My friend, we will work on it but life is too short to be involved in gardening at your age. Gardening is for old people who love plants and trees and clearly then can be nothing more boring than that. Am I, right?'

Marcus nodded and added a sigh. 'Have you met Laurentius? the senator himself?'

Marcus shrugged. 'No, he is hardly ever at the villa apparently. They have another home on an estate, not far from Rome but I am not sure where it is. The matriarch of the home is stuck up but every now and then I see her looking at me. Her daughter is a great beauty but she guards her like an old dog.'

'That surprises you? I'd protect my daughter around you as well.'

Marcus laughed as the tavern manager brought a small bowl of water and olive oil for him to tend his wounds. He took the towel and wiped his nose and mouth. He looked over at Felix who shrugged in the manner, to let him know there was still blood.

'Your lip is still split. You need vinegar on that wound.' He called out to the tavern for vinegar that promptly arrived. Marcus applied it and held the rag against it to stop further bleeding. He stood up to stretch. He was tall with that particular build born to be quick and agile.

He finally sat down and rubbed his jaw and his nose. 'That giant hit like thunder.'

'Better you than me with that great ugly brute. Vicinius will not let the debt rest and I think we both know that. How long ago did you start owing him?

'Well as I have said to you, Felix, gambling is my weakness and I love it like no other. I had been here one night, I think, and I had gone for a drink at a tavern in one of the streets off the Argiletum.'

'Game of Twelve' Felix proffered

Marcus shook his head 'Tesserae' he noted sourly as the food plates arrived and both of them started to eat. Marcus winced as the food hit his lip. They ordered another jug of watered wine.

'*Tesserae*', Felix mumbled to himself wondering why anyone would play that half-witted game. Ten throws, each man and the highest throw won each time and then the player with the most wins took the Denarii on the side of the table.

'On my travels to Rome, I won over seventy Denarii in one night, believe it or not, and now I have lost it all. And, I am in debt.'

'You have no debt with Vicinius.' Felix proffered.

'There are others.'

Felix whistled softly. That is a lot to win and to lose in one night, my friend.'

Marcus nodded. 'This game I joined was a fast game and I wasn't playing I was betting on the side. The man I bet on was certainly going to win and he did.'

Felix looked surprised. 'So why didn't you get up a leave with the coins in your pocket?'

Marcus slumped and looked skywards. 'By the strength of Jupiter, that is my only weakness. Even when I am ahead I don't stop. It is the lure of the Goddess. I blame her for everything.'

'So'

'So, I waited for the next game to start and bet on the side. I thought would win and this jackal sidled up to me and started talking. He noted I was betting what I had just won and over the course of the conversation he gave me an offer I could not refuse.' Two to one.'

'He was offering you double your money if you won, and then only take your bet if you lost?' Felix looked at him with amazement.

'Did it not occur to you that the bet was impossibly on your side? No wonder you couldn't you refuse it?'

'My man was winning and I mean winning by a long way. Every time he threw the dice they came up high numbers. By the fourth throw we were winning by all four. If the table hadn't changed in five more throws he would have been off. Then the game started to change.'

'You had already taken the bet?

Marcus nodded glumly. 'The game almost reversed.'

Felix laughed. 'Ah, my friend, you have been done like a lamb on a hillside spit.' Marcus looked at him with real surprise on his face. 'Meaning?'

'You were set up, as were almost all punters at that table. Did you notice the dice had changed?'

Marcus shook his head with surprise. 'No, and to make matters worse I was once accused of doing the same thing. I guess you are going to say they were fixed dice?'

'Boy, you must be some dumb hick from the country. This is Suburia, Marcus; most of the games are fixed. Vicinius, set you up and he probably did with most at that game on the double up, debt. Do you understand?' Marcus nodded dumbly as he listened.

'So, he wins not just your stake but a debt you owe him as well. The dice are changed beneath the table. The opposing player sends the dice down with numbers he knows will come up. What happened then?'

'Well, I had lost my bet and I thought I would win next time.'

'So Vicinius gave you a loan for the next bet.'

Marcus nodded and he gave me the same odds. Two to one.'

'They must have seen you coming, you idiot. Might I add they saw you coming, a long time off. Suckers like you are a rare find. You must be the only honest man left in Rome.'

'And the most stupid, it would appear. How would I know it was a cheat's game with loaded dice?'

'Ha, Marcus, by having a friend like me.' Felix gave him a broad smile. 'But experience is our teacher so next time you will know. I hope'

'So; where to now?'

Felix finished his cup and put it down, belching as he did so. 'I can offer you a comfortable single bed, so unless you want to head back to the stables let's be off. Tomorrow is a holiday and I am tired and my head hurts. I think the wine has made it worse and my old, but comfortable bed, awaits.' Felix rubbed his head for good measure as he arose.

They both rose stiffly from the table and Felix paid the tavern for the meal. Together, they walked up streets of inner Suburia towards where Felix lived. They spoke little, each in their own thoughts.

Marcus felt the pang of embarrassment, due to his stupidity and his face flushed when he thought about that night. Was he really that dumb that he could not have picked up that the game was fixed?

When he thought back on the game, the way in which he was set up, the way Vicinius arrived just at the right time, with an offer that could not be refused and then the idiocy he showed in increasing his debt, he was amazed at his own lack of insight and obvious stupidity.

Felix was right; he was just a farm boy who had no experience in the city of Rome. He did not understand the ways of a large metropolis. For the first time, he ruefully admitted to himself that he understood hens, and horses, and wheat. But, very little of cosmopolitan life.

He trusted in a place in which trust was not readily apparent and he lived his life as he did on the farm. You worked, your family worked and shared in the produce of the farm and the love of the family. Rome, clearly, was very different.

He knew that it was his desire for gambling, that caused the problem and there was a simple decision and that was to give it up. That thought remained in his mind as he looked for alternatives. Or, he could try to gamble better, and to understand that there were cheats everywhere and he would quickly learn. An offering to the Gods might assist; he mused and vowed to make that offering the following day.

He looked across, at the man who limped beside him and wondered what life he might have had if he had complied with his family wishes.

Both had left their family for another life, both were surviving on their wits and both had jobs that left a lot to be desired.

He clapped Felix on the shoulder, which he noted made him wince.

'How long Felix? Is it the other side of Rome?'

'Next street, my friend.'

'What about Vicinius's beautiful daughter?' Marcus added with a smile.

Felix laughed heartily as he turned the corner with Marcus in tow. 'Ha, his daughter is mine and since she might like you, because of that farm boy innocence you use, you need to stay away from her. After all, you almost fed her father's balls to the crows.'

They walked several more minutes, to the front of a brown coloured building with a plain front wall. In the background, he could hear the whining of a dog.

Felix, with the attitude of someone who knew the abode, plunged through the wood gate, into the small courtyard beyond. Marcus looked around in the dim light, to stables to his right and a house to the left, which looked to be the house of someone with wealth.

'This is where you live?'

'Sort of,' Marcus said with a half-smile 'Follow me.' Felix said with a limp that was more pronounced than it had been. "Now my hip hurts, worse than my head. You?

'I was feeling better until I found out I was sleeping in stables.'

He followed Felix through the portico and past the stables to a small house at the back of the estate. Felix got to the door and with a flourish of his hand noted to Marcus. 'My home awaits.'

They walked inside to the gloom, save the faint moonlight that splashed lightly through an open shutter. Felix lit an oil lamp and noted to a bed in the main room. It was small and unkempt but Marcus shrugged with fatigue.

Felix made sure Marcus made it to the bed, then retired to the back where there was another room.

'Marcus, I have a friend who stays here now and then, so if he turns up, just introduce yourself and tell him to sleep on the floor.'

Marcus nodded as he lay down on the straw mattress and shifted until he felt comfortable. His long legs extended beyond the bed but that was not unusual for him as most beds were the same.

As he laid waiting for sleep, he tested the areas of his body with his fingers where he felt the most pain. Whilst he was sure he felt pain like the next man he also knew he healed quickly and even his jaw swelling had reduced.

He winced as he touched the cut on his lip but like everything else it would heal.

He thought about the recent fight with Cato. Despite the fact that the giant had the strength to kill him with a single punch, he knew the man was clearly under orders from Vicinius, not to kill him even if the fight had progressed to a drawn out hand-to-hand contest.

He held his own and that would sit in Vicinius's mind for some time to come. It might make the loan thug, think twice before he took Marcus on in another fight.

He remembered the lacework of scars on Cato's upper body. How many came from his time as a Gladiator in the ring was only a guess but from the sheer number of scars on his body the man appeared to have been cut enough times to end his life.

The limp on Cato was more obvious from a distance and one Marcus knew he had used it to advantage but the sheer size of Cato and his strength felt overwhelming. Marcus's natural advantage of speed won the fight but he was only too aware that one well-timed punch from the ex-Gladiator may have changed everything.

He was pulled back from his thoughts by the sounds from the stable that remained so familiar to him; they echoed softly in the night air and Marcus felt sleep finally arrive.

CHAPTER 10

The dim light of early morning seeped through the only window shutter in the room. Marcus could faintly feel himself being prodded on the shoulder.

A deep voice resonated across the room. 'You are in my bed.'

Marcus turned over towards the wall and let out a fart. The prodding continued on his other shoulder and he heard the voice again. This time he knew he was not dreaming.

'You are in my bed'

He looked up at a short man with large shoulders and sporting a beard and unfashionable long hair. The brown eyes of the man glared down at him as Marcus tried to wake himself up.

'Well, go find another' Marcus replied sleepily. 'This one is mine and you are disturbing my sleep.'

'Might be better for you to take your own advice and find one yourself' the man said, his voice amplified by the clay walls in the room. 'If you don't get up I will assist you.'

Marcus came awake and sat up on the bed. He looked at the man in front of him with a smile on his face and as he rose up he laid a hard-right fist into the man's belly watching with some satisfaction as he went down winded onto the floor.

In a moment, the man was up, with his enormous arms around Marcus's midriff as he squeezed the air out of his lungs and tried to pick him up off the floor.

Marcus was much taller and despite the man's efforts he could not get him off the ground and the ridiculousness of the situation made Marcus laugh. As he started to laugh, so did the man holding him in the bear hug. Together they fell to the floor laughing and rolling around.

Felix appeared at the door of the room aroused from his bed by the ruckus. 'It is not possible to get any fucking sleep with this noise!' he spat out sleepily 'it is not past dawn and I have a fight in the house already.' He looked down at Marcus who was rolling around the floor in hysterics.

'Marcus, meet Blandius. Blandius, meet Marcus. By the way you are both fools and no doubt Blandius tried to take your bed off you?' Felix questioned

Marcus nodded trying to catch his breath. 'He tried to get me in a bear hug but he couldn't get me off the ground. He was like a heavy weight with nowhere to go.' With that he started laughing again.

Blandius stood up and looked at Marcus with a grimace. 'This boy hits hard.' He noted with a slight rub of his stomach.

Marcus stood up and shook hands with the man before him. Felix looked at them both. They were the opposites of each other. Marcus was tall and muscular with short black hair and dark blue eyes and Blandius was stocky, massive shoulders and small stumpy legs, long blond hair and dark eyes.

'Blandius' Marcus said with a wink moving towards the door to use the latrine and wash his face.

'Marcus' Blandius said with that booming voice. 'Thank Mars himself that you had the sense to leave my bed.'

Marcus did not answer as he walked towards the stables and the latrines to the side.

Once he had completed his ablutions he washed himself with the strong vinegar water provided next to the latrine and then washed himself with the water from the bucket that a slave had brought from the well.

From a small cup, next to a badly polished metal mirror Marcus rubbed oil onto his face and neck and using a metal blade he neatly shaved and cleaned up afterwards.

He ran his fingers through his hair as he finished and started back to the small house at the back of the estate. He stopped to pat one of the horses that had stuck its head out of the stall in interest at the new stranger.

Felix approached. 'Feeling better, my friend?'

'Much' replied Marcus. 'You have an aggressive friend.'

'No, my friend he is not aggressive he is more playful and the thing about the bed was just a joke that went too far. Who hit first'

Marcus smiled 'Me; But he was aggravating me about the bed.'

Felix smiled. 'Well, now, let us be off to find a place we can sit and have *inentaculum* and since you have more Denarii than I from your adventures last night, perhaps it is your turn to pay. I will let Blasius know if he wants to get out of bed and come to breakfast.

The three set off for a tavern several streets away in the maze of twists and turns of Suburia. The rabbit's warren of streets that made up Suburia; The home for most of the poor in Rome, offered dark alleys and narrow streets that led in opposite directions, each lined by houses and apartments.

The three walked down the street with the familiar smell of rotting garbage becoming more apparent and worse if they passed a culvert or small hill where home owners dumped whatever they did not want. Felix turned to Marcus 'Since this is your first real experience in Suburia let me tell you a little of it. First of all, Marcus, not all of the residents in Suburia are poor like me or farm hicks like you.' Felix pointed to a house on the side of the street.

'Meaning?'

'There are a few rich men in Suburia who choose to live here. They travel to their rich estates outside of Rome for the holidays of which, thankfully, there are many in Rome. Behold the streets' He said with a flourish of his hand. 'Each street is different and no street is the same.' He said loudly, as he walked along.

As they strolled down a wider street towards the tavern, Marcus noticed the homes were all adorned with shutters and were usually doubled in height with broad arches as entrances whilst some had small porticos protected by heavy oak doors.

The colours of the city appeared defined by individual houses which were coated in shades of ochre from deep red to light yellow and hues of blue in between. Broad expanses of bougainvillea with small delicate flowers of red and violet crept up the side of many houses, reaching up from street level to surround the high windows and verandas with their thorny plumage an added deterrent to thieves.

The colours of some of the homes varied to a pale white which came from the ochre clay they used to wash stone or brick. From the outside, many of the houses appeared ornate dressed with terracotta pots, holding fruit trees and flowers.

At a number of houses Marcus paused momentarily to peer in from the street. It appeared that the more fastidious and wealthy owners tiled their front door entrance in deep red terracotta tiles which invariably led to a courtyard beyond. Most entrances were designed with carefully planted fruit and ornamental trees with many a slave working to ensure that the house was kept in the finest order.

'If you walked beyond the entrance of these wealthier houses, they are invariably built around a central hall and an atrium but most of their time is spent in the courtyards. A good life if you own one with servants.'

Marcus reflected briefly on the Laurentius villa. In the Laurentius household the atrium lay open to the weather and if the rain had been heavy the slaves collected the rainwater from the trough built into the floor for that purpose. Most of it used for drinking and washing water. The rooms of the villa ran off the Atrium hallway and like the rest of the house it was kept scrupulously clean.

'That might have been you.' Marcus said with a smile. He touched his tender nose and rubbed his shoulder where he had been hurt the previous night.

'Sore? Me too.' Felix replied. 'Yes, that might have been my life but it was not one I wanted.'

'I know how you feel!' Marcus shouted at the top of his voice for all to hear. He thought briefly about his new life and it made him happy.

'I consider myself lucky, Marcus, as I don't live in a *insulae*.'

'*Insulae*?' Marcus questioned.

'Two room hovels, Marcus. That is where the poor live. They call them apartments but they are shitholes. Big enough to sleep in and if you want to use a toilet rather than the urinal that sits on the *insulae* floor or a bath you have to go to the local baths. There is no access to water in the apartment. And, they usually eat at the local as there is no place to cook either. The poor man's house in Rome is a simple affair so consider yourself lucky to sleep in a warm bed.'

'How did you find the little house you live in?'

'I tend the stables twice a week as he does not think the slaves can do it well enough. I have lived there for two summers so far. I also fashioned his prized Gladius for him which he wears on special occasions. And, I should add he is a friend of my father's so I guess the hovel is there as long as I want it.' He pointed his hand in the direction of an alley 'Down there lies our breakfast.'

Marcus walked down another road in the inner section of Suburia. It was paved in rough stone blocks set higher closest to the houses to ward off water when the rain became heavy and acting as a barrier to the heavy thunderstorms that beset the city.

He thought about the hard times on his family farm and how difficult it became to manage the farm when rains did not come to soak the crops. There were no issues like that in Rome.

His farm came briefly to mind as they walked the last distance to the tavern. He had left at a time when the farm offered the crops that came from dressing the fields and planting; the rains had come and the crops had been high and if there was such a thing as a convenient time to leave then he had made that decision at the right time.

As he looked around the road side and the houses on his way to the tavern he could not help reflecting how easy life in the city was in comparison to the farm and the utter dependency on the benevolence of the Gods to offer the seasons and their gifts of sunshine and rain.

'Over there.' Felix noted as he took a step to the right.

At each small street intersection, lay walking stones raised higher than the rest so the citizens of Rome could keep their feet as dry as possible when crossing a rain-soaked street to a house or shop on the other side.

Felix pointed out that the stone blocks were the curse of chariot drivers as many a wheel and a horse's leg were broken as they gingerly moved the chariot wheels through them to continue down the road.

The clatter of chariot wheels frequently combined with loud curses from drivers echoed across the buildings when the stepping-stones had been badly set by careless road builders and not set wide enough to allow the chariot wheels to pass between the spaces of the large lumps of stone.

107

Blasius motioned to Marcus who followed the other two and crossed the stones to the tavern and walked inside with his companions. The smell of freshly baked bread filled his nostrils and hunger set in as they sat and waited for the meal.

Presently, the table was set with dates, honey, olive oil and wheat bread pancakes and within minutes little remained. Marcus ordered a jug of honey water and together they sat to talk about the coming day.

Felix was the first to speak as he downed a mouthful of the water. 'Since today and tomorrow are holidays I suggest we go early to the *Populis* Stadium and then there is a party afterwards at the *Neum* tavern which is near there. It is time for watching a contest then women and song.

'Good morning, Felix.' Came a voice from the side of the table. They looked up to find a young woman dressed in a red tunic with sandals and straps up to her knees. She stood there with a tray in her hands. She was darkly skinned with her voluminous, curly black hair pulled to the top and the side, as was the fashion of the day.

She radiated youth and beauty and Marcus noted that most of the male patrons were watching her with interest. Felix stared at her with a smile.

'Luciana, I have thought about you, day and night.' he replied half standing.

'That's nice Felix 'She said coolly 'Can I offer you further breakfast or honey water?' She said eyeing Marcus and then Blandius.

'Boys?' Felix asked with his smile diminished and shifting uncomfortably on his seat.

'Were you going to introduce me to your friends?' She said with a sultry flick of her hair. She stood with her hands on her hips, standing tall at the head of the table.

'Not unless I have to!' Felix replied, smiling but admonished 'This is my old friend Blandius and my new friend Marcus Attilius.' She smiled at them and put the tray down momentarily to put the cups and plates on it. 'You have such handsome friends, Felix, why have you kept them away.'

'Good question, Luciana,' Blandius noted with a smile.' Why is that Felix?'

Felix went quiet as she smiled and took away the tray.

———

Blandius watched her go with his eyes firmly fixed on her. 'You are a lucky fox, Felix, how do you know a beauty like that?'

Felix laughed 'Well, Blandius, Marcus knows her father as well.'

Marcus blanched and then looked at him. 'No!'

Yes, Marcus, you, country bumpkin. That beauty, is the daughter of Vicinius.'

CHAPTER 11

The vision of the huge timber stadium in the distance, beheld a sight that filled him with anticipation. On most holidays, the stadium, which held the largest crowd in Rome, was open with games for the afternoon and Matralia was one of those days. The heat was stifling and the area thronged with citizens in high spirits.

They neared the stadium and Marcus stopped momentarily to view what was before him. The massive walls of the structure stood high as high as three houses on top of each other. The sides were festooned with flags of all colours, wafting lazily in the light breeze.

He looked with amazement at the massive crowd of men and women, some with children and others already with a belly full of wine. They saw the queue at the front of the bottom arches of the stadium. He watched with amusement as people tried to jump the lines, only to be ushered back by attendants.

Occasionally a nobleman's chair, carried by sweating slaves, moved past, accompanied by their heavy breathing as they walked briskly to the side of the stadium under heavy cloth shades. As they approached, they were instantly allowed passage to another entrance near the main gates, to find access.

Marcus watched the envious eyes of the poorer citizens, who glanced at the fabric-covered platforms as they trundled past. They moved past in procession towards the gates, with attendant slaves holding the high chairs of men and women of high status and obvious wealth.

The platform chairs, covered in colourful fabric, with heavier fabric on top, shielded the morning heat. The sides held curtains so that the occupant could be carried in seclusion, peeking out when the desire took hold.

One by one, the procession of slaves carrying the heavy chairs, reached the entrance to the stadium. The chair was set down and the fabric curtain set aside. Another slave walked beside the chair, at the side of the carriers waiting for instructions. It appeared his job was to ensure the chair settled correctly and curtains moved aside as the passenger was assisted from their cushioned enclave.

The heavier passengers, took several slaves to be assisted from their platform and to be led to what he guessed, was an area that held watered and honey wine, with food before they were taken to their seats.

As he waited in the queue, he noticed with some interest as Lucia Laurentius alighted from a chair, with dark skinned, sweating slaves beside her. She glanced around and then smiled widely at a short man, with greying hair. He assisted her from the chair and accompanied her inside. He guessed it might be Laurentius himself.

To the side of the building he saw the arrival of chariots. They were mostly drawn by two horses, with their reins held by slaves, who drove the horses as the nobleman stood at the back with their tunics flying in the breeze.

Attendants rushed to take the reins, as passengers stepped down from their ornate chariots and made their way to the entrance. The slaves walked the horses to the stables, situated at the back of the arena where they were watered and fed.

The side of the stadium held entrances for nobleman, under the shade of broad sail cloth. Common men and women, such as he, Blasius and Felix waited in the queue in the hot sun. He could not help thinking that if Felix had taken another choice, he would have alighted from a platform chair and not stood in the heat, with the rest of them, waiting for entrance to the contests.

The smell of excitement filled the air, permanently mixed with the scent of beast and sweat. It was a hot day and even in the late morning the heat from the crowd, combined with the relentless sun, made the waiting difficult as patrons shuffled their feet and complained.

'As you can see, Marcus, the idea is to be a nobleman and use the side entrance and should you make it to that status, Blandius and I will assist you, so we walk in with you.'

'Given my skill as a gardener, Felix, that may take some time.'

Blandius just grunted and took a look over at the area Felix was describing. 'You could have been there now, Felix, you are a dumb fool.'

Felix shrugged as they neared the stadium area. Blandius nudged Marcus out of his thoughts and motioned to the side of the path. They stopped at a food stall on the side of the queue and purchased fresh bread, cheese and a small goatskin of watered wine.

Marcus paid the six As and waited for change which took a while to come. He looked around to see that the other two had walked off. He grabbed the parcel and took off after them.

They joined the long line, with Felix and Blandius ogling the women who stood in line with everyone else. Marcus spoke to a man beside him who waited impatiently for the line to diminish.

'It is said that Britanicus, a crowd favourite, will compete today.'

'He is a champion? 'Marcus questioned

'You have never heard of him? He is ferocious, strong and has won eight wreaths so far and he has a very powerful benefactor.'

'Who?'

'The richest man in Rome, no less; Cassius Laurentius. It is said Britanicus intends to retire soon but who knows with these men. They seem to love the smell of blood and sand.'

'Who does he fight?

'Apparently, he fights Calis today. But there are many to choose from my friend. There are many Gladiators but not many are champions. In fact, very few.' The man replied with a twinkle in his eye. 'Romans only love gladiators who win, we discard those who lose, very quickly.'

'I believe I have met him. On the road to Rome.'

The man looked at him with a suspicious look on his face. 'Of course. With flying pigs in attendance, I suppose.'

Marcus smiled; his eyes on the queue that was quickly diminishing. 'Well, I have met him and what's more I have never witnessed a Gladiator match'

'Now that is rare. You were born in Rome?'

'No, I arrived in Rome months ago. I come from the North, from a farm several weeks travel from here.'

'Then you have much to learn about life in Rome young man. Gladiators are the heart and soul of the circus you will see today. Don't believe all that you hear in the farmlands. They train hard, all week, they get fed the best food available and they are expected to perform on the sand more than a few times a year. There are many different types; did you know that?'

Marcus shook his head, listening with interest.

'Ah, well. You have heard of the Bestiarii, have you? No, well they specialise in fighting wild beasts such as lions and tigers and wild dogs, now and then.'

'Bestarii only fight beasts?'

The man nodded. 'They fight with a spear, sometimes a dagger only and there are many who have tried, but the great Carophorus is perhaps the best known. Have you heard of him?'

Marcus shrugged at his lack of knowledge as he listened to the man expound on his. 'You don't hear much on a farm, citizen.'

'He is a big man and very, very strong. He is able to take a great deal of pain, even if he is clawed or bitten on the way to conquering the beast. If you like slaughter, the Bestiarii is the most exciting. You would have slaughtered animals on the farm, would you not?'

Marcus looked at the gleam in the man's eye and replied ruefully. 'Of course, but only for food and pelts; not for pleasure. Have you ever slaughtered an animal?'

'Ah, no not for me; a little too much blood. What is your name, young man?'

'Marcus Attilius'

'Attilius; That is not familiar, but a good name, I suppose. My friends call me Flavio. Anyway, as I was saying there are also many different types of Gladiators. My favourite is the Murmillone but there are also Thracians, Retiarii, Secutores and others as well. If you attend the games over a period of time you will gain favourites as well. However, I won't go on and spoil your fun. You will see. The women love them, you know!'

'Really, that seems odd.'

'Who else do they have to love? Your ordinary Roman man with a big belly who treats them badly? Compare that to a gladiator who is strong,

113

brave and masculine. Let us not forget their well-defined physiques.'

'But they also fight for a living?' Marcus replied as he looked over at Felix and Blandius who were talking to several girls at the front of the queue.

'Of course, that is their life. They are the bright lights in the sky of Rome. Very sought after. After all it is not often you meet someone who's life depends on their skill and the ability to inflict injury on another and could die the next time they walk on the sand.'

Marcus nodded and started to listen to the conversation between Blandius and Felix and finally joined in.
'Where do we sit?'

'Wherever we can, Marcus. Come, we are about to be pushed in'

The three entered the corridor that led to the seating on the three levels above them. The sounds of growling animals, could be clearly heard from the alcoves, to the left of the stairs. Through a gap in the panel, Marcus could see the head of a beast as it snarled at someone from outside the cage.

Saliva dripped from its jaw as it stood, back arched, tense and ready to strike. The hind leg of the lion was marked with blood and the size of the beast took up the length of the large cage.

'What sort of a beast is that?' Marcus asked as he kept his eyes on it.

Blandius rolled his eyes 'You have never heard of a lion?'

Marcus had heard of a lion as a child but had never seen one and the size of the beast astonished him. For some reason, he had thought they were smaller and less ferocious but that may have been the description from his mother who had seen one in her early days in Rome before she met his father.

Blandius motioned to the stairs to their right. Marcus looked at hard wood steps leading to the first level and on reaching the first exit, Felix nudged him up the next level with a grunt. 'Only for the rich, keep going.'

They climbed to the second level and again Felix nudged him in the back pushing him to the final level of the sunlit stairs. 'Keep going; this level is for the Romans wealthier than us and as you know that is not hard.'

They emerged from the stairs into the harsh sunlight of the third level and made their way to the middle of the stadium, which, Felix noted, was the best position to view the action below.

Marcus settled himself onto the hard wood bench and took in the sights of the stadium, which was already more than half full with a wait until the start of the games.

Below him, the two levels were busy with people milling about the seats, waving and shaking hands with others. Vendors moved around with trays of honey water, wine and food.

The lowest level which Felix noted was for the *opulentam nobilemque*, the rich and famous of the city of Rome. The view held a mass of togas, with their wives preening themselves, as they waited and watched for the start of the day's proceedings.

On the highest level where they sat on that day, they were surrounded by the poor of Rome. Most women were prohibited from sitting on the lower tiers unless they were the wives of politicians and wealthy businessmen so the sections were filled with women exclusively.

He looked for his mistress, Lucia Laurentius. He finally located her on the opposite side of the stadium sitting in the platform area that jutted on the level above the sand. She sat with her daughter but the man who met her outside had disappeared.

Blandius pointed to a sign on the third level near the stairs. 'Bestiarii first, Marcus, and that will be an excellent match. If you have never seen this before it will be well worth the wait.'

The bottom of the stadium was a large oval area of hard packed, light brown earth, that showed spots of reddish discolouration. The side walls of stadium held shuttered heavy oak doors in the ochre, coloured walls. Felix told Marcus they led to the underside of the stadium where the beasts and Gladiators waited for the appointed time that they would be required to enter the stadium.

Marcus could feel the tension in the crowd mixed with the building excitement of the coming events. He could only guess at the apprehension felt by the competitors, held in the dark of the underbelly of the stadium as they prepared for battle.

Felix told him about how the day's activities usually progressed. He knew from the experience of watching many fights that the Bestiarii would

115

enter the arena first. The first contest of a Bestarii, with no shield and lightly armed with only a spear and dagger or very short, sword, would be pitted against the lion of the size he witnessed in the cage below.'

'Who usually wins?' Marcus asked casually

'Certare usque ad mortem.' A fight to the death between the two, Felix replied. 'But mostly the Bestarii wins.' He added for good measure.

The man Marcus had spoken to outside the stadium was two rows behind them and he called out. 'Not bad eh; young man?' Marcus looked behind and nodded. 'I have never seen anything like it.'

The man smiled 'This is nothing, my boy, rumour has it that they will start work on the big one.'

'The what?' Marcus replied.

'They are calling it the Flavian Amphitheatre.'

'Bigger than this?' Marcus questioned.

'Twenty times bigger; at least twenty times.'

The view of the stadium from their seat was breath taking. He could not guess the size of the audience but it was more than Marcus had ever seen anywhere.

Perhaps in the thousands, he thought. He tried briefly to work out how to count them and finally gave up.

As they sat there an attendant came around giving away hard loaves of bread with the constant refrain to all; 'Consul Vespasian, wishes you good fortune and a long life.'

'Same to him' Felix replied with a snort as he accepted his loaf and broke it in three to pass to his companions. 'I may be cheap' he added with a hoot of laughter 'but I can't be bought with a loaf of bread. You two, however, could be bought with a small bread roll and cup of water.' Blandius nudged Marcus in the ribs as he turned his attention to Felix

'Well, Felix, we have most of your bread and we also have a loaf each, so if you get hungry we will see if you can be bought.'

'Make my bribe in wine, thanks Felix.' Marcus said, with a smile as he shoved a large piece of bread into this mouth.

'I want a girl as well.' Blandius said as he looked around the benches at the women of Rome.

CHAPTER 12

After a while, six, armour clad Gladiators walked out into the stadium and proceeded to walk the sides of the walls. After every several steps, they hit the rim of their shields with their swords in unison, causing a sound to reverberate as they walked.

The crowd responded with enthusiastic support, standing and clapping each time the swords hit the shield side.

In the middle of the lower level of the stadium, atop an elongated platform festooned with colour from flowers and hanging cloth, held a group of noblemen with one of them sitting above the others in a chair.

He rose from the chair and held out his hands. The crowd hushed as his voice carried, but only faintly, to the top tier. 'Good citizens of Rome, on this sacred day of Matralia, let the games begin.'

'Emperor Vespasian' Felix nudged him. 'Everyone likes him; In my humble opinion he has achieved a great deal in his short time at the top. Marcus looked over to see the emperor speaking with Lucia Laurentius and another man. 'It is the first year of his consulship and he is emperor, as well as a great warrior.' Felix said with a shout.

'That woman over there; Consul Vespasian, is speaking to is my mistress. Who is the man next to her?

Felix sighed. 'To my reckoning that would be her husband, Cassius Laurentius, you hick. Who else would it be? Have you not met him?'

Marcus shrugged and smiled. It was a new world he was living in and one, in which he had no experience, but he was learning. They were a handsome couple and clearly high in the noble order of Rome.

As the Gladiators neared the end of their circuit, two large slaves appeared; each holding a chain that held a collar in place on the lion that Marcus had seen over an hour before. It reared and tore at the chains. With the distance held by the two attendants, it was impossible for the lion to move to either side against one of the men who held it tightly by interloping the chain in the collar.

Finally, as the lion settled one of the slaves let go as the other, while holding the chain, moved to one of the doorways and pulled the enormous lion towards the heavy oak door.

A moment later the arena trumpets sounded and a sole Bestarii walked out onto the hard earth, of the arena. Shouts of 'Caelinus!' could be heard around the arena tiers.

'Bestiarii' Felix noted with genuine excitement 'Let us see if the lion wins.'

It was hard to tell the man's size from their position on the highest level of the stadium. His right arm was covered by a metal greave; held by straps that wound around his shoulders. His leg and shins were bare and his feet adorned with heavy boots. He wore a leather brace as well across his chest, with his loins covered by a heavy, leather skirt.

He cradled a helmet in his left arm. In his right hand, he held a long spear with a highly polished tip, that glinted brightly in the afternoon sun, as he walked into the middle of the arena. He appeared heavily muscled and without doubt, Marcus thought, as he remembered the fight with Cato, he would hold the scars of battles past.

He raised his arm in salute to the crowd and Marcus rose with the rest, cheering as he donned his helmet, swung the spear, feeling the weight and preferred point of balance. Raising his arm as he walked to the middle of the ground.

He stood erect, in the middle of the arena, as he saluted the occupants of the regal dais before him and they rose with the crowd, joining in the cheering. Marcus looked down at emperor Vespasian, residing in his purple toga, and not watching the spectacle before him. Marcus guessed his mind was set on other thoughts, as the man sat back with a wine in his hand, waiting.

The gate opened and the lion, released from its chains, charged out into the arena and then stood still, as it sniffed and growled at the arena noise. It eyed the Gladiator warily, snarling, hungry and with the scent of blood in its nostrils. The lion had clearly been jabbed several times as blood seeped from several small wounds on its back.

At that instant, the lion charged the Bestiarii with enough force to make the man stop in his tracks and await the blow, which came in an instant. The lion reared up to its full height as it opened it jaws trying to get a hold. The snarl from the big cat filled the stadium, as people clapped and stamped their feet.

The sweating Bestiarii, pushed the lion off and pulled back. The lion started to circle, growling and crouching as it worked its way around the Bestarii. Every time the Bestarii put his spear out, the lion swiped fiercely with its claws. The crowd erupted as the Bestiarii and the lion circled.

The man had experience, Marcus thought, as he shadowed the lion watching its movement as it, in turn, circled its quarry. Sweat glistened off the gladiator's skin as he changed position and started to move towards the lion, spear forward and his protected arm, held high.

The lion moved low on its legs, and when the point of the spear came forward the lion lashed out with claws, while growling in frustration. Salvia fell from its mouth to the hot sand below, and each time the spear came near it a heavy paw came up to swipe it away and the snarling increased. Slowly, it circled, watching and waiting.

Marcus studied the lion. It was a majestic beast. It stood there growling, in the relentless sun, with a sandy coloured pelt, almost the same colour as the earth of the stadium. The mane of the beast reached down half way to the ground and framed his head so that the beast appeared bigger and more imposing.

It stretched out, at least a spear length, standing on its four legs to the height of the hips of the Bestarii. Taut muscles flexed beneath its fur and despite being thrust into an unfamiliar arena, with the fear and uncertainty it surely felt, it radiated proud dominance.

The big cat, sensing this was a fight against an enemy it did not know, started growling heavily, which increased as it circled and finally crouched away from the gladiator.

'They don't get fed for a week' Felix said excitedly, waiting for the fight to start in earnest. 'It weakens them a little and once they smell blood of a man or beast they attack.'

In a blur, the lion sprinted towards the Gladiator and as the man raised his arm against the onslaught of the lion with its claws forward, it hit him with its full weight. Trying to find a hold, the lion clamped its jaw on the lower leg of the Bestiarii.

The man grunted so loud it could be heard at the top level, as the pain took over. The jaws clamped into his flesh, at the back of his naked leg.

The lion started to viciously shake the bitten flesh, causing the Gladiator to fall over on his back, losing the spear in the ferociousness of the attack. In a blur of speed, the massive weight of the cat pounced on him moving towards his neck.

With blood seeping, out of the bleeding bite on his leg, the Bestarii desperately held the snarling jaws away with both hands, as the cat used its weight to gain advantage and move its jaws towards the gladiator's neck. Finally, it sunk its teeth into his shoulders and as the blood lust took over the lion bit harder.

Flavio, the man who had spoken to Marcus at the gates leant down and whispered. 'Ten Denarii, the lion wins.'

Marcus looked around almost unable to take his eyes off the brutal spectacle before him. Felix nudged Marcus hard in the ribs. 'Forget the bet, my friend, the beast often wins.'

Marcus smiled quickly at the man. 'You are on, my friend.' He turned back to watch the battle as the growling from the lion filled the stadium, combined with the shouts of the patrons, as they urged the fight on.

The crowd rose to its feet, shouting obscenities combined with others urging the Bestiarii to get up. Over the sound of the shouting people, the guttural sounds from the lion grew louder, as its weight pushed down onto the Gladiator below and its jaws sank slowly towards the Bestarii' neck.

The length of the lion was as long as the gladiator beneath it. Despite the gladiator's hands still holding the head of the huge cat slightly away from his neck, he appeared to be losing strength.

Marcus watched, fascinated by the contest and willing the Bestiarii to gain control. Slowly, almost imperceptibly the contest changed as the gladiator slowly pushed the weight of the cat to one side, holding its snarling jaw with one hand, in a desperate embrace.

As he did so, he grabbed at the spear beside him just below the spear point, using it to rise to his feet. In an instant, the lion was up and standing away from the gladiator who stood, exhausted, bleeding profusely from his leg and shoulder. He stood breathless and trying to gain control.

The lion struck again, driven by fear and hunger, it came claws first into its quarry. The Bestarii stood up against the weight of the cat, plunging the spear blade hard into its massive neck, as it reared on its hind legs against him.

The animal refused to yield and it became more savage with its jaws snapping at the wound on his shoulder. The cry of pain from the Bestarii could be heard above the desperate snarling of the bleeding lion.

In the next instant, the large cat began to falter, unable to spring forward. The Bestarii moved quickly as he thrust the spear head again, and again into the neck of the cat and slowly the beast yielded, sinking to the sand beside him.

Exhausted, he sank to his knees, and then with considerable effort rose unsteadily to his full height. He looked at the bleeding carcass of the lion on the reddened sand at his feet. He hefted the bloodied spear up, as an offer to the crowd, who were clapping and stamping their feet. He then pulled the lion's head up by the ears and slit its throat.

He was a mess of claw marks and two belching wounds. With dignity, he moved to the front of the platform, saluted and walked towards the largest door at the side of the arena. As he neared the door two attendants came quickly out to support him into the underbelly of the arena.

The scene below Marcus, on the sand, gave the crowd the view of the magnificent form of the male lion stretched out, bloodied and dead in the near middle of the arena. There were blood spills around the area of the final fight and blood poured from the lion as it lay motionless on the sand.

Across the arena, lay the blood red trail that came from the seeping wound on the Bestiarii's leg, as he finally limped over to the door. The crowd rose in unison stamping on the floorboards, shouting his name but he did not re-appear.

'Caelinus! Caelinus!' Came the unified shout.

Felix turned to Marcus. 'You see, my friend, you have witnessed the best Bestiarii in Rome. Born a slave and now a hero. Caelinus Felix. We love a hero, in Rome!'

'Will he survive? He got badly mauled.'

Felix shrugged. 'That, Marcus, is in the hands of the Gods.'

Marcus looked at the prone body of the lion as attendants came out to pick it up and remove it to the side of the arena. It was not a fair contest, he thought, a lion with a strong jaw against a man with a grieved arm and a sharp spear. There was courage in the man but more courage in the lion.

Calm descended on the arena and Felix distributed bread and hard cheese to all of them and they drank from the goatskin of wine. He swivelled around on the bench to view the stadium. He had never seen so many people in one place.

It was full and he understood, for the first time, what it was like to live in a city choked with people living their own lives. He understood for the first time the difference it made to live on a farm where life was simple.

Perhaps, his father was right. Maybe the life of Rome would be too different for him after the farm. Only time might tell. At least, he had gained friends and he had experienced life outside of tending the fruits of nature at the call of sunrise and the finish by the very late afternoon, in the seeding season.

He turned to the man behind him. 'What is your name, again?'

'Flavio' came the reply 'At least give me a chance to get my money back.'

'On what?' Marcus asked with indifference.

'On what?' The man said with some surprise. 'On the next match, young man, on the next match. Since we have not yet seen the combatants let us make a bet prior. There are two types in the first match. A Thracian and a Murmillione. Take your pick.'

Marcus shrugged as he received a nudge in the ribs from Blandius. 'Foolish betting Marcus, he knows more than you.'

Marcus shrugged again. 'I will take the Thracian I guess. And the bet?'

'Let's liven it up. Say, fifty Denarii?'

'That is a large bet!' Felix said sternly, looking at Marcus who was shaking hands with the man behind him.

'Done.' Marcus replied and turned to the front.

Blandius who was sitting to his right and directly in front of the girls tapped him on the leg and leant in close.

123

'Are you crazy? How do you know the Thracian will win? In these types of contests, the Murmillione are usually more successful, because of the armour.'

'Oh.' Marcus replied casually. 'Well, you never know.'

Blandius rolled his eyes and moved back to a conversation with the raven, haired girl, behind him.

CHAPTER 13

Attendants cleaned the arena by laying down new sand. Finally, with the expectation of the crowd displayed by clapping in unison, heavy bass trumpets sounded the next contest in which Gladiators would fight.

Felix had headed for the latrines and Blandius was leaning behind him, speaking to a young woman, who spoke to him but kept her eyes on Marcus.

Marcus smiled at her and she returned it with a flourish of her hair. Blandius pretended not to notice and Marcus turned back towards the arena, waiting for the action to start.

'Who is your friend?' The raven, haired girl, asked loudly enough for Marcus to hear.

'A dumb, farm yokel; From the faraway hill's, many day's travel from Rome. He is a dullard. Can hardly keep a conversation going.'

'Oh, and you?' She asked slyly, looking at Marcus, who sat on the row beneath.

'I am a sword maker by trade.' He said in a loud manner. 'I make swords for many of the regal occasions. We have made swords for many noblemen, even Consul Vespasian himself.'

'You make all of those yourself?' She asked.

'Oh no, I am part of a large business that makes swords. I work with the man who was here before. His name is Felix. We are both work at the foundry. So, what are you doing after the games finish?'

She smiled and pointed to her friend who sat demurely beside her. They were very different looking, Blandius noted, as he smiled at the other girl. Both were beauties but one was fair haired and the other dark skinned, with raven hair.

'We have not thought that far ahead.' And you and your friends?'

'The nearest tavern for refreshments, I hope. Why don't you join us?'

The girl looked at her friend who shrugged and giggled. 'Maybe'

'I feel sorry for the lion.' The raven-haired girl said.

'I think the Bestarii must be very handsome and that beautiful physique.'

Blandius rolled his eyes at Marcus, who looked up as they spoke. 'How would you know he is handsome?'

'They are all handsome.' The girl said gushing. 'If you trained every day you might be handsome as well.' She said, with a glint in her eye.

The arena came alive again with four Gladiators moving out of the arena doors onto the baking earth of the central area. They clashed their swords against their shields as they walked the perimeter. The trumpets blared and the arena noise rose from the crowd as they cheered at the spectacle below.

Even under the shade of the sails lofting above his head, Marcus could feel the heat rising from the baking earth of the arena below. Honey water sellers were doing a big trade that day, he noted as the vendors walked down the aisles, with their strong voices

'*Aqua, Aqua*' Once in a while they would stop, take the payment and offer a ladle of cool water, lightly flavoured with honey.

Felix returned from the latrines and sat down. 'Since you are a farm boy, with no education or understanding of anything,' He said with a wry but humorous smile, 'Let me educate you, on the battle we have before us. 'You girls might want to listen as well' He said gesturing to the arena and smiling at them until he got their attention.

'Listen to the school teacher, girls' Blandius said, with a half-smile. 'But, you may not learn anything.'

'The battle of the gladiators down there is a very simple process. They pair off and each of the fights has a s*umma rudis,* a referee, who rules the fight. Once a gladiator has been put into submission, either by a blow or by exhaustion, the *summa rudis* can stop the fight altogether, or show by a hand signal that they must fight on. The stick that he holds is to indicate the contest start or finish.'

'What happens if one gladiator is mortally wounded? Marcus asked.

Blandius smiled. 'Then it is off for the hammer.'

One of the girls looked at him surprised. 'The hammer?'

Felix sighed and looked straight at her, as two gladiators walked out to the arena and stood in front of the official dais. 'They are put out of their misery.'

'Oh' The dark-skinned girl said, with a strange look on her face.

'However, I need to explain the rest of the match for my friend here.' Felix motioned to Marcus, who noted the raven-haired girl was smiling at him again. 'Of the two gladiators on the arena, we obviously have two different types. You see the one who has greaves on his legs and that small round shield? He also carries that curved Thracian sword, with the visored helmet. They are called Thraex. They are strong fighters and move fast.'

Marcus nodded as he took in the sight. The Thracian looked larger than the man he was fighting.

'The other Gladiator is obviously a different style. They wear a helmet with a crest which is fashioned to look like a fish, hence the name; Murmillo. They wear the right arm guard, no leg greaves and they have a longer, oblong style, shield. These are called Murmillones.'

'What sort of sword?' Marcus squinted in the bright sunlight.

'Just a basic Gladius and probably made by us; the finest swords in Rome you know.'

'Well, I might be a dumb hick from the country but I can tell a salesman when I meet one.' Marcus smiled sideways at Felix and flashed a smile at the girl behind him whilst turning to find the thunderous face of Blandius staring at him. 'Is one type better at fighting than the other?' Marcus asked as he returned his gaze to the men in the arena.

'That is up to the Gladiator, my friend' Blandius noted with a grimace. 'They train all day but some are just better than others. But given your bet, we all hope the Thracian fight better!'

The spectacle continued below, with each of the two gladiators standing off a short distance between each other. Standing to the side, the summa rudis in a white toga with leather strapping across his chest raised his stick between them.

127

The two men came to attention in the middle of the stadium, facing the regal crowd that had risen to their feet on the platform. Vespasian motioned to another nobleman, who turned out to be Laurentius.

Dressed in a white toga, with a scarf in his hand, he moved to the front and beckoned to the crowd who rose to their feet. 'Good citizens! On behalf of emperor Vespasian, the battle begins.' His voice boomed out, but faintly heard by most.

The referee motioned to the two men. With a downwards swipe of the stick, the contest began with the men circling and manoeuvring. As each changed position, the other changed in turn, and finally the Thracian raised his curved sword and struck towards the Murmillione who easily parried the blow with his shield.

Marcus could clearly see the men labouring, with the tell-tales signs of their torso rising and falling to their heavy breathing combines with the sound of their shouts as they parried, relented, parried and stepped sideways, again and again.

It was almost a dance, Marcus reflected; a brutal and vicious dance nonetheless. The sound of the sword, clashing hard with a heavy shield, reverberated across the stadium and the crowd rose to its feet as the contest began in earnest.

Each of the gladiators changed position, attacked and changed position again. This change in the fight continued for a long period of time with no result as the blows resounded and the audience clapped, hissed and booed the two men.

Finally, the Murmillione, the larger of the two, feinted to his right, as the Thracian brought his sword down, slicing into the large shield of his opponent. With a sweeping strike of his curved Thraex sword, the blade finally bounced heavily off the top of the oblong shield, slicing the arm of the fish headed gladiator.

The Thracian moved to take the advantage and repeatedly parried his long, curved sword into the shield of the Murmillione before him. He staggered back under the continued attack.

Both men were breathing hard as they shared blows, looking for a weakness. The crash and sound of steel on sword and sword on shield continued until they broke off again and started to circle.

As the Thracian came in for a hard-overhead strike, the Murmillione, slowed by his heavy armour, parried the blow with his shorter Gladius turning faster than a man of his size might. He made a sweeping sword strike into the front leg of the Thraex before him.

The man instantly buckled, holding his bleeding leg and collapsing to the sand. He held his shield up as the Murmillione continued his attack. Surprisingly, at least to Marcus, the crowd started to boo and hiss with the exception of the man behind him who cheered the Murmillione on to victory. Words of complaint erupted.

'*Surgere*' cried one. 'Get up'

'Knee Trembler' cried another

'Coward' cried another.

Gamely, the Thracian raised himself to his feet, to oppose the heaving body of the Murmillione before him. He continued to use his longer sword to parry the increasingly heavy blows. On the next blow, the Thracian's sword shivered from its hilt, broken in half it fell to the ground.

The Thracian raised his half sword to fight. Marcus watched as the sword of the Murmillione, shining from the sun, smashed into the Thracian's shield. As the man staggered back the Murmillione back-handed his sword across the Thraex helmet with a loud crack.

The visored helmet of the Thracian, flew off and fell a short distance as the man fell to his knees again. The Murmillione moved in with his sword in the kill position as the Thracian lay on the ground. As custom dictated, the Thraex lifted one index finger on his hand above him to show surrender.

The referee intervened between them with a hand movement to note the end of the fight. The sand beneath the two men held churned and red with blood, as the wound on the leg of the Thracian bled, near the area that the fallen lion had laid.

The Murmillione dropped his sword and shield, standing upright to the crowd who were on their feet, shouting at his victory. From the top of his arm, blood seeped down across the leather sash, causing rivulets to form across his sweating torso.

He finally removed his helmet and stood before the platform at the centre of the stadium. His body glistened in the afternoon sun.

'See. He is handsome.' The girl said as she got to her feet to join the applause.

Vespasian got to his feet, applauding the Gladiator before him. The crowd hushed as he addressed the man. 'Hail, Gladiator, what is your name for the crowd?'

'Britanicus, Lord'

'Of Brittania?'

'Nay sire. From the land highest in Northern Gaul.

The Gladiator bowed slightly and gestured to the crowd who started to cheer. Vespasian looked around at the response. 'Then a prize, Gladiator, of two hundred Denarii to you for your efforts as well as your Ludis fee! As Romans we know you but for those who have not witnessed your skills before I commend you on your contest today.'

The gladiator bowed slightly again and went to pick up his sword. He stopped momentarily as Vespasian continued. 'Halt, gladiator, I have a request of you. I would like to offer the considerable amount of another sixty Denarii for any man in the arena to fight you, sword to sword. But, no death shall come of it. Do you agree?'

The Gladiator looked up at the platform 'As you wish, my lord'

The crowd hushed as Flavian Vespasian, resplendent in his purple toga, called out. 'Who will take on our injured champion, Britanicus, in a fight with sword and shield? Someone, who has no Gladiatorial experience. Is there such a man who will do this?'

The crowd hushed and waited. Finally, a small boy stood up. 'I will, my lord.' Vespasian looked over at a small boy. in one of the front rows beside him.

The crowd laughed as his mother pulled him down next to her.

'Maybe next year, citizens; what do you think?' Vespasian said laughing at the courage of the boy. 'Will there be no one else? I will offer the same Denarii to the challenger!'

There was a hush to the crowd as they looked around at each other to see who might be the first.

To the surprise of Felix and Blandius, Marcus stood up raising his arm. 'I will fight!' Marcus shouted out and the stadium erupted into cheers and laughing.

Felix tried gamely to pull him down 'Are you out of your mind, you idiot! He is a trained gladiator and you are a bumpkin from a country farm. You can't even use a sword, can you?'

Marcus shrugged. 'I never thought of that but now you mention it I guess I will have to move faster than he does. Perhaps a sword lesson from you after this would be a good idea.' Marcus smiled at Felix and at the girl behind him.

Vespasian looked over in the direction of the shout. 'Yes, young man, come forward and prove your courage. Citizens, behold a courageous, young man'

The crowd stamped their feet and clapped. 'Idiot' Felix said in reply. 'Try not to get killed.'

'How brave.' One of the girls said behind him. 'What is your friends name?'

'Idiot.' Felix replied

'Come; Come, forward, citizen and join the battle.' Vespasian shouted again to egg the crowd on as an attendant motioned for him to follow.

Marcus looked at Felix as he turned to join the attendant. 'You forget, Felix, I owe fifty Denarii behind me and I cannot pay. Did you have a few Denarii you could lend me?'

Felix shook his head and shrugged. He watched Marcus disappear from view to walk down the stairs to the ground level. Blandius sat down with a disappointed look on his face. Felix turned to him and patted his leg. 'Well, at least you can use a sword. By the Gods, this idiot will rue the moment he made this decision.'

'Can he fight?' Blandius asked.

'Against that!' Felix said motioning to the standing bulk of Britanicus who awaited instructions. While he waited in the arena, the gladiator removed his shield and helmet and slashed at the air with his gladius in slow, coordinated movement.

CHAPTER 14

Marcus descended the final staircase, following close behind the attendant and glancing at the stadium tiers above him. The crowd returned to normal, with people milling around and changing seats, as they waited for the entertainment to begin.

Above, the sun arced the heavens to lazily sit in the middle of the sky, above the height of the stadium, to produce the hottest time of the day.

The attendant motioned for him to follow, through one of the heavy oak doors near the staircase. As they moved from the dazzling daylight into the interior beneath the stadium the cavernous area beneath, appeared gloomy and depressing.

As his eyes adjusted he could make out two rows of cages stretching into distance with the flickering of oil lamps throwing ghostly shadows against oak clad walls and across the bars of the iron cages.

The corridor led towards the back of the stadium. It was covered in dirty hay with the sounds of the caged, wild animals clearly heard above the noise filtering from outside.

The air inside held a scent that felt as comforting as it did familiar, from the farm. The heavy smell of hay lining the corridor, running past cages mixed with the pungent smell of dung, from the caged animals remained in his nostrils as he followed the attendant though the maze underneath the building.

He could sense something else but it was not something he recognised. He thought it might be the smell of fear, or perhaps the sweaty anticipation of fighting men or animals, but it remained as a foreboding scent in the passageway. It was to become a scent that he would always associate with the smell of the fight.

He glanced at the cages on their way to the gladiator rooms. Some were empty and some held the darkened forms of heavily panting cats. In another cage, he looked through to see a small mountain bear. Fascinated by the sounds and scent of the underneath of the stadium, Marcus followed the attendant further into the darkness with neither of them speaking.

Occasionally, he could hear the voices from the outside through the cracks of the flat rooftop, combined with an occasional, high pitched cry, from a vendor. As he walked along, he realised the first tier held the seats of rich patrons, sitting above the cesspool of animals and men as they walked along. The irony cast a thin smile on his face.

They walked far enough for Marcus to believe he was at the opposite end of the stadium and waiting for him, sweating and swearing, was one of the shortest men he had ever seen. The man had no neck but massive arms and shoulders with a bald, sweating head.

The arms room lay adjacent to the wild animal cages and held the quiet forms of the gladiators, who stood or sat around the room in quiet reflection, of the fight to come. Some spoke to others and some whispered to themselves.

They ranged in sizes. All, were muscular and glistening with sweat, as they moved through various stages of dressing and fighting positions. Several of the standing Gladiators used the time in stretching or swinging their sword arms with heavy weights on the end.

Two large attendants, moved around the room ensuring the gladiators were attended as a smaller, thinner man with an elaborate tunic, moved around them taking a count and addressing them.

The attendant spoke to him as they stopped. 'Marcus, this is the master of arms and he will explain to you how…'

The man waved the attendant away 'Are you the idiot that volunteered to take on Britanicus?' The man shouted, looking directly at Marcus from his much lower height.

'I am 'Marcus replied with a smirk that was not returned from the short man before him.

'Well, I admire your courage and you will be happy to know there are rules. Have you watched many fights?'

'I have never watched one. The Bestarii before, was the only contest I have ever…'

The man cut him short with a wave of his hand. 'You really must be stupid. I don't know whether not seeing a contest is good or bad. Here is some of the best advice you will receive in your life. Stay away from him and go down early.'

'Why?' Marcus replied.

The master-of-arms shook his head in disbelief and continued. 'But, first we must dress you. You!' He motioned to an attendant who served water to the gladiators. 'Get him in Thraex uniform.'

'While you are being dressed I want you to remember a few facts. You will wear the garb of the Thracian and you do not start fighting until the referee gives you the signal by dropping the rod he holds in his right hand. Understand?'

Marcus nodded.

The man dropped his hand several times to emphasize the point. 'You are fighting a very skilled gladiator. The reason for this, is to give the patrons a little light entertainment. Therefore, I warn you again. You need to stay away from this gladiator. You know? Have a few jousts and then drop your sword and shield and give up. If you don't he will give you a hell of a beating. Got it?'

Marcus shrugged and waited for the attendants to assist him with the outfit of the Thracian. The man looked at him with an impatient look on his face.

He drew close, looking up at Marcus from his short height. 'Listen, idiot, you don't seem to get it. The man you are about to fight is a champion of ten championship fights, with eight wreaths and four of them ending to *mortem*. With one blow, he could cripple you for the rest of your life, and if he gets angry he could kill you. So, shrug your shoulders, you fool, but listen to my advice.'

'Where is the previous Bestarii? Marcus said as he put his arm out to have the greave placed on.

'By the Gods, do you ever listen?' The master said under his breath. 'Don't know; don't care. He was severely injured, so he may not have gone for the *Malleo*.'

'Hammer?' Marcus asked surprised.

'Boy, you really are inexperienced, aren't you? Said the master of arms. 'If one of the boys is mortally injured, we take them off and give them an offering to the Gods. The quickest way to say farewell is with a hammer to the head. It's the most merciful way of sending them on their journey to the black waters.'

Marcus nodded his head as he did not know what else to say.

'All you need to care about, young man, from now on, is to stay away from that gladiator because one heavy sword stroke from him, will easily bust your arm or your leg and probably maim you for life. Don't go out there thinking this is a real fight: it's not. Got it?'

Marcus looked at the man. 'The way you describe it I should stay away and not fight, otherwise, I will end up on the side of the other side of the stadium with a hammer to my brain.'

'That's, if you have a brain.' The master of arms said as he tightened the arm greave and rolled his eyes. 'This is not a brawl or a tavern room fight. This is a professional killer you are up against. My suggestion is that you try very hard not to make him angry. Do you work for a living?'

Marcus nodded. 'I am a gardener at the estate of the noble Laurentius. I came to Rome at the start of the season.'

'Jupiter save us! Why would a gardener want to take on a gladiator? You must be out of your mind.' Marcus looked at him sheepishly as the attendant attached the last greave to his left leg. He moved uncomfortably in the garb.

The greaves dug into his legs and the shield, which had been placed in his left hand, felt heavy and unwieldy, as did the greave on his right arm. 'I have a gambling debt to pay.'

'Did it occur to you that it might be smarter not to gamble and then not have to meet Britanicus in the ring? Saying that,' the man said stroking his chin reflectively, 'I have partaken in a little gambling myself from time to time.' For the first time, he smiled, albeit, grimly.

The man moved around Marcus, checking the fastening of the greaves and the position of the leather strapping around his chest. 'This will feel uncomfortable for a while. but you will become used to it. Trust me, when I tell you the protection is there to help you; Not the other way around.'

Outside the trumpets sounded. A sword and shield were thrust into Marcus' hands and a helmet passed to him, which he started to don but with difficulty as it hurt his head and ears as he pulled it over a felt cap.

The master of arms grabbed the helmet and thrust it onto his arm. 'Now, listen to me, boy. I have checked you out. You are young and strong and you have the physique to take a little punishment. When you get out there, you do as I say. You have a few goes and stay away and then drop your sword. Got it?'

Marcus stood, frozen in fear as he realised for the first time what he had stupidly decided to attempt. His feet felt like lead as he waited with the attendant at the door of the arena. There was enough space to open and peer out.

The view almost paralysed him as he awaited the call to contest. Britanicus stood, relaxed and smiling, in the middle of the arena close to the dais.

He continued to swing his Gladius as he walked to and fro, waiting for his contest to arrive. From the bottom of the arena the view held a great difference from the top. The size and grandeur of the stadium felt mesmerising and at his shoulder the master-at-arms looked out with him.

'Different from down here, isn't it?' He said with a malicious smile.

To make matters worse, Marcus realised he was fighting in front of his mistress, Lucia Laurentius and her husband and for a reason he could not explain he had not thought about it before. The call to contest came too quickly as the door before him opened wide.

The master-at-arms was still at his shoulder as the door opened. 'See the platform over there with the high and mighty? Put your chest out, walk over there and stand beside Britanicus and then get on with it. No doubt the rich will want to say something before you start, but don't listen. Whatever they say will about as helpful as a bad duck egg. Good luck and if it is any help to you, you look the part.'

For some inexplicable reason, Marcus started to recall the days that he and his brother played at sword fights and the times he pestered his father to make him a sword. He tried to remember the thrust and parry game they played but it was long ago and the sword in front of him was metal and much heavier. He tested the edge with his finger and it was sharp.

'Good luck, you are going to need It.' The master of arms said as he opened the door to the spectacle of the crowds and hard earth beneath.

'What did you say?' Marcus gasped as he started to move.

He was pushed out into the brilliant sunshine and his instant thought was the feel of the brown earth beneath his feet. He stared up at the safety of the seating rows of the third tier and the company of his friends wondering at the foolishness of his decision to take on the arena. He had no experience and this was the first time he had walked onto an amphitheatre let alone a stadium packed with spectators. The effect was overwhelming. With the drenching heat of the afternoon heat, penetrating the metal of the greaves, and the anticipation of the fight before him, sweat was pouring from his body as he made his way towards the dais and Britanicus who still had his back turned.

As he walked across the blood-stained earth to where the huge bulk of Britanicus stood before the dais he tried to calm himself. He seemed to have no energy and the shield and sword lay heavy on his arms. As he neared the dais, the stadium erupted.

He stopped next to Britanicus who stood and waited for the clapping and hooting to stop. Emperor Vespasian, was the first to rise and he quieted the crowd with his hand.

'What is your name, Roman?' He shouted out.

'Marcus Attilius, sire.'

'Where do you come from, Marcus Attilius; Are you a city born citizen?'

'No, sire. I come from a farm in the North.'

Marcus looked up at the noblemen who stood up with a commotion within the group. He watched Laurentius moved over to where Vespasian was standing and whispered in his ear. To his left he could see Lucia Vespasian watching over the railing with her daughter next to her. They were both laughing.

Vespasian raised his hand to stop the commotion that started and smiled as Laurentius moved away to the back of the dais. 'Is it true that you are a gardener in the home of the honourable Cassius Laurentius? And you were born a free man?'

'That is true sire' Marcus replied as he watched sweat dropping onto the hard-packed earth below his feet. He glanced sideways at Britanicus. On his torso, he saw again, the same pattern of scars he had witnessed on the gladiator that night before the fire when they met on the road the Rome.

The man was of similar height to Marcus but heavy set with massive forearms and wide shoulders. His torso, held by a thin, leather strap, was immense in size with a large gut that showed the faint outlines of broad muscles. The giant before him swung his Gladius as if it was a feather.

'This is not a fight to death, Marcus Attilius, but you must attempt to fight our current champion, Britanicus.' At the mention of the name the crowd went into applause and once again Vespasian raised his hand. 'So, step into position and begin.'

He motioned to the referee who stood behind the two. Marcus to his left and the referee motioned him to turn the other way.

The weight of the greaves, sword, helmet and shield made him feel uncomfortable and there was no getting used to it, he thought to himself. He listened to the same instructions as the master-at-arms had told him before he walked onto the stadium.

As he stood on the arena, with the sound of the crowd filling his ears, he realised that any fear he had felt was diminishing. Above everything else that had battered his senses that afternoon, he understood the mastery of the man before him and his own lack of experience.

In his mind, he saw Britanicus let the arrow fly that killed their evening meal on that night together on his way to Rome. It made him shudder to think of it.

As the referee made the final points and set a place for both of them to stand Marcus looked over at Britanicus who was smiling at him. 'Listen boy,' he said with a low gravelly voice 'I don't want to injure you. But, if you make my life difficult in this fight, I will hurt you. Understand?' The smile turned to a snarl.

Marcus nodded and tried to take his helmet off as it did not fit and it pained his skull and ears so he threw it to the side.

'You must put that on, boy.'

'Put in on!' The referee ordered.

Marcus shook his head. 'It hurts too much'

The referee looked at Britanicus who shrugged his muscled shoulders and took his helmet off as well. The referee stooped to take the helmets from the area and pass them to attendants waiting on the side. At this gesture, the sound from the crowd was almost overwhelming.

'We... we, have met' Marcus said uncomfortably. The huge size of

Britanicus peered at him. 'Where?'

'On the road to Rome. You were taking Aru home.'

Britanicus nodded.' Ah, now I remember that night! Listen, young'un. That night means nothing on this arena. After this bout, we can sit and talk about that night, but there are no friends on this arena. There are only opponents and I don't want to hurt you/'

The referee returned and set the position with a slice of his rod. Immediately, the crowd went wild with calls and stamping of feet. The noise was deafening as Marcus waited for the first onslaught by Britanicus who stood back, sword raised and shield at the ready.

Overwhelmed by the arena and the pandemonium of the crowd, Marcus realised that the size of the man before him, lay shadowed by the size of his shield. Britanicus appeared impenetrable, given the space it occupied in front of him.

The size of the man felt completely intimidating as the gladiator stood there, with his shield high and his sword hanging loosely.

The *Summa Rudis* moved towards them and looking directly at Marcus. 'Is there a problem?'

'Only one 'Marcus breathed slowly as he kept his eye on Britanicus 'I don't know what to do.'

He saw the half smile crease the face of Britanicus and before he knew it Marcus fended a sword strike off his shield.

The force of the strike made him lose his grip on the leather thong on the inside of his shield. Instinctively, he took a stride backwards to re-position himself as Britanicus moved forward with a hard look and another overhead strike.

The attacks resounded with the sound of the crowd in unison as each strike rendered a welt in the brass of the shield held by Marcus. He had backed more than ten steps away from the gladiator under the force of the assaults.

'Had enough?' Britanicus said roughly, with his eyes intently on Marcus.

Marcus feinted to the right as the gladiator moved forward for another attack and he struck out with his sword which was swotted away.

Britanicus moved back slightly and Marcus moved in for the attack. His long curved, Thracian sword, spun in the sunlight of the arena. He threw strike after strike at the short sword of the giant before him and stepped forward as each blow struck the metal of Britanicus' shield.

Each contact against the shield rang out across the stadium with a resounding clash of steel on steel and with such force that Marcus could hear the reverberation from the lower walls, around the arena. 'So, there is life in the young pup.' Britanicus noted with a grunt as the curved sword struck against the heavy metal and oak of the shield held by him. 'Now, let's see what you have got.'

The fight changed; Britanicus changed his tact and parried the blows by Marcus and paced forward after every thrust of his curved sword. Marcus could feel the change in the man beside him as his strength started to exert itself in the fight.

Britanicus possessed brute strength, which he used to advantage, to move forward and gain the advantage.

Marcus circled, watching Britanicus closely and he noticed that each time a sword strike rebounded off the oblong shield held by the Gladiator, the man moved back rather than moving to strike. Once the gladiator steadied himself he would then strike again, with a hard over-shoulder blade.

The effect, as each heavy blow hit Marcus with shattering violence, brought a sudden tiredness to Marcus as he moved backwards and left and right.

Each time, he was caught by the heavy blade across his shield and when he parried the incoming Gladius strike with his curved sword, the force made it barely possible to hold his sword up.

The shield thongs that encased his arms bit into his flesh as he tried to reposition them but without success.

The sound of the crowd was gradually diminished by the breath coming out of his own mouth. The sound of his rasping breath became the only thing that Marcus could hear above the noise from the crowd and the weight of the greaves and armour, combined with the heat rising from the arena sand under the midday sun, made him feel faint and dehydrated. Sweat stung his eyes as he retreated.

'Time to give up, young'un. Just drop your sword and wait for the applause. You can be a hero for a day.' Britanicus said the last word and changed stance, Gladius forward.

He moved closer to Marcus with his sword thrusting and alternatively his shield smashing hard into the Marcus' sore left shoulder and arm. Finally, the shield was smashed from Marcus's grip and it lay on the ground as he backed away.

'Last chance.' Britanicus growled and motioned him to pick up his shield, from the hard earth. 'That's to make things even.'

Now, Marcus could hear the crowd and see them in the distance on their feet chanting '*Habet, hoc habet! Habet, hoc habet*, He's had it!'

In the distance, Marcus could hear one loud voice shouting. '*Mitte! Mitte!* Let him go!' The breath rasped in his throat and the sword felt heavy in his hand as he took a little distance between his stance and the aggressive move of the Gladiator before him.

Britanicus, sensing the weak and inexperienced man before him, moved in with a sword strike, the force of which bounced off his curved sword and slicing into Marcus's leg, as he moved to his left.

It was not a deep wound but it started to bleed down his leg in the background all Marcus could hear was the deafening noise of the crowd surrounding him. He looked down at the cut, realising he could not feel it. 'Your souvenir of the fight, young un. Had enough of the fight?'

Britanicus hefted his shield up and every time Marcus came in for an attack he smashed the shield down into his weakening left arm. Each blow from the giant caused him to stagger back under the weight and violent force of the shield.

Each collision was met by shouts from the crowd and finally with one last attack, Britanicus pushed Marcus to the ground; He lay there panting. 'Now, stay there.' Britanicus said, as he started to raise his shield to the crowd who were on their feet.

Marcus could feel the anger growing and he got to his feet. Within a moment, Britanicus was on him again and smashed his shield down. As the sweaty, dirt stained bulk of Britanicus came close to him, Marcus changed his sword and shield hand, so his sword was now in his left.

As Britanicus moved into striking range, he moved with surprising speed to smash an elbow into the scarred jaw of the giant. The blow staggered Britanicus. Marcus moved quickly into attack.

He rained blow after blow onto the shield and short sword and suddenly, with the same speed as before, he landed another punch into the face of Britanicus, who, momentarily stunned, shook his head at the effect and bewilderment at the blow.

Marcus circled as Britanicus dropped, clearly dazed, to one knee and with his free hand he wiped the sweat from his eyes. With a roar, he raised himself up and moved forward towards Marcus. He raised his sword and stuck hard downwards onto the Thracian curved sword with a force that could be heard around the stadium. Again, it glanced off but this time the point of Marcus's sword continued its journey burying itself into Britanicus' knee. With a loud grunt from the pain the man raised himself up and grabbed Marcus by the arm greave and smashed a hard fist into his jaw.

Marcus had seen it coming and had moved his head to deflect the blow but it almost knocked him senseless. He staggered back, watching as Britanicus stepped in on him again. This time, with his face in a tight grimace and his sword raised level, Britanicus dropped his shield and moved towards him.

Marcus realised this was no longer a fight; it was now a battle and the only way to win would be speed. He parried the blow from Britanicus with his arm greave and hit the gladiator twice as he came in towards him.

The second punch hit hard into Britanicus' left side. Dropping to a crouch he let loose an uppercut that lifted the big man before him, off his feet. The gladiator hit the solid earth below with a sound that could be heard clearly around the stadium as his size impacted with the sand. He lay groaning as Marcus stood above him, blood down his leg and panting like a caged animal.

Slowly, the gladiator got to his feet. His bloodied nose spread blood across his face as he smiled at Marcus. 'Big mistake, Marcus, because now we have a fight.'

Marcus looked at him surprised that the man had actually got to his feet. He tensed, ready to change from his left stance, as Britanicus moved in towards him.

This time the giant made a move to grab Marcus by the arm in close and as he did he feinted to the right and before Marcus could react a hard, left fist, came over the top and landed square on the young man's jaw.

Marcus sensed the punch but it was too late and, in a moment, the force landed him on the ground on his back. By the time he regained his senses Britanicus had his heavy foot laid on Marcus's neck and a sword pointed at his head. He could hardly breathe.

Britanicus bent down towards Marcus. 'Listen boy, in a real fight you would be dead so get up and thank the Gods I am in a good mood.' He said, spitting the blood across Marcus' face that poured from his bloodied nose. Marcus lay there panting from the exertion. 'If you try anything, I will slit you from the balls up.'

Marcus rose slowly, unsteadily to his feet beside Britanicus. 'You fight well for such a young age but you can tell your children you once took on the great Britanicus' The giant snarled as blood started to pour from his nose.

They stood up and faced the dais. Flavian Vespasian came to the fore and raised his hand in salute.

'Well, Marcus Attilius, you have done well against a great champion and Britanicus I am sure you went easy on our young man. Citizens of Rome, I applaud Marcus Attilius and the great Britanicus as a tie in this contest. Our champion, the great Britanicus remains a champion of Rome.'

Vespasian listened intently as an attendant whispered in his ear. He nodded and with that gesture he went to sit back down and await the next battle as Marcus staggered across to the door at the side of the stadium with Britanicus beside him.

Behind him, from the regal dais he heard a voice thundering out to the hushed stadium; 'Our next battle will be between two gladiators who have not fought in this ring before. They are the champions pick of the Tirones.'

As they neared the door to the stadium the two, young gladiators, waited inside in together, not speaking or looking at each other and both sweating heavily, as the heat from the arena blew in like a furnace. The master-of-arms surveyed them both and made several quiet adjustments as the trumpets sounded for the start of the spectacle.

'*Morituri te salutant*' He said to the two men addressing them before they started the short walk to the centre of the arena. '*Those who are about to die salute you*'

143

'*Morituri te salutant*' they mumbled in reply. One of them turned 'Aqua, per favore, before I go' The master of arms grabbed a ladle and gave it to the man. He gulped it down and together they walked out.

Britanicus and Marcus entered the gloom of the passageway and sat on heavy wooden benches and gulped water.

The Master of arms inspected Britanicus first and assisted him in taking off his armour and closely inspected the knee wound, which refused to stop bleeding.

'That is too deep. We will need to stitch.' Britanicus grunted at the news as if it was an everyday event and the master of arms nodded to the attendant who brought a wood bowl with a long bone needle and thin, sinewy thread which looked the colour of dried wheat.

The attendant washed the cut with water and then doused it in medicated oil. He threaded the needle and proceeded to stich the knee wound from one side to the other. Once he had finished he tied off the thread and bound the wound. Britanicus simply lay there and grunted and asked for more water.

He then turned his attention to Marcus as one of the attendants washed Britanicus in the murky light of an oil lamp. As they washed him he appeared to fall asleep and started to snore.

The attendant focussed his attention to the wound on Marcus' upper leg. He muttered as he inspected it, pushing and prodding after he wiped the dried blood.

He washed the wound with vinegar water and watched to see if it continued to bleed. He poured olive oil on the wound, binding it with a clean white cloth with a pad underneath to staunch any fresh flow of blood. He did the same to a smaller wound on the left arm and then left with instructions to change the leg bandage three days hence.

How is your jaw?' Britanicus asked as he awoke from his nap

'Sore, but not too bad.'

'Next time, remind me and I'll break it.'

The attendant took Marcus's garb off him and washed the dirt and blood from his body. He was given a meal of lentils and lamb in a tasty sauce and a cup of full-bodied wine. He ate quickly and dressed in his own clothes. 'How do I get paid?' He asked.

'I pay you' said a light voice from behind. He turned to find a slim man in a very stylish tunic. His oiled hair and light beard shone from the light of the oil lamp and his eyes glittered as he looked around him.

'I have to say you look very much the worse for wear but you did well out there Marcus Attilius, very well indeed. Now you are owed ten Denarii I believe.'

'Sixty Denarii was my understanding.'

'Ah, yes, but then there is the fee.'

'Fifty Denarii is the fee? Marcus said disbelieving. He stood up to his full height standing well over the man before him. He had taken on a champion in full view of emperor Vespasian himself, his employers and four thousand Romans for ten Denarii?

The man nodded. 'But I am forgetting my manners. I am the Lanista of the Ludis Gallica. I am Aetius; I am the owner of the gladiators you see before you today with the exception of the giant over there on the bench. Britanicus is not my gladiator but all of the other champions you see before you today, these are my men.'

'How does that change what I am paid.' Marcus said, towering over the man before him. He grabbed him by the tunic and pulled him close to his face. 'I was promised sixty Denarii and that is what I will be paid by you or someone else or by the love of Mars we will continue the fight.'

Britanicus woke up and watching the two men he rose to his feet and grabbed Marcus from behind. 'I know this boy and I apologise for him *Dominus*, he is too stupid to know better'

Aetius stepped between them looking like a small tree in between two large oaks 'Now, now, calm down. There is a cost to the fight, Marcus Attilius, and that cost must be deducted before you get paid by the Lanista of the fighters.'

'But consul Vespasian stated publically that the fee was clearly sixty Denarii.' Marcus said disengaging himself from Britanicus as he sat down heavily on the stool behind him.

The man before his stroked his chin thoughtfully and sat down on a stool next to Marcus. 'He did, but consul Vespasian does not have to pay for

Britanicus or for my gladiators. For their board, I mean, as well as training and food and all the other very expensive areas of not just one man, but so many others.' He stated almost painfully.

Aetius picked at his fingernails as he took his time in replying further. 'So, do you have interest in being a gladiator? The Gods have equipped you well to fight in the arena. Why not give it a chance?'

'Once is more than enough for me. I have no interest in meeting another brute like Britanicus again let alone someone else who is bigger and better.'

'Ah' Aetius announced with a flourish of his hand. 'Britanicus does not belong to me he is from another school. The owner of that school is over there.' Aetius pointed to one of the men standing near the door as they watched the Tirones fighting in the arena. 'There is word that Britanicus may retire soon,'

'Ha' Britanicus guffawed 'There is no one better than Britanicus. If I retire anyone can claim the prize of foremost gladiator of Rome.'

'But that is the point, Marcus Attilius.' Aetius continued. 'At this stage there are very few, if any, who are better than him. Britanicus is certainly one of the best we have seen and you took him on with no experience and that is the sort of talent I need.'

'Well' Marcus said slyly. 'You pay me the sixty Denarii and if I decide to become a gladiator I will consult you first.' Aetius stroked his chin and walked over to where the two men were standing. They exchanged words for a moment and then he returned.

'Well, I have asked Polorus to agree on the owed Denarii on one condition and that is you make me a solemn oath. I have one of the most successful gladiator schools and I am looking for new blood if you will excuse the reference. I will ensure you get your sixty Denarii but you come and see me tomorrow to discuss it. Agreed?'

'Agreed' Marcus replied looking over at Britanicus who had taken the moment to lie back down on his makeshift bed and drift back into slumber.

The Lanista looked at him carefully as if weighting his options. The boy was big and very fast and he could handle himself. After a period of time reflecting on the offer, he took the Denarii from his waist pouch and counted them out

'Make sure you come, Marcus Attilius.' Aetius looked around the room and abruptly left with Polorus.

Marcus stood to get dressed as the huge shape of Britanicus moved next to him.

'Listen boy, you are too young for this game. Take your fee and go and do something else.' Britanicus looked around for Aetius who had disappeared. He shook his hand and went back to lie down.

'Go back to the farm, Marcus and live a good life.'

'Goodbye Britanicus.' Marcus replied as he donned his tunic and sandals and started the weary walk back down the corridor to where he had entered.

The gladiators who awaited battle paid no attention to him as he left. He listened briefly as they were addressed by a trainer as he followed the attendant to the end of the corridor.

He walked out of the large oak doors and to the entrance to the steps. Felix was waiting for him as he emerged into the stark sunlight. Blandius stood beside Felix and was intently speaking to the girls who Marcus had met some time before.

'You couldn't wield a real sword to save your life, Marcus, but by the love of Zeus himself, you sure can fight.'

He moved to give Marcus an embrace and together they walked towards the exit barrier in front of them. Marcus felt a touch on his shoulder and he turned to find the man he had bet with and he dropped forty Denarii into his outstretched palm.

'Learnt your lesson yet?' Felix said with a laugh.

Marcus nodded and winced as he moved his leg. He was sore but happy that he had put up a fight without getting killed.

He felt his shoulder which was already turning black and blue from the bruises inflicted by Britanicus as the giant had purposely pummelled his shield arm. 'Where are we going?' They exited the gates and towards the hill in the horizon.

'To the baths.' Came the reply from Blandius. 'And then very drunk, if possible.'

147

Marcus stopped briefly on the road. 'Felix, there is one little matter in which I would like your assistance. There was a deal on the Sixty Denarii. I am obliged to go and look at the gladiator training barracks tomorrow.' Marcus said as he fingered the pouch, containing the twenty Denarii.

'You can't be serious; We have dumb country boy who made the mistake of going to fight the most successful gladiator in Rome on a scorching day and then to get the money he was owed in the first place he is requested to attend the gladiator school the next day.

'May I ask what for?'

'We sort of had an argument as he was only going to pay me ten of the Denarii promised by the Emperor. He said it was due to the costs in holding the contest in the first place. So, to get the full payment of the Denarii, I agreed to go and have a look. Given his position I am glad I agreed. I guess is he wants me to enter the school.'

'You want to become a gladiator? You are aware it is made up of slaves and prisoners-of-war? You are a freeman.' Blandius said as he sat beside Marcus and put his hand on his shoulder.' The idea of a gladiator may sound romantic but let us put you straight; it's not. They train seven days a week, dawn until midday and then they lock you in your cell so you can't get out. However, there is an upside.'

Felix flashed a smile. 'Ah, yes; the women will love you with that country bumpkin look, and big muscles and you have the perfect body for scars, of which there will be more than a few.'

Marcus stopped and sat down on the side of the road. 'No, I don't want to be a gladiator but I don't want to be a gardener either.'

'Gardening is safer than gladiatorial work, my friend.' Blandius noted looking directly at Felix and shrugging.

Felix, noting the mood was getting heavier stood back from the other two and in his normal fashion waved his hand to get attention. 'Well, tomorrow is tomorrow. Since I won a little on a side bet on my friend here, it is my Denarii at the tavern tonight' Felix made a flourish of his little pouch of coins.

He helped Marcus up the road as they walked together with Marcus recounting, blow-by-blow, the fight with Britanicus.

As they neared the top of the hill near the tavern Marcus stopped momentarily 'When I was inside getting treatment after the fight I met with the Lanista of the gladiators, a man called Aetius. Is he well known?'

Blandius whistled in admiration 'A very famous man. But he has, by far, the best troop of gladiators in all of Rome. But, he has no current champion in the making, as far as I am aware. If he wants to meet you, you can take that as a compliment. Remember you are one of very, many men who could carry a sword for him and could easily give up your life for entertainment. As I said; gardening is much safer.'

'Where does he get all these men?' Marcus asked as they walked together towards the baths.

'You are not the only stupid man in Rome who wants to become a gladiator.' Felix said with a smile.

'I didn't say I want to become a gladiator.' Marcus replied with a haughty voice.

CHAPTER 15

The baths filled quickly, with the mood of the patrons high on the blood sport many had just witnessed, earlier that afternoon at the stadium. The crowd, thronging mainly from the nearby stadium in that late afternoon, were noisy when they arrived.

Those who had come early from the stadium were looking for a respite, as the late afternoon sun in Rome was stronger than in the morning.

The heat of the day's proceedings, showed on the sunburnt faces of those who did not have the coins to purchase seats, under the shade of the sails that covered the more expensive areas.

Marcus, and his two companions, joined the queue of men who were awaiting entrance to the baths. The building containing the pools was situated near the Tiber, on the *Campus Martinus,* holding one of the largest of the free baths in Rome.

Felix took over instruction as they neared the entrance. 'Do you have public baths on that flea-bitten farm of yours?' He asked with his usual charming smile and glint in his eye.

Marcus looked at him with one eye, as the other was blinded by the swelling and bruising he had received from Britanicus. He shook his head, attempted a smile and waited for his friend to continue.

'Most of the larger baths in Rome have similar interiors, so you can go to one, and it is much the same as another. Did you know the baths are subsidised by the state? No, I didn't think so. This is the place for health, and of course, a little relaxed business.'

'More business than health on most days' Blasius noted, looking for the girls he met at the stadium. He had lost them on the walk back to the baths.

'The one we are waiting to get into, Marcus, has a gym where they provide uncomfortable straw mats for exercises, including ropes and heavy balls. Somehow, I don't think you will be using those today.' He said with a wry smile. 'Thankfully, we were not stupid enough to stand up and agree to a bout with the great Britanicus.'

Marcus noticed a sign outside the baths, which he read as he listened to Felix drone on about the public baths for noble men. The sign explained the available rooms.

Three rooms for patrons to use. They included a t*epidarium*, relaxation room, a *caldarium*, hot water, room, and a *frigadarium*, used exclusively as a cooling bathroom after the *caldarium*.

The baths proudly noted that only experienced slaves were used to maintain the heat in the various hot rooms. The management of the baths welcomed all and expected Romans, in these communal baths, to spend time, relax and most of all clean themselves of the dirt, that accumulated at such a fast pace most days.

The queue finally relaxed, as some moved off to other bath houses rather than wait. Finally, they were ushered into the front vestibule, where they paid six As, each to enter. They followed the queue, as they entered the main room, with cubicles of all shapes and sizes adorning the wall of the room.

'I thought it was free.' Marcus said tiredly, as he followed the others.

'Bathing is free for cheapskates like you, but if you want the added services you have to pay.' Felix replied. 'And since you are the rich one, from your adventure in the arena, you should have paid for us.'

'Yeah' Blasius said, as he looked around to see if he knew anyone.

They went directly to a free area, sat down on the bench, undressed and naked, they followed Felix towards what felt like a hot room.

'Boy, you have some bruises on you.' Blasius said as the two of them looked at the legs and torso as Marcus stood there naked. His long legs and lower torso were covered in large welts and dark coloured bruises. His face, reddened by the punches from the Gladiator, showed swelling around his jaw.

The wound had stopped bleeding but again, a large welt showed around the area. His eyes were also swollen and his left shoulder appeared black, from the bruises he received earlier that day.

'He will heal.' Blasius said, with a wry smile.

They entered the cadarium and waited until several had left the bath. Marcus watched as Felix climbed gingerly into the bath, slowly taking himself down into the water. As he finally sat, he turned to Marcus who was taking his time, lowering himself into the hot water.

'The only time to hesitate, Marcus, is when the water gets to your balls. That takes a little longer, but you get used to it. If you are as stupid as Blandius, you just go straight in, but then he has no feelings below his head.'

Blandius chortled at the barb and dunked his head under the hot water. 'Unlike, Felix.' He said as he came up spluttering 'He has no feeling from his neck up. He is too stupid for words.'

'I agree with both those descriptions.' Marcus replied with a half-smile as he gingerly walked down the steps, into the hot water, which was fed by pipes from a furnace behind the wall.

'Where are the girls?' He asked, as he sank gently into the comfort of the hot water on his broken body.

'Through that wall, my friend, through that wall over there, which makes it difficult to see them. But there are ways.' Felix replied with a wink. 'Keep in mind that if you ever accompany a woman to the baths she will take at least twice as long as you.'

Marcus started to put his head under the water, but the heat made the pain around his eye worse, so he thought the better of it. He luxuriated in the warmth as he moved his tired limbs around.

For the first time that afternoon, he felt less pain in his shoulder and right leg, both of which had taken a battering, when Britanicus fell on him repeatedly, with his shield leading the attack.

Still, he reflected, as he let his arms float out from his body trying to soothe his painful shoulder, he enjoyed the experience. There was a part of him that wanted to be at the front, to be first and to win whatever the circumstances.

He did not doubt the prophecy from Britanicus that the next time they met, he would kill him but for at least part of the fight, he held the giant on his back foot. The welcome warmth of the water seeped into his tired body, repairing his wounds as he sat back on the seat of the bath. The warmth of a summer day on the farm, lay in his thoughts as he realised it had been a scant seven months since he left. He could no longer remember the face of Manilus, or his mother, Aurelia. He could faintly remember their voices and the way they walked, but he could not visualise their faces, and for the first time since his arrival in Rome he missed them and the farm.

He raised his head to push himself out of his thoughts and looked over at two men, who sat close to the corner of the bath, on the other side. One called out to him with his grey hair plastered to the top of his balding head. 'Hey, you, young man!' Was that you on the sand against Britanicus?'

Marcus nodded, without welcoming the question. 'It was.'

'You did well', said the other 'and we were just discussing how well you went. You have talent at the game. Very few could have stood up to the size and strength of Britanicus. He is the current champion of Rome, you know.'

'Not as good as the other, in my opinion.' The man with the grey hair said back in a questioning voice. 'Doesn't have the same power.'

His companion looked at him in surprise. 'Are you referring to Hilarius, the champion of Nero?'

The man nodded his head. 'I have watched both and the great Hilarius is better; in my considered view, anyway.'

'Nah' The other said. 'Britanicus is by far the better of the two and might you remember, you, old cod; Britanicus is younger as well. This is a game for young men. Not men who get sore legs in the morning.'

'Hmm, you are entitled to your opinion, even if it is flawed. But, young man,' he said addressing Marcus again. 'You should think about it, if you get the offer. God knows, we need new blood in the ring.'

'Would you go into the arena to fight?' Felix asked, as he rolled his eyes at the other two and they smiled in return.

'Not me, young man. I can hardly get out of the bath. But there was a day.' He said with a toothless smile.

'In your dreams.' The other replied. 'Good luck to you, young man.' He said as Felix rose and started to get out of the hot bath, complaining his fingers were turning into an old olive, in appearance. Blasius nodded and Marcus followed.

They walked into the frigadarium, with steam from their hot skins, following them in the cooler air. They laughed together about the comments from the men in the bath, with Felix doing a mimic of the older one, which sent the other two into hysterics.

Marcus laughed and then coughed up blood into his hand. He told Felix to stop the humour.

In the next room, they laid on narrow raised beds, while slaves rubbed them down with scented olive oil and massaged their shoulders. Marcus asked them to concentrate on his left shoulder and finally, when they had finished, they used a broad blunt blade to wipe the excess oil and the dirt that dripped from their pores.

They walked to the cold pool. Felix walked over to the side and dipped his toe into the clear water. 'There is only one way to do this, Marcus.' He said, as he dropped straight into the water and held himself under for a moment before he surfaced.

The other two, followed suit, and Marcus came up with a gasp, as the water hit his injuries and made his body recoil from the unwelcome feeling of cold water on hot skin. He made his way over to the side of the cold-water pool, and spent the next moments stopping himself from getting out of the pool.

They stayed in the cold water, until it permeated their limbs, then they left and walked towards the large pool that sat in the middle of the baths.

It was a long pool, with the water the colour of emerald green, radiated from the colour of the tiles that adorned the walls of the huge bath. The water was not deep and he watched in a tired stupor, as a number of patrons swam slowly up and down the pool, by using their arms in front of them as they rippled the water on their journey.

Around the pool, sat wide stone columns fashioned with inscriptions on the bottom and sides, as well as chiselled depictions of discus throwers and runners, on the sides of the columns.

The pilasters rose to hold the roof, allowing a view of the sky above with darkened, shaded areas, around the bath area where they lay.

Around the perimeter of the pool stood marble sculptured statues of the Gods. Felix who reclined lazily on a large piece of straw matting, looked around for the first time at the sculptures.

Twelve Gods, stood around the green water of the bathers, looking towards to the pool, save Zeus who looked towards the heavens.

The marble of the pool surrounds lay bleached by the water. The statues of the Gods were of a darker colour, due to the rain and sun that beat down each day, on the open pool staining their marble facades.

'Hey Marcus. Do you know the appearance of the Gods? Each of these represents the Gods of Mount Olympus.'

Marcus shook his head unable to lift his tired and sore body from the ground. He moved his head to the side and was able to see one side of the statues, on the edge of the pool.

'Which is Zeus?' Felix asked

He raised his head and looked around. The large man with a thunderbolt in his hands, stood regally at the end of the green water. 'That one'

'Very good' Felix parried 'Now, here is an easy one for you.' Where is the Goddess of fortune? You know, the one that deserts you, almost every time you gamble.'

Marcus, tiring of the game looked around slowly. 'Not here.' He said smiling 'Fortuna is not here but that does not surprise me.'

Felix winked at Blasius who shrugged in return. 'She is my friend. But, you have to look harder.' He motioned to the statue of the Goddess at the far end. 'If you can't find her, how can Fortuna find you?' He looked over at the statue of the Goddess, who stood veiled so she could not see. She held the decision of good or bad fortune, without the sight to know which to bestow.

'As long as she knows I am around, that is enough for me' Marcus replied as he drifted off to sleep, exhausted by the morning activities.

Late in the afternoon, with storm clouds rising over the distant hills, they walked out of the baths and down one of the narrow streets, towards a tavern that Blasius recommended.

They ordered wine and a meal and the drinking began in earnest, with Felix taking up the lead with an old Roman game. A song was carried by all at the table and the person to miss their cue, was required to drink a full tumbler of wine before the singing would start again. This continued until the pitcher emptied and then started again. The drunker they got, the more they missed their cue.

By the end of the night, the entire table of eight men were beyond redemption.

Felix was speaking to Blandius and from the far room of the tavern, Marcus could hear shouting.

As the waitress came back with another pitcher of wine he stopped her.

'What that' noise?' He said, drunkenly swaying.

'I can't say' She said with a smile at his drunken look.

'A game?'

She nodded and moved off towards the stone laid bar at the back of the tavern. Immediately Marcus was up and staggering towards the room. Blasius saw him move and went after him. He caught him before he entered the room.

'Marcus, leave it alone. You are too far gone to be gambling.'

Marcus nodded drunkenly at him, pulled his arm away and entered the room feeling for his pouch as he did.

He sidled up the table and a broad grin on his face. The dice game was in front of him and his mind flashed the win at the roadside tavern all that time ago.

He waited until one of the players tired and he sat heavily in the chair and pulled out his pouch to inspect the contents. It held nine Denarii, so he put five down and watched as the others followed. He threw the dice in turn and won on the tenth throw.

Felix and Blasius stood drunkenly by the table swaying slightly as the game continued. 'There is no fool like a drunken one.' Felix whispered to Blasius, as they watched the game continue. Marcus took the profit of five and left his original bet on the table. Again, the dice were thrown and half way through he increased his bet to seven which was within the rules if the bet was before the sixth throw. The other side of the table met his bet
and again, he won.

Felix bent down to him. 'Now is the time to leave my young friend and if you don't, we are. It is a work day tomorrow. If you stay here, you may lose, whereas if you leave with us you win and we can retire for the night.'

Marcus looked up at him with a leery grin. 'Have we not had this conversation before. Are the dice loaded? I don't think so and besides I am winning. This is my game, Felix; the last time I played on a roadside tavern I won…' He burst out laughing as he downed another cup of wine.

Felix interrupted him.' Yes, Marcus I know the story. However, this is Rome, not a wayside tavern and you are not playing with fools. I am drunk enough to understand it is time to go. Are you coming?'

'Chicken shit' Marcus replied with the same leery grin. 'I will see you tomorrow evening. Richer and a bit less drunk.'

Felix sighed, looked up at Blasius and walked out of the tavern.

The game continued, with the three starting to change in wins and losses. Finally, Marcus laid the total of his pouch on the table of twenty Denarii and promptly lost on the last throw of the dice. He slumped at the table and started to rise drunkenly to his feet.

The bartended moved forward. 'No need to rise, young un' if you want to keep playing. We can offer you some credit if you wish?'

Marcus viewed him through his drunken haze. His shoulder no longer hurt and for the first time that day he felt better. He nodded and sat down on the stool. 'How much do you require?'

'Twenny Denarii' he replied with a distinct slur. The bartender passed the coins over and poured him another wine. He returned to the bar in the other room and filled the tumbler of the man at the bar with the giant beside him.

'How much?' Vicinius asked with a thin smile. 'Twenty'

Vicinius smiled. 'Good. Keep it going and don't stop. He will lose tonight.

CHAPTER 16

The following dawn, after his drunken night at the tavern opposite the baths, Marcus raised his sore body from the floor. He had fallen on the floor, very late the previous night, depressed by his losses and drunker than he could remember.

He woke up a short time later, as dawn rose from the Eastern sky of Rome. He held his head for a moment as he rose up.

Despite a very sore shoulder and arm, he tried to loosen up the joints of his body, most affected by the shield attacks he received from Britanicus the day before.

It seemed longer than a day, but the pain he felt in his body reminded him every moment he moved in a direction where he felt it.

'You look very much the worse for wear, young nephew.' Tacitus said to him as they sat at the table to eat, before commencing work. 'One of my good friends is travelling past your farm over the next month. I asked him if he could take the time to visit the farm and let your mother know that everything is going well.'

Marcus nodded at him trying to quell his pounding head and nodded weakly. The thought of working in the sun that day, was enough to make his retch, so he downed his maize pancake which he liberally drizzled with honey and drank a large pitcher of water. Feeling better, he ate fruit and drank as much as he could take.

'You are holding a few injuries and bruises, Marco. I did not attend your foolishness yesterday but I hear from reliable sources that you fought well and made a few admirers on the way.'

'Who?' Marcus asked weakly.

Tacitus shrugged his shoulders. 'That matters little, nephew. You need to get to work and we will take time on your injuries tonight, to apply a little salve.'

'Ready to go?' Marcus sat there, tired and disconsolate.

Tactius rose from the table. 'If you finish the orchard today I have other work for you, so come over if you complete the job. By the way the feedback I have received, is more than generous in its praise on your work here, so that is good news. A happy master is a generous master. Remember that.'

Marcus nodded, rose from the table and sauntered outside into the early light of day. He picked his tools from the row against the shed wall, hefted them onto his shoulder and walked the distance to the orchard.

He stared at the last area to be cleared and prepared for later planting and drank from his flask again as he waited for his aching head to calm. He dropped his tools as he surveyed the scene before him.

The orange trees that stretched before him, made up the last section of the orchard and over time many had been overgrown, by grass and creeping vines.

There were seventeen trees in the group and most were bearing fruit but needed to be pruned and checked for growths on the stems. His father had been a hard teacher back on the farm, and as he surveyed his repair of the orchard, he realised he had learnt well.

The sun was rising in the sky and Marcus, with his head throbbing, sat down on a stone block to drink water and hold his temples to try and stop the pain.

The thought of the large number of Denarii he lost the night before flashed before him and it filled him with dread. How he could possibly repay it? How long that might take unless he kept gambling to try and win the amount and pay it back? At his current wage, it would take him through to eternity and back, to pay. He berated himself again, recalling that he wanted to keep in the game, but the tavern owner called a halt to his playing due to the debt.

Then, a fight broke out and all he could remember was the soreness in his shoulder and in the midst of it he bolted out of the tavern and started to run. He remembered stopping only at the foothills near the Laurentius villa, breathless and retching into the dry earth, on the side of the road.

He cursed his stupidity once again out loud, as he sat in the morning warmth. He was drunk, very drunk and did not listen, as usual, to Blandius or Felix.

The lure of the Goddess, as she cooed and called softly to pick up the dice, was too much to ignore and he paid the price. Were the dice loaded? Not likely, but possible and he was too drunk to remember.

He pulled his tunic off because of the increasing heat and sweat on his body, leaving only his loin cloth. He wiped his brow to flick the sweat away, and as he crouched up to pick up his mattock he heard a sound from behind. He turned to find his mistress Lucia, standing a short space away.

She stood there, taking in his form with a puzzled look on her face. She wore a colourful tunic under a flowing white robe, which highlighted her dark hair with makeup accentuating her wide, darkened eyes. By the Gods, she is beautiful, he thought to himself. The low sun accented the robe and the way it lay seductively, against her breasts.

'I came to see the young competitor.' She said coolly 'You don't seem to have many injuries given the duration of that contest with the great Britanicus. How does that beautifully bruised body, feel?'

'As it looks mistress. Bruised and sore.'

You have become quite the talk of the city, Marcus Attilius.' She said moving towards him. Marcus kept his gaze steady. Standing with his mattock in hand and the sweat falling from his face to his chest.

'Mistress.' He said, dropping the mattock handle against the stone. She moved over to him and raised his chin with her hand, looking deeply into his eyes. 'The other wives could not take their eyes off you; did you know that? They are jealous, now that they know you work on this estate. That is sort of effect you had on the women folk yesterday. Interesting, don't you think?'

She looked up at him with wide, green eyes. She allowed her hand to fall from his square chin to slide down his torso, lingering on his chest. 'So, Marcus, you have made quite a stir and everyone wants to see you back in the arena.'

'Everyone except me' Marcus replied sternly. 'I surely have no reason to enter the arena again. The truth is that Britanicus could easily have killed me with one blow. I consider myself lucky to have got away from him, and today I am paying the price. I can hardly move.'

'Where is the soreness?' She smiled widely, letting her hand move across his chest to his shoulder. 'Is it there, or here?' Her hand moved up to his cut lip.

Lucia's eyes looked into his. She pushed the black hair back that hung over his forehead and moved even closer to him, as her hand moved softly down to the string tie on his loin cloth. She used her nail, to softly lay a thin white line on his skin, as she smiled seductively.

'Well, Marcus, you have never been trained. If you were properly instructed and coached I think you could win almost any contest. A body like this should be on display in the stadium'

'Given my display yesterday, mistress? I am not sure you saw the same contest I was in.'

She laughed 'I have seen enough gladiatorial contests to know a future champion when I see one. I believe we could find a way to sponsor you, so come to the house tonight and let's discuss it. But come later.'

'As you wish, mistress but I have made up my mind.'

She reached up on her toes and kissed him softly on his cheek whispering. 'Marcus, you are brave boy and always, a mind can change. Please hear what I have to say and then make your own decision. Remember that sponsorship means that all the costs of the training and the kits would be borne by my husband. Your only responsibility would be to fight and for that, you will be very handsomely paid. If you are successful, you would never have to worry about money again. You could pay for the farm, and your mother would never have to work either.'

Marcus looked down at her with the thought of his mother foremost in his mind. Lucia let her hand slide across his chest and with a smile, she turned and walked slowly back to the villa.

Marcus sat back down again. He felt confused and still badly hungover. Her offer to sponsor was hard to ignore and if what she said was true, he could earn enough to live a comfortable life. What did he know of fighting on the sands of an arena? He was untrained and gladiators learnt from an early age. Earlier than his age, anyway.

The feeling of her hand on his chest remained in his mind as he started work to clear the end of the orchard. The heat of the day permeated his skin and his shoulder started to feel better as the day wore on. He stopped for a moment, to wash his face and take another drink.

He picked ripe fruit from the orchard to fill several baskets for the kitchen and picked several of the best fruits for lunch. In the early afternoon, he stopped his labour and inspected the work he completed during the day. Satisfied, he picked up the tools and returned to the work shed to unload them.

Tacitus sauntered back at the same time. They stopped at the table outside the small shack they called home.

Tacitus pulled the muslin cloth off the food, that had been left by the kitchen staff. Together, they ate slowly with the late afternoon sky, displaying the first colours of a sunset, which boded well for the following day.

They discussed the previous day's events with the familiarity of old friends. 'It was some battle, I hear.' Tacitus muttered with a careful eye, surveying his nephews lip and bruised shoulder. 'You have become something of a Roman hero overnight. However, people forget quickly and are always looking for someone new. We will rub hot olive oil into the bruising and that lip will heal soon enough.'

'I need to leave tonight for a while.'

'Not gambling, I hope.'

Marcus shook his head slowly. 'No, mistress Lucia wants to see me.'

Tactius raised an eyebrow as he looked at his bruised nephew. 'Be careful of that one, Marco. Most of the time she is up to no good. She has a sadistic husband, who also happens to be the richest man in Rome and our *patron*.'

'I can take care of myself, uncle and I feel much better this afternoon.'

Tacitus nodded with the mild jealousy of the old admiring the energy of youth. He rose to heat up a saucer of special oil for Marcus. He mixed it on the stove of virgin olive oil, turmeric and garlic. He returned to the table and rubbed the oil into his nephew's shoulders and calves. He noted the scar forming on his nephew's leg, and the level of bruising on his arm and shoulder.

'It would appear that you came off second best, Marco; Did you give him hell on the way?'

Marcus smiled for the first time that day and looked at his uncle with a reflective look. 'He knew I was there, Tacitus. It is hard to fight someone with such a level of skill. For every move, I made, he countered it with two and he was going easy on me.'

'They train them very hard, each and every day and they become hardened to the life. No wonder you found him hard to fight. I believe he is the champion of Rome.'

'You don't go to the games?'

'Not me, young nephew. I have seen enough fighting to last a lifetime. Your mother probably did not tell you that I was in the Roman army, at the start of the Gaul campaign and that must be fifteen years ago now. I resigned from the legion many years ago and found this job. Your mother only knew I was here, several years ago, when I sent her a message when my life as a Legionnaire were over. That is where these scars come from.'

Marcus looked at his uncle's legs as he pointed out the white scars and removing his tunic he showed a long scar across his back. 'This one still hurts' he said with a smirk 'The man that gave it to me has crossed the river and is whipped by Vulcan, to this day.'

'I seem to be getting a few as well, and I am still under twenty years of age.'

'Yes, but you heal at your tender age. Try getting a wound later in your life. It stays around forever.' Tacitus picked up the saucer of oil and the remaining plates to take them inside. 'Come' he motioned 'We must give thanks'

The two of them sat in front of a small shrine, under the stone veranda of the house and lit a candle, in the early evening darkness. They mumbled their prayers, left a small offer of food and flowers to the Gods and left the candle alight as they rose.

Their discussion that early evening, centred on the work he could start the following day now that the orchard was finished. The matter of the three hundred and twenty-eight Denarii weighed on his mind as he listened to his uncle. The thought of how he was going to repay such a large amount seemed insurmountable. At his pay rate, the amount equalled more than three years work on the villa garden on the estate. When he thought about the debt of the Denarii, which equated to over one thousand and eighty Sestertii, it made him sweat. It was a fortune. A thin film of sweat formed on his forehead as he thought about it. No matter which way he turned, the event in his mind he knew he faced more trouble.

———

CHAPTER 17

Later that evening, after he washed and clothed himself in a new tunic, he made his way from the outhouse to the main door of the house and walked in. A servant saw him waiting and ushered him into a room off the atrium which was filled with couches. He was told to wait, while she informed the mistress that he had arrived.

He stood at the window of the upper storey of the villa, waiting for Lucia Laurentius and looking out into a clear, still evening sky.

From the window, he could see most of Rome and the flickering fires on the hills around the city. Suburia itself, at the bottom of the city, glowed from the myriad of oil lamps in the tenements and houses that lined the streets.

He looked up at the blanket of stars sitting above the city and despite the warning from Tacitus, that it would likely rain late the next day, he could not foresee it but then Tacitus was very rarely wrong when it came to the weather.

'You like the view?' Came the voice behind him. She joined him at the window in looking out with him into the clear Roman sky. He could smell something unusual when she joined him. It was alluring and different. 'You like my new perfume? It comes all the way from the province of Espania.'

Marcus could do little but nod as he stood there next to the open window.

She looked up at him with those large, green eyes. 'You have much to learn, Marcus; This perfume comes all the way from Gaul, of all places.' She brought his head down to her neck to smell it on her skin.

'Amazing, mistress'
Lucia lifted her head slowly and kissed him on the lips. He could feel the heat rising between them, and he knew he should not continue. She was his mistress and he a labourer on her estate, but her scent and the way she moved, was nothing like he had experienced before.

She led him over to the couch and they sat together. She was wearing a tunic of the sheerest fabric, and in the lamp light, he could see her breasts rising and falling as she breathed beside him. She wore makeup and her hair was the fashion of the day. Curls cascaded down her wide face, held up by a tortoise shell comb at the back.

'So, Marcus, did you think over our talk today? Moving closer to him, she laid her hand on his bare leg and waited.

'I did mistress.'

'Lucia, Marcus. Call me Lucia when we are alone.'

Marcus nodded, swallowed and continued. 'It is a generous offer but I don't know whether I am capable of such a life. Felix tells me that it is a difficult life; training every day and with little freedom and the loss of life, and limb, is high.

'Felix?' She asked

Marcus shrugged. 'Just a friend.'

Lucia shrugged and waited before she spoke. 'Yes, most of that is true, but there are great rewards not just for you, but for this household as well. Do you understand the rewards of what we are offering?' She asked softly.

'I think so, mistress.'

Well, let me explain. If you agree, we pay all costs and we take a percentage of your winnings which can be substantial for both of us.

'Britanicus could easily have killed me when I went down and as he told me afterwards, he was only playing.' Marcus said, looking into her eyes. 'I doubt, I could ever fight like that.'

'I doubt he was playing, Marcus. You hurt him and that was for all to see on the day. Do you want to take care of your family?'

'Of course, I do.' Marcus replied, affronted by her question. 'But what good am I, dead in the arena?'

'Are you saying you don't want to join a gladiator school?'

Marcus shook his head. 'No, mistress, I just don't know if it is a wise course.'

'So, you want to remain a gardener for the rest of your life?' She said mockingly.

'No, mistress.'

Lucia brought his head closer and she kissed him again. 'Lucky for you, we are here to support you and there will be, as you will see, some fringe benefits for a handsome, young man of the arena. Now what can I do to get you to agree to being a very successful gladiator? Hmm, now what about the three hundred and twenty-eight Denarii, you owe from last night.'

Marcus pulled back astonished that she knew and wondering how she knew.

'Now, now, Marcus, do not get upset. We understand what happened to you. My husband has spies everywhere. Vicinius wants his coins and if you do as I ask; we can forego that debt.'

'Vicinius!' Marcus stood up abruptly with a storm of anger crossing his face. "That fat bastard. How did he get involved?'

Lucia pulled him gently down onto the couch once again as she ran her hand over his leg. Then in a moment it all made sense. The fight at the arena, the game at the tavern. Vicinius was behind it all in the background, pulling the strings.

It was Vicinius that allowed him the credit, not the bartender and this time the fucker had passed his debt to someone else, who was trying to manipulate him into something he did not want to do.

'Marcus, don't be upset. I am doing you a favour because I like you and I want to help you go forward with your life. If you think about it, you have great opportunity in front of you. At this moment in your life, you have a large debt, you work as a gardener and there is little future unless you take up this offer.'

Marcus noted her voice rose when she said the word, 'future', and he understood for the first time in his young life what she meant.

Do it and his life would go forward and he might achieve his dreams. Go against it and he looked forward to dealing with Vicinius, and the Laurentius family. Fighting Britanicus, all of a sudden, seemed an easier choice than what he had before him.

'I guess I don't have much choice. Where is master Laurentius?'
'why do you ask?'

'Is he not involved in this decision?'

Lucia seductively slid the light folds of her tunic off her shoulders, to let it fall softly down her brown body. 'I have his agreement, Marcus and that is all that matters. My husband is away at our estate. While he is away, I am mistress of this house. You need to be sponsored, otherwise you will spend your life in servitude as a gardener until you get too old. You are a farm boy from the country and you do not have much choice.'

Marcus nodded with his mind reeling. That dog, Vicinius, yet again behind another of his drunken gambling debts and now he was held by Lucia, for the same debt, and faced with a life in the arena. Where was the choice?

'Enough talk, Marcus, for tomorrow I will make the necessary arrangements for you to enter the best Gladiators school in Rome. Together we will make you the best; Not just of Rome, but all of Italy. I will make you a champion. There are some benefits to this arrangement' She said softly, as she stood up from the couch and gently brought him up with her.

He looked at her beautiful face, watching as she slowly, carefully moved her hands across his muscular shoulders, letting his tunic fall to the floor.

She stepped back to admire his body, letting her hand move across his muscled skin. She pulled his head to kiss her waiting lips.

He picked her up and laid her on couch. His mind did not welcome the future but there was little he could do to change it. He needed to accept that his life would be controlled by others, and as he looked down at the beautiful woman below him, he decided, at that moment, to take what was on offer.

He kissed her and then took her with the same passion that dwelled in him all of his life. Lucia moaned softly and as the passion increased, they joined again and again.

Later, Marcus lay exhausted on the couch beside Lucia as she lay softly stroking his hair. Out of the corner of her eye, she saw the movement of her husband, in his white toga who had watched the entire time, behind a curtain from the other side of the room.

———

He moved away from where he was standing, to softly pad across the red terrazzo tiles. She smiled at him as he nodded to her and left the room, without Marcus even looking up.

She rose softly from the couch and redressed. He watched her rise and with some reluctance, he raised himself off the comfortable couch and joined her at the door.

She reached up, kissed him softly and taking off a ring from her middle finger she placed it in his palm, closing his hand around it. He opened his palm briefly to look at the size of the jewel, held by the setting.

'Take it, Marcus, it might help you in the future. We have an agreement, don't we?'

He nodded sombrely and turned on his heels to walk back to the slave's quarters, his uncle and his job as a gardener.

'What happens now?'

'I want you to go and see Aetius, who you have already met, and I know he wants to see you tomorrow. He is a highly successful Lanista of one of the oldest Ludis in Rome called the Ludis Gallica. I promise you, he is the best Lanista in Rome and a personal friend, as well. Tomorrow afternoon, finish early and head to the Gladiator school. Do you know where that is?

Marcus shook his head. 'No, I don't think so.'

'The school is at the back of the Stadium.' She said softly. 'Once you get there, tell him you are there on our behalf and by that time, he will have received a message from us. He will show you the school and we can make a date for you to start to become a champion. Don't let me down, Marcus and tell no one, save your uncle Tacitus.'

She kissed him softly on the lips and lightly hugged him. Marcus nodded his head. His life was about to change again and after gaining his freedom from the farm, and his father, he was to be controlled by the Laurentius family. That meant he was to dedicate his life to winning in the arena and the thought of it scared him.

The words of warning, uttered by Britanicus on the afternoon of the contest, moved through his thoughts as he made his way back to his uncle's hut. '*Boy, you are too young for this game. Take your fee and go and do something else.*

CHAPTER 18

The following day, late in the morning, Marcus raised his sore body from his stone seat next to the garden bed he was working on, to be ready for his attendance at the Ludis Gallica, the Gladiator school run by the Lanista, Aetius.

He wanted to speak to Felix about the decision. He had worked from early that morning so he washed, shaved and despite a sore shoulder and arm, he tried to loosen up the joints of his body, most affected by the shield attacks he had received in the arena.

It was early afternoon by the time he reached the factory where Felix and Blandius worked. He walked inside under dark clouds that stretched across the sky of Rome. The inside of the forge held a gloomy stench, with heat that cast a sweating glow on his face as he ventured further into the workhouse.

Despite open windows and the doors at both ends of the building pulled open, there was little light in the that part of the building. The heat remained oppressive and his mouth felt a metallic taste.

The fire in the brick furnace to his right, glowed brightly, as the blacksmith pushed and pulled the bellows, pushing air beneath the raging fire of coals. Each time the bellows compressed, the coals flowed brightly and the fire above rose, only to settle with increased heat as the air expelled from the forge.

The blacksmith pulled a long, narrow piece of steel from the fire before him with forceps, expertly applying his hammer to the sword blade. As each hammer blow descended using the power of his muscled arms, it widened the piece. With methodical cadence, he pulled the piece along the anvil to be hit with a resounding clap, as the hammer head hit the steel.

When the last hammer blow hit the steel, he raised it up to inspect it, and then plunged it into a barrel of water that sat beside the anvil. Finally, he returned it to the fire. Sweat poured off his body as he neared the fire, to find another sword length.

Marcus approached the forge. 'Hot Eh?' The blacksmith said as he reached for another blade. 'What are you after boy? There are no jobs here.'

'I am looking for Felix.'

The blacksmith motioned to the other end of the factory. Marcus nodded and walked towards the next section of the factory, watching as each table held the handles and hilts, and another the final finish as they polished them, with the finest sand.

Before he made it to the end, he stopped to watch the sword blades honed on a large wheel. The sound of the wheel, brought the memory of his father back, and the old wheel he used in the barn to sharpen the farm implements. Again, briefly, his thoughts turned to his mother and Manilus. If it was in his power, he would return to see their faces and enjoy their laughter.

The man before him laid fine powder on a heavily honed blade in his hands. Marcus watched as he changed wheels, running the edge across a smaller, finer wheel to fashion a final, sharpened edge to the blade. Even in the gloom of the factory interior, the new blade shone in the dim light.

He finally saw Felix, who was sparring with another man he had not seen before in the courtyard. He stood at the doorway watching as his friend jousted with what looked like a new sword. The blades flickered in the bright sunlight, as they arced and collided reversed and returned. On each of their arms they held metal greaves for protection.

He watched his friend, realising for the first time that Felix held real skill with a sword. This was the man who had turned his back on a comfortable life in upper class Rome, spurned his birth right, and now moved cleverly and powerfully, in the sword fight before him.

He moved with surprising speed as his body turned, and his arms rose and fell in a rhythm of sword attack and defense. The bone handled sword in Felix's hand, rounded and pointed, rose and fell, to block any of the attacks and moved deftly to take up the advantage.

In the sunlight, the swords sparkled, slicing through the hot air with the whooshing sound until the weapons of metal collided with force as the blades met. In an instant, the swords left their brutal collision to continue their arc.

Sweat fell off their faces as the men danced, the blades arced only to meet savagely, again and again. Finally, Felix brought his sword overhead with both hands, ripping the sword from the other man's hand as it clattered to the stone tiles of the courtyard.

Felix, breathing heavily, looked over at Marcus with surprise on his face. 'What in the Gods are you doing here? There are no jobs for fighting gardeners in this forsaken place.'

'To be honest I wish that was the only problem I had at this moment. I have greater troubles. You handle a sword well.'

Felix handed his sword to Marcus as he wiped his brow. 'Well, country boy, that Gladius holds the symbol of everything Rome stands for as ultimate power in the world. This Gladius, forged in fire and created in steel, gives the common man, nay even the most basic soldier, protection against death and an equal fighting chance. These blades give the promise of courage in combat, of power and of force.'

Felix saw the look on his face and immediately took the Gladius from his friend's hand and put it down on the bench, next to where they were sparring.

The bone handle, was scribed with silver and the hand guard, at the top of the handle, black in colour and shined like a polished onyx stone. It was a beautiful looking sword.

'That is for Per Landinus, a nobleman of great wealth. He wanted the newest steel and it is just that. Much harder and keeps its edge longer.'

Felix picked up both swords to show him, noting the edge on his Gladius against his opponents. The edge of his sword, showed far less dents in the steel edge, against the other. 'This is not your normal fighting sword, Marcus, this one is made for show. Pick it up and try it.'

Marcus hefted the sword in his hand marvelling at the workmanship. The edge showed little denting in the hardened steel, and the weight and balance was like nothing he had held before.

He looked down the straight edge, smiling inwardly at the difference between the sword in his hand, and the one he used against Britanicus. It was impossible to compare, as he swung the blade in the air.

Felix picked the other up and gave Marcus a look.' Come on, let's see how good you are.' Marcus swung the sword through the air again and parried the first blow from Felix as his blade came backhanded through the air. 'Do you know what the word, block means?'

'Sort of.' Marcus said, rounding the sword down onto the upcoming sword of Felix. With a resounding smack, the swords collided and Marcus felt his weight glancing off Felix's sword and with a deft movement, Felix brought his sword up and held it under Marcus's open throat. 'You have to be the worst swordsman I have ever seen. You need lessons and quickly.' Felix said as he laid his sword back down on the bench. He sat and wiped his brow and smiled.

'So, what is the news'

'Not here' Marcus replied 'Can we meet at your place later?'

'If you feel like waiting we can go together. I need one of the boys to sharpen and do a final polish for this sword for Per Landinus and then we can go. He wants it ready for some big party coming up. Probably, so he can strut around like he can use it. Wait here my friend, I will not be long.'

Felix arose from his seat and passed a piece of cheese and bread. 'The bread is a day old but worth eating.'

Marcus sat forlornly, looking at the chunk of bread and cheese in his hand. 'Where is Blandius?' Marcus finally asked as he chewed.

Felix shrugged. 'Somewhere around. I think he went on a delivery of one hundred Gladius.'

Marcus smiled and wiped his mouth. 'Who would want that many?'

'The army, my friend.'

After waiting for a while, Felix returned and together they walked out of the factory, with Marcus speaking from the time they left the factory to the end of Suburia.

'I don't know what to do, Felix. I am in my usual difficult position of owing money and having no way to pay it back. It started in the arena, paying that man back and now Vicinius has got his claws back into me again. What is this? Why can't I stop? It is almost as if the Goddess has part of me that she controls, whenever I see gambling. It is a sickness.'

'Well, you can't say you have not been warned and I don't know what is worse. Your gambling or your drinking. Come, let us at least go and have a look at this shithole they call the barracks. The worst is your bedding of mistress Laurentius. Now, she has control of you in more ways than one. If you don't want to do this… Should I say if you really don't want to train, then you will have to disappear and quickly.'

'Where?'

Felix shrugged. 'There is always the farm.'

The day changed as the clouds disappeared and promised clear skies. They both felt the worse for wear for different circumstances, but their mood was heightened by the weather. In better spirits, they trotted off in search of the gladiator's school.

Walking through the streets at the fringe of the Suburia sprawl, they made their way towards the stadium, finally walking through the *Hortus Nero*, the large gardens built through the insistence of the deceased emperor. The gardens stretched almost six times the size of the stadium they walked towards.

The end of each small path, within the gardens held a circle of stones. The areas were surrounded by ornate fountains and at each circle lay small amphitheatres, built so that poets and citizens, alike, could take the time to relate their thoughts to audiences.

The two stopped to sit on one of the raised seats, to continue their conversation. As Marcus spoke, occasionally shaking his head Felix listened, nodding and suggesting alternatives. 'Did you say, three hundred and twenty Denarii?' Felix almost shouted out.

Marcus nodded his head slowly. 'Three hundred and twenty-eight to be precise. I don't know how it happened.'

'I do. You were drunk as a whore on a bad night. You must have been at that table for a long time, Marcus and you must have lost at the table, the whole night.'

Again, Marcus nodded dumbly and lay back against the stone seat. 'To put it simply I cannot swim against such a tide. I am the fool who cannot stop gambling.'

'That is some debt, friend and it appears there is little any of us can do about it. Do you want to become a gladiator? Lots of coins and women from what I hear.'

'I have no experience, Felix, and whilst I fought on that sand with Britanicus, he taught me one lesson and that is fighting at that level requires skill and age. He actually told me not to join the school. He said I was too young.'

'Well, it's true you are young but younger than you have been gladiators in the past. However, in saying that, it might be worth mentioning that many of them, did not last long. You are not much of a sword fighter but you are ferocious with your fists and that might help. And, they will train you?'

'You mean with the cost of my life if I don't compete. They don't care, Felix. What they care about is the earnings and if I don't win they will step over me.'

Finally, they stood up. 'You may be correct, Marco, but let us see what that son of a jackal's bitch has to say, before we make any decision. Now, follow me Marco; We drop off the sword at Per Landinus and then off to the barracks. What is the worst, young Marcus? You disappear and come back when things have calmed down. However, Marcus, I have some jealously when it comes to Lucia Laurentius. She is a highly regarded beauty.'

The gardens remained a work of art as far as Felix was concerned. The avenues, inside the gardens, decorated with trees from as far away as Africa. The stonework on the paths, demonstrated the fine Roman workmanship that was evident only in the richer parts of the city.

On the journey down the main path of the gardens they counted over fifty workers, labouring to keep the garden in order. The statue of Nero, dominated the centre of the gardens and stood high on a solid stone block. The statue was the worse for its exposure to the elements with bird excrement, and dirt, adorning the top of his head and shoulders and the bronze turning the colour of dark clay.

In the distance, from the south end of the garden complex the stadium appeared in view and they walked off in the direction of Vicus Longus. After walking for a while they stopped outside a large house, daubed in a yellow ochre colour, and rising high above the street.

The house was surrounded by a high wall, with heavy oak gates at the front entrance. Felix made Marcus stay outside as he entered the gates to deliver the sword. He showed him the sword before he delivered it. Unwrapping the cloth protection, he handed it over to Marcus to inspect. It was a true beauty. The ornate bone handle inscribed with silver, matched the scabbard in black lacquer, offset by silver, inscribed with the *Landinus* crest.

'How much?'

'Two hundred Denarii.'

Marcus whistled softly. 'Now, that is an expensive sword.'

Felix shrugged. 'We make more expensive ones if you want gold inscribed.' He wrapped the sword, delivered it and the two walked off once again.

Around the stadium lay the markets, the largest in Rome and in the far distance they could hear the shouts of the vendors as they tried to attract shoppers to their fish, meat and vegetables.

They stopped at one of the stalls selling olives and cheese and asked the way from the girl at the front who was serving. She shrugged her shoulders but the stall owner walked over.

'You want the way to the training school?'

Marcus nodded, as Felix tried his luck with the girl who declined to listen to him. Persistent as ever he kept up the banter, completely ignoring the conversation beside him.

Marcus nodded politely. 'I am to meet with the Lanista this afternoon. He said it was close to the stadium, but we have walked a bit and can't find it.'

The man nodded and then turned to Felix 'That is my daughter and she is trying to serve!' Felix looked at him sheepishly and walked away from the stand. 'Aren't you the young novice from the other day with Britanicus?'
Marcus smiled grimly. 'It was not much of a contest.'

'Nonsense, you did very well. I was there to witness it and I can tell you, you made quite an impact on the those who watched. You showed great bravery and might I add some skill, as well. Britanicus has never been defeated, so you were up against the best of the best.' He pointed in the direction to the right of the large edifice before them, so they moved off to walk a well-worn track. across to the road.

CHAPTER 19

'They have just started the new one, you know' Felix said, feeling the anticipation as they neared the school. 'It is going to be known as the Flavian Amphitheatre and the tallest in Rome including the new Forum. Five stories in all.'

In the near distance, they saw the gates to the school. Beside it, running the length of the school to the rear and high above the walls, sat one of the largest aqueducts in Rome.

Marcus nodded. 'Well, that will be something to look forward to. At least the school has water.' He added pointing to the aqueduct carrying fresh water into the city of Rome.

With the afternoon sun behind them, they descended a small path to the side of the road on the *Caelian* hill of Rome and entered the gates to the school. Above them, the sign was easily viewed. *Ludis Gallica.*

'That's enough to inspire fear and dread.' Felix chuckled as they walked underneath the wood carved gate and into the school.

From what Marcus could see, the substantial grounds held a broad rectangular, dusty field surrounded by barrack rooms, each of which had bars on the windows and doors. As they walked further they saw another sign above the inside gate. *Caserma Dei Gladiatori*. 'It seems we are entering the House of the Gladiators, my friend.' Marcus said, as he took in his surroundings.

The squat building, was topped by a low sloping terracotta tile roof, supported by wide, square timber columns around the entire perimeter. Underneath the broad veranda roof, stood barred doors, that led to rooms off the stone floor.

Looking above the roof line, Marcus could see several of the hills of Rome rising above the barrack walls. In the far distance, some of the buildings were visible at the top of the city.

At the back of the dusty field before him lay a circular wall which he assumed held an arena, smaller in size than the field before him. With a deep breath, he moved forward with Felix beside him.

The last sign, held the largest inscription chiselled roughly into a broad dark plank and affixed the wall above the final gate to the compound. The sign was aged and streaked with bird droppings.

'URI, VINCRI, VEBERARI, FERROQUE NECARI'

'By the Gods on the sacred mount, that is one scary pledge' Felix said with a shudder. Marcus looked up at the sign and read it out loud. 'I will endure to be burned, to be bound, to be beaten, to be killed by the sword'

'Burned, bound and beaten?' Felix said as he walked on. 'This is what you want to do? You must have been cracked in the head, in that fight with Britanicus.'

They walked towards a small outhouse near the barracks and as they approached a servant walked out. 'Hail, friend, my name is Marcus Attilius and I have been asked to meet with the Lanista, Aetius.'

The servant, a large man with visible scars on his body nodded. 'I am not your friend, friend; This is a gladiator school, so understand that before we go any further.' He walked off with a pronounced limp, after motioning them to stay where they were.

He came back some while later. 'Just you, Attilius.' He said and started to walk off. 'Your girl can stay here in the shade. Follow me.' Felix shrugged at the barb and promptly sat down on the stone with a sigh.

Marcus followed the servant down the long stone walkway, to an entrance at the opposite end of the barracks. The stones were worn from foot traffic over many years. When he looked across at the wall, that surrounded the school, he noticed smears of faded red on the surface with iron rings bolted into the surface of the wall.

The servant saw his interest. 'Many a beating has taken place over there.' He said abruptly. He opened the door, ushered Marcus in and followed him up the stairs. His limp was so severe he could take only one stair at a time and held onto the railing as he climbed.

A rich scent assailed the nostrils as Marcus stepped onto the floor above. The scent was unusual and wafted from a brazier, on the opposite side of the room. The opulence of the lodgings surprised him, as he stood with the servant beside him waiting for the Lanista to arrive.

The floors were bedecked with lush, colourful rugs, with furnishings around the room of varying colours. The room looked out to the smaller, fighting arena below and led to a deck built out from the Lanista's room. A large, black dog lay beside the table growling softly at the two of them as they waited. The servant indicated for him to stand while he stood at the side of the room.

Aetius arrived some while later, flustered and with an aggravated look on his face. He walked into the room and glanced briefly at Marcus, waved his hand at the servant who walked back the way they had entered.

He sat heavily at a large table, on an ornate cushion and patted the dog as if it had the ability to calm his mood. The dog wagged its tail contently, while watching Marcus from its sitting position.

The area before Aetius was strewn with sword handles, paper and a set of manacles that appeared perilously close to falling to the hard wood floor below. 'That was a quick decision, young man but I guess others had some influence. Take a seat over there.' He motioned to a stool at the side of the desk which Marcus took holding his gaze at the Lanista before him.

'I already know a little more about you. It appears, in several short days, you have found yourself a sponsor as well and might I add a very important one at that. Once you have the right hand of the Laurentius wealth, everything changes. That was quick work!'

Marcus shrugged unable to decide what to say. 'I wasn't aware his wealth was that great. He has a large villa on...'

Aetius raised his hand to stop his from speaking and continued. 'He is perhaps the wealthiest in Rome and wealth in this city speaks louder than anything else. His wife, Lucia, sent me a note outlining your position and she seems to have a strong interest in you. As you know, I watched you the other day and you also know I was impressed but there is a big difference between a playful fight between a great champion, such as Britanicus, and yourself, and what it means to be a professional gladiator, in the arena and fighting every other day in training or in the ring. Understand?'

Marcus nodded, as he briefly reflected on the night of the gambling and cursed himself yet again.

The seal of the Laurentius household stood above him, and before him a man, a manager of others' lives and one who dealt in the commodity of death, who also could clearly see the benefit. Marcus realized he had become a commodity for sale.

Aetius smiled grimly. 'Of course, that was no battle, boy that was a walk in the garden. The question remains; do you want to do this?'

Marcus sighed and looked over the table at the man, who would carry his future. 'I don't have much choice, Lanista and given another area of my life, which has caused me misery, I have only two roads I can choose from and that is either I join, or I remain a gardener.

Aetius looked at the boy before him and laid a piece of paper on the table in front of him.' What you have there, Marcus Attilius, is a contract between you and me. Do you read well?'

'I can read.' Marcus replied defensively.

'Good, because what it says is that I, Aetius, as your Lanista and this school known as the Ludus Gallicus, own you and what you do as a Gladiator for a period of time which is four years; but, the contract can be renewed at that time. Understand?'

Marcus nodded as Aetius continued. 'In that time, you agree to fight a minimum of eight times a year and in the style, which we believe you will be most successful. At this stage, I believe that style will be as a Provocator or perhaps, a Thraex. Aetius picked up a quill pen, dipped it in ink and passed it to Marcus who took it reluctantly.

'Pay?' He asked

Aetius sighed, as he continued. 'For those services, and training six out of every seven days, the school will pay you two hundred Denarii every month and five hundred Denarii for every win, but no payment for any loss. And, Attilius;' Aetius said, with a louder voice to emphasize his pitch. 'We give you barracks, clothing and food so this becomes your home. And all at a nominal cost.' He added with emphasis.

'I need to think about it, I, I think...' Marcus stammered, as he tried to read the document in front of him. All his mind could return was the debt and the choice before him. If he did not sign contract what then? What did he do with his life.

'You need to think about it?' Aetius said back sternly, with his anger rising again. 'You owe a fucking huge amount of money, to the most powerful businessman in Rome, who will quite probably kill you if he does not get his debt. That debt, I remind you young man, was bought off another piece of shit by the name of Vicinius.

179

'But…'

If Laurentius doesn't kill you Vicinius certainly will because the word is out about your gambling debts. And now; you want to think about it!'

'Aetius, I…'

'I am doing you a favour, boy and all I am getting is this doddering crap from you. Get out.'

'I am not sure, Aetius?'

'By the strength of Zeus, what is it that you don't get?'

'Am I old enough?'

'This is not a day at your school, this is the business of gladiatorial contest. You either want to be part of the *gladiatorial familia* or you don't. Simple as that. Sign, Marcus, and get on with your life, because the first month will pay most of the debt. Now sign it or get out!'

Marcus looked up at the anger across Aetius' face and with a trembling hand he signed his mark at the bottom of the board. As he did so, Aetius snatched it away blowing on the ink, to dry it.

The look on Aetius' face turned into a dark sneer 'In future you address me as Dominus and if you don't I will have you whipped, got it?' He rose from the table with the dog at his feet and walked to the balcony.

'Doctore,' he screamed 'Get them out of the shade and into the sun. I don't give elephants balls how hot it is. They don't fight, in the shade! Ever!' He screamed.

He looked over at Marcus as peace returned to his face. He patted the head of his dog and spoke softly for the first time 'Listen boy, this is not a not a gardening exercise. If you hadn't already worked out, this is a gladiator school and you are now part of it.'

'I understand, Aetius.'

The anger returned instantly to the Lanista's face and the voice raised to its high pitch yet again. 'Dominus, you fucking address me as Dominus. There is not a God on Mount Olympus who will save you, unless you learn some respect. Got it!'

Yes, Dominus, I, I, understand.' Marcus stammered as he looked at the reddened face of the man before him.

Aetius walked over to the desk, poured himself water from a jug and returned to the balcony next to the table. The view looked down onto the clay coloured arena below and the view of the gladiators training

'Get over here, boy and have a look at your life.'

Marcus joined Aetius and looked out as instructed. He could see the hills in the distance and beneath him, he heard the grunts for the first time. The gladiators below, picked up large, heavy poles on their shoulders and walked to the end of the arena, dumping the large poles off their shoulders and walking back to the other end.

Then another would pick up the pole and repeat the process, as another picked it up to repeat the process. The sun, was just above the line of the fence, and the dry heat permeated everywhere.

'They train every day. Make no mistake, when I tell you that I own them all from the hair on most of their lazy heads, to their toes. I am the master and if you disobey me or any of the trainers I will thrash you within a hair of your head. This is a tough business and it is the business of facing death.'

Marcus nodded, watching as the men repeated the process of picking up the poles. They grunted as they lifted them, sweat poring off their glistening bodies.

'How do you conquer fear, Marcus Attilius?' Aetius asked as he stood there quietly looking at the labours beneath him.

Marcus shrugged. 'I don't know the answer, Dominus. Why do you ask?

'Because by the time you get to your first real fight, you will need to find the answer. That is the only way you will get though. If fear destroys you, as it does many in this business, you will pay the ultimate price of death. If you don't conquer fear you will be disabled permanently and probably quickly. Do you understand?'

'I think so'

'Dominus!' Aetius screamed at him. 'You address me, as Dominus!'

'Dominus' Marcus blurted out with his face reddening.

'Did you fear Britanicus, when you met him in the arena?' Aetius asked with colour draining from his thin face.

'It all went by so quickly, Dominus. I cannot be sure.'

'You will need to do better than that, boy. That broken slave that took you from the front house to this floor was one of the best, perhaps the very best, gladiator in his day. Did you talk to him?'

'He did not say much, Dominus.'

'He let fear get to him. A man of far lesser ability, sliced his hamstring in two and down he went. He considers himself the unluckiest of men. Why? Because gladiatorial combat was his life. He was highly paid, he had his choice of the finest women and at least one nobleman's wife fell in love with his ugly face. As soon as he was sliced, it all went away and now he works as our spear trainer and trains these men every day, and wonders what he might have been. Do you understand?'

Marcus nodded, as he watched the men below in the tall timber, clad arena.

'So, you have a sponsor which makes life a little easier as you don't need to buy your equipment or your food and I get to make an excellent partner. They get a young man who has the capability to be a strong Novicus candidate, maybe not a champion, but only time can tell.'

Marcus watched the shifty eyes of the Lanista counting the Denarii in his own head. The attraction of the jackal before him, lay in the relationship with the Laurentius wealth. For the first time, he knew that he held the bridge to the Laurentius wealth. His capability in the gladiatorial ring remained a secondary concern.

'When do I start?'

Aetius looked at him, with surprise on this face, and made his way back to the desk the size of which dominated the other side of the brightly furnished room. He picked up a book, inspected it and then slammed it shut. 'Today' he said softly, with a smile on his face.

'Now, Dominus?' Marcus replied, surprised at how quickly the decision would be made. 'I have my belongings to pick up.'

'You have some hours of sunlight left, but at sundown, when the sun falls behind the hills of our great city, you will be here. Understood?'

Marcus nodded 'When do I get paid?'

Aetius looked at him with surprise. 'If you address me again, without using the word Dominus I will have you whipped. This is your last question and here is the answer. At the end of each month.'

Marcus nodded dumbly, at the small man in front of him and turned around, to head for the door.

'Sundown' Aetius said with anger crossing his face. As Marcus walked out the door, all he could hear was Aetius snarling at the trainer in the small arena below his balcony.

Marcus walked out of the office, descended the steps and made his way back to the gate where a weary, bored Felix rose as he saw him walk quickly down the stone veranda towards him.

As he got there, the older man, he thought was a servant, came out from the hut to meet him. He motioned to Marcus to approach and waited for him to arrive.

'How old are you, boy?

Marcus regarded the wizened face of the man before him. There was a kind look on his face 'Seventeen'

The man studied his face momentarily, stroking his chin in review 'By the Gods you look older. Seventeen is too young for this game. You need to be older because the best age is middle of your third *decennium,* then you have the muscle and strength. However, with your size and the Laurentius family in the background, Aetius will certainly bend the rules.'

'I have signed the contract.'

The man looked at him in amazement. 'It is not my place to say this but you are too young to be in this game. However, you have made your choice, so welcome'

'Marcus grimaced and hung his head. 'I. I don't have much choice.'

The man looked at him with a light smile. 'There is always choice, young

183

man'. You have been told to be back at sunset?'

Marcus nodded glumly.

The man looked at him for a moment and then drew closer 'Then listen to me.; if you ever tell anyone I said, this I will deny it. Many have entered at your age or younger, and many are killed in the first year; and some had more experience than you. You have a choice but it means you must get out of Rome.'

'But what about the contract?'

'They will survive without you, young un. Get some experience and come back.'

'I can't. I have a debt.'

'Then that is your choice. Hail young man, and I look forward to seeing you in fore night.' The man sauntered back to the outhouse as Marcus turned on his heels to get Felix, who had sat down on the cool, stone veranda, once again waiting patiently.

They left the barracks together in deep conversation. Felix put his arm arounds his friend's broad shoulders as they walked. There was little he could say but listen to the story. They finally stopped inside the gardens, at the small amphitheatre they visited on the way.

'If I go to that school I will die.' Marcus added plaintively to the conversation with his head in his hand. 'I am just blood fodder for the school and all that bastard, Aetius cares about, is the relationship with Laurentius and his wealth, as does the Lanista, Aetius.'

Felix listened carefully and nodded as Marcus made his point. 'Of course, would we expect anything less? So, you don't have to join, do you?'

Marcus looked at him blankly. 'I signed the contract!'

'You did what?'

'I signed it. Aetius was determined to make me sign it and kept talking about the debt and Laurentius and he pushed it in front of me and for some reason I signed it.'

Felix shook his head slowly. 'Maybe go and speak to Tacitus. He might have a solution. Other than running out of Rome, I cannot think of any

---

184

other way around this unless you join as you have agreed. You can hide in my house if you like.' He gave Marcus a reassuring smile. 'Why did you sign the fucking contract?'

Marcus frowned and stopped walking. 'I don't know. Somehow, I thought it was expected of me and when he told me to sign it, I did. I am not only dumb; I am stupid as well.'

'Maybe not.' Felix replied with a pat on his friend' shoulder. 'You have a debt and you are feeling the pressure of these people, as they try to organise your life. Personally, I understand. But now, you have to make a choice.'

Marcus smiled thinly for the first time that day and produced the ring he received from Lucia the previous night.

'You stole it?'
He shook his head. 'She gave it to me.' Marcus looked up to the sky as it started to rain. 'I must go, Felix, thank you, dear friend.'

Felix started to protest as Marcus grabbed him by the shoulders, hugged him and left. He made directly for the Villa and his uncle who appeared in his mind, as his only hope. He was confused and frightened when he thought of the future. The old gladiator was right, as was Felix. But where did it leave him?

He arrived back at the Villa, breathless and distraught. He found his uncle at the back of the property fixing a blade to a scythe, for the grass cutting the following day.

Agitated, he pulled him aside, sat and told him the story as it had unfolded over the past several days. His uncle listened, nodded and sighed as he thought about it. 'How much is the debt?'

'Three hundred and twenty-eight Denarii.'

Tacitus whistled softly. 'Marco, that is a fortune. How did you gain that debt?'

Marcus looked at him blankly and shrugged his shoulders. 'Uncle, I can blame others but it was me and my stupidity. I never seem to be able to stop gambling once it gets a hold of me. I lose all sense!' He shouted out in frustration.

'Calm, Marco, calm. All, will be well but we must act fast. You must not go back to the Lanista as you are right he just wants the relationship with the Laurentius family and by all that I know, you are too young to fight in the arena. You will not last a month.'

Marcus looked at him with a perplexed look on this face. 'What path do I take, Tacitus If I stay here Lucia will push me to the Lanista and if I refuse I will go to jail, for the debt.'

'Then you must return to the farm. No one knows it's location and I will not tell them, even if they try to get it out of me.'

'No!' Marcus said firmly as he thought of his father and how much he hated the man and life on the farm.' That is not for me.'

'That does not leave much choice, Marco. I do not want you running off as they will find you somehow. You have that dog, Vicinius, the Lanista and the Laurentius family against you and you must find a way out.'

Sweat formed lightly on his brow as Marcus looked at his uncle. 'I am sorry, Tacitus, I have put you in a bad position as well.'

Tacitus looked at the young man before him and patted him on the arm as he thought briefly about the options. 'I may have a solution. Leave it to me, Marco, I will make preparations. Go pack and we will leave.'

CHAPTER 20

Marcus turned over, to move the side of him that lay half-roasted by the fire, to the freezing cold and allow the warmth of the flames to apply its heat across his cold body. It was so cold he could hardly feel his feet.

His mind crept fitfully back to the night of his escape from Rome, just less than a year before ending up on the sands of Judea.

Tacitus had rushed him from the Laurentius villa and hidden him at a friend's house, on the outskirts of Rome. The travel from the city, which started two days later, became difficult and hazardous as each stop beckoned the wrath of the Laurentius family, and one of their thugs waiting to return him to his agreement.

'The arena is littered with the dead bodies of those who have entered the gladiatorial ring as young novices.' Tacitus said sombrely, as he spoke to Marcus that night. 'Youthful fodder,' he had said sternly, as he advised Marco on the next move. 'I trust the word of Britanicus and the old gladiator at the school, before I would trust the man of this house, his wife or that snarling piece of shit, Aetius. The legion is your only chance or the farm, for that matter, but you have denied that path.'

'I can't return to the farm, Tactius.' Marcus said, sombrely. 'I can't. If I do I go back as a failure and I incur the wrath of my father and I refuse to do that!'

'Then it must be the legion. I know they are on their way to Judea and I can get you in, but you will need to move quickly and that means tonight.' Tactius started to grab Marcus's belongings to put in his sack.

'What about the debt? Will it come back on you?' Tactius shrugged. 'They can afford it, Marco. And, no, it can't come back on me because I will tell them I haven't seen you since yesterday. Understand, you are now part of the Laurentius quest for power and notoriety. Be aware that Laurentius also knows that you are too young for the arena, but another bout with Britanicus to the death would assist his wealth since he will promote it. Also, he gets you out of his wife's clutches. If we don't do this, you are doomed.'

'Lucia seems to do what she wants.'
Tactius looked at his nephew sternly. 'Listen, Marco. Laurentius is a man beset by the need for power. He will do anything and dispose of anyone, who gets in his way. With power comes control. He is a man who is used to controlling. You are in his way. Get it?'

Marcus nodded, holding his head in his hands. 'This is all my fault.'

Tactius sat down beside him. 'Marco, we all make mistakes and this is one you have made. You have a decision to make and I believe you are making the right one by joining the legion. You are too young for the arena and the Legion will certainly make you a stronger man.'

Over the night they discussed the issues and each of them came to agreement that the legion was the only option. They left early the next morning and most of the next day they made his way to the port of *Hacea* to meet with his uncle's old core, the Fifth legion. They hurried to join it as it lay in bivouac, in the port waiting for passage to Judea aboard large, troop ships.

Every time the dray stopped on the trip to the port, he waited to see if he was recognized but they made it to the port by very early the next morning.

Around him, as he followed his uncle, lay a sea of standing soldiers, tents, horses, drays, cooking utensils and worried officers walking around, barking orders. As the neared the main camp, Tactius asked for directions and finally he found the tent he was seeking, leaving Marcus outside to sit on the grass.

Inside, Tacitus sat with one of his old mates from the legion. Over a cup of mead, he explained the need of his nephew to leave Rome and the reason behind his hasty exit.

Marcus watched as they walked outside after the talk and shook hands. Tactius nodded to him and he waited for the next step.

His uncle sat with him for another hour while they discussed the army and his future in Judea. Tacitus grabbed him and hugged him warmly before Marcus jumped up on the dray, sitting back for the short ride from the administration tent to the port bivouac area.

He was given instructions from the supply tent as he waited for the next person to speak to him. He waved to Tactius, who headed back to Rome as quickly as possible, watching him until distance made his form hazy and then, finally, the last link to his old life, disappeared. When he arrived at the at the next tent he was presented to the *Optio*, a man by the name of Varius Aquinius who walked around as he inspected Marcus.

Finally, he nodded his head and called a Centurion who transferred him to another smaller tent to wait. Later that day a quartermaster found him and kitted him with the dress and armaments of the fifth legion.

His first day in the army, found him bivouacked at the port itself, beside two, large troop ships making ready to sail. He studied the ships intently, fascinated by the myriad of furled sails hanging from booms, above the deck.

Men moved around the ship deck, working on the sails and taking on stores, required to make it ready for sailing to another land.

He looked up, to find more than twenty men around the masts, pulling the white sheets down only to refold them and set up the ropes for the voyage.

From the edge of the dock, he could hear the gentle creaking of the ship timbers, giving the ship a life of its own, floating against the tranquillity of the lines that held it to the dock.

The next morning, he was introduced to another Centurion, who inspected the gear his uncle had purchased for him and a doctor entered to look at him physically. An hour later he was passed.

'The mess tent is open, Attilus. Make your way there and presently you will meet your Centurion, Brutus Cenaus.'

Marcus finally found his way to the large tent with long benches and stools and walked cautiously inside. One of the cooks motioned him over, gave him a bowl and indicated for his to sit on the other side of the tent.

He sat at the rough table looking at the soup in front of him. It was blacker than the rocks he turned over as a boy at the farm. The soup was sour and full of lentils which made his stomach turn at each mouthful. It was a fight between his hunger and his mouth as to which one was winning.

Finally, he pushed it away and sat back staring angrily, at the bowl. He was hungry, disorientated and unhappy.

A booming voice issued across the tent from another table. 'You, boy!' Marcus looked over at the man, standing near the middle of another table. He was a huge man, with small eyes and a large, wide mouth. 'Our soup no good for you, *Novice*?'

Marcus looked at him in surprise. 'I, I don't like the taste.'

The men in the tent started to laugh in unison. The Centurion moved over, picked up the bowl and threw it at Marcus, who ducked slightly, but most of the liquid ended up on his tunic.

He then pulled out a cane and slashed it across his back. Wincing from the pain Marcus got up and retreated to the tent flap and outside the tent.

'Move out there, boy, and by the will of Mars I will run you through. I am going easy on you because this is your first day. If you do that again, I will whip you until the flesh is coming off your back. Now, go and get another bowl and eat it while I am watching you and make sure you look like you are enjoying it.

Marcus, shocked and numb from the beating moved off to get another bowl at the steaming vats at the end of the tent.

'You know who I am?' Came the shout as he walked off. 'I am your Centurion and these men in this tent are part of your century. These are your brother's boy and you disrespect them if you don't eat the same food as them. Who, the fuck, do you think you are?'

The centurions voice moved up the scale as he shouted at Marcus. 'You are a single part of eighty men and by the Gods you will eat and fight as required. You are a *legionarius* and you are part of a group of *legionarii* who are your brothers. If this wasn't your first day I would smash your face in. Got it?'

Marcus nodded, looking at him in fear and astonishment, and with tears forming in his eyes he picked up the bowl of soup, eating it slowly as the Centurion watched.

'Eat it. Slowly!'

Marcus nodded his head slightly, keeping one eye on the cane in the hand of the mountain of a man, before him. The Centurion raised his foot and pounded it into the bench next to Marcus. As big as he was the Centurion was bigger and a ferocious man.

Finally, inside the tent, the Centurion relaxed as Marcus finished his bowl. 'We have not been properly introduced.' He said with a mild tone, betrayed by the look on his face. 'I am your Centurion, boy, and you are under my charge as a novice soldier. Put a foot wrong and I will beat you. If you do not get up or you do not train properly I will whip you within a small space of your miserable life. You are not in a nice place. Understand?'

Marcus nodded dumbly and continued to eat. He watched as the Centurion returned to his table and made a comment which sent gales of laughter around the mess tent. Marcus held his head in shame, intent on holding back the tears.

Tactius had spent time on their journey, to explain to him in detail, about discipline in the Roman army. 'Hard punishment is supported from the *legate* down. Your Centurion holds significant, if not the ultimate power to chastise or beat men in the century unit. Your *century*, Marco, which will comprise eighty men. The century will hold ten *conturbenium* of eight men and you will be made a member of one. You understand?'

Marcus nodded trying to absorb the information as he waited for his uncle to continue. 'Listen, Marco; You cannot fight with these men because they will make your life a misery. I know that from my own experience. If you get on the wrong side of a Centurion, it makes your life twice as hard.'

As he remembered the words he put down the bowl, looked briefly over at the Centurion who was laughing with one of the other legionnaires, and made his way outside to gather his kit with tears streaming down his face.

As he picked up his pack he was told his first training session would start after the meal. He donned his boots, breast plate, helmet, sword, shield and spike and made his way to where the rest of the men were gathering in formation.

'You, novice!' Marcus looked over at a short man with large shoulders and a scar across his face. 'Get down there with the rest of the shit pickers.'

Marcus moved down the line to an area where he saw the other novices stood. They all looked miserable and they all held the look of wide eyed fear, on their young faces.

'What do we do now?' He whispered to a man next to him without looking.

Ovidius looked briefly at him and shrugged his shoulders as he came to attention.

'Shut up' Came the bellowing voice of the man before them. 'Most of you know my name and for those who don't, and I make reference to the stupid mules up the other end, my name is Albus. What that means to your miserable lives is a very simple meaning. I am the training officer of this century. If you do not train or you do not train correctly, I am entitled to beat you until you do. Once I have finished I will pass you to our Centurion, Brutus Cenaus, and he will finish you off with one stroke. Got your attention?'

Albus looked across the group and noted with satisfaction that all had come to attention as he paraded up and down in front of them. 'This will be the best trained Century, in this legion. And for those *novices* who know no different, the Fifth is the best legion in the Roman army and over the coming months, I will prove it to you. How? You may ask? Well, I am going to train you until you wish you had died and gone to the black waters of the river Styx. Any questions?'

Albus moved up and down the rank as he spoke. 'Didn't think so. Now, there are three basic positions, which all of you know with the exception of the *novices*. We will practice these until you can dream them. You, *legionarius*!' He pointed at Marcus. 'Get out here'

Marcus moved quickly to position himself in front of Albus, who walked around him slowly.

'Do your bloody helmet up!' He screamed; which Marcus did immediately.

'Shield up.'

As Marcus raised his shield, Albus smashed it with his spike, which sent it out of his hands and into the ground below. The man then smashed the side of the spike across Marcus's back, sending him sprawling.

'Now, get up novice and start again. You never! Never lose your shield!' He screamed loudly at Marcus, who rose swiftly from the ground. 'Never! That shield is your mother, your father and your wife and lover. Lose that in battle and none of those men, will ever see you again.' He pointed to all of them to emphasize the point.

192

Marcus picked up his shield and held it firmly as Albus hit it again, with his spear. 'Better. Now, ladies, get in formation and let's get some marching in before we start practising with the Gladius.'

As Marcus fell back into line he felt the ripping pain of a cane across his back. He turned to find Brutus, who walked up from behind the formation. 'I am watching you, Attilius.' He then swiped it hard across the back of Ovidius, who stood motionless after the strike. 'No talking in line, novice. I am watching you, as well.'

The training continued until the late afternoon. As the men finally returned to their tents, they collapsed one by one, into the hard earth of the port.

The following day was the same, with screaming and shouts from Albus and swipes from the back by the Centurion.

Sword practice started, with downward strikes then upward strikes, followed by side blocks and finally lunges. Each movement held its own instructions and each movement was scrutinized by the teacher and by the Centurion, who prowled up and down the ranks, looking for lack of technique or practice.

'Stop' Albus said sharply.' You, novice? What is your name?'

'Ovidius, Centro'

'Get out here and Alinus, get out here as well.' Albus said pointing at one of the regular soldiers. 'We are going to have a sword fight here, and since we don't want to hurt our new boys, we will use wooden swords. Ovidius, your job is to beat Alinus here who has great experience. Let's see how you go.'

The two squared up and Ovidius started to circle finally raising his sword to strike. Within two blows, his sword fell to the ground, as he held his wrist from the blow by Alinus.

'Now, ladies, you all understand. We will practice until you can sword play in your dreams. Each day we will drill, and each day I will personally flog the man who does not use passion and strength, in his sword movements. Any questions?'

The sword play continued for another two hours, until Albus stopped them yet again and brought them into rank and file. He then turned them, towards the far hills and brought them up to a run as they set off on another forced march.

The exertion made each man sweat profusely. The parts of the body that held the armour, from the small patches of thinning hair from the weight of the helmet, through to the greaves on the legs, that bit into their calves, made their presence felt.

By the time they reached the port barracks, exhaustion had set in. Albus made them stand in line for another hour and then dismissed them.

'Rest tonight because tomorrow we go on a march twice the distance of today!' He called our cheerily, watching with some satisfaction, as one by one they fell to their knees or moved to the dockside fencing to sit and remove their armour. 'Your shields had better be shining, ladies, or Hades will be your payment.' He shouted as he walked towards the main tent with the Centurion who towered over him.

Ovidius was the first to sit and pull off his armour. He was almost as tall as Marcus but thin and long in the face. 'That man is an animal.' He said dropping his leather chest brace to the ground.

There was a murmur of assent around him, as sweating men let out a sigh of agreement. Marcus sat heavily against the wall and nodded his head.

'This is the seventh Conturbenium?' A man said as he lowered his spear to the wall. Marcus nodded. He felt weary and the question was unwelcome given his exhaustion.

'My name is Sextus. I have been told to join the seventh. Is this the right tent?'

'You, poor bastard.' Ovidius said with a smile. 'You want to join that mass of sweating, farting, snoring idiots?'

'Apparently.' Sextus returned. He took a seat so he could pull his helmet off. 'Which conturbenium are you in?' He asked Ovidius, who then started to laugh which set Marcus laughing with the others.

'The seventh.' Ovidius replied rolling on his back as the laughter overtook him.

CHAPTER 21

As he lay on his straw paliass, watching the canvas in the lightly buffeting tent roof above him, his mind returned to the first night of the voyage to Judea.

The sea stretched before them, shining like the face of a polished sword under the mantle of the fading light. Deep hues of orange and red, gifted from the dying sun on the horizon, beckoned the ship as it rolled slowly across the swell with a mild breeze behind it.

It was the first-time Marcus had been on a ship, let alone traversing the seas to another land. The land of a country he did not know the name of, let alone where it lay. He had tried to stay away from the centurion before the voyage and he had opted to sleep up on deck.

The word from the men on the voyage, concentrated on the Centurions who commanded each century. It was urgently whispered that the Centurions, were professional long-term soldiers, and the vast majority across the five legions attending at the siege of Jerusalem were tough, war experienced men but most of them took delight in belittling the soldiers in their command.

Beatings were brutal, commonplace and applied liberally, one of the old veterans had said bitterly. The practice was so common, Marcus was told by another veteran of the Fifth, that each Centurion carried a personally picked olive tree branch, stripped of its bark and seasoned in the sun.

'Get on the wrong side of one of those Centurions and you will regret it every day' The legionnaire with the grizzled face had said quietly, as they stood in line with the same message that Tacitus had passed to him at the camp.

Marcus nodded, looking over at the man who commanded their conturbenium. The Centurion commanding his century was a large man; obviously strong, disciplined and tough, but not brutal, according to the other men in the Century. Unless it was necessary and then he came down with the force of a siege machine.

Marcus had felt the brunt of the olive rod many times, over the previous month they held at port. There was little doubt in Marcus' mind, that the huge Centurion held an unknown grudge for him and that meant staying out of the way.

Necessity and discipline had nothing to do with it. Marcus was a 'marked' legionnaire and he knew there was little he could do about it. The welts across his back held a constant reminder of his need to stay away.

Despite the low swell, the dark timbers of the wide planked deck, held the prone forms of soldiers, either snoring softly or moaning loudly, from sea sickness.

Food was prepared on the deck, using large cauldrons with fires stoked beneath, to cook what was perpetually, barley soup with vegetables and very little meat. Many of the men held rations in their packs, which they used to supplement their meals.

Marcus had nothing except his kit, that Tacitus had hurriedly pulled together from some of his belongings and the rest were purchased at the dock from the quartermaster.

He noted that the other novices in his Conturbenium had the same kit and no extra rations in their empty packs. However, he quickly started to enjoy life on the ship.

It was very different to his life before and he felt at home, under the open sky and the sun that blazed across the decks, interrupted by the shadows cast by the billowing sails.

Now and then, Albus would come on deck to inspect the area, grumble and step back below to the cabin he shared with the Centurion. The days passed slowly, with the uninspiring event of a small island, sitting forlornly to the starboard or port of the ship and now and then, a pod of dolphins appeared playing with the bow wave of the ship, disappearing, just as quickly.

The sea displayed azure blue in the day and in the late afternoon, the broad expanse of ocean, took the deep, grey colour of faded timber as the light lost its lustre.

As he looked out at the sun falling into the horizon, he remembered the smell of the wild flowers of his farm. It was if he could taste the walnuts, plums and oranges they picked off the trees, when they were young.

He could remember his mother assiduously boiling the olives, to remove the bitterness and then how she deftly pressed them, to gain the first olive oil.

As he thought about it, he realised yet again that he could no longer remember their faces and it saddened him. He shook his head in disbelief, as he realised the events of the past months in Rome. A month before he was a gardener on the estate of the richest man in Rome and now he sat on the bow of a ship, sailing across an ocean to a far-away land as a *novice legionarius*, in the Fifth legion of the Roman army.

He shook his head again as if to pull himself out of the dream. It seemed imaginary, yet here he was, grasping the rail and rising with the swell as the ship ploughed on towards Judea. He stifled an emotional gasp, instead, looking to the distance. He could see dark clouds forming and for an instant, he wondered if the clouds were foretelling his life.

Late the next night, a storm hit. Marcus held on to the rails as hard as he could, as men dashed around tying up loose ends, after they had furled all of the sails except for the one that billowed like a loose sheet, on the bow of the troop ship. There was no room downstairs and those who had chosen the top deck on the voyage, quickly came to understand why the experienced ones preferred the gloom beneath the decks, for the duration of the voyage.

'I sure as Hades did not sign on for this' The man shouted out next to him as he spat out a mouthful of seawater. 'Join the army,' He sang 'See new lands for the glory of greater Rome. Well, that is a load of pig crap. All we get is training, marching and a Centurion who delights in using the cane. Just one night, I would like to get him alone.'

Bolts of lightning, arcing across the sea, highlighted the size of the waves as the hull of the ship ploughed into one, only to come up and enter the middle of the next. Water streamed across the deck, with driving rain that made looking anywhere but downwind, difficult.

'What's your name?

'Ovidius. You?'

'Marcus.'

'Call me Ovi'

Marcus shrugged. 'Call me shit picker or Marco.' He shouted back against the wind.

Ovidius laughed as he looked out across the turbulent seas. 'I would like to get that piece of shit alone as well.'

'I can think of a number of boys who feel exactly the same.' Marcus shouted, as he braced himself against another huge swell that washed across the deck. 'Where do you come from?'

'I am Thracian by birth, Marco, and down on my luck I thought I might try the army. You?'

Marcus stood silently for a moment. 'Born North of Rome on a farm and wanted to find my fame and fortune.' He started to laugh at his situation, standing on a ship in a heavy storm and waiting for wave to take him overboard. 'I was down on my luck as well but as I look at it now things were not so bad.'

He and Ovi laughed together, more at the danger and the situation they were in other than anything else. As they watched, a sailor made his way carefully along the rail.

As another monster hit the side of the ship he braced himself finally meeting the two men. Rain lashed against the ship deck with the surface turning into a mixture of heavy rain and the swell that washed heavily across the hard-timber planks.

'Tie yourself on, soldiers.' He said abruptly, as water washed across the deck. 'This is only going to get worse.' He showed them how to set a knot across their wrist to the rail, so that he could undo it easily if they needed to escape. 'She may go down, boys and if she does you grab whatever you can to stay afloat.'

'Welcoming news.' Ovi said, as he and Marcus started laughing again.

'Join the Imperial army and see the world.' Marcus grumbled.

Ovi patted him on the shoulder. 'This is our new life, Marco' He said with a wide smile.

The waves stood larger as dawn approached. In the early morning, the ship, rocking and rolling into the massive swell, got hit by a rogue wave amidships and the vessel lurched to port with its massive mast hitting the water and then slowly, inexorably, it finally righted itself, before it was hit by another.

Two men went overboard, swept away by the waves and howling wind as the water washed over the foundering ship. Marcus could hear the shouts from the men and then there was the same sound of wind, whistling across the masts and the hard thump as the ship hit swell after swell.

He looked around to see the rest of the men hunched down against the rail and most of them calling out obscenities to Neptune, as the sea smashed into the ship.

By the middle of that morning, the storm abated and despite heavy seas, the sailors put the rest of the sheets up and the ship responded by increasing speed across the swells, that continued from the South east. The wind subsided and calm returned to the deck. Marcus looked below deck which appeared to be half full of sea water. Men were shouting as buckets were sent down to remove the water below, by filling them and passing them up to the top deck. They were then emptied and passed back down.

By the middle afternoon the dolphins had returned, with their wide smiles on their snouts, darting around the ship.

It was over a week later when they spied land. Marcus, Sextus and Ovi and several other soldiers were sitting on the deck eating a bowl of barley soup, when one of the sailors high above on the mast shouted out and pointed.

Presently, in the distance they could see the outline of land. A cheer went up on the ship as one of the sailors turned to his mate next to him at the bottom of the mast. '*Caesarea Maritima*, at last.'

By late afternoon, the ship had pulled down most of its sails, as it neared the harbour entrance. Rowers, on either side of the ship, took over as it navigated between two long breakwaters on either side of the entrance to allow safe mooring inside the busy harbour.

Many of the men came up on deck to watch the ship moving through the boats at anchor. They looked out, fascinated, as ships transited in and out of the spacious water.

They pulled alongside a wide, long jetty with the ship finally coming to rest with a crunch against the jetty side. Marcus watched, as sailors jumped off the ship to tie the boat up and planks were put in place, to provide walkways. 'Thanks to Neptune it is over.'

Marcus turned to find Luca, one of the men in the his conturbenium, standing next to him resting heavily against the rail. He was older than Marcus and his age was hard to guess. Like all soldiers, he wore a permanent frown 'I was sure we were not going to make it. Can you swim?'

Marcus nodded. 'A little but only in the rivers at home. You?'
'Not a chance. Had this leaking bucket finally given up she would have taken me with it. By the way, brother, it seems you and Brutus have an issue'

Marcus nodded. 'Can't you tell by the scars on my back' He said with a smile.

'I have more scars than you, friend. I am the favourite whipping boy of a previous illustrious piece of shit, in another war almost a year ago today. However, I was present that first day, when you decided not to eat your soup and I knew it was your turn.'

They all laughed at the image as Luca clapped Marcus on the shoulder with a look of sympathy. 'You are big enough to handle it though.'

Marcus shrugged. 'What I hear from the men is that the first novice year is the worst. Once we prove ourselves, they will leave us alone.'

Luca raised his eyebrows. 'I have fought in this man's army for twelve years and they never leave you alone. However, we have talent in this conturbenium, so let's see what happens.'

'One day I will kill that brute.' Sextus said grimly 'One day I will have my revenge.'

'You will need to get in the queue, because there are a few before you.' Ovi added as they waited for the orders to come to leave the ship.

He shifted his position wincing with pain from his left knee. He looked over at the other two. 'Nothing a good long march wouldn't fix!'

Marcus looked into the crystal blue of the sea below him, watching as a fish swam lazily beside the ship only to dart away as another chased it. He looked at a shape near the pier which looked like an amphora, which was probably dropped from a trade ship and left to spoil in the sea below.

The reflected afternoon sun from the stone city dazzled his eyes, turning the light drenched buildings to the colour of white, rose petal. The city extended up from the port, for as far as he could see from the top deck of the ship, to hills that rose from the West and flatter land on the other side.

The tall limestone buildings at the port served as busy warehouses, with any manner of goods moving to and fro between the ships that lined the quay.

One worker dropped a cart, holding several amphorae and they smashed to the ground leaking olive oil, onto the stone paving in front of them which caused a few choice comments from the men on the deck of the troop ship.

'Lard fingers!'

'Watch your footing!'

Marcus and Ovi were astonished at the difference between the men that worked the quay that day. They ranged from long haired, blue eyed giants to men whose skin held as black as onyx.

Women with ornate bangles in their ears and the bright reds and blues in their dress walked by, with ornate sandals on their feet.

Finally, they moved out of the afternoon heat and disembarked onto the wide port area, before the boat and sorted themselves into centuries with each Centurion barking orders to get them in line. As usual, Brutus held the thick cane in his hand and moved quickly to use it.

'Listen up ladies, we bivouac behind this building and we leave for Judea as soon as we are given orders. Once you have set up, the mess tent will be inside this building behind me and there you will sit and stay, unless training, until we move to Judea. There is a curfew in this city for Roman soldiers and that is after meal times at which time you will be heading for your tent.'

The Centurion looked at the men before him swishing his cane as he moved back and forwards holding their gaze. 'Any questions?'

There was a murmur of agreement from the men and he turned on his heels to head off to the building. He stopped momentarily. 'What the fuck are you waiting for? Pick up your gear and move through that building to the back and set up the tents. Be on the ground at dawn, in full gear.'

The eighty men followed their respective Conturbenium brothers to the back of the building and erected their tents before nightfall.

201

They ate out of their packs that night and the next morning, set up for training at the field of the Amphitheatre, on the other side of the city.

CHAPTER 22

The air held a frosty edge that following morning with men shuffling to get into final place. Six centuries of eighty men stood with their battle gear on, waiting for the drill centurion to arrive which he did promptly.

No matter how many times Marcus suited up he found the battle dress cumbersome and difficult as well as uncomfortable to wear.
He wore heavy sandals, a heavy leather skirt, metal breastplate, his Gladius seated in its sheath on his waist as well as his pilum, a long spear with a spike on the end designed to bend on impact so it could not be used by the enemy in return.

As well, he held his heavy bronze plated shield, which was fixed at the back, by a small leather thong that fed through the arm to a handle, grasped firmly by the left hand. The weight on his body almost fifty pounds once the rations pack was added.

Oviidus and Sextus stood beside him on the parade ground with the tall form of Albus, the training officer, before them and screaming as usual. Now and then he would dart towards a soldier picking out some part of his dress which was not correct or held correctly.

He stood in front of one of the new recruits who stood to left of Marcus. 'Name, boy?'

'Ar..Arius, sir?'

'Well at least you got that right.'

'My na… name?' The boy stuttered

'No, you bloody idiot. My name which will always be 'sir,' to you. Have you g,g, got that?' Albus mimicked the boys stutter. 'Fix your helmet and make sure it is fixed from now on. Next time it is not put on properly, I will beat you. Come out here in front.'

Arius followed the trainer, who walked with the practised gait of someone who was used to being in charge in the front of the four hundred and eighty men, who made up the *cohort*. He held himself tall and looked fit with long muscular arms and in his hand, he held a *pilum*. His battle dress appeared to be perfect with everything in place and shining like new. His voice boomed across the ground.

'Now let us start with this before we take a stroll through the Judean countryside. This spear is your friend and not your enemy as I note many of you see it as. You see it? This wonderful pilum, this saver of lives and killer of enemies'

Albus picked up his spear and held it aloft for all of them to see. 'Some of you might regard this friend of ours in battle as unnecessary and heavy but that would make you more stupid than you already are. This pilum is the barrier between you, and the enemy. From now on when you are lucky enough to be in the battle line, you will hold it at his point.' His hand moved to a point above centre of the hard, oak handle.

'When you engage you move the pilum to the right of your shield, just above centre and you change your grip to here as you do so.' Again, he motioned to his hand position. 'For those of you who are unable to work out in your feeble minds what to do with it, you move it forward in thrusts and towards the sides of the enemy's shields. You do not strike towards the head. Why?'

He looked at the men before him and finally raised his eyes towards the heavens. 'May the Gods give me patience.' He said as he looked at them. He struck the pilum forward, towards the head of Arius who stood before him. The pilum struck his shield several times.

'Because it is a waste of bloody time, that's why. You strike to the side of the shields as deeply as you can. You are after their arms and preferably their sword arm, and if not, then anywhere else will do. Get back to rank, novice.' He said to Arius who had stood as straight as a building wall, while Albus had used him for demonstration.

Albus moved away from the Centurion towards the men. 'Once the pilum is bent and I remind you it is designed to bend; you drop it and move to your sword. It is designed to bend. Why? Well, let me explain it to you morons. So, the Judeans cannot use it against you!'

He nodded to the various Centurions, who moved through their respective ranks, using their canes against anyone out of line or whispering.

'Pilums up!' Came the order and the men in the front row moved theirs to a horizontal position. 'Strike' Again the men pushed their spears forward and waited. 'Back' Next'

The next line came forwards and repeated the action. Each time someone faltered, the sound of cane against the back of the man resounded off those next to him.

Some while later he blew a wooden whistle held around his neck by a strand of leather. 'Back in line, ladies.' Albus said as he strutted in front of them. 'Time for a march and we thought, and, well, decided between us that it was time to do something different today. So, allow us to take you up that hill over there and then back. About sixty miles but that would be the same as a walk in the forest for us, correct.?'

The men murmured in front of him and finally let out a half-hearted cheer. 'You are the men of the fifth and we are the best Legion in the army. Repeat after me. Fifth is us!'

Low murmurs uttered from the men 'Fifth is us.'

'I can't bloody hear anything you pack of lazy shits. Fifth is us.'

The song rang out as the men picked up their marching line 'Fifth is us.'

'Standard bearer?' He called out as the eagle mounted standard rose up at the front with the red and black of the flag, raised so all could see it.

The standard with the letters SPQR beneath it, started to move and each century of men, followed keeping up with the standard bearer.

They followed Albus, as he took off at a light trot. With four abreast, the sound of the clanking armour and deep breaths filled the area as they left it. For a long while they walked at a fast trot, slowed, ran and moved to a fast trot again, finally moving into the rhythm of the march.

Some hours later, they reached the top of the long hill that led out of the city and down the coast. In the clear air of the Judean landscape, they finally came to rest at the bottom of the next ridge.

Albus walked in front of them as they came to a halt. From the hill

top they could clearly see the coastline. Before them, held an expansive view, with sparkling blue sea to their right and on it the distant blurry images of ships, as they moved to and from the large port, carrying cargo and passengers.

To their left sat the ruins of an old house, sitting forlornly with half of its walls, crumbled into the dry earth.

_____

'Right, pair off. Pilums forward. Practice. Pilums down, pilums forward, practice and down.' The exercises continued until the sun started to decline from its perch and head towards the ocean.

'Shields down!'

Slowly, the regulars loosened their grip and let the shield fall to their left foot and balanced it against their leg. To let a *scutum*, drop to the sand beneath your foot was regarded as the largest sin of them all. Albus shouted each and every day as he held his shield up for all to see. 'Your shield remains your constant companion. You hold it close and you polish it, each night. This brass companion, your ally, in easy and difficult times is the only difference between life and death in close quarter battle. Love, it, like you love no other.' Albus held up his immaculate shield, with its red front and brass engraving. He turned it, to show the handle and leather arm thong.

 The novices tried to follow suit until Arius, another of Marcus's conturbenium dropped his shield onto the hard earth. He stooped to pick it up and within a moment, the Centurion was on him dragging him in front of the other men.

'This is what happens when you drop your shield.' He pushed the new recruit to the ground in front of him with a snarl on his face. Sweating from the march, he raised his cane and slammed it across the boy's legs, who howled as he did.

'That is what happens when you drop your shield at any time. The *scutum* is never dropped and this message is for any of the men here. You do not, ever, drop your shield! That shield is your lady; it is your lover, it is your unborn son and it is your life. Do you get it?' Arius looked up at him with fear on his face. 'Yes sir.'

'Now get up and get back to your squad. Anyone here want to argue? You never drop your shield. The only time you drop your shield is when you die and you had better be holding it at that time as well.'

He looked around at the sweating men in front of him and the shields that lay against their left legs. 'That shield is the difference between your life and taking your enemies life. Don't forget it and since Arius here, decided to be so careless with his shield, we will all run, not march back to Caesarea together. If one man falters, complains, stops or cheats I will personally ensure his squad does not eat tonight. Right, get back into line.'

Of the *cohort* of four hundred and eighty men there stood five centurions, experienced, long serving professional soldiers who commanded their *century* of eighty men each, with ten *conturbenium* of eight men each.

The fifth also held Albus, the training commander, the standard bearer and several non-combatants, including a physician, in full battle dress, who ran back with the men through the thirty miles to Caesarea.

When they reached the outside of the port they were stopped by Albus, who brought them back to formation and dismissed them. It was early afternoon, and those who could keep walking moved back to their tents at the back of the port building, to get water and stow away their gear. Most dropped to the ground, exhausted and mumbling under their breath.

Marcus, Ovidius, Sextus, Arius and Luca shared the same tent and once they had rested Marcus got up and started to leave.

'I'm going for a walk to have a look at the city. Any takers?'

Ovi got up, stretched, nodded and followed him while the other three lay forlornly on their straw filled paillasses. They left the tent and started to walk slowly around the streets, that filled the back of the port area.

*

The architecture of the town was greatly different from the stone paved streets of Rome. The houses and buildings were built of high, vaulted arches with flat roofs. The streets were lined with single story buildings everywhere they looked.

The workmanship on the buildings, appeared ornate in contrast to Rome. Most of the buildings were built of large, white limestone blocks steaked with dirt that supported ornate lintels and facades that adorned the more expensive buildings. The use of colourful plants created a palette of colours. Bougainvillea in pinks and red splashed out on the sides of many buildings with high blooms as they climbed the sides of buildings to the roofs above.

Marcus noticed that with the exception of Roman soldiers in dress, there were very few locals on the street. He rarely saw a woman, as they walked down the roads and towards the top of the narrow streets of the port area and towards the back of the city.

Finally, they found a tavern on a corner as they started to make their way back. They decided to stop for refreshments. It was late afternoon and the seats made a welcome respite from the soreness, gained from the march that day.

The shop keeper who spoke reasonable Roman, Latin, came over offering a spiced wine, with bread and cheese.

'When did you arrive?'

'Yesterday,' Ovidius noted with a grimace. 'I thought it was tough on the ship until we got here. We marched this morning.'

'Heard it before.' The man said with a smile. 'You get used to it, apparently' Ovidius looked over at Marcus and they both laughed. 'Not likely'

They ate the bread and cheese for several minutes, both in their respective thoughts. Finally, Marcus called for more wine as his thoughts returned from the farm and his brother. 'Why did you join the army, Ovi?

Ovidius smiled as he thought about the answer. 'I have a wife and child in Rome and I was unable to get a job when I arrived, so I thought the army might be the solution. Two hundred and eighty Denarii a year doesn't hurt, less expenses, of course.'

'Of course.' Marcus mimicked. 'A Centurions wage is better though. Three thousand five hundred, I am told. I am surprised you are married. I thought that was against the rules.'

"it is, Marcus, but they don't know. What about you?'

Marcus looked across at his companion with a raised eyebrow. 'Gambling debts mainly, Ovi. Oh, and they wanted to draft me into gladiator's school, so it was time to leave.'

Ovidius took a deep breath in. 'Gladiatorial combat is one way to make good money, but it is not for the faint hearted. At least in the army you have your mates around you. I thought of it myself, but they said I was too young. You?'

'Well then, it wasn't just me. They wanted me to start, but one of the experienced ex-gladiators told me I was too young as well and I took his advice. I was put up for the job by Cassius Laurentius, who was just using me for fodder anyway.'

Ovi whistled softly. 'Nice to have friends in high places.'

Marcus snorted. 'They were no friends of mine. Did you sign up for long?'

'I was the last of the six-year option and after the last four months I can happily say that unless death cheats me, I will be leaving at the end of that time. You?'

Marcus downed the last of his wine. 'The same; I hear it is changing to twenty-six years' minimum.' He left several Denarii on the table and they started back to the bivouac site.

Marcus stopped to take in the view from the top of the city. The sun descended slowly into the horizon, radiating a deep orange, which softly highlighted the deep blue of the ocean.

They could hear a loud voice coming over the walls and with rising curiosity Marcus saw a door near the end of the building and went through.

They walked down a small passage and entered the outside of a small amphitheatre, set back against the hill. A booming voice could be heard easily from where they stood. Several more steps, took them to a vantage point, under a colonnade where they hugged the wall behind them.

They looked up to see a man, short with large shoulders and a wide commanding face, in full battle dress. He was addressing a crowd comprising of Centurions and the *Optio*, Varius Aquinius, who commanded the legion under the legate.

'We'd better go.' Ovi whispered quickly. 'If they find us here, they will beat us to death.'

Marcus grabbed his arm to hold him in position. 'They can't see us and if they rise we will take off.' They stood back to listen. 'Who is that?' Marcus asked, nodding in the direction of the man in front of them. 'Fuck knows.' Ovi replied, looking towards the passage they had just taken to walk in.

'Gentlemen, let me make myself very clear, regarding the siege we have undertaken, under the direction of emperor Vespasian. This is not a small enterprise we have before us and I can assure you, the Jewish soldiers will not give up their holy city easily, but our days of a drawn-out siege of this city have finished. It is time, to take the battle to them. My spies tell me there are at least twenty thousand soldiers in the city as we speak. However, I cannot vouch for the quality of their men. We all know, this siege has been continuing for too long. We are going to change our tactics and that means we move in with all we have with siege machines and then we go in Legion by legion if need be.'

The man paused, to let the murmuring cease, and finally held up his hand to quell any further discussion. 'We march in four weeks, so you need to get your men fit and ready. Our strategy is clear. After the watch forts are built, starting with the Mount of Olives, we will start apply the siege machines in earnest and our engineers are not under any illusion as to their jobs. Do not take this one lightly, brothers.'

The man cleared his throat and shouted out, in his deep voice. 'There are three walls to gain entrance to the inner city of Jerusalem. And, we will have to battle all three to get through. We will be building three forts at the Mount of Olives, the Eastern Gate and opposite the Psepphinus tower. The engineering boys will be hard at work and each of you will be given instructions, once we arrive.'

Varius Aquinius rose briefly. 'Titus, do we move quickly or try to starve them out.'

'By the Gods. Titus himself.' Ovi whispered.

'Shhh. Marcus nodded.

Titus shifted his step at the bottom of the amphitheatre and took his time to answer. 'My father has tried but we no longer have the time or the patience. You all know he has left for Egypt and with the Fifth now in attendance we will move forward. It is a good question Varius, but our spies tell us, the city is stocked with grain and they have underground aquifiers to feed their wells. My belief is that a fortified, battle hardened siege, is the only option we have. We break their walls and in we go and break them.'

He waited for other questions, but with no response he continued. 'They will be a difficult enemy. They will not meet us on the open field and I can assure you that their skirmishing tactics, will cause us casualties. Any training from now on, must be close quarter with sword and dagger. Centurions, set up your Conturbenium properly and make sure the squad leader, your *Decanus* is strong and willing and if they are not, change them out. Each century is to give forth, five of their best men, for sorties when required and for that I want your best fighters.'

Varius stood up again and waited for Titus to finish. 'How long is the march to Jerusalem?' Titus shrugged. 'Maybe two weeks depending on how quickly we can move each day.' He raised his hand to point at several men. 'Quartermasters, make sure you have provisioned properly and we will need a significant amount of timber at the other end, for battlements and rams.'

He looked around at the large group sitting on the steps of the amphitheatre and with a quick glance at Varius, he put both his arms up in the air. 'That's it, get on with it. Centurions, keep your men in order.'

Marcus and Ovidius moved back to the door unseen, as the others left by the arch at the other side of the Amphitheatre. As they passed the final wall and onto the street, they came across a description which Marcus stopped to read.

'What does it say? Ovi asked as he stopped beside him
'You can't read?

Ovi shook his head. 'Never had reason to learn.'

Marcus smiled at him. 'It says Pontius Pilate, prefect of Judea.'

'Who was he?'

Marcus shrugged as he moved off. 'No idea. Now, there must be a tavern we can have some fun in.'

Ovi put his hand on Marcus' shoulder as they walked down the streets looking for a tavern. 'It is against the legion rules, Marco.'

Marcus nodded and kept walking. 'Yes, it is Ovi, but if we have pain we must have fun. Let us see what happens.'

The two men finally found a tavern in full swing at the top of the city. From the balcony, above, they ordered wine and looked out at the twinkling lights of the bay. They could hear the sound of the bivouac area and the lights from the buildings at the port as they drank steadily, enjoying the scented wine and watching the patrons, who moved in and out.

They looked up at a commotion inside the bar and Sextus was pushing a man out of the way as he walked through the tavern. 'I've been looking for you two. Brutus is looking angry and asking where everyone is.

'What did you say?' Marcus asked, watching a game being played on the other table.

'I said you had gone for a walk.'

Marcus smiled warmly at him 'Well done, Sextus, we have time to play.'

Ovi shrugged and sat back in his seat as Sextus looked at them before turning on his heels and returning to the barracks. The two looked at each other and ordered more wine.

'Let us make it quick, Marco.' Ovidius downed his wine and looked around the tavern.

It was dimly lit and there were very few patrons, with the exception of three who sat at a table playing a board game with two dice. They walked over to watch and listened as they showed how the game was played.

'What is that dice in the middle for?' Marcus asked intently watching one of the men throw his dice and move a marker around the board.

'Ah, friend, that is a doubling dice. If you have a bet on the table, you can double at any time and if your opponent refuses, they lose their bet there and then, and you take it. If they continue then the winner is paid the bet, times whatever was on the dice, which can go up to sixty-four by the way.'

Marcus waited for the new game to begin and laid five Denarii on the table and sat down to play against the opponent opposite. Within minutes he had lost and he paid the penalty of ten Denarii, when he accepted the original double bet half way through the game.

Marcus felt lucky as they started the next game. He laid double his original bet of ten Denarii, on the side of the table. Within several moves, he placed the betting dice so it showed two, as the double. The man immediately placed it onto its side so it displayed four.

Ovi watched the face of his friend and shook his head. 'Let's go, Marco.'
'You go, Ovi I will make my fortune here and return as soon as I can, but I will hardly be able to carry it all in my pouch.'
'Marco, we need to go. We have orders and we are novices. If Brutus gets wind of this, we will cop it hard.'

Marcus looked up at him with a slightly drunken smile. 'Ovi; go ahead. I will follow soon enough.'

Ovidius looked down at this drunken friend debating whether to leave or not.

'Come on!' He shouted

Marcus looked over at him and shook his head. As he reached into his pouch he heard a loud voice behind him. They both looked up at the raging face of Brutus, who picked up the board and threw it across the room.

'Both of you! To camp right now and don't stop for any reason.'

They both stood up and moved out of the tavern. As they walked out Marcus heard Brutus speak to one of the players. 'How much did he lose?'

'Ten Denarii' The man said quietly. 'But he was on the way to losing more until you came in.

The way I see it, you owe me around forty Denarii'

Brutus reached down with one enormous hand grabbing the man by the throat. 'If they come back again you throw them out. If you don't I will be back to see you. Understand?' The man looked up at him trying to rise. 'If you ever speak to me like that again it will be your last.' Brutus drew his dagger from his belt and held it in front of the man's eyes.

Finally, he let the man go, storming out of the tavern, throwing chairs as he did. He looked for Ovidius and Marcus but they had gone and his only hope is that they took his advice and headed back to the tent.

*

The next morning after a forced march over the two longest and tallest hills at the back of the port they stopped before returning. Albus brought them all to attention and waited for the lines to gain order.

The Centurion moved to the front looking directly at the novice line.

'Legionnaire, Attilius. Front and centre. 'Marcus looked ominously at Ovidius, before moving out to the front of the eighty men. 'Drop your helmet, pilum and shield, boy, and take off your vest. Marcus looked at him, stunned and angry. He dropped the pilum to the ground and placed his shield next to it.

'Now get on your knees.'

Marcus faced him, angry and defiant looking down at the brown sand beneath him. 'You'll get on your knees, Centurion, before I get on mine.'

Brutus nodded to Albus, who moved quickly over to stand between the two of them. He landed a heavy punch to Marcus' stomach and together they pushed him roughly to the ground on his face. Marcus tried to move, but the heavy sandal of Albus laid squarely against his neck.

'Now listen, boys' He said to the men in the century standing before the spectacle. 'Before you, kneels a man who does not care about his conturbenium, his century or his legion. This is a man who flaunts the rules. He cares little about those around him. This is a man who cannot take orders and believes that he has the right to shit on those around him. He will not take care of his brothers, he will not take your back and he will run in a fight. This is what we do to men who don't take orders and take care of themselves at the cost of the legion.'

With a whipping motion Brutus brought up his cane and slammed it into Marcus hitting him in the middle of the back. He continued for another nine. The men watched as red welts on his back started to bleed and on the tenth Marcus let out a howl of pain

'From this point on, no one, and I mean no one, talks to this soldier until he changes his ways. For the rest of the time in Caesarea Maritima, he sleeps outside his Conturbenium tent. Any questions?'

The Centurion looked around with a snarl. 'He will eat scraps from the mess tent, after all other men have finished and when we march he marches, at the back, ten steps from the last man. If anyone flouts these orders, I will flay your back worse than this piece of shit below me.'

Albus put the men at ease as Brutus pulled Marcus up by his hair.

'Ovidius Aemilus!' He shouted out. Ovidius walked out stiffly, to stand beside the prostrate form of Marcus. Marcus looked up at him and then at the Centurion. 'Brutus, punish me if you will but it was not Ovidius' fault. He kept urging me to go and I refused.' Marcus croaked and then fell back, pushed angrily by Albus.

Brutus raised his hand, to get the attention of the men before him. 'What was his choice, brothers?' He shouted. 'He had a choice and that was to leave but does one leave when a brother needs assistance? Ovidius drop your pilum and shield and tunic.'

Ovidius gave him an angry look, leaving his shield, pilum and tunic on the ground. Albus pushed him to his knees while Brutus positioned himself with the cane putting ten slashes into his bare back. The sound of the whip could be heard everywhere as the last bit into the flesh of his back. Blood sprayed across the dirt.

'Next time' Brutus said roughly trying to catch his breath. 'You pull your brother out of where ever he is and follow orders. Your friend here caused that whipping and unlike you, he is at the back of the Fifth. Now get back in line.'

Ovidius donned his tunic with a grunt at the pain, picked up his gear and returned to the line.

Albus took his foot away from Marcus' neck as Brutus towered over him. 'Now, you piece of jackal shit. Get up, put on your tunic pick up your gear and get to the back of the file. If you get closer than ten steps from the brothers of this legion, I will whip you until the crows eat your flesh in this dust hole; they call Judea. If I find a man speaking to you I will flay his back as well!'

*

The days of marching continued, with Marcus breathing in the dust, and then eating once everyone else had finished. The sores on his back made it difficult to rest or sleep on his back, and his leather tunic bit into the sores, each time he marched.

Albus, acting under the orders of the Centurion, had taken him on forced marches by himself, up and over the hills with full pack, including rations while Albus ran in a tunic and sandals.

Early the next afternoon, he lay exhausted, bruised, and depressed, outside their large conturbenium tent, on his makeshift bed. It had been over three weeks of silence so no one had spoken to him. He turned on his side to see Ovidius holding a plate to his side.
'You need to eat Marco.' He whispered, dropping a plate with several pieces of meat and a hunk of bread.

'Go away, you must not speak to me, Ovi, otherwise it will be you that gets the beating.'

'Then by the Gods, Marco, apologise.'

Marcus shook his head. 'I will not apologise to that piece of shit. What I did was wrong, but what he did in front of the century, was wrong as well.'

'But, that is life in the army, Marco. You and I were wrong and we paid the price with you paying more than me. You can't fight them all. What is it you don't understand?' Ovidius said with an urgent whisper. 'That is his job, to keep order, and all you do it try to counter it. The next step is jail and you can imagine what that will be like, given this hellhole.'

Marcus shook his head as Ovidius dropped the plate, walking off with a sigh.

Marcus ate the meat hungrily, stowing the plate in his bedding. The late afternoon air, promised a cold night, and the pain he felt each night without the protection of the tent and proper bedding, made his bones ache.

He finally rose from his dirty, outside bed and made his way to the mess tent to get his miserly dinner. He ate it hungrily, thankful that one of the cooks had taken pity on him and given him meat in the stew.

As he was walking back from the latrine towards his tent he pulled his wool tunic tighter, as the chill set in. Before him, the Centurion blocked his way.

Beside him stood Ovidius who raised his eyebrows at Marcus as he approached. 'I brought your mate along because I want to ask you, Attilius if you want to know why you keep getting beaten by me and discarded by your brothers in the legion?' Brutus asked bluntly, as he glared at the two of them standing before him.

The full moon rose above, turned the sand beneath their feet, slowly, into a carpet of silver. Marcus looked at the Centurion with barely disguised disgust.

The Centurion wore a red tunic that barely covered his wide chest and without the battle armour that usually accompanied him during the day. 'The reason is simple.' He continued. 'Both of you have a problem and particularly you, Attilius. You both display arrogance and you don't give a shit about this century or even your miserable lives. We don't put up with that attitude. Pull your words and your behaviour back and we will get along, just fine. How long do you want to tough it out, Attilius?'

Marcus glared at him, with anger rising. 'There is nothing wrong with my attitude. Your attitude, is the problem, Brutus, and the men hate you for it. You go past the requirement of regimentation and move into inflicting pain on others and pleasuring yourself.' Marcus spat the words at him, alternatively watching Ovi's surprised face.

'And that is where you are wrong, boy. My job, is to make sure you all live as long as possible so you can fight another day for the glory of Rome. Your job is to fight for the legion and if that requires hard tack, then so be it.'

'Try a little respect, Brutus, and that may work better.'

He watched as the Centurions face blazed at the rebuke and waited for the response that would surely result. 'You talk about respect, boy? You have no respect for your brothers and then you want me respect you! If you were not so arrogant, I would accuse you of gross stupidity. 'Keep talking Brutus, you are hated more than most.'

'Maybe,' Brutus noted with grunt. 'But then, I have respect and that is what I deserve. You need to be taught a lesson, boy and maybe then you will learn. You are welcome as well, Ovidius.'

Marcus looked at him, his anger rising so he looked at the Centurion with a sneer. 'I have beaten men bigger than you, Centurion.'

Brutus flexed his considerable arms, looking intently at the man before him and then looked casually around him, towards the other tents and latrine area. 'As it happens, we are standing out of sight and I don't have my staff. So, to settle this, let us have a dance.'

Marcus and Ovidius looked at him, at each other and prepared for the fight by moving into fighting position. Fists up and crouched.

The Centurions face smiled lightly, at his own words and he moved towards Marcus with a deliberate movement to take a hold of his tunic and move in. 'However, Attilius, and you Ovidius, if I win, you pull yourself into line, and change. That goes for you Attilius, more than Ovidius.'
'If we win?' Marcus said balling his hands into a fist.

'You won't, but if you do, I will lay off.' Brutus replied.

Marcus darted quickly to one side and brought his left fist into the Centurions hard belly listening as the breath in the man exhaled from the force.

He moved up with his left hand, grabbing the big man's neck, driving another punch into his face before him. Ovidius moved in quickly to support and put his boot into the Centurion's stomach, as the big man went to his knees.

The Centurion grunted and with surprising strength, he stood up and in return, laid a hard punch into Marcus's neck, moving in to knee him hard, into the groin. As Marcus fell, winded from the knee and in intense pain, the Centurion grabbed his hair in one hand and with his right, laid a roundhouse into his jaw. Marcus slumped and went down, unconscious as he hit the hard earth. Blood and spit dripped from his mouth as he lay there.

He then turned to Ovidius, blocking a hard punch as it came around towards him. 'Wrong move, Ovidius.' He said with a loud grunt, and in one motion he swung a hard uppercut lifting him into the air and sending him semi-conscious, to the ground.

Moments later, Marcus woke with a thudding head and sore neck. He felt his jaw realising that several of his teeth were loose. He sighed inwardly. The pain could join the rest of the areas on his body that were racked with soreness and unforgiving hurt.

The Centurion, bent on one knee, looked down at him with a wide smile on his face. 'So, Attilius, you learn another lesson in life. You are not the best fighter in the legion, and you decide to take me on! Either you have not weighed your options, or your stupidity continues, boy, because I was in the midst of battles all over Gaul and the dry lands before you were born. So; Consider yourself lucky.'

He looked down at Marcus who rolled over on his back and tried vainly to get up. He was tired of the fight and tired of fighting the authority that had surrounded him since he joined the legion.

'You will do well to listen to me, boy. You have strength and skill; But, you don't have the common sense of a mule. Are you listening?' Brutus looked down at the man lying on the ground at his feet.

Marcus nodded dumbly as he tried to clear his head and his singing ears.

'You have a choice, Attilius; But not for long. You have a reputation for gambling and whoring, which, maybe you share with others in this legion of soldiers but the difference is you never know when to stop. So, here is some advice. If you want to survive this desert bunghole, take responsibility and use your talents, Given, I might tell you, by the Gods, to improve and not destroy your life. Now, apologise!'

'You don't know anything about my life, Brutus.' Marcus said weakly.

'I know about everyone in this unit, young'un and I know about your life, as well. I can tell by your attitude and your capability and the anger that burns inside. Change, Attilius and your life will change with it. If you don't I will end up beating you to death one day or that anger and stupidity of yours, will get you and maybe me, killed in battle in some forlorn place as we face yet another enemy of Rome.'

The centurion rose from his kneeling position with a slight trace of blood coming from the side of his mouth. 'You hit hard, boy, but not hard enough. You are lucky that I am giving you a choice because not many Centurions in this legion, would give you this chance.' Brutus grabbed him by balls and squeezed hard. He put his face close to his ear. 'Now, let us see if you are good to your word. Apologise, before I smash your face once again and this time it will not be a tap.'

Marcus looked up to the see the Centurions other fist cocked and ready to hit him and he let out a low groan, as the fire in his balls became unbearable. 'Alright, Centurion, I apologise'

Brutus nodded slowly 'Change, boy, and start to lead. If you don't, this desert will be the last thing you will see. At assembly tomorrow morning, you join your conturbenium in the rank and file and you sleep in your tent tonight. If you get out of line again, by the witness of Mars himself, I will beat you until you meet your end and cross the river Styx. Are we agreed?'

Marcus nodded as he half-retched into the ground. 'We are agreed, Centurion.'

The Centurion stood up and put a hard, sandaled kick, into the stomach of Ovidius as he reached him. 'I hope you listened,' He shouted. 'Now, apologise!' He stood over him and waited.

Ovidius finally turned over and looked up at the snarling face of the Centurion. 'You win, Centurion. I apologise.' Brutus spat, on the ground. 'Then that is the end of it.' He walked off towards the tent.

Some minutes later, after the pain had subsided, Marcus rolled over on the dusty earth and took in the view of the stars that were starting to shine, faintly, from above. He grunted as he rose to his knees and crawled over to Ovidius, who was shaking his head, as he formed a crouch in order to try and stand up. 'That man truly hits harder than anything else I have ever experienced.' Marcus nodded, stood up slowly and helped Ovidius rise.

They walked slowly back to the tent line with Marcus holding his groin and Ovidius with a hand on his face. They smiled grimly at each other with Ovidius reaching into his mouth to pull out a tooth, that he calmly flicked onto the ground as they neared the tent.

CHAPTER 23

It was an unusually cloudy day as the legion started a forced march, from the port of *Caesarea Maritima*, towards the city and the siege of Jerusalem. The news circulated that Titus had moved off some days before to check the other legions who were encamped around the holy city. Orders had been passed down, that the Fifth would endure a forced march to make up the legion strength, for the final siege and sacking.

In full armour and pack, the legionaires trotted under the baking sun above. Combined with the heat from the desert floor, the endurance took its toll on them as the army snaked its way out of Caesarea Maritima. In the distance heat shimmers rose from the desert floor and the mountains in the distance held their dry, brown lustre.

'Join this man's army.' Ovidius spat into the dust, one particularly hot morning, as they trotted in line with the rest towards the hills in the distance. Behind him, as the legionaires held their red shields and pilums up, keeping two paces behind the man in front of them, they followed those in front as the line changed course, around obstacles and the winding road, before them.

The march from Caesarea Maritima was to become a trial of hardship as the days, broken only by the shivering cold of the nights started again before sunrise on the long, hot and dusty trudge over the hills, towards the holy city. Centurions and officers rode on horses, while the rank and file such as those before him, marched by foot carrying their kit with them. By the end of each, hot and dusty day, they sank gratefully into the sandy ground for the night.

As Marcus neared the top of one hill, he paused momentarily, as the line in front of him halted to let a cart pass by. He looked back from his position, watching the Fifth legion move across the plain behind him, throwing dust up to the sides and behind it as the carts, pulled by immense bullocks, followed the men.

The legion resembled an immense, scarlet serpent of moving colour as the deep red of the Roman shields inscribed with gold and polished daily, reflected the sun. The line of the walking legionnaires, highlighted the irregular course that over five thousand men were following. Outside the line of the men, the red capes of the officers billowed in the wind, with small eddies of dust crossing the legions as they marched.

At the head of the legion rode the high-ranking officers, followed by the standard bearers, with their colourful flags. The letters of the Roman army, banners decked with the silver medallions of the legion and their histories of war, led the men across the arid, dry land.

SPQR, Senatus Populusque Romans, literally the Roman senate and people, sat high above the legion on banners and staffs as the legion trudged its way across the desert, on the three- week march. In the distance, Marcus and the others could see the bearers of the other banners, the picture of a flying eagle, also framed by gold laurel wreaths, held the number below indicating the legion or the Century that marched behind it.

The standard bearers, each holding golden shields on high lances, marched proudly at the head of the legions; each separated by officers on horses and another, five standard banners behind them.

The venerated Tenth legion, as well as the Fourth and ninth were not in the group. They were already stationed at Jerusalem after holding the city to ransom in the colder and wetter months, at the start of the year.

At the head of the legion sat Titus on a white stallion, with Governor Silva riding beside him. The men of the legions knew Titus held ultimate power and not because of his father, Vespasian, but in spite of him.

Marcus was told by one of the oldest men in his century that Titus, like his father, was renown throughout the legions, as a man who understood the logistics of armies. He was a leader that knew how to inspire his men.

Marcus looked over his shoulder at the legion that followed in the dust and across the broad plain on the way to Jerusalem. They were men he had learnt to regard as brothers-in-arms and men who pursued the glory of Rome.

The legion comprised of ten cohorts of four hundred legionnaires. The legion included six centuries of eighty men and each century included ten conturbenium of eight men. Behind the dust trail kicked up by the legionnaires, followed another one hundred and twenty cavalry horses comprising of messengers and scouts. They were rarely used in battle unless it was an emergency or the Roman legion was in retreat, which was rare and a regarded disgrace.

In the afternoon, the standard bearers set the pace, marching to a grunt every fourth step. The cadence of the grunt, was mimicked by the troops behind them, until the sound flew across the open plains and clearly heard by the scouts, far way on horseback.

Albus seemed to be the man with the most experience in their conturbenium and over the sparse fire they huddled around at night he explained the battle tactics. The soldiers marched in battle at a spaced distance, equal to their own width, to allow the space to throw their pilums and to draw and use their swords.

This *quincunx,* resembled a chess board in battle, using young men in the front row and as each row came into battle and the battle progressed, the more experienced and greater strength of veterans, faced the enemy.

Marcus had begun to understand the Roman ethic and practice of battle formation. The training and drills of the month at the port below Rome and the months at Caesarea Maritima had instilled a discipline that became second nature.

The Fifth legion, under Titus, like all Roman legions, used a standard formation for combat. The troops lined up three lines deep in battle with *Hastati*, who were young and strong but limited experience in battle, followed up by more senior and experienced *Principes* and at the back sat the *Triarii,* who were highly experienced and only brought in when the going became tough or the legion overrun.

All legionaires knew the order of the legion and the army. The youngest and least wealthy became Hastati, the first line of battle in a Roman Legion and the rank held by Ovidius, himself and the rest of the conturbenium.

There was a saying in the legion that Marcus had heard many times, over the months, *ad veteranos*. It was used by the brothers in all kinds of situations, implying that everything else had been tried and found wanting and really said *'for the veterans.'* When the Triarii came into battle, it was a sight to behold.

He had often watched the Triarii in training. Like every other legionnaire, he regarded the experienced shock troops, with some awe and a little jealously. As the battle went forward, the Triarii sat with one knee on the ground, their shields sitting on their front foot, waiting for orders and when they were told to advance they did so, with cold, brutal force.

Each night the engineers, who had gone ahead, set up the camp. Carrying provisions, they set up the meals and encampment requirements which was akin to moving a small city. The only duties the legionnaires held each night was the erecting of tents, cleaning their gear and the boredom of guard duties.

Around Marcus each day he heard the general complaints from the men which were as mundane as they were plaintive. 'Bloody officers. Always in the front and always with the best food. We eat rats and perhaps they should try that for a night.'

'How often does that Centurion have to come down and check. He would be better off taking care of a child.'

'You can't beat a child.'

'He could.' And the laughter would start until the next complaint or an officer appeared on horseback and they all went silent. Just under two weeks later, they bivouacked with the gleaming city of Jerusalem in the far distance. As they came closer on the first day, the city was larger and the buildings and wall taller than Marcus had expected. In the near distance, he could see the myriad of activity by the legions, encamped around the city walls but far enough away from the archers strikes, from the parapets around the holy city.

Late one night, unable to sleep in the tent, Marcus walked outside by the fire looking forlornly into the glowing embers. For the first time, since he had been transported to Judea, he took the time to pause, to reflect and look at his life. The reddening glow of the coals, gave his thoughts comfort.

He sat down beside the fire to enjoy the feeling of engulfing warmth as it radiated across his body. He added a small piece of timber, watching as the sparks flared into the brutally, cold night.

He keenly felt the weight of guilt, about his uncle Tacitus, who had moved quickly to save his nephews life, even at the peril of losing his own position, or worse, ending on the wrong side of Cassius Laurentius and his vengeance.

At his uncles age, jobs were harder to come by and Marcus felt the guilt of allowing Tactius to help him. What choice did he have? His uncle had saved his life and how could one pay that debt?

He thought back to that day at the port and how he and Ovi had stood in the shade of the veranda, listening to the speech by Titus. He understood, perhaps for the first time, the allegiance Titus commanded from his officers and the unwavering commitment each of them showed to Rome, to their legion, Century and Cohort.

It occurred to him, as he gazed into the heat of the coals, that whatever he thought of Brutus, the man was ultimately correct and a man who cared about those in his command. Marcus had disregarded his legion and the men of his conturbenium and that was an unforgivable sin. However, he had learnt, albeit the hard way about the brotherhood and the need for loyalty.

He wondered what his mother might think of him, if she knew where he had ended up on his grand misadventure. Did he now understand the meaning of disgrace? He had walked to Rome, to find his life and ended on the dusty outskirts of Jerusalem, in the Fifth legion with the battle before him.

Ovidius joined him at the fire, also unable to sleep as the frigid air of the desert seeped into their bones. Only the heat from the fire made it bearable. It continued to amaze Marcus, that the ground could be so brutally hot during the day and freeze at night. There was no getting used to it. Around the campfire each night, the usual subjects of past wars, even the subject of officers was discussed in low tones, almost whispers, as it was a punishable offence in the legion. Punishable by a severe beating, or worse.

Ovidius looked around for another log to throw on the diminishing fire and after a little searching found one and threw it onto the glowing coals, watching as sparking embers flew off into the night sky, only to disappear under the stars.

There was very little wood in the area and the fire before them came from spare timber used for the construction of the forts and battering rams built for the immediate sacking of the holy city, glowing eerily in the distance.

They had stolen what timber they could find that day and built the fire in a pit so it could not be easily seen. The unit camped on the dusty land above the Mount of Olives, waiting for the final orders for the siege.

'This land is a shithole, of no use to anyone.' Ovidius said to Marcus as he wrapped his fur coat around him against the brutally cold wind that, at least, fanned the flames.

'I agree with you, brother, and the only person who seems to enjoy this bunghole is Titus and that is because his daddy has told him to be here.'

225

'The rich and famous.' Ovidius replied.

Marcus rubbed some of the sand between his fingers. If the heat from the Roman sun beat relentlessly in the middle of the hot months it was nothing compared to the brown aridness that lay around them.

The dry, dusty and waterless land was even more irritating, as there was not one part of his person or weaponry, that was not coated in the fine dust that adorned their feet like a brown dye.

It even coated his sweating forehead during the long, hot days showing streaks, as the rivulets of sweat traced down his face from the helmet he wore. Water was scarce so washing themselves was kept to a minimum.

He looked over at Ovidius, one of the seven soldiers of his Conturbenium sitting before him on the dry, dusty ground. He listened momentarily, to the light bitching about the food they endured, as he sat by the fire.

As he looked across at the man he called a friend, he knew he could not ask for braver or more resourceful man, to fight the battles that would surely come. The eighth member of their squad had died in Caesarea of a fever. The physicians had tried everything but he had died and they waited on a replacement.

The one lesson Marcus had learned in the legion, usually painfully from long lasting sores, was the formation of the squad and how much it mattered. Life in the Roman army based itself on hardship, friendship and more than a little skill when the fight became bloody.

The Conturbenium, the smallest and most intimate team in the legion, each comprising of eight soldiers, made the difference between a new beginning or the end of life. He finally understood, it was not the legion or the century that made up the brotherhood of the army. Loyalty and care lay in the spectre of life and death, in the embodiment of comradeship, within the squads in every legion and known as the conturbenium.

In that lesson, as well, Brutus had been correct. Trust and support in battle, came from forged friendships in the conturbenium. Your brother protected your back and you protected theirs.

During the day, above the wall, Marcus could see the parapet outlines where archers, bows poised, loaded their vengeance on the Roman legions as they prepared to assault the walls. One day the Ninth and the Tenth had retreated under the pressure of an attack by the Jewish soldiers, when they ventured too close to the wall.

The Jewish defenders waited for the working men to come close and the tactic was to allow them near so they could unleash their firepower. The tactic, so angered the tenth, that during a skirmish the next day they could hardly take a Jewish prisoner, rather than run a sword through them for revenge.

Those two eventful days, had taught the legions a very valuable, and costly lesson, in the life of over sixty legionaires. The two previous days created a disaster and there was little doubt that Titus had spent, at the very least, that night to review tactics. Like all generals, he was concerned about the loss of men, but the siege would go on.

The Jews did not play by Roman rules. They moved in small bands, on the run from small doors, leading from the outer wall of the city. They ambushed, retreated and ambushed again. They were not weighed down by the Roman battle dress the men were required to wear. They wore light coloured garb, moving quickly without the use of horses or heavy weaponry.

Roman battle tactics, confined to the use of the heavy infantry legions, and swift cavalry, gained the most success when confined to open field and siege warfare. In Judea, it was different. The heat and ground did not encourage Romans tactics and the skirmishes by the Jews had caught them unaware several times, at the cost of considerable casualties.

Titus, like his father before him, spent many hours in front of his men to talk of his plans. He regularly moved through the encampment of his men, aware that there was consternation as to the tactics and speed of the Jewish infantry. He felt an explanation of the Roman response would best come from him.

There were a number of occasions, where Titus had ambled by the fire where Marcus and Ovidius sat and took the time to sit and speak, soldier to soldier and share his thoughts with the Conturbenium, as they rested after a hard day's work in assisting the building of the huge siege machines. Titus, clothed in a simple tunic would politely ask to sit down and spent the time to share a meal. He ate little, and no more or less than they. Each time he would rise with some humble thanks and saunter off to another campfire and another conversation.

Marcus, like all of the legionaires loved the stout and humorous general, who sat with them, away from the opulence and food of the officer's tent, to speak to them about their thoughts and his plans. Titus, like all great generals, understood his men. There was a rumour that he was not well liked in Rome but on the field the men respected him.

CHAPTER 24

The next morning, Marcus, who had been appointed as the Decanus, by Brutus, moved slowly down the hill below the Mount of Olives carrying timber with the rest of his squad. It was to be used in the building of the final fort ordered by Titus the previous day.

The work was mundane and boring and his men grumbled, as they completed the bidding of the engineers, who roamed around the fort site with their rulers, plans and persistent nagging.

Some hours later they broke for lunch which was provided at the back of camp within the copious number of olive trees, that dotted the terrain and had already been picked clean of fruit.

Bread and barley soup comprised the meal and with the hunger created by the work that morning they sat contentedly on the tent line, to finish their bowls. Below the hill and across the short, brown plain, lay the city, shining and beckoning to the invaders who camped around three sides of the city walls but far enough away to be free of arrows let loose from the top of the walls. The fourth side of the city offered a deep ravine beneath and it remained free of embattlement.

One of the engineers with muddy feet and a harassed look on his face walked past. 'There is more timber to be taken to the lower level of the fort and we need to lay the foundations by nightfall. Make sure you are ready to move.'

Marcus looked over at Sextus and Ovidius and smiled broadly. 'You have been told, boys.'

The smiles came back as a commotion started from down the bottom of the hill. As they looked down, they could see Jewish soldiers in the distance pouring out of a heavy oak door, at the bottom of the Eastern wall.

As they exited in numbers from the door, they raised their swords and voices moving towards the soldiers working on the fort, not more than a long javelin throw from the wall structure.

Another shout gained their attention as Brutus came thundering through the tent line and down towards his men. 'Time to dance, boys' he called out. 'Grab your swords and shields and follow me. No time for armour. Attilus, group your men.'

Quickly and without panic the men grabbed their swords and shields from their position near the tent and moved down the hill, following the Centurion as he ran down to the melee at the front of the fort.

Jewish soldiers continued to emerge from the wall opening and moving in mass towards the half-built fort. They were chanting, as they met the first line of Roman men, who were not armed and were starting to retreat up the hill.

The Jewish infantry hit the front line of Romans with force, slashing and killing, overrunning the stragglers as the sheer numbers forged through the line, in an arrow formation to start up the incline.

The Jewish force of soldiers followed a single man who sprinted before them, into the midst of the Roman defence line which hurriedly moved to formation when they saw the Jewish soldiers moving in force, across the open ground to fight.

The man stood tall, with long black hair and a full beard, which was streaked with blood and by the time Marcus neared him he had downed two men and was fighting with two others. His eyes shone as he moved deftly through the battle, with a sword in his right hand and a dagger in his left, fighting with skill and force.

As Marcus and his squad reached the fight, the deafening sound of battle assaulted their ears. Shouts and sword clashes, drowned out any orders coming from officers, and the sheer number of the Jewish force fell so heavily on the Roman legionaires that they were forced to step back, against the tide of screaming, grunting, sword-wielding men.

Marcus instinctively knew that the skirmish would end badly. It did not suit the Roman form of combat, which was orderly and relied on heavy suited soldiers in broad formation against enemies, that fought the same fight.

The Jewish soldiers were different, they fought without cumbersome weight and they seemed intent to die in the effort. He stopped briefly as he shunted a spear away from him, stunned, as the Jewish soldiers mercilessly cut down the forward legionaires in their path and even those Roman soldiers on the ground were knifed and beheaded.

Within a short space of time, the battle raged until it reached a standstill with the Romans using the higher ground to advantage. However, they were against greater numbers of Jews, who fought ferociously and with significantly higher numbers of men. Marcus turned to find Roman archers behind the battle line firing bolts into the oncoming Jews, as fast as they could, but the numbers kept surging. Amidst the screams and grunts of pain, Marcus looked to find Brutus who had disappeared into the bloody melee.

As he stood in the middle of the breech with the Roman infantry head-to-head against the Jewish force, he realized no training or preparatory instruction could prepare any recruit for the bloodshed that surrounded him on that early afternoon.

On the other side of the breech, within the grunting, screaming mass around him, his vision held the blades of swords and spears points that surged from the enemy against them, time and time again. When one surge fell back, another phalanx of swords, clubs and spears entered the line yet again from the other side. Men against men, shield against clashing shield they screamed from the pain and from the sheer terror of the maelstrom in front of them.

For some reason, he could not explain, he felt an extraordinary calm in the face of the brutality around him. If he was never to be a farm hand or pursue a more, lofty occupation he realized at that instant he was made to fight and fight, he could do very well. Perhaps it was the lure of the savage dance before him or the constant surge of adrenalin but the tougher the fight became the more he excelled at the pursuit of killing. In a momentary gasp he realized he had found an occupation in which he excelled.

He moved forward into the battle line, urging his squad to advance around him as they used the force of their shields to move forward. At the front, he slashed and fought against the oncoming spear ends and sword blades slapping and thrusting, against the heavy metal of his shield, and off his helmet. The sound of metal against metal and the sound of men falling to the earth as the battle reached fever pitch drowned out any other sound, even their own breathing.

He heard Ovidius grunt loudly and turned to find him with his hands around the throat of one, not even noticing the sword cut on his left arm. Marcus turned and drove his sword though the Jews torso, watching in slow motion as Ovidius kept his hands on the man's throat to the reddened earth below.

230

The grunts and shouts of the men, as they wielded their swords, came into focus as he found Sextus next to him fighting into the middle of the line.

He glanced momentarily to his left and all he could see were the screaming shapes of the enemy, pouring forth from the direction of the wall. In turn, each man of the Roman legion sank their feet into the sandy earth below, shields forward to take a stance against the impact that surged and waned and then surged again. Above the clash of steel, as swords and spears connected with brutal contact, the whinnying of horses could be heard from the side of the battle line.

Every time Marcus took a man down another took his place and he was starting to tire. 'They fight hard.' Sextus said breathlessly, with his sword dripping with blood, from his last kill. 'There are too many. What now? Do we retreat?'

Marcus tried to speak but with the onslaught of swords against him he could do nothing but brace against the oncoming attack and wait for reinforcements. Here and there, he could hear the cries of the horses above the sound of battle, deafening and alarming as the beasts came close into the skirmish with wide eyed terror.

He looked down at the ground which was awash with red and the gore of the battle. The pungent smell of blood and gore gave way to the realisation they would not win the fight with the number of Jews against them. They were losing ground and with the force of men pushing against him he could no longer hold his feet on the line.

He looked around for Brutus, who he finally saw across the skirmish, some fifteen deep and fighting his way forward with Sextus who had moved off in that direction. Marcus changed course, hacking his way across to where Brutus stood and taking two of the conturbenium with him.

Suddenly, in front of him he encountered the leader of the Jewish force, screaming at his men to move forward. He looked over at Brutus who had dropped his shield as he was hit across the head by a club and only his helmet saved him from dying from the full force of the blow. As he staggered to his knees with blood pouring from beneath his helmet, Sextus pulled him up by the arm and pushed him backwards, into the Roman line behind him.

As Brutus started to stumble back, he raised his arm as he shouted out to Marcus. 'Get him, that is Simon of the Jews, kill him.'

Marcus glanced over his shield only to duck again as a spearhead came over the top of his scutum, breaking in pieces as it fell to the ground. He moved forward, towards the tall man who used his sword with such force.

He slashed his sword towards Simon's legs who deftly sidestepped in the middle of the fracas using his sword to deny the blow. He moved quickly, bringing his sword down on top of Marcus's shield, with a strike of such force that it ripped the cord from the inside of the shield, nearly sending it to the ground.

In such close proximity to their leader, Marcus felt the surge from both sides of the Jewish line to defend him. He was under attack from the centre and even with Sextus back at his side, the force was too great and slowly, inexorably the Jewish forces were pushed back and the surge of battle changed.

Each time, Marcus held the front with his men, by digging their hob-nailed sandals into the blood-soaked earth but each time they were pushed back by the force of the Jewish soldiers, only to try and hold their ground again.

The ebb and surge of the battle went on to the point that Marcus had lost the sense of time or self. As the men at the front of the battle on either side, were run through or injured, others fell to their knees in exhaustion.

The ground beneath them was a blood-stained morass of those who had fallen from wounds or gained death from the onslaught. Through the haze of his hard breathing, Marcus looked down to see he was ankle deep in gore.

Marcus tried to pick up one man from the ground, as they retreated several steps, but the man simply shook his head and fell back to the ground to be speared by a Jewish soldier as he passed over him. He heard the sickening scream, as the spear strike entered and moving with greater speed than he thought possible he plunged his gladius into the side of the man, watching as he sank in front of him to the ground.

He looked to his right, to see Arius fighting against a giant of a man, using a club head to smash against his shield and drive him back into the line. A final blow broke Arius' shield and with a loud grunt, the man pulled his dagger, thrusting it into Arius's neck and the boy went down.

'No' Marcus screamed as he moved towards Arius with Sextus taking up the fight to his left. By the time he reached the boy, he was bleeding to death from a deep wound and collapsing to the ground. Marcus pulled

Arius by the arm and pushed him back towards the Principes behind him, as they, in turn, pulled him to the back of the battle line.

Marcus surged forward towards the giant and moving his shield to the left he brought his sword up to strike, only to feel the full force of the club head on his damaged shield. The man was laughing hysterically, speaking in gibberish, blood soaked from head to toe. The club head rounded again, and struck his shield on the side smashing it out of his hand.

Marcus pulled his dagger and ripped it into the man's belly with as much force as his waning strength could muster. With his remaining strength, he forced the knife strike up and into the man's shoulder watching with some satisfaction as the giant fell to his knees. Sextus finished him with a sword to the neck.

His arm felt numb from the effort of the continual sword strikes and with his right-side dripping with his enemy's blood, Marcus looked again for Brutus, who he finally found unconscious on the ground behind him. Suddenly, Ovidius with blood streaming down his face from a sword cut on his forehead grabbed Marcus's arm.

'The cavalry' He said breathlessly. 'Are coming through.'

'About bloody time.' Marcus said trying to get his breath back, as two soldiers beside him took up the fight directly in front.

Within a moment, horses and riders appeared towards the right of the skirmish, riding through the morass of soldiers and animals standing and lying prone, dead or severely injured on the gore of the desert floor. In an effort to get the centurion out of the way, Marcus turned and pulled the dead weight of Brutus to his knees and passed him back to the second line.

The Jewish skirmishers saw the cavalry coming through the right flank. They raised their spears directly into the neck of the oncoming horses, to bring them down and take the rider with it. With the terrifying sound that came from the throats of the speared horses and the Roman riders hitting the ground around them Marcus and his men continued their attack into the melee, trying to hold the battle position.

The sound of horrified horses, whinnying, neighing and rearing against their attackers, their eyes glazed in horror at the carnage overcame any other sound in the battle. With deep wounds rented into their necks by the Jewish soldiers, the frantic sound of confusion and pain increased until it was impossible for Marcus to hear his own breath or his words.

'This must be the entrance to Hades' He shouted to Ovidius, but there was no reply.

The crescendo increased as the effort became close to unbearable, with the shouts and grunts of the men across the battle floor and the wailing horses, drastic and violent. The clash of men and swords rose up and across the Mount of Olives and could be heard above the walls within the enclosed holy city.

Marcus made another surge into the melee, centring himself in front of Simon, and again their swords collided but this time, as he pushed his numb right arm forward, he caught Simon across the shoulder. The blade dug in to leave a gash in the man's upper arm as he fended another blow on the other side of the line, from Ovidius.

At that moment, the line of Jewish soldiers surged against Marcus once again pushing him to the ground. He instinctively covered himself with a shield that lay next to him and in the next instant, he felt a spear strike into his calf. He shouted with pain and tried to rise against the force of the men in front of him, pulled up by those in support to the rear.

Above him, passed the first flash of a cavalry horse, as they moved further into the melee watching, as the rider, a man in a red tunic, fell heavily to the earth next to him. Within a moment, two Jewish soldiers were on him, with a spear that missed the man's head by a dagger width. Momentarily, Marcus started to rise and he and the other fallen rider looked at each other with amazement.

'Lord Titus!' Marcus said breathlessly.

Titus rose up at the same time. 'Throw me a sword.'

With his strength strapped and adrenalin pulsing through his body, Marcus rose to his feet, dropped the broken shield, picked up a sword that lay point down onto the blood-soaked earth and threw it across to where Titus stood.

Using the sword, he picked up from the ground, Marcus brought its bloodied blade up into the belly of the first attacker, and then with a backhand motion, struck across the second, finally severing him at the neck. He used his dagger forcing it into the neck of the next man who moved towards Titus and then he was grabbed by a hand he could not see. Sprayed blood blinded his eyes, and the next instant he felt a heavy fist driving into his jaw.

He went down momentarily, only to see the man in the red tunic rise and reach for his horse which appeared shaky and with blood seeping out of its nostrils. The man leapt up, as two more skirmishers made their way across to the horse.

One grabbed the bridle as Marcus rose again with a shivered spear in his left hand that had laid in the mud beside him and clubbed the Jewish soldier holding the bridle. He instinctively speared the other in the groin, before falling semi unconscious to the ground against a dead Jewish soldier. He looked up groggily to see Ovidius grab the top of his breastplate and drag him bodily back through the lines.

In the next moment, he saw the cavalry again break through the Jewish advance and with over four hundred horses moving through the battle line, the Jewish soldiers started to show panic and uncertainty. Slowly, the back lines retreated and the rest started to quickly follow.

Marcus rose to his feet unsteadily to chase them, but as he tried to pick up a sword that lay at his feet, he fell to his knees in utter exhaustion. His body lay covered in dripping and congealed blood. His sword arm so tired, he could not lift it, let alone a sword.

In the distance, he could see the total retreat, as the Jewish skirmishers made their way back to the wall, and the safety of the archers who sat on the parapets waiting for the Romans to come in range.

The Roman battle line around Marcus fell to the ground, as the cavalry chased forward. Behind them lay carnage, that stretched over a third of the plain between the half-built fort and the walls of the white city. The area at the bottom of the mount of Olives lay a wasted, blood drenched area with dying men screaming and groaning on the ground. Dismay set in as the Romans looked at the broken, bloodied bodies of their brothers who had fallen that afternoon and they started the task of rescuing those who lay, still alive, on the sand.

The line retreated up the hill, with Sextus assisting Marcus, to the back of the fort. There was a broad, bleeding gash on his lower calf and as he sat down on the ground. The only memory that sat heavily in his mind was the picture of Arius as he lay there bleeding with a bewildered look in his eyes.

'Arius' Marcus croaked to Ovidius who sat down heavily beside him. His face, like all of those around him, was encrusted with blood and gore from the battle.

Sextus dropped his sword to the ground beside him. The blade was pitted and cracked. He shook his head 'I think he was dead before he was passed back.'

Marcus nodded and for the second time since he was a very small boy tears filled his eyes, which he swatted away with his hand. 'We should have saved him'

Ovidius patted him on the shoulder. 'We all had men back there we wanted to save but there was no time. We have lost a brother and that is the end of it. We have survived.'

Sextus was grinning through a mass of blood on his face still sheeting down from the cut above his eye. 'Now that was a dance, eh? 'Marcus grabbed Ovidius' arm 'Thanks brother.' He fell back against the earth, finally rising to grab a ladle of water as it was passed around and after greedily gulping as much as he could, he fell back again and passed out.

Moments later, he was woken by a hand shaking his shoulder. He looked up to see Sextus who was pointing to a man standing before them. His red tunic, stained with blood was standing slightly downhill. 'We meet again, soldier' He said quietly.

Marcus looked at him for a moment without recognition. 'It's Titus, you idiot' Sextus whispered to him. 'Get up!'

Marcus looked at Sextus and then started to rise. The man came over to him and gently pushed him back down on his rump.

'In the battle, young man, you saved my life and I give you thanks. I am sure you saved others by the way you fight and in turn, yours was saved. Did you lose any?'

'One' Marcus said solemnly. 'I could not get to him in time.'

Titus nodded sombrely 'It is always the greatest loss when we lose one of ours. My name is Titus, and I shall remember you. What is your name?'

'Marcus, sir, Marcus Attilius.'

Titus smiled thinly. 'I am not a sir, boy. Titus is my name. To you and all.' He walked stiffly down the hill to address the exhausted men.

'Brothers, hear me.' Titus shouted at the top of his voice, so that the hundreds of men sitting and lying on the sloping ground of the Mount of Olives could hear him. 'We have underestimated the Jews, my brave Roman brothers, and they have won this day but we will prevail and we will take them to heel' Titus shifted his position, raising his arms to gain their attention. Even the badly injured raised as far as they could, to hear his voice.

'You have proven yourselves today and the Fifth has, yet again, earnt it reputation as the hardest fighting men in Rome. Rest, heal and be ready as soon as you can, for tomorrow we start the siege, that will bring the Jews down. Forget Rome, forget your woman or your bellies. Follow me and I will take you through all three walls and we will rid this country of those who take the mistaken decision not to submit to Rome.'

He raised his hands up several times as the cheers started and momentarily he had mounted his horse and waited for the noise to subside.

'Men of the legions, we have the enemy behind the walls and when we get through there are two we must seek out and capture. You will understand who they are when you see them by their bearing and the way they are protected. They are Simon of Gioras and John of Giscala. Simon of Gioras was in that fight today. There is one hundred gold coins for anyone who captures either of them. Two hundred,' he added, 'if you catch both, because both will die on the steps of Rome!'

Marcus, resting on his elbows waited until Titus had finished his speech; he fell back against the grassy patch with the late afternoon heat rising from the earth warming his body with his eyes on the cloudless sky above.

The physician of the legion made his way through the men. Inspecting, prodding and ordering his assistants to conduct the tasks he deemed necessary. When he got to Marcus, he inspected the gash in his calf, muttering to himself, he then called one of the orderlies over.

'Why was this man not bound?' The orderly shrugged his shoulders as the doctor eyed him with a steely glare.

'Where is your tent, soldier?' Before Marcus could answer Ovidius turned his head to point at the tent line at the top of the Mount of Olives. 'At the top' He added sombrely wiping his bloodied face with a proffered cloth.

237

The physician turned his attention back to Marcus. He grabbed a flask of olive oil and poured it into the wound. He then pulled a long metal needle and thin gut from his bag and proceeded to stitch the gash, which was deep and as wide as his calf muscle. Once he had finished the stitches, he bound the wound, tied it tightly and probed several of the visible cuts he found on his upper body.

He pulled another flask and lifted it while Marcus drank. 'That will take some of the pain away but that is a deep wound and there is no movement, until the stitches have bound the flesh, otherwise it will open up again.'

Marcus grimaced with pain as he spoke. The physician looked briefly in his mouth and pulled a small lump of wax from his tunic, softened it with his hands and placed it inside Marcus's mouth where the lacerations and loose tooth sat.

'Bite slowly on this and keep your jaw in that position until tomorrow morning. You will be off that leg for some while so report to the sick tent. I will be in to see you in the morning.' Marcus nodded grimly feeling the wax form a solid piece in his mouth and binding his jaw together.

The doctor smiled grimly at him moving to a soldier groaning on the ground near where Sextus sat waiting on treatment for his injury.

The soldiers leg had been severed at the knee and as he watched the doctor applied a second tourniquet and poured what looked like molten wax to the bottom of the stump to stop the bleeding.

The man shouted out in pain, grabbing fiercely onto the men next to him as the wax was applied and finally his head hit the ground unconscious with his teeth imbedded in the olive branch that had been placed in his mouth so he could bite against the pain.

Around Marcus, men were tended and taken away and finally two attendants came to pick him up. He moved to a sitting position and from there on the Mount of Olives he could see clearly where he had stood not so long before.

The brown earth of the plain below showed deep rents where the battle lines formed and where his conturbenium had fought the Jews to a standstill.

Broad patches of blood reddened earth, the significant evidence of the cost of many lives in the skirmish, rendered blooms like petals of a huge flower where the battle had begun and finished before the city.

As he watched, a swirling eddy created a sand storm that confined itself to an area near the West wall. It blew up and over the fortification, only to diminish and disappear as if it never happened.

The holy city, bathed in the soft white of the disappearing afternoon sun made its presence felt. He turned to Sextus who lay back exhausted on the sloping ground trying to massage feeing into his cramping right hand.

'They fight for their God' Marcus said as the men grabbed him by the arms to assist him to the sick tent. 'We fight for glory'

'Perhaps we have all misjudged their only God. No wonder they want to defend it, just as we would defend Mount Olympus.'

'Then they may win.'

Ovidius rose painfully from his sitting position with a straightened back as he leant gingerly to pick up his sword and shield. 'That thought occurred to me as well, Marco, but either way they will defend like their future depends on it. Which it does.' He added haughtily. 'Heal well, brother and let us fight another day.'

Marcus limped away to the sick tent and as he painfully moved along with assistance he looked back at the city for a final time that day. For the first time since his arrival in Judea, he knew they were laying siege to a city built by men, who loved their God.

CHAPTER 25

Some days later, from a distance, came the unmistakable cadence of the battering rams against the outside wall. As the metal heads smashed into the wall, at the Northern end of the holy city, he could hear the sound of falling rock. Some while later, the loud cadence returned as the metal head slammed into the wall to weaken the surface.

Each blow was followed by an eerie silence, then it would start again.

All three towers contained metal headed rams, winched back from their forward position to a point, thirty steps away, only to be released against the wall on a pendulum. Once the ram hit the wall it was winched back into position, and the ram let loose to swing back onto the wall surface again, and again, and again.

Each time the ram hit the wall, the reverberation could be heard across the area outside of the city and more so to the North and East. Each time the ram was winched back, engineers inspected the wall from the safety of the rampart, to note the damage and make adjustments.

The orderlies of the sick tent had become the messengers of the day, telling all who would listen that this time the engineers had built siege towers, more than the height of four houses on top of each other, and two wide.

The front cladding of the siege tower was protected to stop the arrows, sent fruitlessly down from the archers above, and they had fireproofed the front with metal adornments.

The siege had started in earnest and all legions, put on notice of the coming breech. With the siege machines slowly positioned in place by horses and men who pushed the structures from the back, the news was passed early that morning, by one of the orderlies that one of the rams had broken through the back wall. When the Fourth legion started to advance, they were repelled by the Jewish forces and the wall rebuilt from the inside, even as the last Roman was pushed away.

Titus changed tactics, increasing the number of siege machines to four. The Tenth, the most famous of all the legions was given the orders, that the next insurgency inside the wall would be instigated within the week. Prisoners were not to be taken. If the Jews would not submit to Roman rule, they would pay the price.

The following week, as Marcus tenderly rubbed the wound on his calf, they could all hear cheers coming up from the Northern wall. They nodded to each other as they knew the breech had been made. This time, the Tenth, would be entering the first wall.

Judging from the numbers of men who invaded the sick tent, taking Marcus's bed as well, the losses were more than expected and yet again there was a tinge of despondency in the air. The grumbling of the men who entered the sick tent, gave an understanding of the level of resistance the soldiers inside the city were prepared to hold. They fought hard and ruthlessly and gave not a footstep, without a fight.

By the end of the second week, Marcus was able to stand with the assistance of a strong staff, fashioned to sit under his arm and allow him to hobble around the tent and to the latrines when the he needed.

His jaw healed within several days and the wax had been removed. Each morning, with a little effort, he left the tent to stand outside and look down at Jerusalem in the distance. He leaned against his staff as he spoke to one of the legionaries who lay on one of the stretchers, with a deep wound to his leg.

'Let me tell you, brother, those men can fight.' He said, as he waited for the physician to arrive. One of the attendants had wrapped his wound tightly.

'I met them below the Mount two weeks ago.'

The soldier nodded knowingly. 'Ah, I heard about that dance; We lost a lot of the boys that day.'

'And today?' Marcus asked shifting on his support. His leg was healing but his leg reacted, as he shifted weight.

'Not sure, brother, but it must have been in the hundreds yet again. Titus and his father must have a reason for this siege but it has been worse, a lot worse than any of us expected.'

'So, I hear' Marcus replied.

'The next wall will be a bitch.' The man said with gritted teeth, as he grabbed his leg to alleviate his pain. 'The real problem remains, that they hold the keys to the kingdom. If we are not fighting them on the ground, we have a thunderstorm of arrows from above and when we concentrate on the archers we get hit from below. This will not end well, my friend, not well at all.'

'When do we go in again.'

'Each day we breech, until we finally open that inner wall. Then, by the law of Jupiter we will make them pay.'

'Attilius?' An attendant called out from the tent opening. Marcus nodded, patted the man on the shoulder and hobbled out of the tent.

'Centurion Brutus wants to see you at the officer's tent.'

Marcus raised his eyebrows and took his time, to walk stiffly and with the aid of the crutch, to the tent on the other side of the camp. He had not seen the Centurion since the battle and despite the care of the doctors, he had only seen Ovidius briefly on one day, when he came to make fun of the holiday Marcus was having in the tent.

He found Brutus sitting outside the tent drinking a cup of mead. It was late in the afternoon and the heat was subsiding. Brutus stood as he hobbled up and drew up a stool beside him so Marcus could sit down. He gave Marcus a cup of honey mead wine and scratched his beard before he spoke.

'How fares it, Attilius?'

Marcus smiled thinly as he sat heavily on the stool. 'Better each day, *Centuro*' He replied using the more familiar word that noted a sub-officers rank.

'I am better as well. You and your boys fought well the day in front of the fort. I am proud of all in the group.'

Marcus looked at him in surprise at his gratuity. Brutus looked at him with an even eye 'Even Centurions can be humble, Attilius, we lost one hundred and eighty-three, that day.'

'Arius' Marcus replied grimly, with a look of disappointment on his face. He could not hide it and the sadness in him surfaced.

'Not your fault, boy.' Brutus said roughly. 'There is no fault in battle except loss and on that day, we lost and we paid heavily for it. We will have our retribution soon enough.' Marcus raised his cup and clinked it against the Centurions as they sat in silence for a while.

Brutus was the first to speak 'I hear from the Optio that you and your conturbenium will be promoted to the second line and as you are no doubt aware, that carries a different sort of responsibility. You fight well, Attilius and when you get this change you will need to choose one of your other men, to take a second-in-command role, and preferably someone who can hold their line in battle. Try to remember, even in your thick skull that at your age and experience, being promoted to *Principes* is high recognition.'

'I do, Centurio and perhaps you showed me some sense.'

'It gives me some satisfaction that our personal dance made a difference but you still have much to learn, Attilius. If you keep up the capability to fight the way you do, you may make Triarii.'

Marcus looked at the man before him with a sense of detached fondness, for someone who had helped shape his life with surprise. 'Really?'

Brutus nodded and clicked his cup against Marcus as they drank. 'The tenth will hold the Mount of Olives against attack and the fifth fight tomorrow on the understanding that the siege rams get through the central part of the wall. I have witnessed a few sieges in my time but I have yet to experience one like this. Whoever built this fucking fort or a city knew how to build a wall. The Jews know their city, and we don't and that is not a good combination. When will you be back in action?'

'Perhaps a week I am told. The wound opened again the other day and the doctor is now talking about hot poultice.'

The Centurion let out a low whistle and lifted his leather skirt to show a white gash across his knee. 'That was given the hot wax and let me be the first to advise you, Attilius; You had better be hanging onto something at the time!'

'Like a beautiful woman?'

Brutus laughed heartily and slapped Marcus on the shoulder. 'Yes, something like that.'

Early that evening, Marcus made his way to the tent he usually shared with his squad only to find them missing.

He made his way slowly to the mess tent and finally found them, sitting outside on logs as they ate from their bowls. He waited for them to finish and motioned for them to follow him to the tent.

Ovidius, his wounds all but healed, still complained as they had been sent on training march that afternoon, for no good reason. The men were dressed in march gear ensuring the *Caligae*, the sandals on their feet were done up well against the fine dust that seeped into all they held dear to their lives.

Once they were finished and the bowls returned, the grumbling continued as each hefted the weight of their breastplate, shield, Gladius and dagger. They picked up their pilum, helmet and their rations pack before heading off to their tent and a welcome fire.

Titus had ordered fires to be lit each night to ensure the Jewish soldiers knew the Romans were outside the gates and waiting. The fire blaze diminished and the small talk of forced marches and arrogant officers, finally slowed. 'I met with the Centurio this afternoon. There was good news was good for a change. We have been made Principes and we move to the second line at the next battle. It appears that our stand at the fort, has made us something close to heroes.'

Sextus stood up by the fire to stretch his legs. 'Well, this is welcome news and might I add we deserve it do we not?' Ovidius and the others applauded his words and then settled, as Marcus kept speaking.

'We are to get a replacement but it will take some time. I believe they have new blood coming through from Caesarea, but when will they arrive? 'Ovidius;' He said pointing a finger at him. 'They have asked for a second-in-command. I have put your name forward and that means you will have to take on some responsibility with the boys.'

There were laughs around the fire as he finished his words and several claps on the back to give congratulations for the role.

Marcus looked around the fire at the six men before him. Ovidius and Sextus sat together. Vanu, Enius, the largest of the group and without doubt the best with a sword.

Next to him sat Lucanus who sat on one side and one of the newer recruits, a freed slave by the name of Felix sat on the other side had joined them a week before.

'I am told the fifth will breech the wall, just as soon as the rams gain the

---

entrance and that could be as close as tomorrow. If I could walk I would join you but I am told I cannot try at this stage, as the wound is not healing.'

'Too much mead in the sick tent, I suppose.' Sextus said quietly with guffaws around him.

Marcus looked at the man and his mind flashed back instantly to his friend in Rome and the time they spent together when he had arrived in the capital. It was a time that felt so long ago, he could hardly remember it.

'So, it is congratulations to all of us and my direction at this time is to get well and join you in battle. I will let you know if and when, the new recruit comes. Farewell brothers.'

The men murmured their farewells as Marcus hobbled off to the sick tent. When he got there, the physician was there waiting for him.

'Where have you been?' He asked sternly 'With my men, doctor, where else might I be?'

'Hiding, I might have hoped. We need to cauterise that wound, soldier and there is no time like the present. Lay down on the bunk, face downwards and put this in your mouth.' He offered him a soft piece of wood to place between his teeth. The physician undid the binding on his leg and inspected the wound and the broken stitches. 'You have not stayed off his leg as I asked. Have you?'

Marcus mumbled 'I may have walked more than I should.'

The doctor nodded and indicated to the attendant to boil the liquid. 'Then you will pay.' He said blandly to anyone who was listening. He gently removed the broken gut stitches from the wound, wiped it out without listening to the grunts coming from the man on the bunk beneath him and applied a thin stream of olive oil, into the wound and wiped it again. Blood was starting to flow again so he held a new cloth against the wound to staunch it.

Several minutes later, Marcus could smell the same stench he remembered on the sloping ground of the Mount, on the late afternoon of the battle. He started to twitch when the physician moved around to see his face.

'Do not move!' He commanded, as he bound the sides of the wound and in an instant Marcus felt a pain he had never experienced as the hot wax poultice was poured onto the open wound. With quick movements that spoke of expertise, the physician let his attendant pull the wound together as he started to bind the wound again using larger stitches away from the original stitch line.

'Now stay in that position for the rest of the night and you do not walk for five days and then it should have bound together. Any questions?' Marcus could hardly raise a grunt against the invading pain on his leg, so he just clenched his teeth and nodded.

The doctor continued 'We are under orders to get as many of you back to the wall as we can but you have lost muscle so once you can get up, you are to return to your squad and continue training.'

Marcus nodded grimly waiting for the intense pain to subside.

CHAPTER 26

Three days later Marcus witnessed, yet again, the bedraggled, badly injured forms of legionaries who had been ambushed by the Jewish forces, when they entered the second wall. One of the men lying on a makeshift bunk spoke to an orderly as Marcus listened.

'A very bad day, brothers. The Jews built a tunnel under the wall, and all the way out, until they were underneath the siege towers. The earth sank, taking the siege towers with it and then those cunning bastards, set alight the struts in the tunnel to burn the machines. The resulting fires burnt all three siege machines and before we knew it we were under attack once again. I hear that Titus will now put forward another three machines and continue the battering of the second wall.'

One of the returning men who listened, with blood covering his upper body and a deep arm wound, sat back against the tent wall waiting for treatment. He called out as he waited.

'We have them boys, we have them. Titus has called a halt for the next day. The news is out that we are to build a wall around this cursed city and then make a new attempt to go forward. He will pit legion against legion to get it finished.'

Marcus nodded his head as he listened and flexed his leg. It felt better and it was time to join his conturbenium. He walked back to the tent and reclaimed his bed position from Ovidius. The next day would be the start of the wall to enclose the Jewish city.

The fifth legion finished its part of the wall, just beating the tenth who started from below the Mount of Olives. They complained that their terrain was harder for construction.

The men of the Fifth laughed at their words and proudly waited at the finished end of the wall, for the tenth to join. Most of them sat around with their arms against the wall. 'My sister could work harder than you boys' Brutus said with a laugh as the last measure of wall was put in place by the men of the tenth. 'A fine legion,' he added 'Not bad at fighting but could not build a sand pit, methinks.'

One Centurion of the Tenth, moved slowly over to Brutus who stood with a broad grin on his face. 'Perhaps you would like to dance, you great buffoon.' The man said pulling his helmet off.

Brutus turned to his men raising his arm. 'Well, we would, Delanus, but you don't have the time!'

The laughs resounded around the area as several soldiers of the conturbenium moved behind Brutus in case the Tenth decided a dance was in order.

The wall, constructed of interlacing posts, sharpened at the top and placed solidly into the sand below made a menacing sight as the ends met and the Roman legions cheered. The whole city of Jerusalem was encompassed in a wall, within three days.

The siege machines were replaced by engineers, who worked day and night. They were placed up on rebuilt ramps as once again, they toiled to place the machines near the wall. They stayed behind the towers pushing them from behind with bullocks to stay away from the constant shower of arrows that came from the archers, high on the parapets that adorned the walls of the holy city.

That night, the word went around that at last; a breech had been made at the wall between the city and temple that sat nearest the Eastern wall. It reminded Marcus that he had viewed the temple as his first point of familiarity, so many weeks before.

In pre-dawn light, the men fed on cold, grain porridge as Titus had commanded that fires were to be put out the night before. The legions, one by one, were led down the valley, towards the North field and set in place behind the two siege machines, that continued to throw their battering rams against the heavy stone wall.

This time, Marcus noted, the sound and cadence had changed. The cadence was increasing and the sound of broken, fractured stone, replaced the relentless sound of impervious rock hit by the metallic ram head.

The siege machines smelled of smoke and the front of the first machine, still held ravaged areas that had not been repaired from the previous day's attack by archers, with lighted arrows.

The Optio walked in front of the Fifth keeping his back to the wall as a show of defiance of the long-range archers, standing above in the increasing light of dawn. He started to shout. 'Soon the last pendulum will swing and the wall will open. You are to go in conturbenium by conturbenium and be beware boys, beyond these walls, are men who will willingly give their lives for this city and the temple of their God. Our job today is to bring them to their knees. You do not, and I repeat, not, take any prisoners.'

Cheers and raucous calling met his words, as he strutted across the floor of the outer wall area. 'Our commander, Titus Vespasian, saved the day again, several days ago, by leading our cavalry to take out the defenders. This is your day and once you get inside you have three commands. The first it to fight them until they stop; the second is take the walls. The third, and most important, is to move forward to capture the gates to the temple at the top of the stairs from the main square. Everyone understand?'

The Optio looked at the tense men as they waited for the order to move forward. 'Let me remind you all. There are two leaders we want alive. You know who they are. John of Giscala and Simon of Giora. These two are on the top of our most wanted list and if you capture them, keep them alive! Got it?'

The men murmured as they shuffled, edging forward as they listened to the Optio. '*Principes* will take the wall archers and the front supported by the *Triarii*, our finest men, will take the city with the front lines.'

Again, the cheers and noise increased and finally he held up his hand. 'No one and I mean no man, is to enter or touch the contents of the main Temple, or any temple in the city. If you are caught trying to remove the contents, you will be beaten and put to the sword.'

'What about the rest?' One called out.

'That is yours.' The cry went skyward as the men moved into final position, awaiting the signal from the siege tower and the orders went out.

'Shields up and above your heads and swords at the ready.'

There was a final shattering echo as the breech occurred. The iron head of the pendulum finally punched through the wall after hitting it more than a thousand times. The result was a gut-wrenching sound as the wall finally gave way, followed by a fusillade of arrows from the Jewish archers from inside the wall.

Slowly, almost sluggishly, the wall collapsed from the parapets, top down onto the ground around the siege machine and in the early light, Marcus could make out the falling forms of archers, who sat atop the wall and fell with the stone blocks beneath them. Their cries could be clearly heard as they fell beside the siege machine, followed by the moaning of some who survived the fall.

The shouts and grunts of the Roman legionnaires started. Some gave orders, some men spoke to themselves, some held a grim expression in expectation and some men urinated from the stench of fear, unaware that they had done so. On some faces, the excitement created by the wall collapse, radiated into smiles and on many junior recruits, the look of fear and dread at the coming fight caused their features to fall and their eyes to open wide in fear.

Of the troops waiting beside Marcus, on the dark timber rampart, he could hear heavy breathing and on most the heavy sheen of sweat on their faces. The most obvious tussle with fate came from the constant fidgeting, which he now knew accompanied all, but the bravest soldiers prior to battle.

CHAPTER 27

The Optio pulled up in front of them, slamming his Gladius into his shield to get their attention.

'Take formation boys, shields to the front, pilum to level and when I give the word you charge. You move in squads, as it is too close quarter for the line. Each conturbenium moves towards the areas we discussed. The steps to the temple and the road to the city lie beyond this stone breech. This is not normal formation, ladies; This is full force!'

Marcus joined the line with his six conturbenium brothers around him, waiting for the order from the Optio. 'Sextus, Ovidius, Vanu, Enius, Lucanus and you, Felix. Stick with me and guard each other's backs.' He whispered quietly as he waited for the order.

'Right, go!'

The lower front section of the siege machine opened in front of them, and four abreast, they sprinted up the stairs in full armour and into the breech.

As they stepped through the opening, the Jewish infantry stood before the steps to the city, to the front and right. In a split second, Marcus saw a larger force standing in front of the steps that led to the temple. Rigid, snarling and shouting, they waited for the Romans to advance.

In full battle armour, shields and pilums to the fore, they charged at full sprint into the Jewish soldiers who stood waiting, with their spears forward and the line hard and regimented.

In drill, the Fifth as well as the Tenth, the lead groups, had practised this tactic many, many times. The charge represented the formation of an arrow. As the lead legionaries, sprinted shield first into the line they ducked, bringing their shields up and through the line of spears, pointing menacingly to the front of the Jewish soldiers. Once the first went through the spear wall, the others followed them only to fan out left and right to attack from the middle of the Jewish ranks from the side. The frightening sight of the eighty men comprising of ten conturbenium moving in an arrow formation at the Jewish line, made a formidable sight with their red shields up, spears forward and the menacing look on their faces, as they advanced on the run.

The legionaries, did not shout or grunt. The only sound that could be heard below the sound of rushing feet, were the orders within the Jewish ranks as they waited for the onslaught.

'Hold, hold' Could be heard above the onslaught as a shout by the commander to his men.

The noise echoed from the clash of armour as the Roman smashed their way into the opposing line, created a shattering noise that Marcus thought could only be heard in Hades. The echo reverberated, from the white limestone walls, as blood started to spill on the ground around them.

The effect on the Jewish defense line was catastrophic as the legionnaires barrelled into the Jewish defensive positions. This was clearly not a tactic the defenders believed the Romans might use.

As the men at the front took the first two rows out in battering ram formation, the following legionaries took the sides. Within minutes, the battle had changed to a melee of grunts as shield, hit shield, and swords pushed forward to find open flesh.

As the legions poured through the wall, the Jewish soldiers fell back only to regroup and fight again. Line by line, the Jewish forces lost order and control. The numbers of Romans entering the battle became over-whelming and slowly, the Jewish soldiers fell and then the rout started to create an effect, across the entire battle.

The Romans, weary of the siege and still praying for those killed at the Mount of Olives and the breech of the Northern wall, started the pay back which became methodical, efficient and brutal.

Marcus looked down as he made it to the steps of the wall. Above him, the steps rose in a long straight line, to the top of the wall. The sheer height and width of the walls from the perspective of inside the city, made him understand how hard it had been to break though. On the floor of the battle, to his left, lay bodies of the recently dead and severely injured from both sides. He could barely make out the stone below the bodies as they lay, prostrate on the floor of the massive city.

'After me' He shouted, as they sprinted up the stairs of the wall, with shields taking the brunt of the arrow strikes as they rose to the top section. On top of the wall the archers had fallen back to corner positions on three sides, with bolt after bolt fired at the advancing conturbenium.

Marcus hunkered down as another arrow slammed into this shield. Then, he heard the swoosh sound of another and then another, as it split the air above him, barely clearing the top of his helmet. The men held pilums which were no match for the archers on the wall top. There remained little option but to charge the groups of archers as they retreated around the wall, towards the far end of the fort.

Marcus went to one knee, holding his shield directly in front of him and he motioned for his men to stop with him. He looked at Ovidius who grimaced and cast his eyes back, towards their path along the wall, realising that archers were assembling behind them.

Marcus nodded and in the next moment they sprinted down the wall top, which could barely take two abreast and towards the group at the end of the parapet. A group of enemy archers and at least five soldiers stood at the ready to defend the position.

The sound of metal on metal and the bellowing of breath, filled their ears as hand combat took the place of pilums. The Jewish soldiers drew their swords as his squad approached, fighting hard against Marcus and his men.

Within minutes, they were cut down and the conturbenium ground to a halt. Ovidius put his sword into the neck of one man as he fell over the front of the wall and that was the last.

'Anyone badly hurt?' Marcus said with a deep breath as he looked at the men hunched beside him. For the first time, he noticed a drip of blood from his arm where an arrow had sliced lightly across his shoulder on its flight.

Marcus went down again on one knee with the others as they attempted to catch their breath. They looked over to the next corner of the fort and the conturbenium, on the opposite wall, was under archers range from both sides.

'Up!' Marcus said 'Let's go'

They charged across the slain and dying men at their feet and towards the far corner of the wall. As they neared the half way point, Marcus heard the sound of arrows and grunts, coming from behind him.

He glanced behind to see Vanu's shield take an arrow from behind narrowly missing his head and with enough force to pass through the entire shield at the top. He and Enius turned around, with their shields up to take the long arrows, as they flew from the small group of archers who had moved to a position behind them. Lucanus held the back position with his shield, pointing it to the side against the opposite wall.

'Split' Marcus shouted and he continued towards the two archers in front of them, while Sextus, Vanu and Enius moved towards the group at the back with the sudden sound and thump of arrows hitting the front of their scarred shields.

Suddenly, Vanu screamed in pain as an arrow hit his ankle and trying to find his balance, he fell over the wall into the fracas of fighting men below. Enius and Sextus with their shields high at middle level and swords drawn and their mind on revenge, threw themselves at the three enemy archers, some way down the wall. Marcus could hear an eerie howl come from Sextus, as he plunged into the group of archers, head first.

Marcus pulled his shield around to counter the arrows from in front. Within seconds, they were on the two retreating defenders. Ovi drove his sword through one of them and the other jumped over the wall, rather than face the Roman sword thrusting at him. Marcus could hear his scream as he fell and yet again another arrow flew past his head, with that familiar, high-pitched sound like a bird flying past at high speed.

'We are pinned, boss and the only way is through em,' Felix shouted, sheltering most of his huge size behind his shield, as they looked at the next group held up on the far corner, where the two walls met.

'We have no choice, boys. Up!' Marcus said, rising from his crouched position. He could feel the hairs rising on the back of his neck as his vision narrowed on the last group of archers at the end of the third wall tower, some one hundred feet away. He looked briefly over at Sextus and Enius who were rising from the fight with the Jews, who had fired on them from behind.

He looked around the wall top for the other conturbenium squad, who had sprinted up the stairs behind him. He counted ten Roman legionaires on the ground, with two trying to rise. Around them lay as many archers, not moving and with the sun glinting off the rusty colour, of their drying blood.

On the far wall, Sextus was taking the last archer hand-to-hand with his dagger. Marcus watched, as Sextus knifed him and pushed him over the wall to the battle far below. He watched as the archer flailed through the air to hit with thud between two combatants. Felix grunted as they rose from their position and took off quickly into a sprint, towards the Jewish soldiers at the end of the wall. Two soldiers held long spears, joined by three archers, who were firing from the shelter of a hut at the far end of the limestone wall. The final corner had to be cleared and Marcus stopped to try and work out the best angle of attack. They had both wall tops covered and the hut allowed them to unleash their arrows and duck back.

'Stop, Felix' Marcus called out in vain as the big man thumped down, towards the nearest group, shield first into the middle of them and taking an arrow into his leg as he neared them. Two went over the wall under the force he created, as he hit them and the others, three in total sprawled against the hut parapet.

With the breath knocked out of him, Felix started to rise as Marcus and Ovidius reached him. As he rose without his shield he heard, then felt, an arrow, penetrate his shield and into his neck. Marcus grabbed desperately at him, trying to stop him falling but his weight was too much as he slid, still holding his Gladius over the edge of the wall and down to the sandy mound below, at the wall base.

Marcus looked around the wall top and all he could see was the carnage of men from both sides laying on the blood-soaked stone. There were more than thirty bodies lying on the stones of the walkways and he looked across to see the two remaining from the other Conturbenium, fighting Jewish soldiers who had come up the stairs in support.

On the other side of the fort wall he could see Enius and Sextus picking themselves up and looking over at him. He motioned to them, as they jogged around to where Marcus stood still breathing heavily.

'Vanu?'

Sextus shook his head. 'Fell over there.'

'Felix?' Marcus looked down at the raging battle in the square beneath the wall. 'Down there, somewhere.' He said bitterly. For the first time, he felt the heat basking the wall top and he felt the stream of sweat coming from under his helmet.

He looked down at the carnage below as he heard the grunts and cries of the two forces, locked together in battle.

Marcus started off with his shield up as they moved in support of the two legionaires who had taken out the Jewish soldiers at the top of the wide, stone staircase. Ovidius ran one through with his sword as they passed and the other was pushed over the wall with a scream as he went down.

255

Brutus shouted at them from the bottom, motioning to the stairs leading to the temple surrounds, across the other side of the square. As they came down from the parapet top, Marcus turned to see one of his men gurgling blood with an arrow through his chest, clutching at it as he fell from the side of the stone staircase, into the chaos below.

'Enius!' Marcus called out his name as he saw him fall. He looked up, to find a single archer at the top of the steps slinging arrow after arrow into the running conturbenium. He stopped on a step near the halfway point, turned with his shield forward and took the steps three at a time to the top. In moments, he was on the terrified archer, slicing his throat and throwing him off the edge with a loud shout. *'fili mulieris virum ultro rapientis bitch'*

They sprinted down the last of the stairs, fighting ferociously for the last three steps as they fought hand-to-hand the swords and spears held by the Jewish defenders from above and below. Finally, they broke free, and headed for the temple steps.

As they finally reached the top of the wide steps that led to the temple square they were charged by a group of Jewish soldiers who had been waiting. Lucanus, who was to the side of the group, bore the brunt of the attack and holding his shield high he turned to see where Marcus was positioned.

As Lucanus turned, he saw a long blade coming through between the shields and as he ducked the slicing blade made its way through an opening in the shields and into his throat. Clutching the gaping wound with his hand, he fell face first into the stones.

Ovidius was the first to see Lucanus fall and as he tried to lift him from the stones he was speared at the front of the leg.

'Luca, Luca. Get up!' Ovidius shouted, as the blade sliced off his greave leaving a gash. He gasped as he felt Marcus's arm pull his up and away from the scrum of men defending the jabbing spears and shouting faces of the Jews. As they moved away, with Ovidius still holding onto Luca, one of the spears from a Jewish soldier penetrated Lucas' throat and Ovidius dropped his arm as the spear went past his face. 'Come on;' Marcus grabbed him by his shield to pull him away.

They were joined by reinforcements and within moments the Jewish forces scattered to the sides of the square as the Roman legionaires pursued them.

Some fought and some yielded and finally they reached the entrance to the temple. In front of the two, high golden gates, stood two enormous guards. Large men with long beards and heavily armoured.

'We are in fucking hell' Ovidius said hoarsely, as he looked at the two giants before him. Ovidius moved forward only to receive a sword strike from one of them that penetrated his shield with the tip narrowly missing his arm.

Marcus moved into a crouch only to have a shield smash into his arm and the force instantly reminded him of his day at the stadium, and the strength of Britanicus, as he used his shield as his weapon. It left him breathless. He stopped momentarily to regain his breath, as the sweat poured from his head and arms.

'You go forward. I'll wait.' Ovidius said with a half-smile at Marcus who was still trying to stand up straight. He could feel the wash of exhaustion moving across him and the need for a long draught of water.

Sextus moved to the left of the second man thrusting his sword to drive him back towards the oak door leading to the temple. The man let out a grunt driving a club into the side of his helmet and piling a fist into his nose. Sextus went down heavily onto the stone floor.

Marcus stood in front of the first man, trying to regain his breath. He looked around to find they were the only ones at the door and in the square behind them, the battle raged in earnest, as the Jewish defenders were pushed further towards the city entrance.

He looked down at Sextus, who lay unconscious on the stone, with blood streaming out of his nose and his helmet on the ground beside him. Rising up, he motioned to Ovidius who was showing strong reluctance to take on the man again but followed Marcus as he moved forward.

Marcus crouched down with his shield, attempting to bring it up under the giant's torso. As the guard deftly pushed the shield out of the way, Marcus landed a kick into the man's groin and plunged his sword as hard as he could towards his midsection. He watched in horror as it bounded off the giant's armour and continued into thin air beyond.

Working on instinct alone, Marcus swiftly moved behind the giant, and placing his arm around the man's neck and with his free hand he grabbed his dagger and plunged it in, watching as blood poured from the wound. He could feel the rage of the man as he bucked and wrestled to take Marcus from his hold, but slowly the rage calmed and he fell to the stone on his knees and then finally, on his side.

Marcus released his grip, to fall on his back breathing hoarsely, with sweat pouring down his helmet, into his grime encrusted face. He realised there was not one part of him that did not hurt as he raised himself to his knees.

He looked over at Ovidius, wondering instantly what had happened to Sextus, until he saw that he was on the stone under the giant, with his fist pounding into his face, while the guard held Ovidius by the throat with his massive left hand. Ovidius, after scrabbling for his sword handle, finally found it and thrust the blade hard into the man's side.

Marcus looked for his dagger, finding it next to his shield. He moved over and plunged it into the giant's neck, again and again, until the man fell on Sextus with a grunt.

With fatigue setting in, Marcus pulled the man off him and inspected his face as Sextus rolled over and started to vomit. 'No one will compliment you on your good looks from now on.' He said with a grimace helping Sextus to his feet.

'No one ever did!' Sextus replied as he spat on the ground and finally got to his weary knees. He looked at the other two, showing several broken teeth. 'I have never seen a man that big.' He said, looking down at the large mass at his feet.

Ovidius pulled himself using his shield and rested on it momentarily. 'Maybe there is more inside.' He looked over at the other two, noting a slight moment of recognition on their faces. 'You go first.'

Marcus dropped his helmet to the ground and wiped his sweat soaked hair. His blue eyes shone against his sun darkened skin, and for a brief moment he felt a calm unlike he had felt ever before. They were at the doors of the temple of the holy city and for a reason he felt unable to understand, he knew they had desecrated a place of worship. This was not his God but the unease stayed with him.

He looked at the massive door in front of them and with surprise he realised it held no lock or barrier. Together, they pushed the door open and walked into the temple entrance.

The three of them moved slowly into the temple with swords at the ready and shields high. The sound of their armour, clanked off the walls of the surprisingly small space. The temple held an altar at one end and on it sat a large, gold, multi arm candelabra. On each side, long narrow windows in perfect line, splashed light into the room highlighting the ornate carpets on the floor and the fine fabrics that adorned the temple.

Objects of gold of various sizes sat on tables around the perimeter of the temple. Marcus walked to the altar and looked behind it to find another door, smaller and ornate. He opened it and walked in and all they could hear was a long, low whistle. 'Now, this is what Titus is after.' Sextus said as Ovidius nodded.

They walked in behind him, to find chests of gold coins and golden cups amongst jewel encrusted necklaces, and amulets. Chest upon chest, laid against several of the walls, held coins or jewels. Ovi dragged his hand through the coins in the trunk that Marcus had opened, watching them glint in the light from the door.

'No wonder!' He said aloud.

From the back, they heard an unmistakable voice. Brutus called out from the oak door. 'Brothers, is there anyone here?'

They walked out of the door and towards where Brutus stood, leaning heavily against one of the front doors. 'Treasure?' He said bluntly as he held his left arm. It was bleeding from the top with dried rivulets of blood down to his elbow.

Marcus nodded his head and pointed to the room at the back. 'Wealth like we have never seen.'

Brutus nodded. 'They are sealing the area and heading into the city. We are needed, so follow me. Titus will be here presently.' Brutus exited the door with Sextus and Marcus behind him. Ovidius looked reluctant to leave.

'There is retirement back there, Marco. We just have to take a pouch full, that is all.'

Marcus looked back at the room with a sigh. 'My thoughts exactly. Maybe, we come back.'

As they exited the oak door and raised their shield they heard the unmistakable sound of arrows flying swiftly through the air. In front of them, Brutus had not raised his shield and he stopped in mid-stride with a bewildered look on his face, as three arrows in succession, penetrated through his chest plate and into his chest. In slow motion, he fell to the

259

floor with the arrows imbedded and trying to pull one out. As he hit the ground, his helmet fell off his head. It clattered away coming to rest against a bloodied and shivered sword.

Marcus ducked down with Ovidius beside him, under the shelter of their shields as he looked at the Centurion on the ground beside him. His eyes were open and glazed and out of respect, Marcus placed his hand on the Centurions eyes and closed them.

Ovidius pointed to the archers firing from the other side of the square. Without a second thought, the three of them rose and sprinted towards them, with shields held high and swords in their hand. The group of archers were hit by legionaires on two sides before they could fire another missile.

Suddenly, in front of him at the other side of the square, near the entrance to the temple, he saw the tall form of the man he had fought on the ground, near the Mount of Olives so many weeks before.

'That's him' He said looking intently in his direction. 'Who?' Ovidius said, quickly scanning the area. Of the group of archers who were attacked by the two conturbenium only one archer still stood. He dropped his bow and fell to his knees in front of the legionaires. Marcus watched, detached, as one of the boys beheaded the man with his Gladius.

'The other one. Move with me.' Marcus shouted and without any further sound he took off in the direction of the man and his two companions. As the three reached the bottom of the stairs that led to the top of the far wall, Marcus at full speed and shield up, threw himself into the three soldiers, instantly bowling them over.

As Ovidius took on the other two, Marcus slammed a fist hard into the face of the big man and with his other hand around the man's neck, he held him to the ground. With surprising force, John of Goran, rose up with his sword ready and the fight began in earnest.

Blow-by blow they traded as each tried to gain a superior position. Marcus moved to his left to strike at the big man's legs, only to be blocked and find the reverse occurring.

The man could fight hard, he thought momentarily and he was bigger and stronger than Marcus. The question was whether he was as tired?
A final overhead blow came from John, down onto the sword held by Marcus above him. It glanced off onto shield, passing by a whisker from his head.

He parried it and using the same move that Britanicus had used on him, so long ago, he withdrew his shield to his side and moving forward, slammed it into the man's groin and then up into his jaw as John bent forward from the first blow. Marcus repeated it until the Jewish leader hit the ground.

Within a minute, two men from the other squad, joined the fray as one was taken down and Ovidius ran one through with the force of his sword swing. The second, fell within moments and John, dazed and disorientated, backed to the wall surrounded by the three of them.

'Drop your sword.' Marcus said fiercely. Realising the man did not know what he was saying he motioned to him to do the same.

Hate blazed in the eyes of the man before him, who stood with his back to the wall, his long hair matted with blood and bleeding cuts, to his arms and shoulder. Slowly, sluggishly, he sank to his knees in front of them as his sword clattered to the ground. His face told of utter exhaustion but the hatred of defeat, showed just as clearly on his dirt, ridden face.

Marcus kicked the sword away and sheathed his with the same state of tiredness overwhelming his body. Around them, the sound of battle and cries of pain and triumph, slowly ceased as those who were left of the Jewish garrison dropped their swords or fought finally to their end.

From the vastness of the temple square, all of them could hear the screams of terror and anguish from the inhabitants of the city, as the legions poured into the streets and the homes of the besieged city, to wreak revenge.

CHAPTER 28

A young man, handsome, black haired and tall, shouted out the name of the conquering hero in unison with the crowd as Titus rode very slowly, past the crowd on his way to the Piazza, at the head of a long procession.

A look of confidence showed on his face as he smiled at the crowd. He had proven himself, on more than one occasion on the battlefield, and his men respected him and in Rome that was triumph, in its essence. He had the backing of the legions and as his father had taught him from early in his life, a phrase he used often. *Ductus exemplo.* Lead by example.

'He looks like his *pater.*' One said, as he looked up at the massive white stallion that bore Titus, on his march of triumph that day. In the distance, the unmistakable figure of Flavian Vespasian stood at the top of the steps, to welcome his son's return.

This staged return to Rome and the triumphal march, from the end of the Appian way to the centre of Rome, took far-reaching planning and organisation. Both of which, rated highly in the talents of Emperor Vespasian.

Romans, Flavian reflected, as he waited for his son to reach the steps of the white marbled plaza, were a fickle bunch when it came to politics and power, but by the fortune of Zeus, they loved a show. And when it came to shows the practice held to make them bigger and better each time. Not always easy, he mused, but it made excellent political sense.

Trailing behind Titus, on his cloud white stallion, followed a procession of riches and displays of Roman dominance in Judea. Behind the son of the emperor, on beautifully crafted drays, pulled by the best horse flesh in Rome, sat some of the riches plundered from the city after the end of the three-year siege.

On one dray sat the golden table of Shewbread. An ornate table, over two cubits long made with fine Acacia wood, overlaid with gold so that it sparkled of wealth and conquest from the dry lands.

It was a prize possession and not just for its worth. The table was the icon of the Jewish religion. A table designed to hold twelve loaves of bread to represent the twelve tribes of Judea.

Behind the Shewbread table, on another smaller dray, held a large seven-branched candelabrum with a range of gold artefacts, looted from various temples within the city of Jerusalem.

Behind the drays, that pulled the massive chests from the stolen treasury, came the manacled Jewish prisoners brought all the way back from Jerusalem to show the patricians the meaning of Roman conquest. The successful sacking of Jerusalem.

The prisoners, gaunt faces, cast downward as they endured the endless taunts and stone throws from the Roman crowd, that jeered as they crept past. Their faces showed the inevitability of the arrival in Rome and the realisation that the city offered the end of their journey and their lives.

At the very front of the Jewish prisoner column, walked two single men. The Jewish leaders of the siege defence of Jerusalem. Simon of Giora who alternatively glowered at his fellow internee, John of Giscala and the crowd that constantly jeered and threw objects at them. They were both surrounded, by two large Centurions.

Both wore a noose and the tethering rope was held behind them, by each of the Centurions who had great delight in pulling it now and then, to stop his prisoners from going forward.

The prisoners, thin from the near starvation the Roman guards inflicted on him, on the voyage back from Judea, stood erect with their faces showing a resignation of their fate as the procession neared the steps.

'Cut him up' One old man shouted as he walked past in the procession.

'Make him pay' Came another shout, as a well-aimed stone hit the top of Simon's head, causing it to bleed.

Titus swivelled to his right, to smile at a small boy walking beside his horse, not far from the Piazza steps. He leant down, picked the boy up with one muscled arm and sat him on the neck of the horse. The crowd went wild at the sight. Here was a general of the Roman army, a leader of the legions, letting a young boy ride with him.

With the steps, almost before him, Titus let the boy off and held up his hand to stop the procession behind, which took some while to settle. He dismounted and walked quickly up the flight of forty steps, to the wide area in front of the tall building. It was good to be back in Rome after such an absence and he walked directly to his father, embracing him in front of the crowd.

Titus, resplendent in battle dress and a red robe hanging handsomely across his shoulders, stood aside from his father and waited for the applause to diminish. Everywhere he looked, there were people standing and chanting. The noise was deafening and only abated when Vespasian raised his hands.

He turned and whispered to Titus. 'One day, my boy, you will be emperor and this is just the start. This is what they like and this is what keeps you in power. However, never forget the legions, as they are the source of power.'

Vespasian smiled and held his palms up to stop the shouting. 'Romans, this is a proud day. Titus has brought all of us the riches of the Judea rebels and some of the worst offenders will be crucified as a lesson to those who defy the will of Rome.'

The crowd erupted again as Vespasian waited for it to settle. 'There is no doubt that the siege of Jerusalem has been a great success. As proof of the efforts of the great Roman legions, we have before us some of the treasures that were gifted to us by our success in that war. '

Again, the crowd erupted against Vespasian's booming voice. 'I give you Titus, conqueror of Judea.'

Titus moved forward raising his arm in salute as he waited for the crowd to subside. 'In the wagons before you, Romans, lies treasure unlike any of us has seen since the Anglais wars. The wealth we gained from the Jews, will be used for the good of Rome. With this wealth, we can purchase grain and build roads. This is the glory of Rome!'

Titus and his father exchanged glances as they waited for the crowd to settle. The noise finally started to subside. Titus looked over at his adjutant with a nod and the Centurions brought the two Jewish leaders up the steps, to the middle of the large square, with their noose trailing behind. At their side, the Centurions held their swords ready, if one started to escape.

Titus noted with mild satisfaction, at a flicker of fear crossing the face of the Jew. He had proved a worthwhile adversary, Titus thought to himself, as he stood there listening to the erroneous voices coming from the crowd. Finally, the noise hushed in anticipation of what was to come.

A worthwhile adversary in a dusty shithole, Titus mused, as he waited for the sentencing to begin; Jerusalem sat in a land that few cared about, save

Rome. Perhaps the Jews would learn that fighting Rome was a worthless occupation? Unlikely, he thought, with their devoutly religious fervour.

However, there was a cost to Rome as well. He had lost well over a thousand men himself and unfortunately, many from the tenth legion, which had proven their worth under great Caesar.

Standing next to him on that sun filled day, under a cloudless sky in Rome, was his ramrod straight father, who seemed to care less about the losses. His father was pragmatic enough to understand that the campaign was successful in routing the Jews and finally sacking the city of Jerusalem. The elder Vespasian was a man of admirable discipline.

The spoils, gained from the sacking of Jerusalem were immense. Collected from the various temples in the city, they made up the size of forty-eight, full drays, plus what his men had taken without his knowledge. Clearly, there were times his men pilfered treasure but who was to blame them? As long as the prizes of antiquity and gold from the Jewish treasury returned to Rome, the rest could be taken for the legions retirement funds.

There were many times on those long nights under the stars, sheltered under the cloudless sky of Judea, when he joined the campfires of his men to sing songs and share in their meals. He preferred them to his own officers, most of which had their sights firmly on a political career. Only a fool did not know that the military was the most successful route to power. Some were good, he thought as he stood there. The rest were useless or blinded by ambition.

The years of siege, necessary to implement Rome's will and residence in the country, remained the added benefit of the political capital and the addition to Rome's treasury. The further advantage lay in tax collection, which continued even as he stood on the weathered marble floor, on that very day.

Titus moved forward to where Simon and John stood, near the top of the steps of the marble tiled square, looking down into the crowd. He nodded to the Centurion, who pushed the men forcibly down onto their knees.

He looked around the expansive crowd that seemed to occupy every nook around the stairs and the large square beyond. As Simon and John were pushed to their knees, the crowd moved to silence, save several who called out for vengeance.

"I give you the leaders of the Judea rebels. They were captured on the last day of the fighting as we entered the inner wall and against a foe, that understood the meaning of fighting to the death. I give you Simon, son of Giora, the Jew and John of Giscala, the other leader of the resistance.

Titus raised his hands against the persistent jeering from the crowd as they shouted obscenities against the kneeling prisoners. 'What say you, John of Giscala? Do you surrender to life imprisonment?'

Cries could be heard from the assembled masses around the steps. '*Occidere eum*. Kill him! Kill him!'

'Get rid of the scum.'

Titus held his hand up to quieten the crowd. 'Citizens. Let him have his say.'

John looked up at him silent and obstinate. 'You have won, Titus Vespasian. Is that not enough?'

Titus turned to the translator and listened to the response. He nodded as he listened.

The crowd started shouting obscenities as Titus motioned to the other man kneeling before him. 'What say you, Simon, son of Giora?'

The man glowered at him from his forced kneeling position. Weak from the forced march and hunger, he tried to rise but was roughly pushed back down by the Centurion, as the chains that bound his hands and feet clanked against the hard-stone tiles. He spat at Titus's boots, until he was grabbed by his long hair and pushed away. Simon looked up at Titus and shouted but he could not understand the Aramaic tongue.

He looked over at the scribe standing next to him. 'What did he say?'

'We will have our day.'

'Not today'. Titus replied brusquely, as he nodded to another Centurion who moved over to the kneeling man, placed his sword at the top of his collarbone.

The starved, gaunt form of the Jewish commanders, who had held Jerusalem during the three-year siege, slumped forward across the top step of the square. The crowd rose and clapped in unison with derogatory shouts at the fallen prisoners. Titus raised his hand in salute to the crowd. He looked at the scribe for a moment, as the man returned his stare with a questioning look on his face.

'Sire?' He asked.

'Did he say anything else?'

The scribe shrugged. 'No Sire.'

'I respected him; but in his place, I would have died on the wall of Jerusalem rather than come here and die like this, in front of these jackals.'

'So, the law is decreed. John of Giscala will be imprisoned for life and Simon of Giora will be thrown off the *Saxum Tarpeium*, this very afternoon. His body will lay in waste at the bottom of the ravine for all to see what happens, when you defy the right of Rome.'

The square broke out in clapping and jeers at the two men, who were pulled to their feet. John was still bleeding from a thrown stone from one of those who lined the procession and Simon, still struggling and swearing, spat at John's feet. '*Gehenna* for you, for eternity' He gasped as he was pulled in the opposite direction.

The tall, bearded man to his right, caked with grime and a light trickle of blood down his long face, looked at Simon in disgust. 'I don't know who of us is worst off. You, to be thrown off the *Tapeian* rock or my servitude in chains in a stinking, Roman prison for the rest of my life. You might be right. Hell, would be easier.'

He looked at the man, who he had hated for all those years, and out of desperation had partnered in the defense of Jerusalem with him. He shook his head. '*Gehenna* for you as well, Simon. For our defense of the holy city we will reach heaven and for our sins we will meet hell. Go in peace, brother.'

Simon spat at him again as he was towed away by his chains. The scribe nodded, as Titus left the scene to join his father on the Forum. The procession continued, with the treasure moving slowly to the palace treasury rooms. The haggard faces of the Jewish prisoners stayed in his mind, as they shuffled down the steps of the

Capitoline hill, onwards to the *Ancus Marcius,* towards their fate in the prison which would likely lead to crucifixion for all.

After the usual round of pleasantries, Vespasian and Titus retired to the

267

palace. Once inside the opulent surroundings, Vespasian called for a servant who removed his sandals and washed his feet as he sipped one of his favourite honey wines, while sitting across from his son.

Titus had removed his heavy battle leather and sat in his toga across from his father. He waved the servant away as he neared to wash his feet, waiting until he had departed before they started to speak about the future.

Vespasian was the first to speak. 'I hear that you were almost killed in the advance one afternoon.'

Titus nodded. His countenance held similar to his father. He was stout and short of height with a broad face and a slightly balding head. He had unknowingly adopted some of the traits of his father and wiping his brow and across his head as he made a point in conversation, was one of them.

He raised his eyebrows. 'Yes, father it was close. I was saved by one of our legionnaires, who pulled me out of the spear line and cut the man to pieces. The legion was in trouble on that afternoon and a cavalry charge was the only way to break up the rout.

'Was this at the start of the final siege?'

'Close to it, but it was actually the day I rode down from Mount Scopus, to review the land near the city. All of a sudden, the Jews poured out of the city walls and came onto the men near the fort and, might I add, in force. They hit the middle and a battle started in earnest. I went in with the mounted escorts and thankfully, the Goddess was with me that day and we routed them back.

'Were there greater numbers of Jewish infantry?' Vespasian asked 'Many more, father and they are not infantry as we know it. They are more like skirmishers. I did not have my battle dress on and therefore, they did not recognise me. We fought our way in to free the men, near the fort, and over an hour later we broke out of the melee and made it back to the main group. The Jews were dispersed and ran back to the wall entry. I took a few out on the way but it was close and we made it back to the main group at the bottom of the Mount.

'You led the charge?' Vespasian smiled proudly at the man opposite him, noticing as he always did how physically similar they were.

Again, Titus nodded. 'I did and perhaps foolishly but those Jews fight like the heavens are before them. I can attest how hard they fight and they know the terrain is very difficult to operate in.'

Vespasian nodded, relying on his memory of his days in Judea before he passed the command to his son. 'Yes, I remember the areas around that city are covered in levies, olive groves, fences and old buildings and unfortunately, we are best on open ground and battle lines in place.'

Titus interrupted this father as he sipped his wine and spoke. 'They are ferocious fighters and they have no formation like we do. They work in small units. They are agile and fearless.'

'And Simon the Jew?'

'He fought hard with his men on that final day. It was only through a stroke of luck from the Gods on Olympus, that we actually caught him alive, as he was going over the Eastern wall when we caught him. Had he gone over that drop, it is unlikely he could have survived it.'

'Well, he is gone now.'

'Let us be careful father,' Titus said leaning forward to emphasize the point 'The Jews are zealots and they are not easily tamed. If we don't take them down totally they will arise again. They have their religion and their God; And they fight hard to honour him.'

Vespasian rubbed his jaw thoughtfully as he pondered the information from his son. 'What about Judea?'

Titus grimaced and shifted uneasily in his seat. 'We have one large group left which I have written to you about. They are tough and, in my experience, as relentless as those who defended the holy city.

'Sicarii?' Vespasian, queried

Titus nodded 'The Sicarii; those dagger thieves must be destroyed or they will re-populate and bring the rest of that dust hole back into their way of thinking. Remember well, father. Simon is now a martyr and the Jews will not stop unless we stop them.'

Vespasian smiled grimly, knowing that the tax revenue and produce from the region depended entirely on the success of the next war. He had read the scripts sent by his son over the previous year and he was well aware of the Sicarii rebels.

'Will they fight in the open?'

269

Titus stood up to stretch and called for another wine and something to eat. 'No, father they will likely hold up in a high fortress position called Masada and if that is correct it will become yet another siege. It is very high up on a mountain and can only be attacked via long, steep and for them, defendable trail.'

'Then how?'

Well, I have my best engineers over there working on it. Either way, it will not be easy and we will lose lives in the process.'

'Do you want to finish this off?' Vespasian asked knowing the answer before his son gave it.

'This is my destiny, father, and I will complete.'

Vespasian filled his cup with wine as he smiled at his son 'As we discussed, I have issued a new coin for Rome known as the *Judea Capta,* so any Roman who uses it will be reminded of your glorious victory. I have also conferred with treasury and we are implementing an additional tax on the Jewish lands, it will come into effect immediately. They will pay more than once for their defiance. Which was the stand out legion?'

'The Tenth, of course, followed by the Fifth.

Vespasian nodded. Of course, the brave men who formed under great Caesar and made a name for themselves. 'Were they first through the wall?'

Titus nodded, rubbing his shoulder absently against the pain that had started again. He had so many injuries, it was hard to know which one to treat first.

'When do you intend to sail?'

'On the next full moon and after a rest.'

Vespasian smiled widely at his son and rose to take a bath. 'Then tonight we will drink your good health and success. You conquer the Jews and I will take care of Rome which incidentally, is your heritage. Finish off the Jews and the transition to power after I die, will be secured.'

Titus nodded at this father. 'How is mother?'

'She is well, Titus but still suffering from those headaches she gains all the time. I will take of her and you take care of business.'

Titus retired to his rooms and a long bath and thought about the coming siege of Masada. Three more full moons, and he would be there. It was just a fort, he thought to himself as he gratefully immersed himself in the heated water.

Across the other side of Rome, Simon was shackled tightly, as they dragged him screaming up to the Southern summit of the Capitoline Hill. The site overlooked the sight of the Forum under construction. Below the edge of the *Saxum Tarpenium,* lay the sides of a steep cliff with jagged rocks that stuck out at all angles.

Far below, the sparse vegetation of the ravine bottom was the only feature of the barren area.

One of the Centurions, pulled Simon by his hair and held him over the precipice for a moment with a smile on his face and then let him go. No sound came from Simon as he plummeted to the bottom and after looking briefly at his broken body on the ravine floor, the Centurions picked up their gear and headed back to barracks.

CHAPTER 29

Elezar Ben Ya'ir, leader of the Sacarii, gazed out from the wall of the massive complex of the mountain fort behind him and down into the deep sloping valley, stretching as far as the eye could see from the mountain top, fortress of Masada.

In the long distance, he could see the cloud of dust kicked up by a group of horsemen which he knew instinctively brought yet another Roman presence. Judging by the speed and the colour of the band of riders, it was someone important.

He sighed deeply and walked behind one of his Scarii generals, as they inspected the Roman embattlements far below, on the Western and Eastern approaches. There was only one way up the mountain and that was via the old, goat road that wended its way like a long white snake, up the mountain from the side and up to the gate of the fortress itself.

Still, he reflected ruefully, the Romans had arrived and they were ensconced in the fort with nowhere to retreat when they viewed the tents and fires of the various bivouac sites around the bottom of the cliffs far below. They seemed to grow larger every day. The stories of the sacking of Jerusalem sat foremost in his mind as he looked down at the Roman jackals surrounding the high fort.

They walked together along the solid battle wall that surrounded the Sicarii garrison. The wall top was the width of two men, lying head to head and the stone fortifications more than eight men high. It remained impregnable without a siege machine to break its thick walls and getting a siege machine up a sheer mountain side was impossible, even for the Romans.

He waited for one of his aides to catch up and the man finally arrived breathless and an anxious look on his face.

'What is it?' Ya'ir said abruptly.

'You need to take a look at this sir.' He said, and without a further word, he about turned and walked off in the opposite direction, waiting for his commander to catch up.

They walked quickly down towards the Western side of the fort. He looked over the wall side, to a view he knew only too well. The side of the mountain was sheer and unencumbered by boulders which fell to a culvert and then up the side of another high hill, opposite the fort and the peak of which, stood just below the line of the floor of the fort.

'What is it?' He asked as he peered around.

'Look! look down there!'

Ya'ir looked down and for the first time felt the prickle of the hairs on his neck rise, and a sudden fear engulf his bowels. Far below, workers, and presumably Roman prisoners gained from Jerusalem, were dumping soil into the culvert. He watched as others wet the soil from buckets, brought up from the aquifers the Romans engineers had diverted from the fort itself.

One of his generals met him on the wall. 'What is the problem?

'Look down there. For some reason, I did not see it this morning either.' Ya'ir said softly, as he pointed down to the scene far below.

'What are those Roman bastards doing?'

'They are building a road to launch a siege ramp.'

'That is not possible!' Yehuda exclaimed loudly, with disbelief on his face.

Ya'ir gazed down for a while before he answered. 'If I am not mistaken, they intend to fill that chasm down there, with enough earth to build a siege road up to the fort level.'

Menahem Yehuda, a Sicarii general, looked directly at Ya'ir and then back down at the activity at the bottom of the chasm. From their position on the wall the men far below looked like insignificant ants scurrying to and fro, as they threw soil from their baskets and walked away to gain another load.

He stroked his short beard in contemplation. 'It is not possible to build such a road, Elezar. It is too deep and too long. I mean, it is probably half the length of our fort and ten times as deep. To build something like that, and let's include the fact that they need to send a heavy siege engine up such a road to the wall, they would need to move enough earth to make such a road. It is not possible. It must be the heat and they have gone raving mad!'

Ya'ir looked at his general while he looked beyond the threat, to the long, dusty plain beyond. 'I don't think they are mad, Menahem; I think they are a strong and resourceful enemy and they will stop at nothing to ensure we are defeated. That bastard, Silva is under the direction of the Roman murderer, Titus. And, that means we will meet them soon enough. If I am right they will build that road and that now depends on what time we have left.'

'Meaning?'

'Meaning, one day we will meet them at the wall.'

'So?'

'So, first things first. Get our best archers up here for continued target practice and let us go to the war room to work on the best strategy to stop them. But, I tell you now, that I don't think we will be able to make a change to their progress. We may kill a few but it won't be enough.

'Surely...' Yehuda said, before being interrupted by Ya'ir

I don't intend to become a Roman dog, as I am sure all of us are the same. I know a lot about the Roman war machine just as you do. We have learnt over the years, brothers, that they are nothing but persistent and brutal when they take control. So, our sole purpose must be to stop them.'

'And if we don't?'

Ya'ir pushed his long hair back from his squinting eyes. 'I cannot think that far ahead and I am not sure I want to.'

Yehuda barked out several orders to the man next to him, to get the archers to the Western wall. The instructions were simple. Gather their weapons and rain arrows down on the Romans and anyone else working on the road.

'But some of those are our countrymen.' The archer captain said.

'I don't care. The road must not be built. Do your duty!' Yehuda shouted angrily as he turned, on his heels, and followed Ya'ir down the stairs from the wall and to the barracks at the other end of the long space.

As they neared the barracks Ya'ir motioned to him and walked down one of the corridors towards the granaries. As he neared the door a man motioned to him as he stopped.

'Do they come?'

Ya'ir looked at his quartermaster in the dim light of the corridor outside the grainery doors and nodded. "I don't know when, but sooner rather than later. Don't worry as we have plenty of time and it is not as if we did not know they were on the way. The Romans want a fight and it is our duty, all of us, to ensure they get it.'

He walked back slowly with Menahem, both in deep thought and both with the tacit understanding, although not spoken, that the situation was dire no matter what face he showed to his men.

He thought for a moment about the tactics they had used before and after the siege of Jerusalem. The Sacarii, literally, the *dagger men*, hunted the Romans in packs though out Judea and with success. The Roman legions were too ordered and too slow to fight against the skirmish tactics of the Sacarii.

Ya'ir had devised those tactics many years before and yet, they had worked until they had retreated to be holed up in the fortress he stood in on that very day. Hit and run, he had told his men countless times, and the more they wounded the beast of Rome, the angrier it got, which was exactly his plan.

The Romans started to make mistakes. Like the Roman empire, overlords of the worlds they conquered, they were unable to change, even against war mongering that clearly did not work in their favour. Their stupidity continued as the beast remained unable to change against the Sacarii tactics and losses mounted, as the Sacarii did their job. Hit and run, hit and run.

In the desert, the Sacarii were superior, but he knew, deep down, that the brute force of the Romans would win out in the end. He knew, even years before, that the fort where he stood, would become the stage of that final conflict. If courage alone could win a war, they might have won it several times over. As he walked with Menahem, past the last of the indoor, granary rooms he knew that force required courage and discipline to be successful.

That applied to the Sacarii as much as it did any war machine and the Romans had conquered the world with that combination. There could

275

never be a compromise with the bastard Romans. It was fight or submit. Simple and easy for both sides to comprehend.

He briefly recalled the last skirmish, which occurred less than half a day ride from the fort and how they ended up outnumbered and without an escape route. The Romans had chased them with their cavalry ending up against a cliff in a dry, desolate gully. Both of his closest friends, Yosef and his brother Shimon died that day, run through a number of times by the Roman riders who had caught up with them.

He and four of his men had narrowly escaped, down the canyon narrows where the horses could not get though. That day, they lost fifteen brave Sacarii soldiers. The Romans had no interest in Sacarii prisoners; those bastard Roman soldiers would put any of them to the sword. There would be no such thing as a prisoner left alive.

After the skirmish, they retreated back to the fort on the belief that it was impregnable and from there they could mount another reprisal against the invading Roman legions. There was no possibility of sending a siege machine up the winding road, the fort doors sat impregnable and the fort too high with archers lining the parapets.

The more he thought about the siege road the Romans were building, the angrier he felt. If they finally finished it, it might become a wonder of the world. The audacity! No matter how much he hated the Roman machine he grudgingly admired their undeniable capacity to make war and conquer.

He opened the last door of the wide room and inspected the grain, that lay in mounds across the broad floor. He mentally counted the amount and it was enough for a year so they had water and grain. At least they would not starve if the Romans did not make their way through the outer wall.

The only question that remained was anyone's guess? How long would it take for the Romans to build the road? The sheer daring of the Roman engineers impressed him. To build up a level road, of some one hundred and twenty cubits deep, at a length of what would need to be, no less than nine hundred cubits, was not only impressive but laced with extraordinary ambition.

'The question is how we defend.' He said to Menahem as they entered the planning room sat at the long table. A cup of steaming, sweet tea was placed in front of them by a woman who tended the room. He sipped it gingerly and laid his head back in the chair.

Yehuda sipped his tea slowly making drawings on the table, with his right finger. 'We have no heavy objects to throw down, unless we dismantle the wall and that won't work so that leaves archers and spears but how effective is that going to be given their siege ability?'

'Not much my friend, so it appears we are looking at our doom. Make no mistake about these Roman shits. They will put us to the sword, as good as look at us, and we have just under a thousand on this fort and that means a strong slaughter day, for our Roman dogs.

'At least we have four hundred soldiers but the rest are citizens as you know.'
'They won't care, Menahem. They will slaughter everyone so we don't rise again and whilst I love our men they will be unable to fight these Romans in close quarters. Let's see what our architect has to say.'

Ya'ir got up from his seat and called out. Gerau!' He returned to the table and waited for the man to arrive. He was a small man with a wide intelligent face and shining eyes under a bald head.

'Did you inspect the work below?'

'From above and at the bottom of the fort, from outside one of the portals. We almost got hit by a Roman arrow we were that close'

'How long will it take for them to finish the ramp?'

Gerau produced a sheet with scrawling on it. 'It will depend on the labour force and of course they will be whipping the holy, city prisoners, each day to get it done.'

'Do we know how many were taken prisoner at Jerusalem.?'

'Some ninety thousand is the figure I heard from one of our spies.'

'How many were slaughtered?'

Gerau looked at Ya'ir with a perplexed look on his face. 'Does it matter?'

'No' Ya'ir replied.

'Over twenty thousand, I believe. Add to that the sacking of anything remotely precious and the raping of our women and you get the picture.'
Gerau replied.

Menahem sighed, placing his arm on Gerdau. 'How long?

'Maybe two months.'

Ya'ir sat bolt upright. 'Are you sure? Only two months?'

'Or less.' Gerau replied, and since they are now finishing off a wall around the base of the fort hill, there is no escape for any of us.' 'Water aquifiers?'

'From my last inspection, they are all blocked off.'

Ya'ir looked at Gerau for a moment and then at Menahem, who shared the same look of shock at the news.

'Then we must prepare for our death.' He said matter-of-factly. 'No one must hear of this for the present. Let us make preparations with a brave face and then we make the final plans.'

'But we have over a thousand on in this fort Elezar. They need to know.'

Ya'ir sighed deeply and looked over at the two men. 'To know that the Romans will be on our doorstep soon? What will they do? Leave? There is nowhere to go.'

CHAPTER 30

Cassius watched, deep in thought, as a slave appeared with a brief bow to him as he pulled the bridle of the horse with a whisper to them to take them forward to the stables at the back of the sumptuous villa. It was late afternoon and his visit to the foundation building works on the Amphitheatre, had created his good mood.

At long last, the gardens dedicated to Nero, by Nero himself, had been trampled by the workers on the Amphitheatre site. He made a special trip just to watch the statue Nero had dedicated to himself, be pulled down behind two large draft horses and with a resounding thud, it hit the muddy ground. Bird shit, bronze and marble was all that remained.

He inspected the fallen statue briefly and the only thought that came into his mind, beheld the statue as a reflection of Nero's legacy, to the Roman world. The pompous, fatuous and totally self-absorbed emperor was finally removed from the gardens and in the very least, from his mind.

Now, he thought, Vespasian and his militant son, Titus, were an entirely different matter. A different class, with strong military ties and holding the political and military power in their grasp so tight, it was impossible to infiltrate.

Still, he reflected, as he walked around the amphitheatre area which showed a broad landscape of moved earth and large stone blocks laid into place with shouting workers milling around, he had spent much of his time influencing senators and the political circle.

He realised early in the reign of the emperor that Vespasian and his son were the straightest of arrows. As far as he knew, neither had any real vices.

No whoring or gambling and the worst he witnessed over the years came to watching Flavius Vespasian, leering at dancers but they had to be very lithe and very blond and that was not the easiest combination to find in the city of Rome.

The truth, of course, was very different. Vespasian had a long-standing mistress, who was not only beautiful, but far more adept in social life than his wife. Laurentius, of course, preferred a more bountiful figure and when the mood took him, perhaps more than one. He had never taken to boys, unlike many of his peers, who whored around with anything they could find.

Vespasian had agreed in the company of another senator, Gaius Sabinus, to attend the villa that night to attend a party in the honour of his wife's birthday. He passed the message to the emperor that Sabinus had a new dance troupe on display that would be to his liking with the hope that the thought of new dancers was enough to get Vespasian to come along with his wife.

Like all powerful men, Vespasian offered his wife in the formalities of Rome but he favoured another. He had married Flavia Domitilla, who was native born in Sabratha to a motley bunch of Italian colonists who had moved there, during the reign of Augustus, or so he had been told. She was the daughter of Flavius Liberalis, who was a simple quaestors clerk and the rumour had it that in her earlier life, his wife was mistress to an African knight.

But then, Laurentius noted to himself, there was no way of measuring taste or choice and clearly Vespasian's wife Flavia, had little in the way of those. Still, she did well with Vespasian and clearly, she held the intelligence to see his promise earlier than most.

He smiled inwardly at the thought of the emperor's mistress. Antonia Caenis, a woman of no standing. But, that choice of woman, overtly displayed the emperor's attraction to lower class women. She was a former slave and secretary of Antonia Minor, who in turn was the daughter of the famed Mark Anthony and Octavia Minor, niece of Augustus, no less, and the mother of the incompetent, stuttering fool, Claudius.

But who married a slave whether she was beautiful or not? He laughed out loud. The emperor, that's who! By the Gods, here was the most powerful man in Rome, who liked the low classes and drank from a working man's cup.

Cassius dropped the reins of his chariot, stepping down with a careful glance at the ground outside his villa on the seventh hill of Rome. He arrived home earlier than he thought, but there was little to do that late afternoon, after his visit to the site of the Flavian Amphitheatre.

He wiped his forehead of its light sheen of sweat below his close-cut, greying hair. Hoarse and heavy breathing could be heard from the two horses in front of him and the sound made him a little happier as he briefly listened.

He whipped them hard on the ride up from the city and there was nothing like taking a whip to chariot horses, to shock them out of their inherent laziness. Horses and slaves, he thought, as he walked towards the villa. Both held the same tendency to be naturally lazy and indolent and a stout whipping now and then, kept them in place.

Laurentius sat down heavily on the stone wall near the villa. He rubbed his ankle which refused to rid it itself of pain and looked briefly out at the fading sun behind the hill of Rome. The city stretched out beneath him, with oil lamps coming on and fires lit, to start preparation for the customary late meal.

The fruits of his business empire lay before him, from the high two storey villa clothed in orange and red ochre render and high plumes of red and pink bougainvillea, down to the stables at the back of the property, which held the finest horses that money could buy. The property held over one hundred slaves, who worked the house and long reaching vegetable and fruit gardens, surrounding the estate with five of his slaves, cooks, rated the finest food preparers, in all of the lands of Rome.

Any other man might be happy with the surroundings but he was not; not the man who sat on the heat of the stone wall that afternoon. He would trade it all, he thought, for more years of youth and to build something like the Forum and the Flavian Amphitheatre with his name sculpted on the front, for all to see long after he crossed the River and met *Mania* at the banks of the black water.

Yet, the honour of building those edifices, would be bestowed on a man who held none of Laurentius's wealth but held the ultimate power of Rome and that was the trust and respect of the Roman legions. Control of the army made a difficult, but solid key to the doors of power. The legions were never happy and Vespasian would not be the first emperor to give them the titbits necessary, to keep their complaints at a minimum.

Slowly, he raised himself from the wall and walked, as was his custom, through the slave's quarters to see if they were working and to punish any if they slacked off. He noted with some satisfaction that as they bowed their heads to him, there remained that glint of fear. Fear remained the most powerful motivation in his business empire. It worked socially as well, he reflected.

He walked through the long corridor in the bottom of the house finally rising up the steps, past the larders on the right. He heard the unmistakable sounds of moaning as he passed the second door. In the first instant, he thought it might have been slaves at each other yet again and he gripped his whip in his left hand to open the door with his right. Then he heard a sound he knew only too well.

Clearly, his wife was starting the party early and knowing her desire for young, muscular men he knew what his eyes would find if he opened the door. His desire to see the scene moved the door handle quietly and he peeked in.

There she lay, naked on the sacks of wheat with her head back, moaning loudly with her black hair, cascaded across the hessian sacks. A young man, dark haired, short and muscular, pounded her with long powerful thrusts as she convulsed in pleasure with each plunge, her hands on his butt, pulling him inwards.

He watched for a while with a slight smile on his face as he retreated back to the stairs. He walked up to the top level, called on the slaves to run a bath and made a quick review of the festivities to come.

As he bathed, Lucia walked in with her hair a mess and the flush of sexual gratification on her face. She dropped her tunic to the floor and stepped into the bath with him. He could not help but admire her curves and the darkness of her skin, highlighting her eyes. She was a rare beauty, even in her middle years of life.

'Any good?' He asked with a smile

She returned his gaze steadily and returned the smile. 'You heard?'

Laurentius nodded without taking his eyes off her. 'Too quick.' She replied 'They are all the same when they are young. Hard and quick.'

'Better than soft and quick.' Laurentius laughed and with surprise, noting he was growing hard for a change. There was a time in his life he could not keep it down and now he could hardly keep it up.

'Get on your knees, Lucia.' He said, starting to rise.

She looked up at him with her large, brown almond eyes and nodded.

He entered her, with the warmth of the bath water surrounding his flanks and her soft moaning filling his senses.

CHAPTER 31

That night, Emperor Vespasian arrived, as his habit dictated, as the passenger on a beautiful chariot, emblazoned with his crest and two of his finest steeds leading the carriage. He remained a man who understood horses better than most. His mother had been the matriarch of their equestrian empire and he was able to ride before he learnt to walk.

Behind him, a larger chariot kept close with three Pretorian guards as security, watching him and his movements with close interest.

He alighted and strode purposefully towards the front entrance of the Laurentius villa. He inspected the grounds as he made his way and as always, the grounds were in spectacular condition. The soft evening light, fell across the olive grove on the back hill and above it the moon started to peek, with a silver halo to announce its arrival.

Without doubt, his host of the night was a man of discerning taste and ruthless ambition. A perfect senator, he thought briefly with an inwards smile and the thought that the price of the senatorship lay in the wealth of favour, or both.

Rome had never been built with the view to *maius bonum*. It was built on the proceeds of division and conquest and the personal ambitions for political longevity, by the various emperors and senators who served the state for their own purposes. Everyone, in political life, held two agendas. The first was the outer face of public concern and conviviality. The second, usually hidden deeply, was an unquenchable thirst for power.

There was no *maius bonum*. no greater good, no matter how many times he heard that phrase or anything like it. All change came back to personal ambition and the personal greater good, of those who made an effort. He had learnt early in his political career that power inevitability corrupted. It was just a matter of how much power was on offer.

The act of war, he knew from personal experience, served a purpose outside of Rome's aggrandisement. It was the accumulation of silver and gold, making the difference between a city of poor and belittled citizens, to a grand city offering public buildings, sewerage and water aqueducts and care for the ordinary plebeian.

Vespasian admitted to his son, Titus, before he left for Judea for the second major siege, that for the first time in his life, he felt old and felt it every single day. When Titus asked him what he meant, he made it clear. His familiar, old supply of energy was waning and the old wounds making his life hell, no matter how the doctors treated them. It was harder to rise from his slumber and more difficult to continue his punishing schedule, each and every day

He candidly explained that the purpose of the arena, the Flavian Amphitheatre, more magnificent than the world had ever seen, was to ensure the name Vespasian could live on in the eyes of the world, for more years than he might survive.

The cost of both buildings continued as an issue, with the price running well beyond, several hundred thousand Denarii. However, the welcome gold from the Jerusalem temples made the difference, as would the patronage of the host of the opulent Casa, in front of him.

The only question remaining was how to get his host to release some of his staggering wealth, to assist in the finalisation of the Amphitheatre. He gave his whip to a servant at the door and entered to find Cassius Laurentius and his beautiful wife waiting for him. 'Am I the first to arrive?'

'Ah, no, dear Flavian, you are close to the last but we are pleased to see you at any time.' Lucia said with a wide, welcoming smile and a lingering kiss on his cheek.

Flavian handed her a small gift of a lapis lazuli, bracelet. She took it and immediately put it on with a broad smile. She held the Roman ideal of beauty with a white face, bright red lips and with dark eye makeup accentuating the colour of her eyes. Her scent reached his nostrils and she had obviously washed prior to the gathering, in water perfumed with cinnamon and balsam. There was a hint of rose and orange and another scent that he could not make out while he studied her seductive face.

'You are too generous, emperor Vespasian.' She cooed softly.

Vespasian dismissed her with a wave of his hand. 'Ah, Lucia it is your birth day today is it not? It is a small present with my heartfelt respect.' He looked at her briefly again admiring her beauty then he turned to look around the villa room and then back to her eyes.

'My thanks.' She wore the standard garment of the upwardly mobile women in the empire of Rome, which was a *Stole*, a long-pleated dress that was draped around her shapely body and pinned together by tortoiseshell fibulae.

Brooches that gathered the fabric were strategically placed under her ample breasts and at the point of her hips. The colour, held a bright green with gold bands.

Her heavily made up eyes, complemented her high eyebrows and wide face. Sometimes her beauty took his breath away. Without doubt, Cassius remained a lucky man, he mused and no doubt his wealth did not hurt the success of the marriage.

'Where is your good wife?' She asked with a perfumed hand on his arm

'Unfortunately, she is ill. Something to do with her head. I am told she is on the mend and she sends her apologies.'

'We wish her a quick recovery, so please pass that on.' Vespasian nodded and walked towards Laurentius who had been waiting patiently for the interchange between his wife and the emperor to finish.

'Flavian, welcome to our humble abode.' Laurentius said, offering the arm-to-arm handshake that many used on a welcoming greeting.

Vespasian looked at his host with mock surprise. 'Dear Cassius, there is much we can say about this magnificent villa, but humble is not one of them!'

The two men laughed together as they walked down the hall. They passed under the chill air of the open atrium above, where a hint of cooler night air fell from the open area of the ceiling. Vespasian admired the ostentatious wealth of the house. It was not to his more plebeian and minimal taste, but it was adventurous and grand on scale he did not love but could admire.

Long, colourful tapestries hung down the walls. Along the long corridor, the finest marble mosaics were inscribed into the floor with scene after scene of gladiators and animals, inlaid into the floor. Incense burned from several pots on the walls and the scent seemed everywhere.

'Is this new?' He asked stopping at one particular panel. The mosaic showed a panther lying on the ground beneath a Bestarii and his spear.

'Very new, Flavian.' Lucia said. 'We had it commissioned in your honour.'

Vespasian smiled at the lie and continued his walk.

They entered a door tended by two large, dark skinned slaves. The interior of the room was the same as many he had entered in his adult life. Along the sides of the room, sat eating couches and a large entertainment floor, with white Terrazzo tiles and black curtains. Lamps on long poles created cascading light down the walls.

The couches were complete with serving tables and flasks of wine in front of each of them. Dark wood, combined with mother of pearl inlay, made Vespasian think of the cost of such fine furniture. But, at the same time, realised that the entire villa was a testament to the wealth of the man before him.

The feast on the table made his mouth water as the dishes were brought out one-by-one. Suckling pig, an assortment of sweetmeats, pheasants with top feathers still adorning their carcasses, wild boar hindquarters and as much dressing of cold vegetables and sauces as they could fit on the table.

Behind them, a tune was played on a fiddle which was low enough to be in background and to assist the mood of the night.

Flavius Sabinus Vespasianus, moved across to the guests and shook their hand. Senator Lucius Rufus, dressed in his toga smiled warmly at the emperor as he rose to take his hand. Vespasian nodded to him and bent down to kiss the cheek of Rufus's wife. She was a large woman, overweight and weighed down by the jewelled bracelets that adorned her arms and wrists.

He moved to Senator Gaius Sabinas, who moved from his prone position to rise as Vespasian moved to take his hand. He was a large man towering over the emperor. His time in the army and a sparse diet showed in his wide shoulders and strong, muscular physique. His greying hair was left unfashionably long with curls, that fell across his wide forehead.

Vespasian bent down to kiss his wife, who equalled Lucia Laurentius for beauty but with a basic taste in fashion which more suited his preference for what women chose to wear. He lingered momentarily, as he embraced her from above and lightly brushed her cheek.

'Antonia, beautiful as usual.' He said graciously and unaware of the look between Claudia, the wife of Rufus and Lucia, who winked at her when he made the remark.

After a stroll to inspect the long table of food, Vespasian made his way back to his allotted couch. As he sat down, Lucia sat beside him and poured him a long tumbler of wine.

'You remembered? 'Of course.' she replied. 'Your wish for a basic cup is always in my mind because it is so unusual and so refreshing.' She smiled.

Vespasian nodded as he gazed briefly into her eyes. She held an air of seductiveness that he sensed in very few women and if the rumours were true she acted on it. His eyes fell to her breasts, barely touching the fabric of her tunic top and the emerald green of her large eyes.

'Please drink up, emperor Vespasian.' She said breathlessly. 'We have looked forward to having you here tonight. 'Girls' She called out. 'Fill the cups of your men and let us drink in honour of the emperor who has graced us with his presence tonight.'

'Let me return that favour and a drink from all of us, to you, on your feast day.'

In turn they raised their wine and drank deeply to Cassius Laurentius and his wife.

Cheers surrounded the emperors couch as he sipped his wine and chose from several delicacies sitting on a dish, in the hands of a beautiful girl who stood semi-naked to his side. She was blond with blue eyes and without any doubt, he had rarely viewed such a beauty.

'My Lord' She said without looking directly at him. 'What will be your choice?' He pointed his finger at several of the sweetmeats which was handed to him in a small bowl by another attendant. The blond girl stood to his side, looking towards the performance floor.

'Do you dance tonight, girl?'

'I do.'

'Then I will look forward to it.'

He turned his attention to Laurentius who lay on a couch opposite him and raised his cup in appreciation of the feast. 'Ah, Cassius you might

---

287

wish you were a senator because today one of your esteemed guests gave the speech of the year.'

Laurentius looked over at him and then at the other two men who were pushing food into their mouths as quickly as it was served. 'Don't tell me, Flavian it must have been Gaius.'

'Ha, how could you have guessed. By the power of Jupiter, he was in fine form. A rousing speech on the future of the great city of Rome and how we should employ the funds we have gained from Judea. What was that mention you made in the speech, Gaius?

Sabinus shifted his position on the couch and took a long swig of wine. '*carpe noctum*. Let us seize the night upon us and make Rome as powerful as possible.'

'A nice play on *carpe Diem*, Gaius. Using the night term rather than the day. You write all your speeches.'

Gaius looked at Laurentius with mock surprise. 'But of course, Cassius. I don't have your wealth to purchase speech writers.'

Laurentius smiled at the slight, turning his attention back to Vespasian. 'So, Flavian, all is well in the state of good Rome?'

'Never well; Always a sick patient.' Vespasian scoffed. 'At least the senate has an honourable man like Gaius who will stand up and make a statement that is to assist all and not just himself.'

Rufus laughed out loud. 'That's because you can never shut him up at any time let alone in the senate.'

They chortled at the remark as wine cups were refilled and the suckling pig came from the oven. It was laid on the table quietly by the servants but the scent of the honey, glazed meat filled the noses of all around the seating area. The attendants filled the bowls, which were passed to the guests with haste to keep the meat warm.

'How goes the building?' Laurentius asked, over the discussion between Lucia and Antonia. 'I think you know only too well, Cassius, as my spies tell me you have visited the sites on a number of occasions.'

Laurentius smiled at the remark and looked up to the ceiling. 'You flatter me too much, Flavian, but I like to keep my eye on things in the city. I also have an offer for you Flavian if you would like to hear it.'

The emperor nodded and with a flourish of his hand. 'Do tell us your offer.' He said with an air of mild interest but inside he felt the pang of expectation.

Laurentius sat up on the couch and with his eye on the three of them, he refilled his glass and sat back. "Well, in order to make the Flavian Amphitheatre, the wonder of the Roman world, we need to offer it so that Romans will be lined up to attend and the world will hear of its grandeur.'

'Agreed.' Gaius added as the wine started to dull of his senses.

'I was thinking that we open it with one hundred days of games and yes, I understand that this is a large cost. However, the Flavian Amphitheatre will be opened, in such a way, that the world will see for what it is.'

'And what is that, Cassius?' Vespasian asked

'A wonder of the world, Flavius. A genuine wonder of the world.'

"Large cost, Cassius.' Gaius said quickly. 'A very large cost indeed. Whilst the opening is far off, it does make sense to make it bigger than most of us might expect. But one hundred days of games. By the Gods, that is beyond anything we have ever offered.'

'Makes sense.' Vespasian said, as he popped another small cut of pork into his mouth. He roughly wiped the sides of his mouth with a cloth and let out a deep sigh. 'Expensive though.'

Laurentius smiled at them. 'Yes, a great expense indeed. However, for naming rights of the opening with the name Laurentius across the placards and inscribed in stone in the Flavian Amphitheatre, I would be willing to assist in the cost.'

'How willing?' Gaius asked with a wide smile.
'Half.'

'Half?' Vespasian blurted out. 'I have underestimated your wealth, Cassius, but I am heartened by your support of the city of Rome.'

'Plus, a senate seat.' Laurentius said with an expectant look on his face.

'Ah, the wolf has a lamb's coat.' Rufus laughed, watching his wife rise to join Lucia and Claudia.

'Hmm, When?' Vespasian asked quietly.

'Business, always business.' Rufus' wife said abruptly, as she changed couches.

'By the time the Amphitheatre opens, Flavian, because it works for all of us. I get a seat in the senate, the games are underwritten by my wealth and it would be shown that I assisted with the funds, and, let me emphasize that Rome gets the games for one hundred days. What could be more magnificent? Imagine, one hundred days of bread and wine, of Bestarii and large chariot races. Not to mention the extraordinary number of gladiatorial contests.'

Vespasian looked at him with a broad smile. The First Gladiator of Rome flashed into his mind. The question remained as to whether Cassius Laurentius could be managed. He hid his wariness of the man across from him.

This was a power play and nothing was surer that if he succeeded his next move might be a higher position which included emperor. However, he did not have and would never have, the support of the army. His mind reflected his son, Titus. Could he manage this man? The answer was in the affirmative.

'What say you Gaius and Felix. Is this a reasonable offer?'

They nodded and Vespasian smiled at his host. 'Well, let us work on it and while we are, why not bring the dancers on? But, before you do, Cassius let me explain that in order for you to take a seat on the Palatine hill you will, unfortunately, pay dearly. I might add that such a senate seat is unheard of unless you have a background in the law and this is going to take some manoeuvring.'

'How expensive?' Laurentius asked moving to the front of his couch.

Vespasian looked over at the two expectant senators on their couches with a light smile on his face. 'Seventy-five percent, of the cost of the one hundred days.'

'Seventy-five percent? Flavian, that is a large sum!'

'It is, Cassius but the cost of a senate seat is expensive as well and that is included in that offer.'

'Not with your influence, Flavian.'

'But, exactly, Cassius. It is my influence and your money.'

Vespasian watched as Laurentius went through the sums in his head. He looked over at Lucia who nodded her head, turning her attention back to her female guests. Finally, he turned to his three guests. 'I agree and it will take me that long to save the funds.' He laughed and they joined in.

'Then we have agreement, Cassius?' Vespasian asked, surprised at how quickly his host had agreed. He should have gone for more.

'Happily, Flavius, we have an agreement?'

Vespasian looked over at the two senators sitting on their respective couches and raised one eyebrow. 'Well that creates a question. Would we have support of the senate gentlemen?'

'Unknown until we tout it.' Lucius said as he received another bowl of roast pork.

'I think we could pass it.' Gaius said reflectively. 'We of course, would have free access and patronage for the games?'
Laurentius shrugged. 'But of course, dear Gaius, of course. That will be open to all senators.' Gaius sat back on his couch. 'Yes, I think it will work and why would anyone oppose it. Lucius Rufus, what say you?'

'Yes, I believe it will be accepted.'

'Then we have a deal.' Laurentius rose from his seat, took the wine jug and personally refilled the glasses of his guests. He then raised his in return. 'To the games!'

Vespasian smiled thinly at Laurentius. 'You are a sly dog, Cassius but I believe we have a deal. Now the dancers?'

'Of course.' Laurentius nodded to one of the attendants. 'While we wait for them to start, please update us on the Judea situation. I believe Titus has returned to the country.'

'He has and I received a message only yesterday and the siege of Masada is starting. My understanding is the high fort offers the last stronghold of resistance, in that hell hole and my order to Titus is to take the fortress and put everyone to the sword. There are logistical problems with this one, as the fortress was built high on a mountain and there are steep sides to all parts of the fort, save one road, a wide goat track, that winds around the fort and it is easily guarded from above.'

What then?' Laurentius asked

'They are in the process of building the longest, and might I add, deepest rampart to one side of the wall that any of our engineers have ever attempted. In fact, they have just started construction. Not bad, eh?'

Laurentius looked at Vespasian with genuine surprise on his face. 'They are building it out of solid earth?'

Vespasian nodded. 'It's the only way to get access but these Sacariii rebels will pay with their lives.'

'How many does the fort hold?' Lucia asked, with her attention moving from the two women sitting beside her.

'Over a thousand I believe, but I may be wrong. Come, let us not talk any more business.'

Laurentius took the sideways look from Lucia and she clapped her hands. The musicians came through the curtain and started a slow cadence, as the women, all blond and all beautiful, started the dance.

Laurentius moved quickly across to the couch inhabited by Vespasian. 'She is a beauty, is she not?'

Vespasian took in the view with his eyes firmly on the legs of the woman who had served him before. 'She is.'

Cassius whispered to his emperor. 'Then she is yours and across the line of the curtains is another room. At the end of the night she will be waiting for you. I am told she is very practised and very, very accommodating.'

'Ah, Cassius, you are such a generous man but tonight I have other duties to attend, once I leave.'

Laurentius smiled at his emperor and then gazed at the dancers for a moment. 'Of course, Flavian, but she will be there waiting if you wish to meet her. We will be retiring by that time but if you would rather go then we will be there to farewell you. You have been very kind to come along in the first place.'

Vespasian nodded as Cassius moved back to his couch with a smile at Lucia. She joined him on the couch. 'Yes?'

Laurentius shook his head. 'She is there for you and me.

292

CHAPTER 32

Marcus and Ovidius sat by a fire, looking absently into the glowing coals. Each in their own thoughts and with the view of the fortress of Masada, high on a mountain above them.

Luminescence, cast by the full moon, radiated across the sandy countryside. Far above them, the moonlight highlighted the walls of the fortress. The light cast an eerie glow across the mountain sides, that fell steeply from the base of the fort walls to the desert far below, where they sat, side by side, warmed by the fire.

The only road to the fort, hardly a cart track, wound up the mountain side like a coiled serpent up the Western side to the fortress. The road, washed to a whiter hue by the moon light, stood out against the darker grey of the cliffs.

Marcus rubbed his hands in front of the fire, eyeing the tent and his uncomfortable bed with yearning. He had endured, well over a thousand cold nights and hundreds of battles, in the land of Judea. He could scarcely remember how long it had been since the sacking of Jerusalem and the loss of his men. Two years? Three? Now he felt more tired than he could remember since that fateful voyage from Italia so long before.

The desolation and inhospitable climate of the land bore down on his energy, as it did almost everyone else. The sentiment was shared by the legion, with grumbling and complaints higher than he had ever heard or witnessed. The corps were tired of the land of Judea, and the Roman generals, in their fateful resolve to wipe out any remaining resistance pursued the Sacarii with vengeful purpose.

The news, older than the meagre meat they gained in their meals told the story of Flavius Vespasian, the fifth emperor with several years and the stronghold he and his son, Titus held on the city and its constituents. The years had passed to the point that he was not sure of the month or the year in which they bivouacked, fought, marched and bivouacked yet again. He spat on the dry earth by the fire, watching as it spread out, unable to sink into the dry, hard soil.

The food was inedible and despite a number of furloughs, when they returned to Caesarea, he found the women dark and unattractive. A visit to a whore, made a brief and uninspiring interlude and each night he found himself longing for the farm and for Rome and his friends. Even the thought of gambling no longer interested him.

Before the march to Masada, Sextus had fallen ill from food he purchased in one of the markets and died from dysentery some weeks later. The conturbenium was no more and he thought that one more death might make little difference but as he looked across at Ovi he realized how much he missed Sextus and the others. It did not matter how the conturbenium brothers died, Marcus reflected as he placed another log on the fire; it was a loss of yet another brother.

The farm stayed constantly on his mind. In a recurring dream, he sat on a stump near the old stream speaking to his brother. Afterwards they would walk back to the farmhouse where his mother was waiting with a meal. Above, the sky was blue. It was summer, with the heat dissipating in the lazy afternoon and the outside table adorned with picked blossoms, with the food he loved to eat.

His brother entered his thoughts one afternoon, as his arm was bound from yet another wound from a Sacarii ambush, and for the first time he looked at his legs and arms realising, they were almost the same as those livid scars he saw on Britanicus on that day in the arena. He wondered what his mother might think of him now, scarred and tired of the battle.

He rubbed slowly across the new bandage, trying to reduce the wincing pain and lay on his back to look at the Judean sky. It was no different to the farm save the fact that there was rarely a cloud except in the very late months and early months of the year in the Mount Olympus forgotten, bunghole.

The sky held a lesson which crossed his mind. His time in the legion and the constant battles and skirmishes had changed his life irrevocably, as those forces in turn, had changed him. He no longer felt scared and he had lost, probably forever, his boyish enthuasism and he found little joy in what he did.

He realized it must be more than four years that had passed after that last day in the temple square, of the holy city, Jerusalem. In his mind, he could still revisit the battle of that day and the enduring loss of a man, he respected and four brothers that he loved, as part of his Conturbenium. The loss of Sextus had all but darkened his mood, to the point that he could not laugh.

They had trusted him and like Arius before them, on that fateful day at the bottom of the Mount of Olives, he had not been able to protect them properly. Despite his grudging respect for Brutus, the loss of that man affected him more than the others and perhaps for a very good reason. The man had taken the time and respect to show him the value of loyalty. Whatever he did in the army from the day of Brutus' death, on the stone floor of Jerusalem, was in honour of the Centurion.

The legions had met their duties and sacked Jerusalem and for that they received the generous sum of a meal, and a march, to the East of Judea to chase the Sacarii. Some had purloined treasure and coins but anything larger of value was taken by the Centurions to assist in their retirement. The rest, including the treasure they had witnessed in the temple, was escorted back to Rome for a triumphal march on the return of Titus.

Of course, Titus returned to take the praise, while they marched to fight the Sacarii. This had stuck in the craw of many a soldier, in the months following the final day at Jerusalem. A triumphal march, without the legions who fought, to celebrate the day.

For his part, he and Ovidius had stood guard over the fallen leader of the Jerusalem rebels as the rest pushed on to find the other leader, Simon. He was found and finally captured, trying to escape.

By the time they were relieved, of guarding the exhausted Jew and moved to the city, there was little to find in the way of gold or jewels that could be stowed out of sight. Each of them pilfered a few coins and Ovidius, a small statue made of gold, but it was far less than the most of the others. For the capture of John of Giscala? Not a mention of the one hundred gold coins. If he complained, he would be whipped and he knew it.

From their position on the square that day they heard the sounds of Jewish soldiers put to death by swords and daggers and the loud shrieks of women raped as they tried to escape Roman revenge. There was not an officer in any of the legions who might put a stop to it. Only the strongest prisoners were kept and the rest put to the sword.

From that time on, and through the monotony of day-by-day marching, they continued into the dusty, brown terrain of Judea. The only break in the monotonous countryside, was a team of camels led by a local tribesman, or the welcome relief of a Wadi break in the land, offering water and vegetation.

This was a land forsaken by all of their Gods, as dry as an empty barrel of wine and with less appeal. Only three legions were left in Judea, being the famed Tenth, the Fifth and Fourth. The others were despatched years

---

before to Egypt, to take up the Roman cause in another dry, unforgiving and featureless land.

The landscape held little attraction for any of the men and since the Sacarii used skirmish tactics, it meant that they were on edge every time they marched through terrain, where the rebels could hide and provide cover for an attack.

When the Sacarii attacked, it was fast and brutal and by the time the side of the legion had recovered, the Sacarii retreated. The sides of the legions were now constantly on the watch and the governor and legion head, Lucius Silva, finally relented, posting horse guards at the side, with their job to watch the hills and culverts as they passed on foot.

The cloud raised up by the legions could be seen from any distance in the dry land. Since Lucius Flavius Silva, was also the siege commander and governor of Judea, he believed in travelling in force. The legions were commanded to march together.

Ovidius had grumbled almost every day that the dust clouds would offer evidence and advance warning to the enemy. Even the Gods on Mount Olympus could see like everyone else did, the hazy, dust storm kicked up by the men and the accompanying drays.

Late that year, they had taken up residence around the bottom of the Masada fortress to the West, on the higher ground where the fifth legion set up camp and had hurriedly built the wall, on the Western side.

The Tenth, were located at the East and they had barely beaten the Western legion and the Fourth, to finalise the wall around the base of the steep hills, that led up to the Masada fortress. Most of them looked at the three and half mile wall with grumbling admiration, because the earth was so sandy it was built from hacked stone blocks.

Marcus could clearly see the siege road, built by the Jewish prisoners in the light of the brilliant moon. With a squint of his eyes, he could make out the ongoing work, day and night as they filled in the culvert. They intended to build a road strong enough to take a large siege machine, which had been transported from Jerusalem behind a team of fourteen draft horses.

They had already lost quite a few engineers and workers, in the process of building the siege road, as the Sacarii archers were accurate and gave no favouritism to their own. If they were digging or dropping earth, they were fair game, and many a time Marcus was at the start of the road assisting with the timber supply, to hear a shout or cry and see a worker fall down into the ravine, with an arrow sticking out.

The scared engineers would hurriedly move back behind the barricades, waiting for the archers to pause, before moving out again onto the road.

The engineers had constructed armaments at each stage to protect the workers but within the first four months the '*ants,*' as they called them, were in range and the Sacarii waited patiently for any opportunity to unleash. There were some times of the day, the archers disappeared, and no one could work out why. In those times, the work was feverishly fast.

The word had been passed around the legionnaires, the day before, that the siege machine was finished. They all watched from below as it was rolled up from behind by men and horses, up the Roman built culvert road, to the wall. He heard word from one of the men working behind the colossus that the engineers held their breath, as the massive machine was pushed up the long road. If the road collapsed, the siege machine would be destroyed, along with the horses and one hundred men pushing it.

When the cadence of the ram started, it held a familiar sound from years before outside Jerusalem. The massive steel head of the ram, attached to a long, four-cubit square post, was winched back behind the stout timber and iron wall, to be released to fly through the front of the siege machine and hit the massive stone wall of Masada, with shattering impact.

Each concussion, sent an echo through the fort and down the valley to where the legions were camped. The cadence was slow and continued unabated. The wall would breach quickly, according to the engineers, and the Tenth would be the first to go through, with Tirarii on the sides.

CHAPTER 33

Ovidius and he, had been given the great honour of being made Triarii; They were promoted after the sacking of Jerusalem and in that award, they were escalated into the elite fighters of the Fifth legion. Their promotion had been assisted by the losses of Triarii at the final battle at Jerusalem and many of those lost Triarii, had been killed by the Jewish archers in the first hour of the raging battle.

The Triarii kept at the back of the battle lines, shield to the fore and one knee on the ground until they were called in. Then with cold, brutal efficiency they moved through the ranks and once in front of the enemy, their killing skills were ruthlessly administered.

They no longer sat in the Conturbenium squads and they were without a Centurion to command them. They worked in unison as they knew each other's skills intimately, as they held the skill set necessary to kill efficiently and quickly, without remorse and with prodigious speed. It was a known fact that the sharpest swords and daggers kept the company of the Tirarii.

Marcus likened the Triarii movement, as each battle progressed much like a deadly dance. After fighting as many battles as he and the other men had encountered, they could almost forecast the moves made by the enemy.

As Triarii, they were highly conditioned killers. They understood the parts of the body where a kill was quickly administered, or at the very least, a mortal injury that took a man to the floor with no hope of rising. They were conditioned over countless battles to control, where others panicked, creating the savage, unrelenting movements of their razor-sharp swords to create a breech.

When they entered battle, many of the front-line legionaires pulled back to watch them with awe.

Marcus looked over at Ovidius. He had pulled a piece of bread and hard cheese from his pack and he passed half over to Marcus, who ate it contentedly by the fire on that cold night. The Sacarii, he knew from experience, were not battle experienced fighters and they could only fight with a short sword and dagger. One of the old-timers had told him that the Sacarii meant 'dagger men' for a very good reason. In hand-to-hand combat, the skirmishers moved with deft speed and with a flashing knife in both hands.

Many of the Roman Triarii learnt quickly; that a flashing right hand by the Scarii feinted away to hold the attention, whilst the left was cutting up into their torso and before they realised the move it was too late. At least several of the boys had been disembowelled, while fending the high hand that held the larger knife.

They soon learnt, that as soon as a high hand with a knife moved, they took a small step back and drove through with their shield to uppercut and block the lower hand and then upwards with their Gladius into the neck of the assailant.

Whilst they were held in awe by the front ranks they were unusually calm before a battle, with many a joke being told before they were ordered to move forward. Long experience in battle, Marcus realised, allowed a relaxed approach to killing and each of the Triarii had favoured moves in battle, which many in the front ranks copied without success.

The Triarii moved forward, in formation, with each man knowing what the other was doing, when to assist and when to gain assistance. The one goal they all held was to move forward, so that the enemy that were wounded could be finished off by the lower ranks, as they took the position behind the Triarii advance. Battle continued with cold blooded movements that either killed or mortally wounded those in the way

CHAPTER 34

Eleazar Ya'ir started to give orders to his men, as he stood high above, calmly looking over the wall at the massive siege engine sitting squarely on the siege road and listening to the force of the ram as it slammed full force into the wall. He remained astonished at the audacity and capability of the Roman war machine, beneath his walls.

'We do not have long' He said slowly and with a tiredness in his voice.

'Where do we start the defence?' One of them asked. Ya'ir shrugged as he looked down at the siege machine once again.

'First of all, we should fortify the wall behind, with another row of blocks but it may not make a difference. I want you to tell everyone this morning that we have little in the way of choices here.'

'I think they know that, Eleazar.' One of them replied.

Ya'ir nodded slowly. 'Once the Roman dogs breech the wall and make an entrance, it will be the end. They are not here to take prisoners and let me tell you now, my friends, it will be a slaughter. There are only two choices and I understand that one of them is much against our religion but the alternative is not going to be fun.'

'Meaning?' The officer replied

'Meaning, we have a choice and everyone is to know that and I trust you to spread the word.'

Yehuda smiled grimly at the inference and made his way to the bottom of the wall. The concussion from the ram was deafening and could be heard, from one end of the fort to the other. He went over to one of the engineers who was standing closer to the inner wall than the others. As the ram was drawn back for another pulverising blow, the voices of the engineers behind the siege machine could be heard clearly.

'How long?'

The man held a terrified look on his face. He winced as the ram exploded against the outer wall again. 'Maybe until late afternoon, maybe a little

---

later but sooner rather than later.'

Yehuda nodded. 'Will a new inner wall hold?'

'Barely'

'Will another wall assist?'

The man shook his head contemplatively. 'No, I don't think so. Once a wall starts to fall it takes much of the construction with it, so it will not create much difference. Once this part of the wall falls, under the weight of the above parapets, all will fall with it' He used his hands to emphasize the point.

'Do it anyway.' Came the reply. 'At least it will give the engineers something to do.'

'They are not, engineers, Yehuda. I am the only engineer.'

Yehuda smiled at him. 'Yes, I know, but you know what I mean.'

Suddenly from above they heard a shout. 'Fire, fire!'

Yehuda ran up the steps with the man behind him. As they reached the top, they saw that the Roman engineers had set up a fire against the wall, to create heat against the stone.

'Can we use water?' Yehuda said quickly, without being able to think of any other way.

'Too far away, friend. Too far away.' He looked up at Eleazar, who remained calm as he always did under severe stress.

The engineer tugged at Yehuda's sleeve. 'Feel; The wind is changing.' He said excitedly and as they looked the flames from the huge fire, set against the wall, as it started to turn back on the siege machine and within minutes the mid-section of the hard-dried timbers, were alight. As buckets were produced to quell the burning timbers, the Sacarii archers let loose, killing anyone who showed their body outside the siege machine wall.

Ya'ir ran down the stairs with Yehuda close behind him. 'We may have a chance brother. The only option I can think of, is to let the women and children out and anyone who is not a trained soldier then let them walk in mass down the road.'

301

'The Romans will slaughter them.' Yehuda replied calmly, as they walked to the wall section across from the siege point, so they could look down.

'No, I don't think so. Not if they walk down in mass. They are after us and the fort and we can take that chance.'

As they inspected the doors, and the old road that led down the mountain, Ya'ir put his hand up into the air. 'It's changing again.' He said grimly and started to sprint back to the wall position over the siege machine. The flames had returned to the wall side with the siege machine front smouldering, but not alight, and the cadence started it's jarring once again.

'This wind is gaining strength and that helps the Roman dogs.' Ya'ir said slowly and without emotion. 'Tell everyone to prepare tonight, because tomorrow morning at first light, the Romans will be opening the door.'

'What about sending the people out?' Yehuda asked as he watched the smoke rise from the wall base.

'It is too late, Yehuda.' He said, with a hand on the man's shoulder.

'Then?'

'Ask them, my friend. I cannot make such a decision.' Yehuda looked at his friend as tears rolled down both of their cheeks. 'Tomorrow, we make a stand. One way or another.'

Yehuda looked at Ya'ir, a man he had fought alongside for ten years and he knew without doubt what he meant. Tears rolled down his cheek onto his beard, as he turned to let the council know the situation, so a decision could be made.

CHAPTER 35

It was the twelfth day of Aprilis, as the tenth legion and attending Triarii, crouched behind the siege machine which had finally busted through the Masada fort wall. The acrid smell of smoke and burning timber, permeated though the air.

Marcus checked his shield tie, which had become loose, and for some reason. the day felt eerily like that day behind the barricade, at the final siege point in Jerusalem. The only difference that Marcus could discern, was the lack of sound coming from inside the fort.

The orders, before they made the march, under shields towards the massive black timbered machine at the top of the road, were made with hard edged certainty. The Triarii would assist on the sides, of the *Legio X Fretensis*; The tenth, as the famed legion of Caesar, would be the only legion to move in, whilst the other legions stood, fully clothed in battle gear, at the ready on the hill top at the start of the ramp.

The rumour held that Titus had returned to Rome with full command given to general Silva. No one had seen him so that was the assumption. Unlike Titus, Silva did not lead from the front. He was *dux explendos ritus tabernaculi*, a 'tent general' as the men referred to him in a less than respectful manner.

In the light of the early morning, they could look down to his tent complex, which was bathed in light from oil lamps that lit the outside and inside of the canvas structures, to a dull glow. Inside, one of those tents, and probably the largest, sat Governor Silva as he studied the plan and barked orders. No doubt, he would attend once the battle had ended.

With the wall breeched and the Legio X Fretenis and attending Triarii at the ready, the order was made to move in quickly and there was a tacit understanding from the top down, that there were
no prisoners to be taken that day.

Everyone; man, women and child were to be put to the sword.

Still, there was a strange silence that hung over the low mumbling of the men, as they stood, at the ready, for the attack. It was unsettling to Marcus, as he stood there on the side of the three men in columns, who made up the Tenth. There were no shouts, no archers, no fires inside to stop their progress. From what he could see, there was no welcoming party and that could only mean an ambush, somewhere inside the fort.

The way the wall had collapsed, had infuriated the Roma engineers, as they were forced to build steps to get into the breech. The bottom had fallen away and the stone blocks too heavy to move. They moved quickly to set up temporary steps and finally progress was allowed.

On command, they went in. The Tenth crouched in formation, with the Triarii from the other legions, at their side and with a shout they entered the breech, by vaulting up the stairs three at a time.

They passed the gloom of the inner wall and into the fort. They kept formation as they sprinted down the steps to the fort complex, with grunts and heavy breathing coming from most. A shout went up and the forward officer stopped suddenly, as all those following did the same, coming to a breathing standstill.

Across the top floor of the fort and in the light of the early morning sun, were fallen bodies, casting their fallen shadows. The ground was littered with the fallen corpses of nearly a thousand inhabitants.

Stunned and shocked by the scene, the Romans picked their way through the bodies, turning each over to see if they were really dead. Some appeared to have been poisoned. The congealed foam that came from their mouths told the story.

Some had committed suicide, by falling on their swords, whilst others had been run though at an angle they could not have completed themselves. Much of the blood had dried which meant it had occurred the night before.

Some of the Tenth legionnaires snorted in derision at the Jews who had suicided to avoid the fight, while others, shaking their heads at the vision, understood the meaning of the act. Marcus walked around with the other Triarii, turning the bodies over to check. He noticed only briefly that general Silva had followed the troops in and was standing slightly behind him. He had made it out of the tent.

'By the will of Zeus.' Lucius Silva said, with a low voice. 'What sort of an act is this?'

'An extreme one.' One of the Centurions said roughly. 'This is against their religious beliefs'

'I don't think anyone is alive.' Marcus mentioned, as he continued to turn bodies to see their faces. There were no moans or movement. The entire area was still.

'I think this one still breathes, but barely.' Ovidius said to Marcus, as he inspected the body. Marcus moved over to see the body in front of governor Silva.

'No one breathes over here.' Another Centurion called out.

Marcus turned to see who had spoken. As he did, he felt a savage rip through his shoulder that spun him around and sent him sprawling onto his back. Out of instinct that came from a thousand battles, he rose quickly and hardly able to breathe he looked down to see an arrow through his left side chest. It had travelled through his breastplate and protruded out his back.

He reached down feebly to pull it out, but as shock took over he felt his strength ebb and his knees buckle. Suddenly his strength left him and he went down hard to the stone below.

Ovidius was next to him as he fell and he immediately started to pull the arrow head out, calling for a medical orderly.

Marcus was barely conscious as his head rolled to the side. Hazily, in the distance, he could see two legionaires putting their swords into a tall man, with a long black beard, who had unleashed the arrow and then he started to black out.

'Ya'ir,' He heard governor Silva hiss, as he bent over Marcus to assist.

He saw Ovidius get pushed out of the way by a medical orderly, who cut the arrow and pulled it out of his chest. He then moved Marcus quickly, to pull it out of his back. Above him, he saw the orderly put the two halves together. 'Got it'

'Got what?' Marcus thought momentarily through the blood red haze of his eyes. All of a sudden, he felt engulfed by tiredness. Tired of the battles and forced marches. Tired of army food and a life exalted in the struggle of killing Roman enemies and bored in times of peace. He was tired inside, in the core, that gave him strength. Ovidius, always spoke around campfires of the time they would be hit by a sword or an arrow. His time had come and in a perverse, almost dreamlike way, he welcomed it. It was time, overtime, and like all Tirarii, he knew it was coming.

305

He lay flat on the earth of the Masada fort, as his strength ebbed from his body. Ovidius was beside him on his knees as his helmet was removed and his brow brushed with a rough cloth. 'Stay with us, brother, help is on the way.'

'Bad?' Marcus croaked, at his friend who looked down at him.

Ovidius nodded. 'Worse, I think. Keep awake and alive, Marco. Think of the legion and think of me. Who else is going to save me in the heat of battle? Stay alive, friend.'

Marcus felt Ovidius take his hand in a clasp, as they removed his breastplate. They lifted him to pull the back panel off and he heard a scream realising it was his own voice, resonating across the fort and for the first time, he knew he was dying.

He started to lose consciousness. He lay on the floor on the Masada fort, with blood dripping from the gaping wound made by the passage of the arrow. Slowly, drip by drip it pooled onto the cold stones below.

'Get him to the aide tent now.' Silva said quickly 'And make sure he gets the best of those butchers they call physicians, down there.' Governor Silva patted the arm of the Triarii as he lay prone and half unconscious before him. He was lifted up onto a stretcher and taken quickly down the siege road to the tents that lay on the back of the hill top. Ovidius looked at him and Silva nodded, allowing him to accompany Marcus down to the tent, far below on the plain.

Lucius Silva walked slowly amongst the bodies laid out on the stone and earth floor of the fort interior. He was speechless at the carnage, that laid before him. He shook his head, as if it might make a difference, closed his eyes briefly and then walked stiffly to the other end of the open area.

'Check the rest of the fort.' He said to a Centurion and then called out to the legionaires standing near the gate. 'Open it up and start the drays coming up. It will take us days to bury this mass suicide.'

One of his men walked by, still checking the prone bodies on the ground. 'Get me the body of Ya'ir before you do anything else. Hang that piece of horse shit from the top of the fort, for all to see and let the crows eat his eyes.'

He watched, as the large gates opened to the white road beyond. Whilst part of him felt relieved that Roman lives were saved that day and the fort was finally, conquered, he was still confused.

Twice, after he reached the gates, governor Silva stopped to look back at the mass of bodies behind him. It was almost as if there had been a battle and they had arrived well after the slaughter.

He remained astonished at what he witnessed that early morning. It was the strangest and most appalling sight he had ever seen, in twenty years of sieges and battles across the Roman empire. Was this the work of cowards? Were they unable to face the might of the Roman war machine? This was not the roman way but then perhaps, it was the way of the Sacarii. To Lucius Silva, it held the stench of disrespect.

He glanced over at where Ya'ir must have been standing when he unleased the arrow. He realised the arrow was directed at him. Marcus Attilius, at that split second, had got in the way.

Warriors did not take their own lives.

CHAPTER 36

The orderlies pushed Ovidius out of the tent. They told him, in no uncertain terms, not to come back for several days. They left Marcus in the medical tent without a second glance. It would be an easy day, as there were no other casualties, save an engineer who had fallen from the siege machine and broken his ankle.

As they left him in the tent, Marcus feebly heard one of them say. '*Mortem*' as they left him.

Despite the orders, shouted out by General Silva as he was carried away, he was laid on a dirty, badly stained stretcher in the tent; Bleeding profusely and with filthy binding shoved into his chest wound from the orderly at the fort top, he lay there sweating and groaning. Only his helmet and breastplate and shoulder harness had been removed. At the back, where the long arrow had punched through his breastplate, blood continued to pool on the dirty linen beneath him.

Semi-conscious, he tried to raise himself from the stretcher, only to be told by an aide that if he moved again, he would bleed to death. He could feel the binding shoved into his chest and his back and he looked down at the stretcher. It was soaked in his own blood. He said a prayer and fell back into darkness.

He barely felt the stiches applied by one of the doctors but he could hear the comments on his limited life and the size of the wound on his back. He lapsed in and out of consciousness as they packed the wounds, to try and staunch the bleeding.

The following morning, he was moving in and out of his delirium and he could faintly remember two doctors discussing him next to his stretcher. One had said matter-of-factly that they would be able to use the camp bed the next day because it was highly likely he would die in that coming night.

In the back of the tent he heard a commotion as Governor Silva walked into the tent and inspected the cot that Marcus lay on. He was delirious and could not make sense of the high pitched, discussion. 'Who left him here in this state?' Silva asked to anyone in earshot. He waited but there was no response.

'Let me make myself very clear. If that brave Tirarii dies, all of you, and I mean physicians and orderlies, you die with him. He is a Tirarii of the Fifth and I will let them loose in this tent if he dies. Do you understand!' He shouted at the top of his voice. 'Someone has left him for dead and be very fucking clear you bunch of dogs. If he goes I will flail the skin from your bodies before you die. Who were the orderlies that brought him in and who was the attending physician?'

'The wound is weeping badly' Said one voice feebly.

'That is not what I fucking asked. Who are they?'

Several orderlies moved forward with a physician next to them. Silva nodded to his guards who grabbed them screaming, from the tent.

'Now listen and listen well. I don't give a donkey's ass what is happening to him. Get him back from the dead and do it now! Be aware, I will be back each day to check on him. This goes from Titus Vespasian down. He will survive, or you will join him on the River bank and cross the black waters with him. I am leaving my personal physician here and he will be in charge. If he says move, you fucking move! Got it!' Silva snarled at the staff, turned around and left the tent.

A physician sat down next to the stretcher softly taking the bandages up and inspecting his chest. He whispered. 'Tirarii, can you hear me?'

Marcus nodded slightly, unable to raise his head. He felt feverish and hallucinating to the point, he thought he was talking to the doctor in the middle of a battle.

'Watch out for the archers' He mumbled to the man beside him.

The doctor placed his hand on Marcus' forehead and withdrew it after he realised the soldier was burning and that was never a good sign. 'My name is Actius and I am under direct orders to save you, Attilius and it appears a few lives in this tent, now rest on your recuperation.' He turned and told the rest to move away from the stretcher.

'Try to listen to me, if you can. You are very badly injured from that arrow and, frankly, lucky to be alive. The wounds continue to weep and unless we stop that you will die from a fever. The only solution I can think of, is to cauterize the wounds, but the risk is that the wounds continue internally and you will certainly die. However, I see no other option. It is your choice.'

Marcus looked at him though half closed eyes. The man held his gaze and with a hand resting on his shoulder, he watched as Marcus nodded, falling back into a stupor. Early that evening, he felt hands on his body, as he was moved over onto his stomach and he felt a liquid being poured into the wound. A flat stick was pushed roughly into his mouth and he felt the staggering, agonising pain as a red-hot tip was applied to the wound to seal it.

He opened his mouth to scream, but nothing came out, as his teeth bit through the wood clamped into his jaws. The searing heat from the iron invaded his entire body and for the first time in his life, he wished he had died somewhere before this excruciating night.

A dressing was applied to the back wound where the arrow had punctured though and he was pushed quickly onto his back, where the pain from the searing point became more than he could bear.

The same procedure was applied to the front. The doctor stood over him waiting for the next red-hot iron to be brought. 'I have treated both sides with a special oil to stop the weeping and clean the inside of the wound. If it works, you may live but the next two days will tell. You are a brave man, Attilius and I am using all of my skills, but I cannot be certain. I hope you understand.'

The pain radiating from the front of his chest as the red hot, iron was applied deep into the wound, sent him into unconsciousness and he became oblivious to the treatment of the wound site. Again, they sutured the sides and applied olive oil to the bandage which wrapped around his entire torso.

The doctor applied the final knot to the fabric and looked down at the man beneath him. His forearms and shoulders, held a pattern of small white scars from the battles he had endured. It never ceased to amaze him, why a man might put himself through this type of hell. But, they did, and with a level of bravado and bravery that he himself, could never possess.

The doctor turned to the aide as he handed back the hot iron. 'Whether he wants to drink or not, you force it down. If he gets hot again, make sure he is bathed with water and do not touch that wound until I return. Before you do that, change out his stretcher to a clean one and make sure he is bathed with cold water. Let me make myself clear on this. This tent is under direct orders from Titus himself, to save this man. Got it! As an added incentive to you savages, keep in mind that if he dies, we all go with him.'

The aide, wide eyed and clearly frightened, nodded and the doctor left the tent with misgivings as to whether the legionnaire would last the night.

The next morning the doctor returned and called the aide over. 'Is he drinking anything?' The aide shrugged. 'I have tried several times but he refuses.'

'Get me water.' He said sternly. Once he received the cup, he pulled Marcus' head up and forced the water down his throat. As Marcus coughed, he screamed at the pain in his chest but the doctor repeated the procedure, until Marcus pulled his head away unable to drink any more.

The doctor lay the cup down and turned to the aide. 'You are no longer to take care of his man.' He said sternly. He called another aide from the end of the tent. 'Can you at least take instruction?'

'Of course.' the small man said, as he stood patiently at the side of the stretcher.

The doctor stood up and looked the aide in the eye. 'Four times a day you are to force water down this man's throat until he drinks at least three cups full. If he resists, you are to pull his head back and force it down. Understand?'

The aide nodded as the doctor continued. 'If he is still alive tomorrow, you are to replace the upper bandages only. Use this oil on the lower bandage only and then apply a dry bandage over it.' He handed a flask of camphorated olive oil to the aide and left the tent.

'I don't know why they bother' The first aide said with a shrug of his shoulders as the doctor left the tent area. 'This legionnaire is off his scone and is obviously going to die. Why keep going? Just let him pass to the netherworld in peace.' Another aide came over, pulled the cloth from him and returned to where Marcus lay. 'I'll take care of him from this time on.' The other aide shrugged and walked off.

Late that evening, the aide moved over to where Marcus lay. Amazed at the strength the man still held to pull his head away from the water cup. He continued to raise his head and succeeded in getting the cup full of water down. He bathed the broken body from head to foot and pulled the sheet back over him. Finally, he brought his face down to the man's ear.

'Legionnaire, can you hear me?'

When he heard a grunt, he whispered to him. 'I will not let you die, so the rest is up to you. Together we will make you better. Do you understand, soldier?'

Marcus opened his eyes to see the small man beside him pushing his black, matted hair back and stroking his forehead with a wet cloth. He nodded briefly, before falling back into unconsciousness.

The next morning, the doctor returned again and muttering to himself he replaced the bandages and laid his hand on Marcus' forehead. 'You are getting better, soldier and your wounds are no longer weeping, so perhaps we have done the right job.'

Marcus came awake at the voice and hoarsely whispered. 'Thank you.' The doctor nodded at him and rose from the bed side. He turned to the aide beside him. 'You are the right man. Keep up the good work, because he has a long way to go.'

Two weeks later, Marcus awoke from a deep sleep late in the morning and he looked over to find Ovidius sitting next to him, in full armour. Each time he moved something clanked and jangled. The sound of the armour, was somehow comforting and familiar to Marcus, as he looked up in the eyes of his friend.

'It appears you have survived, Marco, and I have told everyone that it is only to get out of further marching.' Ovidius smiled at his own remark and placed his broad hand on his friend's arm. 'It is good to see you dear friend, but it will not be for a quite a while. We march for Caesarea and from there, only Mars knows.'

Marcus nodded, unable to speak properly. The pain through his chest burned brightly and no matter what position he moved to on the camp bed, the pain remained constant.

'It seems you were shot by Ya'ir, the leader of the Sacarii no less. And, there is also no doubt the man misfired and was aiming for Governor Silva. So, when you turned you moved into the arrow flight. However, no thanks from our esteemed general Silva of course.'

'But, of course' Marcus said hoarsely.

'Still, there was not much left of the Sacarii' Once the boys had finished with him and his corpse was hung outside the fort for the crows to pick at in their leisure, there was very little pickings left.'

'When do I re-join?' Marcus asked feebly.

Ovidius shrugged as he heard the call from the outside of the tent. 'I must go friend. Be well and mend well and we will see each other again.' He rose from his seat and smiled.

'Ovi' Marcus croaked

'Yes, Marco.'

'Be safe, friend. Be safe.'

Ovidius smiled broadly and picked up his helmet. 'Ha, you horse's arse. Without you to protect, I have a much easier time in battle to do what I want! Get well, Marco.' He turned on his heels and walked slowly out of the tent. 'One day we will meet again.'

*

The next morning, the doctor came around to change the bandages with his usual fussing and muttering. Marcus looked at him intently for a moment. 'When do I re-join the legion?' He asked.

The doctor looked at him sternly. 'As of the day you received the arrow, you can regard yourself as an ex-legionnaire. Your injury is so great that the army have decided that you are to be repatriated to a farm on the island of Sicilia, to assist in the supply of the army. You will be working on grain farm due to your occupation you noted before you joined the legion.'

'A farm?' Marcus looked up at him with distaste on his mouth.

'Listen to me, legionnaire. You have lost a lot of muscle and cartilage and there is little chance that left arm will be able to pick up a shield, let alone fight in battle, anytime soon. If at all.'

'How long will it take to recuperate?' Marcus asked with frustration in his voice.

The Physician shrugged. 'It is hard to know. Maybe six months and up to a year and you will be required to work on that farm which will help your countenance and your left arm and chest. Your duty is to yourself, Attilius. It is now time to heal, not fight. Once you are up and around, use the time to regain the strength in your arm and shoulder but once you have been repatriated from the legion there is no going back.'

'No' Marcus croaked and stared to rise.

The doctor pushed him gently back, to the comfort of the stretcher. 'The good news is that if you continue with the exercises that I will give you, that arm and shoulder may work again. But maybe not with the strength you had before. That remains to be seen over time. But you are young and strong and that is always a good start.'

'I must re-join' He said breathlessly

'The Fifth legion has left for Caesarea and then probably to Gaul. I am under orders, by general Silva himself, to make sure you survive to live another day. There is only recuperation from now on. You can kiss your army life farewell, and personally if I was in your place, I would be happy at the news because you are very lucky to be alive.'

'Maybe' Marcus replied slowly.

As the doctor finished his review of the wounds he stood and looked down at his patient. 'There are other things in life besides fighting battles, you know.'

He turned to look at the doctor and slowly shook his head. The pain in his chest burnt with the intensity of an internal blaze, day and night. Alternatively, he sweated or shivered, and each time he complained to the doctor, the man simply nodded his head and instructed the orderlies to bathe him and pour a dose of foul tasting oil down his throat.

Was there life outside of the legion? He looked up at the top of the canvas tent undulating in the light wind. Around him the stretchers were empty and despite the conversation from some of the orderlies, he stayed alone in that tent, away from his life and his beloved Fifth legion. The depression set in that he was badly wounded and by himself, after six years of marching, comradeship and the fraternity of the brothers.

Three weeks later he was able to stand, barely, and they placed him in a chair outside the tent. The view of the Masada fortress flooded his mind, with memories of the fateful morning he was hit by the misdirected arrow from Ya'ir. The brown, heat shimmer of the fortress walls brought a scowl on his face as he gazed upon it.

He was still incarcerated in the tent, situated near the start of the siege road they built, to take the huge machine up to the wall. The tent lay on top of the hill, opposite the fort from where the siege machine had been removed after the fort was evacuated. Below him, the plains of Judea stretched into the distance, dry and unwelcoming.

Morose and depressed, he closed his eyes against the shimmering heat of the desert as his thoughts turned to Jerusalem. How many had he lost in that brutal battle for the city? Arius, lost at the battle below the Mount of Olives, Sextus, Vanu, Enius, Lucanus and the free slave, Felix. All for the sake of mighty Rome.

Add to that the spectre of the man who taught him respect, the Centurion, Brutus, and the loss felt, just as substantial to him on that day as it did in the middle of the battle within the city walls of Jerusalem, so long before.

As he sat there lamenting his fate, the Physician walked up to sit beside him. 'How do you feel legionnaire?'

'Better, but still sore.' The Physician nodded as he checked the area where the arrow had entered. The swelling had subsided and the bruising contained itself to the wound site. He felt pleased with his result and it was news he could send to Sulla, who was clearly under orders from Titus to ensure the man survived.

'I have something for you, Attilus. It was given to me by your friend to pass to you when you started to get better.' He passed the pouch to Marcus and walked off towards the officer's tent.

'Ovidius?' The Physician turned and nodded.

Marcus opened the leather thong drawstring and let the contents fall into his hand. Four gold Aurius coins shone in the late morning sun. He picked up the other item. A small piece of animal hide, with writing on it. *Audentes fortuna iuva,* was inscribed in dark ink. 'Fortune, favours the bold.'

CHAPTER 37

SICILIA

He had stood impatiently on the dockside of the port at Maratima Celsina, waiting as the grain ship loaded its last net of grain. He walked up the narrow gangplank to the deck where the captain introduced himself with a grin that showed half his teeth missing.

'Welcome, citizens. My name is Junus, like the month but missing a letter.' He beamed broadly at his own joke. 'There are two latrines, one on the left side and one on the right side and both are situated over the rail.' He laughed again and added. 'Make sure you are downwind and for those of you who have not sailed before that means the end opposite to where the wind blows from. Your sleeping quarters are around the deck,'

He motioned with his hand around the deck area. 'We have a kitchen down those stairs which is for meals only. All cooking is done up here and down there, depending on what we eat. We have a cook with a bad reputation so don't criticize him or you will come off second best. Any questions? No? Good. We will cast off within a short while. Make yourselves comfortable.'

Marcus looked around at the other three men who made up the passengers. As he looked around he realised he may have been the least injured. One had lost his arm, another appeared mostly blind as he was taken around by another man with a pronounced limp which only allowed him a short number of steps before he stopped to take a breath and resume.

As the ship slowly pulled away from the dock he looked up at the island that had been his home for more than a year of convalescence. The grain fields of the middle of the island offered him a home even though it was in barracks. The soil and the seasons offered him solace and time to heal and memories of his childhood and his early life. Many a time he had stopped behind the bullock to adjust the straps of the plough and be plunged into memories of his life on the farm.

With a hard face under his straw hat, he looked up pensively at the sky. Here, on clods of earth, yet again, he stood, a broken and badly injured soldier with no life to which he could welcome. The last six months he had improved to the point that he could walk and run but his left arm remained weaker than his right and the scar on the front of his chest lay livid and white and almost the size of his fist.

That evening they all met downstairs in the cramped galley and ate a meal of maize porridge with mutton and a white wine that came from Greece that was almost undrinkable. He returned to the deck and slept fitfully for most of the night.

Several days later, Marcus stood on the slowly rising bow of the ship as it moved through the swell, lurching up and over another wave, to carry him and the other passengers and cargo, to the port of Rome.

Away from the confines of the grain port of Celsina and the island of Sicilia no longer in view, the craft moved deftly through the head-on breeze, towards Rome. He realized as he stood there against the railing that he had finally completed his tenure in the army, working on the government grain fields and he hoped it might be the last time he held the displeasure of another open sea voyage.

The ship made him think back to his voyage to Judea, so many years before. This time, as a retired Tirarii, a veteran of over several hundred battles, including the siege of Jerusalem and Masada, the sea no longer frightened him as the ship sailed through the low swell with ease, rising and falling as the waves moved smoothly under the hull and the blue sea ran along the side.

The crops, harvested each season from the farms were distributed as grain throughout the empire, to feed the legions on campaign. Men, like him, who worked the farms were known as '*miles amissa*' or lost soldiers. Only the nearly dead, and very injured, were employed as a way of giving them something to do outside of the legion, to finish their tenure and longer if they needed the time to recuperate.

On the island and under the glow of oil lamps, the stories of hardship and life-ending wounds scattered the conversation each night as they sat inside the tenant huts on the colder nights or outside by the fire when the weather warmed a little. In the summer they sat, slapping the mosquitos and telling stories from the sieges and battles they had fought.

By the time Marcus shuffled down the plank of the ship that delivered him to the island, from Judea, he stood hunched over from the pull of the wound through his chest and he still, after several months, held a light fever at night.

317

He walked for the first several months with the assistance of a cane and each night he drank from the medicinal, oil bottle he had been given until it was dry. He had resisted the change to Sicilia but, in retrospect it had recuperated him due to the dry heat and work requiring him to bend and carry.

As he listened around the fire on those warmer nights, it appeared to him that the men who had attended the final two days at Jerusalem were the worst affected. Many held wounds that refused to heal and there were days you never saw them, as they lay on their beds in the barracks under a sweating brow and grey pallor.

He listened to their stories with anger and disgust. Tales of tough men dumped on stretchers by unforgiving orderlies left to bake in the heat of the aid tents. Many were left for dead or attended by physicians who could work better as horse doctors.

Marcus considered himself lucky to have received the attention that he did on orders from Titus himself. Fever was rife after the battle lines dispersed and the injured were left in the tents.

At Jerusalem, water was in short supply so washing was never administered. Camphor oil and bandages and left for nature to make the decision on life or death. Sometimes, the luckiest passed to the black watered river of death in the night, while others suffered at the hand of severe wounds and life-sucking disease.

One night, as he sat in quiet contemplation of the meal in front of him. Tears fell soundlessly from his eyes onto the plate as he tried as much as he was able, but unsuccessfully, to hide a sadness that sought him out at the times he least expected it. The tears farewelled a man who had held his back and saved his life more times than he could remember.

The month before the ship was to take him to Rome, he had sat the table of the farm house to eat the usual meal of mutton or goat meat with plentiful vegetables. In the background, locusts sang with the occasional sound of a bird nesting for the night.

At the table they all looked at the new man as they ate their meals and like all of them he had been sent to the island to convalesce. He sat sullenly at the table with his eyes downcast at his meal and unable to speak. His left leg was missing, as was any pretension of happiness. He sat at the table with the look that all of them had seen before on the faces of those who joined the farm and the life of an ex-soldier.

The table offered the men a mixture of desolation and unhappiness and the absolute certainty that they would no longer join their brothers in the legion they had fought within. The look was most prevalent on the first days on the island as any new visitor realised they were faced with their remaining time of servitude to tend a grain farm rather than fight in some other land.

'Where did you serve, brother? One of the other men asked him.

'In the Tenth, you may have heard of them.' Sarcasm laced his voice. 'If you are wondering about my leg it was lost in a skirmish in Gaul as the Tenth and the Fifth tried to keep the peace.'

The man pointed to Marcus who sat listening to the conversation. 'That man there, Marcus Attilius, he was in the Fifth.'

'Oh,' The man replied. 'How did you get here?'

'I was the one wounded at Masada.'

The man nodded. 'I have heard about you. You were the one, Eh? I thought the Tirarii were invincible.' He said with a wry smile.

'We thought the same of the Tenth!'

The man nodded sagely and looked across the table as Marcus nodded. 'Invulnerable to the last I am here, still recovering.'

'And that appears to be my fate, brother. They sent me here without a second thought after fifteen years of service. The legion doesn't give a shit about us if we get badly injured. Well, brother, my name is Decimus. Dec, for short.' He replied with his mood lifting.

'Marco, brother.' Marcus replied. 'How long were you in Gaul?'

'We arrived four months after the release from Masada. Thence to Caesarea and off to Gaul. From one shithole to another.'

'Did you come by a man by the name of Ovidius?'

'He was in the Fifth.' The man remarked.

'Correct, and he was the last man in my conturbenium.'

'I knew him. He was Tirarii, wasn't he?'

———

319

'He was, as was I.' Marcus replied.

Dec looked at him solemnly and lowered his head as he spoke. 'Brother, I have sad news for you. Ovidius was killed on the same day that I lost my leg. I am sorry to give you the news but over eighty lost their lives that day. It was a skirmish that became a fracas and we were under the command of yet another idiot.'

Marcus dropped his cup onto the table and lowered his head. 'Do not tell me this is true, brother. Tell me anything, but do not tell me this sad news.'

Decimus paused momentarily, then reached across and laid his hand on Marcus' arm. 'If it is any help, he died courageously. He saved the life of two others and finally got an arrow through the neck. The Fifth were in mourning. I am sorry to be the messenger of his death. He was well liked and a considerable loss for all of us.' Tears blazed his eyes as Marcus finally looked up and nodded at Decimus, who sombrely returned to his food.

Marcus walked outside to the warm air and the welcome solitude. As he sat on one of the steps leading up to the hut, looking up at the blaze of stars across the sky, he was too shocked to think of anything but his times with Ovidius and his overwhelming desire to see him again which was now, impossible. He was the last remaining member of his conturbenium and tears flooded his eyes accompanied by racking sobs. For the first time he wished he had died on the high Masada fort. How was it possible that he, Marcus Attilius, had survived?

He hit the ground in frustration with his fist until it started to bleed. Stranded on this God forsaken island, ploughing and harvesting crops for legionaires who he would never see let alone fight alongside. His conturbenium gone and the last remaining member, shot by an arrow and where was he, Marcus Attilius, to save his brother, as Ovidius had saved him so many times. The anger inside him grew until he stood up and screamed at the sky above until he was hoarse.

A large wave on the port side send spray up and across the deck pulling him out of his sad thoughts. He was joined by the captain, who he had befriended on the first day of the five-day voyage. After dropping off half of their cargo in Mycenium, they headed back out to sea and North, towards the great city of Rome.

'You were going to show me your scar' The captain said jovially, as he leant on the rail next to where Marcus stood watching the swell.

The captain wore a low, black cap on his head with a huge moustache and beard that flew back across his shoulders in the wind, coming off the bow. His hair was flecked with grey, which complimented his eyebrows.

'You were going to tell me at which port we finish, so I can look forward to getting off this junk heap.' Marcus replied, with a dour look.

'How dare you talk about my dear ship like that, Marco. She is as good a vessel as you could want to voyage on!' The man smiled with little regard to his missing teeth.

'That depends on whether you like travelling over water, Junus and to be honest, I will be more than happy to never see another body of open water, for as long as I live.' The captain mimicked a frown at him. 'Each to their own, my boy, each to their own. Personally, I could not care if I never saw another road or another horse for that matter. Filthy, brutal beasts if you ask me. So, you want to know our final port, do you?'

Marcus looked expectantly at him and waited. 'Portus, is the answer to your question and it is close to Rome. It's on the North mouth of the Tiber and since you are a land lubber, you will not be aware of the name of the coastline. But, I will tell you, to increase that limited knowledge of yours.'

'Tyrrhenian, I believe is the answer, Junus.'

The captain adjusted his cap as he looked at him in surprise 'Impressive, Marco; how did you know that?'
'Someone told me on the voyage to Judea. I seem to have a memory of things, of no interest to anyone else.'

'Was it tough in Judea?' Junus asked seriously.

Marcus nodded slowly, running his hand though his black hair that had grown to his shoulders. The question made him uncomfortable. 'I lost six men in my squad over the years and they were like brothers. The sacking of Jerusalem and that fort of Masada were hard, but the constant skirmishes with the Sacarii, made it even worse. We lost a lot of men. The truth, if you want to hear it, Junus, is that I have lost everyone I knew well in the legion.

'I hear we got even though.' The captain replied

'That is true. But, any campaign has its costs and each paid dearly.'

'Can I see the scar?' Junus asked quietly.

Marcus let his tunic fall to his waist and turned from his front to his back. The captain looked at the broad muscular torso of the man before him, with amazement. He was tall and handsome, with long black hair and blue eyes but as his eyes descended he saw for the first time, the cost of war. The view of the ex-legionnaire before him, made his breath stop. His chest held a wide scar on his left and his arms were covered with scars, as were the sides of his upper legs. The right leg seemed worse that his left, which he assumed was due to the position of the shield that naturally protected the left-hand side.

The scar on his back was much larger, with a white livid area that took up a man's fist in size, yet his face and lower torso was devoid of any marks save a thin white scar on his chin. He looked at the soldier's arms, noticing his right was much larger than the left.

'Not bad, huh?'

'Is the left arm weak?'

Marcus nodded. 'Much better than it was, but still weaker than the right and I used to have similar strength on both sides. That was why they refused to let me re-join the legion. They made the assessment just before I arrived in Sicilia to the farm. I could not stand well, let alone use my left arm. The doctor was a joke amongst all of us who worked the farm. He would arrive every three months, do his review and leave.'

Junus looked at him with raised eyebrows.

'Well, he didn't care. He just wanted to review everyone and get off the island, as quickly as possible. No matter what I said to him he just smiled that idiotic smirk and left.'

'How long after you were hit, did you arrive in Sicilia?' The captain asked as he stroked his beard into place against the wind.

'I am not sure because I was not in this world for some time, but probably three months. I was in the medical tent for a long period but I lost track of time. I don't remember the first month at all and the second was through a veil of pain'

'The wound?'

'The wound and a fever, which would not abate.'

'And the scars; is everyone like this?' The captain asked, as he looked at the arms of the man before him.

'More or less, but you know, when I think about it, we received less wounds as Triarii than we did as front-line, infantry men.' The captain whistled softly. 'You were a Triarii? Remind me not to take you on in a fight.'

'Apparently, my fighting days are over.' Came the reply. 'But I am told that I was one of the best, but what good will that do me?' Marcus turned his face to the wind, watching as the waves came through to lift the bow, and allow it to gently dive over the crest and into the trough beyond. 'So, Marco; what now?'

'I wish I knew, Junus. That is the question I have in my mind most of the time. I have spent over six years in the army and I am not skilled to do anything, other than tending a farm.'

The captain pursed his lips as he listened to the young man beside him. 'What about the Pretorian guard? You have those skills and from what I hear they don't work too hard; besides a little training and seducing women.'

Marcus looked at the man next to him and laughed. 'Ah, Junus, I wish life was as easy as you make it. To be a Pretorian, my friend, you need my skills and a strong family heritage, otherwise you have no chance. I come from a family of regional farmers, ten days walk from Rome. What chance do I have?'

Junus smiled sourly in return. 'I sympathise with you because I am the same. If I cannot sail and carry grain, what else am I good for? Unless I work on the docks; and that is hard work every day and I am too old for that. At least, you are young.'

'Young and unemployed.' Marcus rose from his bending position on the forward rail with the sun setting off the port bow. They finally sauntered back to the mid-cabin, to eat an early meal.

The cook provided a lamb stew and a cup of red wine of reasonable quality and they talked with the easy swaying of men used to a mess table rising and falling slowly, with the bow. Marcus ate slowly and listened to small talk at the table about the cost of ferrying grain, the slow labour on the ports, and how they intended to unload at Portus and head back to Sicilia for another load. According to Junus, the season of calm seas was ending and soon the rough seas and high winds would begin.

As he rose from the table, Junus pulled him aside with his hand on his shoulder. 'Marco, you are young and strong and very experienced in warfare. So; go forward and find something that allows you to use those skills and make a living. It surely beats farming.'

The next morning, Marcus came up on deck to watch as Junus expertly steered his ship from the open sea, towards the coast. With the use of one small, forward sail, he brought the ship expertly through the waiting boats anchored off the harbour, and towards the port.

'Bring the sail half down' He barked, holding the long tiller arm with accustomed ease.

Junus steered his ship around two smaller craft and towards the port side. The bustle of freight unloading, and loading, ships casting off and moving into dock, could be heard in the distance as could the grunts of the dock workers as they moved the cargo from one and loaded the cargo to yet, another ship.

The sounds of men shouting, combined with loud creaking noises of heavily laden ropes and pulleys holding nets of cargo over the ships and onto the waiting port floor, filled their ears as they stopped just off the dock.

A small, but stoutly built long boat, came alongside. Junus looked over at the man who stood beside two rowers. 'Head down to number three, captain, as they are just about to leave.'

Junus touched his cap in respect and pulled harder on the tiller to bring the small ship to the starboard. 'Sail down' He shouted 'but keep hold of the ropes, because she will need to come up soon.'

They stalled at the side of the port area. The ship drifted slowly without sail and finally, he gave the order and the ship sprung forward, with Junus now standing on a box to get a better view. Slowly, he brought the ship around nearing the side of the port and in one practised movement he thrust the tiller around and the ship gently nudged the side of the port, as the men jumped off, to secure the ties and bring the ship to rest.

Finally, Marcus pulled his meagre belongings together and made it to the gangplank at the side of the ship. Junus was there, barking orders to his men to get the grain unloaded.

'Lazy, filthy brutes.' Junus said, with a snarl as Marcus approached. 'Look at them. By the Gods how stupid can they be? 'So, Marco. Another step on the path of life for you and me, eh?'

Marcus dropped his belongings to give the man before him a hug. He felt affection for the grizzled sea captain and happy, that it was returned. 'If you want an easy way back to Rome just ask one of the dray drivers and tell them it was my idea. If they complain, tell them Junus sent you, because all they ever do is complain.'

'Where do they end.'

'Near the Via Latina, at the grainery.'

Marcus thanked him, picking up his pack to walk down the narrow plank, to the rough surface of the quay. He could still feel the gentle rocking of the sea in his ears as he walked away.

He heard a shout and turned to wave at Junus.

'*A Navis in portum tutum est, sed quid non est quod naves in extructione vallorum!*' Junus called out with a laugh 'Move forward!'

Marcus listened to the remark that Junus called out. 'A boat is safe in the harbour but that is not what it is designed for!' He smiled, nodded and walked away. In the distance, on the other side of the port, he could see the roads that would lead to Rome and his thoughts went back briefly to the brown, sand land of Judea.

Suddenly, behind him, he heard a loud voice and he stopped in mid-step to look around, only to take a deep breath and move on. He realised for the first time since he left Caesarea, he was free. Free to do what he wanted and without the constant presence of Centurions and commanders, waiting with heavy sticks and brutal servings of suppression. For the first time in over six years, he was a free man, and it lifted his spirits for the first time since leaving the wheat fields of Sicilia.

He entered a road that the drays took on their journey to Rome. He picked up his steps towards a tavern on the roadside longing for a good meal, Roman wine, and the sound of Roman voices.

He found a café and sat heavily on the bench, waiting for service. He looked out towards the movement of the workers on the port. In the distance, he could see Junus shouting orders from the gangplank rail, as the grain was lifted out of the hold. The men raised the sacks by block and tackle off the deck and onto waiting drays, with tired men and restless horses waiting for the load to be finished.

In the legion, the days rolled into each other, with battles to be fought and wounds to heal but the future was certain. Marcus realised for the first time, since the fateful day he fled Rome, that while he was free for the first time, in so many years, his life no longer held a certain future.

The thought of working a farm, as he had over the past two years, for the army on the island of Sicilia, filled him with dread as did the boring life of a gardener. In his mind, lay the foreboding that his choice was limited by his skills and the only two he possessed were unpalatable. Farming or fighting.

However, he decided on the voyage from Sicilia not to return to his farm. He could not face his father, with the shame of his earlier life in Rome and that left him with an uneasy feeling. The only path he could take would be to try and make a better life in the city.

Cassius Laurentius and his secret affair with Lucia Laurentius, moved to the front of his thoughts for the first time in years and the debt he still owed. The fact that he had absconded from the Laurentius household, as well as fleeing from the gladiator school with the Laurentius name as sponsors, meant that he would have limited time in Rome before he was discovered.

He remembered, with a familiar rising concern, the memory of the day he had foolishly left his mark on the bottom of the *Gladiatorial familia* contract with Aetius the Lanista of the Rudus Gallica. And in the same thought he remembered the sage advice, from the slave at the school, to leave Rome. Be quick and get away. If you stay, you are too young and you will die on the arena sands.

Enforceable; was that not the word the Lanista had used? He had escaped that life and the question remained in his thoughts, as to how enforceable the contract might be on his return.

He had proven his worth in countless battles in Judea, paying a very heavy price. He thought deeply about his aversion to farming and he knew that it related to his father, to his lack of acceptance of Marcus and his guilt at leaving his mother and brother to work the farm in his absence.

His father had called him selfish all those years ago and, of course, he was right. But, the invisible yearning of youth, his inner voice, to change his life, had held too strong.

In the legion, he rose with Ovidius to the top when they were promoted as Triarii. The experience he held in hand-to-hand combat made his skills formidable. But, without the legion as his home, what else did he hold dear in his life?

Junus, that humble sea captain had been as wise as his years. If he still wanted the success he yearned for as a youth, it must be with his skill and in reflection, as he walked across the port towards the road, he knew that the only option he had left was to turn up at the Ludus Gallicus and speak to Aetius. It was time to fall into the hands of fate.

In this moment of inner thought, he understood the words of the Centurion more keenly than he had before, on the sands outside of Jerusalem. If he was to survive he must meet his life with the skills he possessed. There seemed to be little choice.

With a deep breath, he ordered his first real meal and wine in over six years and waited in quiet contemplation of life in Rome. In his mind, the city beckoned; not with the warm and open arms of a mother but with the angry countenance of a surly giant.

CHAPTER 38

ROME

There was a soft knock at the door as Tacitus was about to wash his dinner bowls. He sat up stiffly and made his way to the door and opened it slowly.

Before him stood his nephew. Much larger in size than when he had left, but with the same handsome face and wide smile. He grabbed him in a bear hug and pulled him into the small hut.

'Marco, Marco.' He cried out as he saw his nephew. 'I thought you were dead.'

'Tacitus.' Marcus replied as he returned the hug. 'I returned from Sicilia this morning by ship and made my way here.'

'Sicilia? By the Gods what were you doing on that island?'

'Recovering from a long arrow that did everything but kill me.'

Tactius hugged him again 'I will give an offering to Mercury to thank the Gods for your safe arrival. Arrow? Did you say arrow?'

Marcus nodded and laid his pack on the floor.

'Did anyone see you?' Tacitus asked solemnly.

'No, not that I am aware. It is dark and I was careful.'

'Please take a seat, Marco. It is so good to see you. I have asked about you but no one had any news. Why were you in Sicilia of all places. I have been there once. Not much to say about it, as I remember.'

Marcus removed the top of his tunic and he bowed to wash his hands. Tacitus winced when he saw the broad scar on his nephews back and his chest. He whistled softly as he touched the scar. 'By the Gods, Marco, that is some scar! What happened?'

'A single, misdirected arrow at Masada.'

'You were lucky it hit the left, but not lucky to have been hit so hard' He said as he inspected the large scar more closely. Were you wearing your armour?'

'The arrow was meant for Consul Silva and I got in the way.'

'You are lucky to be alive with a wound like that. They must have good doctors, in the army.'

'One and he is the one that thankfully treated me otherwise I would be sitting on the banks of the River Styx, waiting for the boatman' Marcus replied with a grimace.

'So, you are no longer with the legion?'

Marcus shook his head solemnly and sat back down to replace his tunic and eat some of the food Tacitus had placed before him. 'When they reviewed the wound was still fresh and they simply pushed me out of the corp. I wanted to stay.'

Tactius nodded with a sympathetic look on his face. He looked momentarily at his nephew's arms and legs which were adorned with the scars of battle; a tell-tale sign of anyone who served in the legion. His nephew held longer scars on his shoulder and a particularly long healed slash across his left leg. 'It was tough?'

'Harder than I could imagine but I fared better than many others. We lost a lot of men in the siege of Jerusalem but I was the only one wounded at Masada believe it or not.'

Tacitus reached out to touch him on the shoulder. 'We heard the news about Masada. And as usual, there was a long procession with Governor Silva and Titus Vespasian, at the front to tell us how well he did at the fort. Titus seemed uninterested to be honest as he stood behind him.'

'That is hardly surprising, uncle. Silva was at best, a tent general. However, he made sure the medical staff took care of me and without him I would, quite likely, be dead. The orders came from Titus himself.'

Tactius looked at his nephew with fondness. 'It must have been a terrible time after Masada.'

'It was, uncle.' Marcus replied, 'But, as we were constantly told; it was our duty.'

329

Tactius put his arm on his nephew's shoulder. 'I just can't believe it is you after all these years. I heard about the siege and I thought you must have died there. A year before, we saw was Titus riding tall on his white stallion, dragging his treasure and the Jewish leaders though the streets of Rome after the sacking of Jerusalem.'

'We heard.' Marcus added with a sly smile. 'It did him no good with the men. We all felt a little cheated. He and the emperor got the treasure and we got a meal and a march to the next battle, and finally, Masada. One of my Conturbenium brothers by the name of Ovidius and I, caught one of the Jewish leaders, John, near the temple. The legionaires who captured him were promised one hundred Denarii. But it never came.'

'Hardly surprising.' Tacitus noted with a raise of his eyes

Tacitus continued using his hands to emphasize the point. 'Well, it was some spectacle and of course the nosy citizens of our good city, came out to cheer and stamp their feet. After the sacking of Jerusalem, it appears that Emperor Vespasian and his son are our true royalty of Rome. The truth is there for everyone to see. They now hold absolute power.'

'I saved his life.' Marcus said casually.

'Who's life, Marco?'

'Titus; He had gone down with his horse on top of him and I moved in to make him safe and took two Jews down in the effort. I did not know it was him.'

Tactius listened as he built a fire against the approaching cold night. Marcus spoke, perhaps as a release of his tormented life after Masada and he retold his life from Jerusalem to Masada and how he was shot with the arrow high on the fort battlements. He spoke with emotion, about witnessing the mass suicide of over a thousand inhabitants of the fort and how the legion thought it was cowardice. Slowly, he reduced to tears.

Tactius listened patiently as he tended the fire and supplied wine to his nephew.

'And Sicilia?'

'On a farm, uncle. To tend the crops for the army, while I tried to recover. I have lost strength in my left arm and side which means the army is now no longer an option.'

'No, probably not, Marco.' Tacitus said with a sour look on his face. 'Life presents many opportunities and you are still young. You can take your choice but given your distinct lack of popularity around here, perhaps you could look outside of Rome.'

'Laurentius still remembers?'

'Laurentius would never forget a debt, nephew and he as vicious a man as resides in greater Rome today.'

Marcus nodded. 'Tacitus, I don't want to go back to the farm. In my father's eye, I will have failed and he won't let me forget it.'

'He doesn't let anyone forget it, Marco.' Tacitus said with a grim look.

'Then you have several options. The first is to become a gardener at another household because you have those skills and the second is to work a farm outside of Rome. Both give you a reasonable living and if you work hard you can become a farm manager after a while. They are in high demand I believe, and no one really knows you outside the farm community. You can find a girl and get on with your life.'

'I want more.' Marcus said flatly.

Tacitus looked at him angrily. 'Marco, how many battles have you been in?

Marcus shrugged. There were so many he could hardly remember them all. 'Hundreds.'

'Then, what could you want, more than a peaceful life after the wars you have been though and to find a girl, to bear you children, and enjoy the fruits of your labour?'

Marcus sipped his wine as he listened and then refilled it from the flask on the table. 'I still have the debt and I still have the contract with Aetius.'

Tactius stopped momentarily to look his nephew in the eye, and then reflectively, he started at the fire for a moment. 'Marco, that may give you fame and fortune if you are successful but it is a profession that is loved by many and scorned by many. You must remember, that if you take that choice it is your life from that time on. Do you understand that? Marcus nodded as he leant back in the chair.

'The problem is that many, perhaps the majority die in the first year. The other problem is the debt with Laurentius. If he finds out, you are back in Rome and let me say to you he will find out; then he will want his debt to try and force you into gladiatorial combat.'

'I have saved up that much, Tacitus, to pay the debt.'

'Gambling?'

Marcus smiled sheepishly. 'A little uncle; but on the farm, there was little else to do and no one had much money so we gambled for duties and unfortunately, I ended up doing more than my fair share. I do not think I can go back to be a gardener or working a farm. The contract I signed all those years ago means that if I am to stay in this city, the Ludus is my only option.'

'If you stay in Rome.' Tactius added plaintively

'I have decided to stay in Rome, uncle, because this is the only home I know outside of the farm. The legion was my home but they don't want me.'

'Well then, you must weight that decision, Marco. Also, with your arm, I think I can help. When I was in the army they treated those injuries with massage to open up the muscles and heavy weights used in repetition on the left arm to build up the wasted area. Did they massage you in Judea?'

'No. I was too sore, uncle and at the farm medical care was unavailable. Where do I go for the massage.?'

'Here, my boy, it is one of my many skills and we will start on it tonight. It will be painful but we must unlock those twisted muscles and release the energy. By the way, your friend Felix has come around on a number of occasions, looking for you. You should see him before you make a decision.'

'I will, Tacitus on the morrow.'

Tactius moved across to his nephew to inspect his shoulder in the light of the oil lamps that flicked shadows across the ochre coloured walls. 'And, then?'

'I will return to the Lanista and join under the contract. I have the skill and I need the money. Let us see what happens.'

'You understand the life? It is tougher than the legion. As tough as the army and it is yet another life of battles.'

'I understand, dear Tactius, but I do not fear it.'

'You should.' Tactius replied sternly.

As night descended softly onto the surrounding hills, the closed door of the gardener's hut echoed the grunts and groans from the ex-soldier, as he withstood the pain of his uncle's fingers working hard into the frozen joints and muscles of his left shoulder. Finally, he finished by working first pressed olive oil and turmeric into the area and bound it with a clean cloth.

'Now go to bed, nephew. You deserve a rest.'

Marcus smiled at him, hugged him and fell asleep as his head hit the folded blanket that served as a pillow.

*

Marcus awoke the next morning with the familiar dull pain in his shoulder, a little less than usual. He looked at it, noting the bruises his uncle had left the night before. He moved his arm realising thankfully that it felt free, but sorer than the previous day. He could move his arm above his shoulder, for the first time.

His uncle had left earlier for his duties and a bowl of maize porridge was left on the table, with a half loaf of bread and fruit. He walked to the door and leaving it slightly ajar, he looked out at the magnificent estate beyond and the large and ornate villa. It appeared the same, with staff walking around, as the estate came to life and work began in earnest.

He returned to the table to eat his breakfast and prepare for the day. As he finished his uncle returned with more fruit in his hands.

'How do you feel, Marco.'

'Much rested, Tacitus, and my arm is better after that brutal massage you inflicted on me last night.' Marcus smiled, as he rose to dress and pick up his belongings. He embraced his uncle who checked outside the door to see if there was anyone close and then gave the signal.

Marcus exited the door and moved quickly to the back wall, climbed over it and headed to the Via Tibatina road, for the walk down to the sun-drenched city below. He could feel the hard stones beneath his sandals, as he made his way down the road assiduously avoiding eye contact with anyone walking up or down and looking away as drays and chariots moved past.

As he walked down the hill he could see the building his uncle had called the Flavian Amphitheatre in the distance. In the haze of the morning sun, he could see the size of the huge structure and the stout posts that held the pulleys for the stone, which was rising upwards to a second level.

He walked directly to the sword foundry, noting that the city seemed unchanged since his hasty departure all those years ago. Garbage still remained piled up in the streets and higher on the corners, as chariots moved recklessly down the cobbled roads and through the stepping stones, raised so that citizens could walk out of the water when it rained.

The front of the foundry, looked much the same with dark grimy doors and the smell of worked iron coming from the front. On top of the building, the chimney above the forge smoked slowly and the sound of beaten steel echoed inside.

He walked in to find Felix sitting at a bench, with thin boards in front of him and in his hand a metal pen, as he wrote on one and placed it to the side.

'Not even a smile for an old friend?'

Felix looked up at Marcus with absolute surprise on his face. His first impression was the size that Marcus had become. Wide shouldered and thin waist with massive arms that obviously had wielded weight, over a long period of time. His blue eyes shone in the light of the window and his black, curly hair to his shoulders.

Marcus looked down at him with a smile on his face. His friend had changed as well. A little fatter and a little balder but with the same smile and amiable look.

'Well, may the Gods deliver us both. Marcus, you, big mule, where have you been?' He rose and they shook hands until Marcus grabbed him in a bear hug.

'It is a long story, Felix a very long story.'

Felix looked at him in mock surprise. 'Well, I have time to listen but I have to go to one of our suppliers and then we can sit and have lunch. Do you have anywhere to go?'

'The Ludus Gallicus.' Marcus said with a tight-lipped smile.

'You could have done that five years ago.'

'Over, six' Marcus replied grimly.

Felix pursed his lips 'Has it been that long, my friend. It seems only yesterday that we made that fateful trip down to that school. I suppose you are sure about this?'

Marcus nodded a familiar shrug of his shoulders and Felix noted for the first time the slightly wasted, left shoulder. He pointed to it. 'Sword?'

'Arrow'

'Do you want me to accompany you to the school?'

Marcus smiled at his friends offer. 'Well, Felix it is my decision and it is better if I go by myself but I thank you for your offer.'

'Of course, my friend. Now let us go and do some business and then you can give me the start to finish of your adventures and I will bore you with mine. I own the foundry now.'

Marcus looked at him and patted him on his shoulder. 'Well done, Felix. I look forward to hearing how you cheated some poor mongrel out of his business.'

'I am still paying, friend, so we will see who cheated whom. I have other news for you Marco, which may or may not mean anything. Do you remember Blandius?'

'Of course, Felix. I remember him well and that first morning we met at your lodgings. Why do you ask?'

He joined the Ludus Gallicus.'

'The same school as me?'

'He had a bout at the Pompeii arena some months ago, as a Tirone. He has changed since we knew him.'

'How?'

'Just bigger in the shoulders even thought that would be hard but he still gets cranky in the morning, so I hear.' Felix said with one of his wide smiles showing perfect white teeth against the brown skin of his face.

Marcus looked at him in surprise. 'Really? How is he faring inside the arena?'

'Very well from what I hear and I saw him some months ago. He is much bigger and I am told he has been very successful in his first tiro year. He won his first contest.'

Marcus nodded, waiting for Felix to pick up his boards and together they walked into the sunshine of the bustling city to meet the supplier and sit and have their meal in the *post meridiem*.

CHAPTER 39

The Ludus Gallicus sat in the distance beyond the building site of the Flavian Amphitheatre. Marcus shook hands with Felix after the lunch, as he ambled off in the direction of the gladiator school, in no hurry to arrive and face Aetius.

In the distance, he could see the dark forms of storm clouds, rolling in from the North and he had no doubt his uncle would be praying for rain, as he had lamented that Rome had been dry for weeks.

High behind the hill, at the back of the Ludus, there was a faint rainbow and perhaps the rain would miss Rome, as it did too often, not to be an act of the Gods.

Tacitus had adorned his altar to Ceres, supplied with food and flowers for weeks, to bring on the rain. His uncle was convinced Ceres had been insulted and she withheld the rains to show her displeasure. She took insults personally, Tacitus once confided to him, when he worked with his uncle in the garden of the Laurentius villa.

He entered the gate of the school, observing that the sign had been refinished and the words of the Gladiatorial oath, deeply cut into the new sign. Around him, work on the gates and surrounding area appeared newly finished and the overgrown shabby entrance to the Ludus Gallicus that Marcus remembered from years before, appeared tidy and far more prestigious.

The slave that had given him the advice was nowhere to be seen and the front hut of the gate, held an arrow that pointed towards a new entrance at the end. Marcus straightened his shoulders and walked down to the gate, opened it and was met by a female slave inside.

'I want to see the Lanista.' He said softly

'He is in the arena with the trainers. Who are you?'

'Tell him Marcus Attilius has returned.'

He was ushered upstairs to the office of the Lanista and if his memory served him well, the room had not changed much. How long had it been?

He thought to himself, since he had visited Lanista Aetius, before he escaped to the port and across the broad sea to Judea, so many years before.

On the walls hung a range of wooden Gladius, each with scars and chipped blades and clearly of some significance to the school. In the background, he could hear the shouts and grunts of gladiators, training in the late morning with the occasional bark from a trainer.

He walked to the edge of the balcony. Peering over he watched the sweating men in sword combat, with the same wooden Gladius that hung from the wall. They practised in the same manner as he had almost every day in the legion, with strike after strike practised and drilled until it became instinctive.

battle, the well-rehearsed and lethal habit learnt in practice, created a deadly skill, offering an instinctive capability to kill and kill quickly.

He turned to find a familiar voice. '*Caelum, non animum, mutant, qui trans mare currunt*' Aetius stated, with a sour look on his face.

'Those who run off to sea change their climate but not their mind'; Marcus reflected on his remark as he stood in front of Aetius watching his eyes. The man had the shiftiness of a Rome sewer rat.

Aetius moved towards him with his eyes intently focused on Marcus' left shoulder. 'Attilius, I had almost forgotten about you. Are you not about six years too late, to honour our agreement?'

'They were difficult times, Aetius... Eh, Dominus'

Aetius walked over to where Marcus stood and inspected his body. He noted the scars and the change in his physique. He pulled his tunic down and inspected the wound. 'Battle blunted, sword?'

Marcus smiled 'Arrow; A gift from the fort of Masada. Straight though.'

Aetius nodded in return and walked back to his desk to sit down. He did so with his left hand clutching his back. 'My fucking back is killing me, as are those lazy shitters down there on ground beneath us. We have not had a win in over a month.'

He turned his gaze back to Marcus, motioning for him to come over and sit opposite. 'You have changed into a man. You are bigger and stronger except for that arm. Does it pain you?' Marcus shook his head absently, putting his hand across the scar. The thin eyes of the Lanista darted from side to side and he mumbled to himself. 'So, Attilius; do we go forward? I should not have left so abruptly the last time we met but….'

Aetius cut him off in mid-sentence. 'Listen, Attilius; I don't give a morning fart about your motivation to stay or leave, all that time ago. You think you are the only one?'

'Dominus?'

'Hear what I say, Attilius; Maybe, I lost a little leverage with Laurentius and there remains a little nastiness but I can handle that. I have other problems and normally in this situation I would have you flogged for insubordination, tear up the contract and leave you at the front gates, which is my right by law and my right as your Lanista. However, Attilius, you are not the first or the last to run. This is not about forgiveness; this is about business. Understand?'

Marcus nodded at him and kept his mouth tight.

'What you don't understand, is that you lost the Laurentius patronage and that was worth an emperor's ransom. Live or die, you would have been a rich man as well as mounting the best-looking woman in Rome.'

'I was young, Dominus.'

'Were you at Jerusalem?'

'And Masada' Marcus replied solemnly.

Aetius nodded as his eyes moved across Marcus yet again. It was almost as if Marcus could hear the mind of the man across from him, turning and calculating.

'What level did you attain in the legion?'

'Triarii.'

Aetius pursed his lips and looked at the ceiling, nodding in appreciation. 'Triarii? Why did they let you go and I am assuming they did let you go? You didn't run from them as well, did you?'

'No, Dominus. I was sent to a farm to recuperate after the arrow nearly killed me.'

339

'So;' Aetius said as he watched Marcus. 'Why come back? Why now?'
'It is either this or farming. I am being honest, Dominus.'

Aetius nodded, stood up and moved across to the balcony. '*Medici*'. Get your ass up here. Now!' He walked back to his seat and leant on the table with his hand on his back. 'Stand up, Attilius.'

As Marcus stood up, Aetius motioned to him to remove his tunic which fell momentarily to the ground. He moved from his position and walked around Marcus several times. 'You are in good condition. except for that shoulder. The question is, whether we can fix it.'

Marcus nodded and replaced his tunic as a man strode into the room. He stood in front of the desk and waited. Aetius nodded to him and the man looked directly at Marcus.

'Medici, this is Marcus Attilius and he has decided after an absence of six years to join us as a freeman. I have his contract and I have made the decision to get him started immediately. Marcus, this is our school physician and if you get injured or should I say, when you get injured, this is the man who will hopefully patch you up. So, physician, first question; Can you fix that shoulder?'

Momentarily, Marcus relaxed, as he heard the agreement to enter the school. He faced the Medici who was a tall man, gaunt, with an intelligent face and quiet demeanour.

'Raise your left arm, Attilius.' Aetius commanded.

The Medici looked him over and noticed that Marcus winced when his arm was raised higher than his shoulder line. 'Massage and weights, Dominus. Some months to get it back to near contest level. Otherwise he is in good condition. He bears the scars of a legionnaire. Correct?'

Marcus nodded.

'Triarii.' Aetius added

'Triarii?' Medici said, with a shrug as if it meant nothing to him. Marcus watched as Aetius rolled his eyes. 'Concentrate on the shoulder, Medici and don't move off it until it is as strong as the other.'

'Of course, Dominus.'

Aetius stood and stretched his back as a slave girl brought in a plate of meat and wine, which she placed on a small table, near the door to the balcony. He looked over at Marcus with his eyes flashing. Show him through and then bring him back up here.'

The Medici nodded and gestured to Marcus to follow him.

'What is a Triarii' He asked, as they walked down the stairs to the compound.

'Elite soldier. We got called in when the front men were under pressure and we learnt to kill quickly and with speed.'

'Well, that is the training for this game, I guess. Some battles go on for more than an hour but the toll is high. Aetius is panicking, because we are not winning in the arena against the gladiators from the other schools. If we don't win we lose patronage so if you are as good as he thinks, you will be under pressure.'

Marcus nodded, as he followed the doctor along the passageway to the barracks which held gated doors, on the front of each room. They entered a room which held a single bed, a table and a rough-hewn chair.

'Why the cell doors?'

The man shrugged as he closed the door. 'Freemen are not locked up but slaves are sometimes purchased to become gladiators. They sometimes try to escape the school. Still happens now and then but they are usually caught and heavily punished.'

Marcus nodded as he looked around.

'This is your room unless Aetius wants you to share with another Novicus. For the first year, you will be a Novo which is novice rank. The trainer, the *Doctore* will show you the ropes but if you have any questions keep them to yourself. You will learn in good time.'

He followed the physician down the wide stone porch to the outside of the arena. They walked through the opening and finally stood at the side of the timber panelled enclosure, watching the gladiators at the other end of the arena, practised, locked in sword play. Marcus counted fifteen gladiators in the group.

'Two of the men are Tiro; First years like yourself and the rest are contest hardened. The two seniors are the men at the back.' Marcus looked over

341

towards the high, timber fence, at the other end of the small arena. The men were large and fit, with dark skin from their training in the sun. 'The one to the left is Atticus, who is still injured after his last fight and is the most promising gladiator in the school. Most of the men here are *Veterani,* meaning they have had at least one fight and survived. Atticus is *Primus palus.* Caius, who is standing to his left, is *Secundus palus.* First and second gladiators of the school.'

Marcus nodded

The Medici called out and waited. 'Severus!'

The man glanced over and with final instructions to the pair he was watching, he sauntered over to where the physician was standing. Marcus looked at him with the eye of man who had encountered hundreds in battle and he knew instinctively, that the man had skill. He was large, muscular and bald with a wide face and a livid scar that fell down one cheek from his ear to his mouth.

'New novicius' The Medici said gesturing to Marcus, who stood erect waiting for the introduction. 'He is ex-Triarii of the fifth legion.'

Severus looked at him with an appraising eye. 'You, poor fuck.' He said with a smile. 'Of all the occupations you ended up with us.' He laughed, shook Marcus' hand and looked directly at the Medici.

'Ex-Triarii and Dominus wants him to be a novicius?'

The medical Medici shrugged as if he really did not care. 'That is the order from the high and mighty.' He said quickly. 'Aetius wants him started tomorrow morning, but he has a left arm weakness, which needs to be tended.'

Severus looked briefly at the arm and nodded as he returned to the group, with a shout that brought them all to attention. 'Meet the new Novo.' He called out to the laughter of the men, who sent a range of insults to Marcus as he and the Medici left the arena, the same way they came.

They walked to the back of the school across the dusty path that lay edged with grass. He motioned to Marcus to follow him through the doors to the kitchen beyond. The familiar smell of stew met his nostrils as he walked past the fires and the bake oven, to the back of the area. 'There are many rules as a Novicus, but one of them is you must serve the meals to the gladiators, until you end your tenure.'

'How long?' Marcus asked

'Usually a year but I don't believe Aetius will leave you in that position for long. He needs winners and perhaps you can help him. We must fix that arm first, though.' They walked out the back to the orchard as a light mist descended from the dark clouds but the sky refused to send rain.

'I will take you back to Aetius and the oath which you must repeat in front of him, and a witness, which I assume will be me.'

They walked back to the office with the Medici silent and Marcus deep in thought as he waited for Aetius to move back from the balcony. 'The contract is on the desk, Attilius, but I have changed the date and now we must finish the oath. This oath binds you to this school, the Ludus Gallicus for a period of four years and if you are still alive at that point we can either re-negotiate this contract, or you can leave. Understand?'

Marcus nodded and stayed standing, as Aetius pulled a board from a drawer in the desk.

'Repeat after me. I, Marcus Attilius, gladiator in training of the Ludus Gallicus, *Uri vincri, veberari, ferroque necari.*'

Marcus repeated the words in front of the Lanista. 'I, Marcus Attilius, Gladiator in training at the Ludus Gallicus, will endure to be burned, to be bound, to be beaten, to be killed by the sword'

Aetius smiled, satisfied with the result and looked over at the Medici, who simply nodded and waited instructions. 'Show Attilius, to his lodgings. Give him his own room and tonight he can start assisting the serving to the gladiators.'

He turned his attention to Marcus who stood waiting. 'Listen to me Attilius, as this is the first and last time I will say it. You are now in a team of men who fight for a living, just as you have in the legion. These men will give you are hard time for a while, but I am sure you can handle that. Take up our family as this is now your *familia gladiatorium.* Take the family in your heart and together we can take Pompeii and Rome by the scruff of the neck.'

'I will Dominus.

'Good.' Aetius said with a flourish of his hand. 'Now, get out of my sight. I have work to do.

———

343

CHAPTER 40

Marcus lay in his bed at the end of the first night, with his head resting in his hands behind his head. The night endured as he suspected with the shouting, jibes and taunts from the gladiators as he and two other Novicus served the food to the seasoned gladiators, who seated themselves around the tables of the kitchen room waiting.

Only two men watched him with the eyes of eagles, as the rest created jibes and hurled verbal insults at him, as he stooped to place the bowls in front of them. Atticus and Caius watched the way he moved and his reaction to the taunts though the mealtime which lasted several hours.

Without doubt, the two senior gladiators knew the meaning of the army term, Triarii, and they knew what his probable skill level could be. Above all else, this was a school that thrived on competitiveness and if the physician was correct, Atticus and Caius were the most competitive and the most skilled. The rest did not matter.

As he lay there, he wondered for the first time why *Mecurius*, the god of travel had led him to this very bed and the Ludus, after all he had been through. Was it not his desire just to leave the farm and make a living in Rome?

Yet he lay on the bed in the Ludus Gallica, with nothing to show for his servitude in the legion, except twenty gold coins he pilfered from Jerusalem and less than three hundred Denarii.

Even the ring given to him that fateful night with Lucia Laurentius, had been sold to pay for his army kit when he left Rome the night after.

For the sum that lay in a pouch in his tunic, he put up with over six years of the hell known as Judea. His environment over those years was a brown sandy landscape that baked during the day, under full armour and freezing at night, so cold it took your breath away, even under covers once the fire died out.

The arrow through his chest was his fault. He had been careless. With the occupants of the fort lying the ground from their mass suicide, he had not thought to inspect the perimeter. Stupidly, he got in the way of the intended target, as the arrow was sent on its way by Ya'ir, the sole remaining soldier of the fort. Why didn't Ya'ir suicide the night before like the rest on that barren outcrop?

No one could have suspected that a person remained alive on that desolate fort, so high up above the plains that stretched into the distance, as far as the eye could see. When they looked at the prostrate bodies on the cold stone floor beneath them, what else could have taken their attention? The Sacarii leader had all the time in the world, to let off that bolt.

It was clear to him as he lay on the bed that night that Silva and his men did not understand the act of those desperate Sacarii. It was not cowardice as they all lamented, in a relaxed and jovial fashion around the fires that night after the breech. The belief, by all the men of the legion and the Triarii themselves, is that the Sacarii had become so scared of the Roman soldiers that they had killed themselves. The truth very much in the opposite.

On the grain ship, that took him from the Sicilia island to Rome, there was a crew member, a man of dark appearance and dour personality and they had struck up a conversation after dinner. It was the day before their intended arrival at Portus and after everyone had left the table. The conversation moved to Judea and Masada and the man bluntly told Marcus the truth. The Sacarii were, above all else, Jews and suicide held against their beliefs. It was written in their religion and they held their religion as the final truth of life

So, why had they killed themselves? An act of defiance, that governor Silva and his commanders could never understand, as it was not the Roman way.

As Roman legions, they fought with significant force and loss of life. They worked in smaller units, such as the Conturbenium, through to the Century and Cohort and into the legion proper, with SPQR emblazoned on gold discs and banners, for all the world to witness.

The Roman army worked on discipline and force, but not the Sacarii. They worked on skirmish and self- defeating suicide. The truth, he thought to himself, as he looked at the ceiling of the small room that was to become his home, was that the Sacarii, at a horrible cost, had won. What would the world remember?

The Roman siege or the suicide of one thousand? It remained in his mind, to be the ultimate act of defiance.

345

They had deprived the tenth legion and attending Triarii of the final battle, after five months of siege road building and planning. They won the day, at a cost which was to the Roman way of thinking; unthinkable. The mass suicide, had linked itself into the minds of every soldier that attended Masada on that fateful morning.

Laurentius and his wife, Lucia entered his mind and the telling words from Aetius, as to the loss of the patronage. As he recalled the events before he ran from Rome they were a blur or emotion and fear and he realised that nothing would have stopped him from his retreat, from the Ludis he now, ironically, lay in. Life was simply a continual path of uncertainty and happenstance.

Laurentius, he knew, was as mad as a cut serpent and his wife for all of her undeniable allure, held her own issues. Anyone who knew Vicinius and his henchman, Cato, were in a group of Romans best stayed away from at any time. Yet, in the midst of his life that mostly appeared as a deep fog, he kept bumping into these people who had some effect to propel him, to the very bed he lay on that night.

As it did, most nights, his mind turned to the farm and try as he might, on that cool evening at the Ludus, he could only vaguely recall the faces of his mother and brother but he could not bring them into focus. The realisation that he could not remember their faces seemed incongruous with the realisation that he could remember, in detail, every rock, fence and piece of furniture in the farmhouse.

If farming was unsavoury to him, at least he held no doubt as to his skills as a Gladiator. He was tall, strong, fit and more skilled in battle that the men in the school. How many of them had fought at Jerusalem and the long road of battles to Masada?

If he was to make a success of that fated walk to Rome, from his farm, he knew for the first time with certainty, it must be in the arena. If Mount Olympus had blessed him with the skill to fight, then it was time he accepted it and used the skills, to further his wealth and future.

With a deep breath and that resolute thought in his mind he closed his eyes and welcomed sleep. He dreamed of the road leading up to the farm gates and the hazy picture of his mother and brother waiting. The road and the land lay washed in blue with a cloudless sky above, and the gates, never open, were open for his arrival.

*

At dawn, the next morning he was awoken by the beating of a loud drum up and down the stone veranda outside of the rooms. His door was unlocked but he heard the sounds of jangling keys outside other doors, as they were thrown open with the grunts and growls of men, as they arose from slumber to meet another day, in the confines of the Ludis.

'Up and out' Came the shout and Marcus, with the others, left their rooms. He followed the men to the arena grounds on the other side of the school. The morning air was mild as he listened to the sounds of the men's complaints. At least this part of the school was familiar to the morning call in the legion, he thought to himself, as he stood waiting.

Severus waited until the line-up finished. He produced a wooden Gladius, which he waved around, as he walked up and down. He quieted them down and waited for Aeitus, who finally appeared on the balcony looking dishevelled and angry.

'Atticus, pay attention.' Severus shouted, sternly
Si, Doctores.'

'Doctores?' Marcus whispered, to the novice next to him.

'You address Severus, as Doctore. Don't you know anything? Each fighting style has a trainer. What fighting style are you?'

Marcus shrugged as he waited for Aetius to begin which he did from his perch on the balcony not far above them.

'Let me call out some names for you, to see if you can remember any of them from the *Caserma dei Gladiatori*. Germanus, Ludus Dacicus. Raecius Felix, Ludus Thracus. Hilarius, Ludus Maelius. Anyone?'

The stony silence from the men next to Marcus was ominous.

'Anyone remember them?' Aetius said again, with aggravation in his voice.

'No!' Aetius shouted out. 'They are all bloody champions and you can't remember their names? Standing in front of me, is the difference, you sons of cows. They are champions and you are not. They get paid the big denarii and you do not. They can get any women they like and you satisfy yourselves with gutter whores. Why? Because they are champions. Given the fact, that most of you would not know a champion until they slit your throat in the arena, I am probably wasting my time; but I live in hope.'

Aetius continued to look each of them in the eye as he took a big sigh and continued. 'Do you have any idea how much it costs to feed and train you? No, I didn't think so.' Aetius took a breath and wiped sweat from his brow with a bright red cloth.

Again, Marcus looked around to see if anyone would answer back, but there was mute silence everywhere.

'So, you will train like you have never trained before, for the next two months, until the night where we have been graciously requested to fight at the senator Sulla residence, in celebration of his beautiful daughter's wedding. If you are lucky enough to attend, you will view one of the most luxurious villas in Rome and you will be pitted against the *gladiatori* from Ludus Dacicus. Six, will attend, and two will fight from each side. I expect whoever is picked to win. Now, get to fucking work!'

The men looked at each other and moved to the centre of the arena. 'Attilius! I want you up here with the Doctore now.'

Severus led the men over to the centre of the arena. In several motions, he showed the men the strikes to be practised on the Palus, the high pole set in the earth. The pole, of which there were six, showed the scars of many strikes with the wooden sword that he held in his hand. 'First this, then this and then uppercut like this. Now get to it! You heard what the Lanista said about the coming bout, at the most magnificent villa in all of Rome. We do not want to lose, and let me tell you, senator Sulla is very generous with the winners. Now, two to a *palus* and I want to hear the strikes!'

'Follow me.' Severus said sternly, as Marcus followed him up to the office.

As they walked up Marcus turned his attention to Severus and stopped him at the bottom of the stairs. 'You have a Tiro gladiator here by the name of Blasius but I haven't seen him.'

'Blasius? He is in Pompeii for spear training at the school. He has been there for some while and should be back soon. You know him?'

Marcus nodded. 'Yes, but it was a long time ago, and he may not remember me.'

Aetius was sitting on the couch touching the hair of a young blond boy who was barely clothed and sat with a fixed smile on his face. As Marcus entered the room Aetius patted the boy's head and pushed him gently off the couch with a word. 'Later' He moved to the desk chair.

'Attilius, I have given some thought regarding which style of gladiator I need you to become. My belief, at this stage, will be Thracian. However, with your build and assuming you can fight, Murmillione might be more suitable. Time will tell.'
'How many different types are there?' Marcus asked a little bewildered.

'Ha, Attilius, there are many, many different types. There is the *Retarius* which is the gladiator with the trident and net and not, I can assure you, to be underestimated. There is the *Murmillo* which is where you may end up. The *Murmillione*, is a gladiator with a fish head on his helmet but utilising a large shield and Gladius and that may work better because of your training in armour and in close battle quarters. A very popular choice for the contests, I might add.'

He looked over at Severus and continued. He stroked his chin as he contemplated the various forms. 'Now let's see there is the *Eques* which is a horseman and the *Secutor* who is really a lightly armed pursuer in the gladiatorial battle. Hmm, let's see who is next.? There is the *Hoplomachus* who fights with a spear and can be deadly, if used properly. Then there is the, *Provocator* who is very similar to a legionary with shield and sword, but light armour for that one and that style would suit a smaller man. Then there is the *Thraex* which may be your calling. The *Thracians* use a curved sword and are usually quick and light footed. Then there is the *Scissores* as well, but not very popular with the crowds.'

Marcus nodded dumbly at him trying to take in the information.

'The truth of crowds' Aetius continued 'Is that they like contrast. For example, they like *Parmularii* against *Scutarii*. You know, small-shield fighters against big-shield fighters.'

'And *Bestarii*, Dominus.'

'Of course, Doctore. We left out the beast slayers, but they are always in fashion as a show starter. They get the blood up of the crowd and sets them up for the gladiatorial battles. By the way we don't train *Essedarius*, the chariot fighters or the Eques. Any questions?'

'What do the Bestarii fight?'

'Anything that will lie down after one spear strike!' Severus and Aetius laughed together at the joke, while Marcus waited. 'Severus, you agree?'

'I do, Dominus. Let us start him as a Thraex and see how he goes.'

'Good. Now, Attilius, several other areas we need to discuss. The first is the fact that you are too thin. You need to put on more weight. Before you ask, the reason is that over the years we have found the heavier gladiators receive and recover from bruises and cuts quicker that the slimmer ones. We think the size makes a difference. Understand?'

Marcus thought back to the arena and the men as they practised. He had not noticed it before, but many of them were of a higher weight. Interestingly, Aetius did not note that the weight might also, make them slower. In the legion, the trainers were hard on anyone putting on weight, as it slowed them down.

'Secondly, I want to see you in action at the end of training today. I want to see a fight between you, and one of the training gladiators in armour, and with wood not steel. Which one, Doctore?'

'Besides Caius and Atticus; perhaps Albus, shows the most promise.' Albus?' Aetius questioned and then nodded. 'Young man from Thrace and a Tiro with a win under his belt. Yes. Good choice.'

'Wood sword?' Marcus said with a quizzical look on his face. Severus butted in. 'The school does not allow proper swords, for reasons such as injury during practice and the only time you get to use steel is the day before a fight. The *Rudis*, the wooden sword is the training tool in all schools. You are allowed to practice only on the *Palus* and in combat training. Since you have used steel in the army, it may take some time to get used to the different weight and feel of the wooden Gladius. The swords are fire hardened wood, so they don't break easily.'

'What will Albus fight as?'

'Murmillione; in normal arena fighting, there are favourite pairs. Murmillione against Thracian or Hoplomachus, or Retarius, for example or Retarius against a Secutor. Sometimes they mix and match in the arena. Everyone has their favourites.'

'Is this hand-to-hand or just swordfight?'

Aetius looked at him with the rage returning to his face. 'This is a gladiatorial contest, Attilius. You fight with everything you have. Understand?'

Marcus nodded, watching the shifty eyes of the Lanista, dart from his face to that of the Doctore. 'You fight like you are in the middle of a battle in Judea.'

'Just asking, Dominus.'

'By the Gods, Attilius. I hope you are not as dense as you appear to be in these conversations, but then, I think you are just foxing an old man like me. Doctore, have we explained the training?'

Severus shrugged as if he did not know so Aetius continued. 'You train from sunrise, until the horses of the sun make their descent off the highest point. You receive breakfast at mid of the morning and the you receive lunch, after the final training session. Now, your arm. I have spoken to the physician and he is setting up a session to work on that arm each afternoon, after the sun starts its final descent and the horses of the chariot are put into the stables for the night.'

Marcus nodded reminding himself again of the debt and the news of the visit to the Sulla villa. 'Do I attend the Sulla villa?' He asked slowly.

Aetius shrugged quickly. 'That depends on this afternoon.' He turned to Severus. 'Make sure his uniform fits and he is not hampered by anything.'

Severus nodded and touched Marcus on the shoulder. 'Let's go; there is sweat to make and men to fight.'

Marcus followed the trainer down the stairs and back to the arena. Severus showed him the armoury where the swords and dress were stored and asked him to pick a Rudis which he did after testing several and finding the weight he liked.

For the rest of the morning after a breakfast of maize porridge and fruit they worked in pairs; each man on either side of the central poles. As one strike hit the Palus, the other gladiator struck against it to counter the blow, from the other side.

As each Rudis hit the pole, the sound reverberated off the hard timber and Marcus could feel the vibration of the rudis up his arm. The harder he hit, the less the vibration so he realised that gladiators were taught to strike heavy blows with their swords, as they were trained on the Palus each and every day.

Water was kept in plentiful supply by attendants. They filled the buckets, as the men drained them. Marcus dipped a ladle into the water, drinking and dropping it back in. As he looked across the arena, the brown backs of the men stood out, glistening with sweat. The grunts and growls of exertion echoed off the timber, lined enclosure.

Training ended early in the forenoon. An antipasto lunch was served, as the men washed themselves down, to get the dust and grime off and sat on the stone deck beside the arena to quiet their aching muscles.

'In the legion, we hear?' Caius looked at Marcus who was sitting beside him in the shade of the awning. Marcus nodded in assent. 'How long have you been here, Caius?' 'What does it matter to you, Triarii.' He replied angrily, looking skyward. 'You think you are better than us, because you fought in Judea? Try it here for a year and then see which was worse.'

'No doubt, brother, both have their hell' Marcus said sourly

Caius nodded as he wiped sweat off his shoulder and across a livid scar on his chest. 'I have a family to support and this is the only way of doing it. Let me tell you something Attilius; All that shit you heard from that scum Aetius? It's a load of pig shit.'

'Like what?' Marcus asked, with the familiar prickling of hairs on the back of his neck before a fight.

'Brotherhood and all that shit. Let me tell you, this is as competitive as the arena and just because we are in the same school, does not mean we are brothers.'

'I disagree' Said a voice from behind. Marcus looked up to see Atticus, standing tall behind them. 'You are a sour man, Caius. If you can't share the brotherhood you should not be here.'

Caius stood up, spat at the ground and sauntered away.

Atticus sat his considerable size down on the stone next to Attilius. He shook his hand and introduced himself. 'We have not met; I am Manu Atticus.' They shook hands again as Atticus stretched his long, heavy legs in front of him.

'Don't pay mind to Caius. He is having a bad day, but then he always has a bad day. It all started when he lost to me and took second position in the school. He is a bad loser and he makes serious mistakes in contests. It will cost him his life one day. He does not like the title *secundus*, second

---

sword, and most of the boys don't like him. But as regards what he said, he is wrong. This is a family. We take care of each other with the exception of Caius.'

'Are you, ex-legion?'

Atticus nodded his head 'Gaul for many years and then back to Rome. I applied for the Pretorian guard, but one must have the money to buy their way in, so I applied here and Aetius accepted me.

'How long have you been here?'

'Hmm,' Atticus stroked his chin. 'Time passes quickly, Marcus, but it has been over a year and I have had two wins in that time. One at Pompeii and one at Triena.'

'Caius? Is he a good fighter?'
'Good fighter but lacks one essential ingredient. He loses his concentration. But, he is excellent with the Gladius and one of the rising stars. You fighting him today?'

Marcus shook his head as Atticus rose to stretch. 'No, a Tiro by the name of Albus'

'You have a fight on your hands, Marcus, so pay attention and keep well, brother. We will all be watching.'

An hour later Severus reappeared and motioned to Marcus to follow him. He walked back to the armoury and seated himself, as Severus put a range of clothing next to him. He looked down at the gear beside him and started to get dressed in the leg greaves, and upper leg protectors. He tried the helmet on, which fitted without any noticeable pressure points. He inspected the small round shield and long curved sword which was wider at the end than at the heel of the blade.

'Leave the sword on the bench, Marcus, you won't be using steel today.' Severus said, handing him back his Rudus. 'The man you will be fighting today has already won an arena bout, so keep in mind, he is Tiro status and a good fighter. As you already know he is fighting as a Murmillo, which means short sword and long shield which is probably where you will end up. You need to be careful of the shield, because the Murmillo can use it as a battering ram, to knock you over.'

'How does the win occur?' Marcus asked, as he tested the weight of the small rounded shield, with his weaker left arm.

'Either of you can yield but I would not recommend it in front of Aetius. The other way is that your opponent, or you, lies, prone on the ground and the attacker's sword at the throat or belly. Are you ready for a dance?'

Marcus stood up adjusted his helmet and looked directly at Severus. 'I have danced with more than you could imagine, in the past six years, Doctore.'

They walked out into the afternoon sun with his opponent, Albus, already on the arena sand, striking the air with his rudis. Marcus walked out to him and held out his hand which Albus ignored. With his dark eyes flashing and distinctive garb, Marcus noted for the first time, the casting of a fish above the crown of the helmet of his opponent. His left arm, held the long shield and his right held firmly onto the rudis.

Behind Marcus, the rest of the gladiators stood in quiet anticipation of the bout. Above them, Aetius stood with his hands lightly clasping the rail of the veranda and his eyes intently on the two men below. He nodded to Severus, who brought them together.

'I am the referee in this match so if I say break, you break. The contest is not over until one of you yield. Biting and gouging is not permitted.' He looked at both of them, moved back and then dropped his hand.

Albus circled Marcus to the right, trying to position his shield and rudis in a strike position. Twice he struck out with the rudis, which Marcus easily moved away from. and then in a blur, Marcus moved in with the short shield bringing it hard up into Albus' stomach.

As he instinctively moved back, Marcus positioned himself, put his left foot behind Albus, and using his shield, he swept the man's legs up, watching as Albus hit the ground heavily with a grunt. Marcus, moved his weight forward bringing his rudis up to the man's throat.

'Yield' He said. He looked over at Severus, who then looked over at Aetius, who smiled and waited for them both to rise. The space of several moments had passed since Severus had dropped his hand. 'Well done, Attilius.' He called out 'Now, another contest.'

Albus removed his helmet and wiped his brow with a shocked look on his face. He replaced his helmet and raised his shield and sword. Marcus did the same waiting for Severus to drop his hand for the contest to begin,

Albus changed his tactics, moving to the left with sword strikes, to keep Marcus away.

Marcus moved back several paces, waiting for Albus to move towards him, which he impatiently provided with an overhand strike. Marcus knew the blow would be heavy and directed, so he feinted to his right, moved to the left and with a resounding slap he drove the flat point of the sword in Albus' exposed flank and then brought the rudis up to the left of his neck and held it there.

'Yield' He said

Albus refused and with all his strength, Marcus brought the sharp side of the rudis around again and hit the man beside him with such force, he dropped to his knees unable to gain his breath.

Severus moved in with his hand forward, to stop the contest, and when he looked up Aetius had disappeared. Behind Marcus, there was constant murmuring from the gladiators and many with astonished looks, as they sat back down on the cool stones.

Severus turned to Albus 'Go and get dressed.' He removed his helmet and spat on the ground in front of Marcus, as he turned on his heels and moved back to the armoury.

The trainer set his eyes on Marcus. 'You are amazingly fast, Attilius but we need work on that arm. Go up to Aetius, he will want to speak to you and do it now. Don't worry about Albus. There is no one in this school who is used to losing that quickly.'

Marcus nodded, passed the shield and rudis to the trainer and walked up to the Lanista. He had barely raised a sweat as he entered the office.

'Triarii, eh?'

Marcus shrugged.

'By the Gods you can fight. You have the strength of a young bull and Triarii, together you and I can make some wealth. We need to get that arm to the same strength as the right. Did the Doctore note anything about your sword play?

Marcus shook his head with a smile. 'I am more used to steel, Dominus.'

Aetius looked at the tall muscular man before him. Importantly, he held the three most important qualities of a successful gladiator. Size, good looks and a high level of skill in hand-to hand fighting, and yet, the man before him contained another quality which was harder to determine. Perhaps, he sensed in him a burning desire to win and it was a quality that was hard to find. If harnessed properly, it could make him the best gladiator in Rome. He had seen many, but it was rare to see a man so intensely confident.

'The next step is to get that arm right. I will speak to the Doctore. That is all. You can go.' Marcus nodded and retraced his steps to the arena below to start exercises on his left arm while Aetius lay down on his cushioned couch and started to dream of gladiatorial success.

The notoriety, when a school held the champion of Rome was incalculable. It allowed for larger fees and the added advantage of attracting high quality candidates whether they were slaves or freemen. Champions attracted champions. It was as simple as that.

Aetius licked his lips slowly in anticipation, because if this man was half as good as he was against Albus, he had the champion in his midst. He called out to his servant to bring him a new board, pen and ink.

As he waited, Severus entered the room. 'Did you see that, Dominus?'

'I did, Doctore and I am still trying to get to understand how fast he moves.'

'It is his style, Dominus. It is unorthodox and when I watched Albus, he was confused from the start. If Attilius had not beaten him so quickly in both contests, I would never have believed it. Attilius has been trained to move quickly and kill quickly and that is what he does.'

'What do you suggest?' Aetius said with a familiar curve of his lip

'We keep his style and train him on sword play and let's see what happens.'

'I think we have our champion so take care of him.' Aetius said. 'It is the depth of his chest that gives him that strength, so let us not worry so much about his weight.' He waved the Doctore away with a swipe of his hand.

If, indeed, he held a champion, the winnings stayed in the Ludis Gallicus and that meant in the pocket of the Lanista. It occurred to him, that at long last the Gods from the mount, were smiling at him.

Yet, even as Novicus or Tirone, champions stood out. One had only to watch the great Hilarius or a Germanicus to understand how superior they were in the arena. They were different; Sometimes it was difficult to understand why they were so successful, but he thought, perhaps it was style.

The great champions brought a different style to the arena, that the rest found hard to beat. Champion gladiators, held the ability to take on a variety of differing opponents, and win.

They held the intelligence to understand the techniques and strengths of their opponents and to uncover their weaknesses, quickly and attack them.

He moved over to the balcony to sip and his wine and look down at the small arena below. Attilius had one other outstanding characteristic as a gladiator and that related to his handsomeness. The women would love him. Aetius had been in the gladiator game long enough to know that good looks were a very valuable asset for any gladiator. The truth remained, that most of them were as ugly as an enraged bear.

Aetius reflected briefly on his father who had been a successful gladiator under Caesar and severely injured in a bout. He became a Doctore, for one of the smaller schools which, in turn, became his life. He wanted Aetius to follow in footsteps in the arena, but Aetius was not a fighter. He understood that the real wealth lay in the school and with his father's help, he had built the Ludis Gallicus over twenty long years.

Over that time, he had chosen and trained many gladiators and he had witnessed how his men faced the requirement of dying, just as his father had died several years earlier, after receiving an accidental wound whilst training a new and inexperienced gladiator.

Learning to die was equally as important to learning how to live for gladiators. For most there was the ominous spectre of death in the next contest and very few of those outside the Ludis or the arena, understood the level of courage required to fight hand-to-hand, under the scrutiny of a crowd against an opponent who had one sole purpose and that was to maim or kill you and at the very least, make you succumb to their power.

He knew gladiators well enough and he knew they fought in contempt of life, chasing glory and wealth. By fighting, they faced both possible fates.

The fate that could bring them glory and the fate that would send them across the river to death. Gladiators fought under *virtuis,* fighting with the acceptance of death. If that was not courage, then what was?

Aetius sipped his honey wine, reflecting on the gladiators who rose to the top of their profession. It was not an absence of fear, because they all felt that companion, whether they admitted it or not. It interested him that the most successful gladiators seemed to have the ability to contain their fear and then use it, to their advantage to concentrate harder. It was not just the level of strength or skill because, again, they all held it in abundance. The best possessed a quality, which remained difficult to define and even harder to understand. It represented the same force which occurred in all animals. Why did one chariot run faster than another, if the horse flesh was much the same?

He returned to the couch. Time would tell, if Marcus Attilius was gifted but the Gods were clearly on his side, so he decided to give a large offering to the Goddess Fortuna for smiling on him. As veiled and blind as she was, she had, mistakenly or not, bestowed good fortune for once.

CHAPTER 41

Crispinus Racus, stood in front of the emperor, with two large boards in front of him and with a pen in hand pointing to several areas of the drawing. His hands trembled slightly, as he marked out an area on the plan.

'Yes, architect, I understand.' Flavian Vespasian replied, with a tone laced with authority. 'But you are behind by some months and we have a finish date in mind, don't we?' Vespasian delivered the message with a sour face with his son, Titus, behind him and standing to his side, a large Pretorian guard, in full battle dress and a menacing scowl.

Racus almost bent double, as he bowed. 'Of course, sire, but we have had set backs with the foundations and the changes, made to the chain lifts and the cells of the prisoners. This is not an easy project, emperor.'

'Hmmm.' Vespasian uttered, as his eyes moved across the board.

Racus looked at the emperor's eyes and then looked quickly away. 'As you requested, sire, we are using Travertino for the floors of the building with tuff for the pillars and the massive radial walls. Then there are tiles for the upper storeys of the amphitheatre walls, as well,' He said as a way of explanation, 'I have had to design new ways to pour the concrete for the lower levels, to ensure the proper strength for the upper building and…'

'Architect; if this was an easy project, I would have found someone far less expensive than you. Now listen to me and listen hard. If you need more men for the labour, put them on. If the quarries are not supplying in time, tell me, or my son, Titus, and if you need to change anything do it. But, it will be delivered on time, architect. On time!' Vespasian's voice raised several decibels, as he stared at him.

'Sire as you are aware' Racus said with a grimace on his face 'The amphitheatre contains fountains changed to your specifications. Latrines, which require us to redirect and connect aqueducts from the hills. As you know, we have had to install substantial arches in the corridors, with barrel vaults in all the halls, to ensure strength and this has taken a considerable amount of time. We have designed the arches to transfer the weight of the structure, to the connecting columns below and because of the need for weight bearing columns, on the lower…'

Vespasian held his hand up to silence the chief architect. 'We are in the middle of the year and if the amphitheatre is not on schedule, within three months, you will be replaced and I will have you flogged and put to death by one of my guards. Do you understand?'

Racus, his face red, nodded and bowed slightly. 'And, architect, let me remind you! You are the architect of the greatest building in the world. Be thankful.'

Crispinus looked across at the massive form of the scowling Pretorian guard, standing just behind the purple robed emperor with a blanched look on his face. 'Sire, of course, I understand your concerns…'

'I am not sure you do, Racus, and you have three months to be back on schedule, so I won't stop you from taking control and lifting the work effort.'

He gave Racus a steely look, watching as the man picked up his diagram boards and moved off quickly, towards one of the building crews.

With Titus at his side, Vespasian walked back through the arches, holding the next two floors to the outside. They then journeyed on his black chariot, towards the other side of the massive building.

With a flick of the whip in Titus's hand, the horses obeyed and started to canter off along the road that circled the structure. Behind him, two of the Pretorian guards rode with their eyes fixed firmly on the precious cargo in front and to the sides, to ensure that a spear or a well-directed arrow was not on its way to find the emperor or his son.

They neared the massive gate on the Eastern side, dismounted and walked up the wooden stairs, to the highest level. The third storey of the Amphitheatre had begun, and the scene below, resembled worker ants crawling over stone blocks, below timber gantries with ropes, swaying like spider webs around the structure.

The gantries moved slowly, holding stone blocks the size of chariots, as they swung across to be placed in position and men laid floors, across the top level. 'Two more storeys to go.' Vespasian breathed, as he watched the scene. 'We could not have done it without the spoils of Judea, Titus and for that, Rome must be thankful.'

The bottom of building held a maze of passages and rooms, slowly covered over, as the floor of the massive barrel shaped structure took shape. The sides of the arena sloped away, as each tier was built to seat spectators, with the start of the second level built as a large walkway that circled the entire complex.

'Patrons will be able to walk right around the Amphitheatre when it is finished' Vespasian said to his son. 'It will be the grandest and most significant structure; the world has ever seen.'

'What about the Forum?' Titus asked with a surprised look on his face.

'Ah, the Forum. Well, Titus that is for the senators and the snotty plebeians. This arena is for the masses and we know that if you want to quiet the masses, you must give them shows and this will be the greatest show that anyone has ever seen, to this time.'

The shouts and curses almost stopped as the purple robes of Vespasian were seen from the crowds of men below. Vespasian turned around to speak to Titus and the noise started again.

'For all of his issues, Crispinus is quite a genius.' He said, to his slightly taller son beside him. 'He has built these lifts, which will take the animals, prisoners and gladiators, from the catacomb depth up to the entrances to the arena. They work via gears of some sort, with slaves doing the hard work below. It is quite magnificent, is it not.?'

'It is, father and a fitting tribute to your contribution to Rome.'

Vespasian nodded, without showing any humility. His son was correct and the building before him was a testament to his ability and vision. In his thoughts, he could clearly envisage the opening with the fanfare, Bestarii and Gladiatorial fights in his honour.

In his mind he could almost touch the opening day of the amphitheatre and on that day, the arena would be festooned with colourful flags, combined with the shields and flags of the Roman empire. There would be a display by the Pretorian guard, to show the citizens the strength of the police force, followed by one hundred days of games. It will be a spectacle the Roman empire will witness and never see again.

The order for wild beasts had been issued, with over two hundred, comprising of lions, tigers, bulls, leopards, bears and elephants to be caught and held ready for the games which would begin just under two years from this very day. He looked down on the yawning chasm beneath him. By the Gods, it was a beautiful structure, he thought to himself.

As they descended the stairs, Vespasian stopped with his hand on the railing and let out a groan.

'What is it, father?'

'This pain again, Titus. It is on my left side and has been with me for some weeks.'

'Have you seen the physician?'

'They talk like they know what they are doing, but I don't think they are any good. Let's continue, Titus' He said with a grimace, almost sitting on the dusty step.

'You need to rest.' Titus said with concern, as he walked his father to the chariot. He assisted him onto the chariot and pulled the reins easily, to set the horses off at a slow trot to keep the movement of the chariot in check, with the Pretorian guards behind them.

'Perhaps you are right, Titus.' Vespasian said softly, holding his side over the bumps in the road. 'The senate is in good order and I have only several things to attend to. There is the occasion of Sulla's daughter's wedding. Perhaps you could attend those as well. Laurentius will be there, so make sure he is kept happy.'

'Of course, father.' Titus looked at his father's ashen face as he flicked the reins to get the horses into a canter, away from the building behind them and towards the palace. As they neared the front gate, Titus shouted to the servants to assist and as they dismounted, Vespasian doubled over again from the pain. Three servants carried him into the palace, with Titus beside him giving orders to be careful. He was placed on a divan in the outer room.

'How do you fare, father? Do I call the physician?'

'Hush, Titus, I will last a little longer than this' Vespasian said as he lay back on the divan and a cup of water in his hands. 'Sit down next to me as I have wanted to speak to you and this seems like an appropriate time.' Titus, with a concerned look on his face, sat down next to his father on a stool as his father looked around to see it the slaves had left, after he waved them away with his hand.

'So, Titus as you are aware I am in my sixty seventh year and my health, after all these years of being so robust, is starting to fade. It angers me, but there is little I can do according to those dogs, we call physicians.

It must be age, because I don't remember being sick even in Judea and Egypt. So, before *Mania,* comes to claim me we must discuss several very important matters.'

The emperor rose from his prone position to sit up and move closer to his son.

'You see, the pain subsides. It does not last long but it is the power of a sword strike when it does. Now, let us talk succession. I have spent some of the past two years placing you in a position where you can take control of the emperorship, and my role, as first man in Rome. There is no one better equipped than you, to take over the reins of power and if it falls to anyone else, there will be trouble in Rome within weeks.'

Titus nodded, relieved that his father was feeling better. 'We have the army, that is for sure. The legions would follow me anywhere. What about the Pretorian guard? It seems to become bigger in force every day.'

The emperor took a sip from the water and put his hand on his son's shoulder. 'That is precisely, why I have increased their numbers. They are my police in Rome and they will follow me to their death. I will make sure they follow you as well. Uprising does not always start in the Roman territories. We have a population of nearly one million in this city already, and the inhabitants of Rome need to be behind you.'

'The two 'S' worry me, Titus, but we will deal with them in due time.'

Titus nodded, reflecting the code word for Sulla and the man who finally vanquished the fort of Masada. Governor Lucius Flavius Silva. They were in his father's thoughts as threats and he knew of no one who could handle and extinguish a threat, better than him.

Gaius Sulla, was a power monger and one to be watched and he knew that Silva had loyalty in the legions, but he did not control them. He was a 'tent' general and there was little in the world the legions disrespected more, than a man who stayed in his tent as the battle raged.

'I understand, father. What else.'

'I need you to promise me something.'

'What?' Came the soft reply. 'Anything.'

'If I pass to the underworld before the Flavian Amphitheatre, or the magnificent Forum are finalised, I want you to swear to me you will

---

363

have them finished and the games funded by that jackal's son, Laurentius.'

Titus picked up his father's hand and kissed it softly 'You will be there father. But, if you are not I will finish the work.'

Vespasian nodded and rose unsteadily to his feet with Titus holding onto his arm. 'Now take me to my office. There is work to do.'

CHAPTER 42

With the physician before him, Marcus picked up the heavy stone once again, to complete another repetition on his left arm to strengthen it. As he finished a count of five, the Medici came over to him.

'That is enough, Marcus. Now follow me to the infirmary and let us start the massage.' Marcus dropped the rock onto the ground, near one of the palus. He followed the physician as they walked towards the outside veranda, where the rest of the gladiators lounged, as they rested their tortured bodies and digested what had been a larger than normal lunch.

'Has anyone here, not had a rub down?' He called out, referring to the medicinal olive oil with camphor that was massaged into the skin and muscles of all gladiators after their sessions had finished. He did not receive a reply, so he shrugged and waited for Marcus to lie on the massage table inside the hut.

The cool of the room was welcome, after the hour spent working on his shoulder outside in the afternoon sun. The sinews of the shoulder were sore, as the Medici worked his fingers into the aching muscles and sinew, of his damaged chest. Defying the searing hurt from the probing and kneading, Marcus looked up at the faded frescos on the wall, trying to concentrate away from the pain.

'The shoulder is much better, I believe.' The physician said with a sigh. It has been almost eight weeks and the strength return; however, we are not there yet.'

Marcus started to move off the table as the Medici pushed him back.

'Bandage first, then you can go.'

'I don't think the bandage assists, physician.'

'Let me be the judge of that, Attilius and you can judge how to use the sword.'

Marcus shrugged at the rebuke. He waited until the bandage soaked in aloe was applied and he rose from his position. 'My thanks for your care.' He said with a smile which the Medici returned and a hand on his shoulder.

'It is about as good as it can be, Marcus. Your strength has almost returned but flexibility will always be a problem because some of the internal flesh has been destroyed, due to the path of the arrow. We still must work on the strengthening and I am going to start you on some stretch positions, to see if we can get a little more flexibility. However, if that arrow had hit you a little to the left, you would not be here today.'

'That makes me feel better.' Marcus replied with a wide smile.

'Are you always in a good mood, gladiator? Because, you seem to be.'

'Not always, physician. Never when I fight.'

'I saw the list on Aetius desk yesterday, for the contests at the Sulla villa next week.'

'Don't tell me, physician; I am on the list?'

The Medici nodded. 'You are. See you tomorrow afternoon, same time, same place.'

'Is there another place?' Marcus asked with wide smirk.

'No.' the physician replied flatly and left the room.

Marcus walked into the sunshine of the arena and towards the kitchen. He had still not received lunch, because of the training on his left arm. As he walked into the kitchen, he faintly heard a voice he remembered.

'Ha, they will let anyone in here.'

Marcus swivelled to find Blasius sitting on one of the stools in the kitchen. He was busy ladling Minestrone soup, into his mouth. 'Marcus, you are a sight for tired eyes.' Blasius said as he rose to embrace the man before him.

'You have changed, Blasius.' Marco said, eyeing the size of the man's shoulders and quickly inspecting the white scars that foretold the vocation of the man before him. Army or gladiator, both held the scars of experience.

'Well, friend, look at the size of you! By the Gods on the Mount, you must be twice the size of when you left Rome. You have no fat on you at all. Are you not eating?'

'That's all I do, Blasius. They try to fatten you like a pig in this place.'

Blasius pushed his bowl away and the bread that lay beside it. 'I wish I could say the same in this shithole, they work you hard enough to keep any weight off. Word has got around about you, in this place and as far as Pompeii. Triarii? That is a high station, in the legion.'

Marcus shrugged and reached for the bread. 'It is fair to say, we all were entitled to it after the siege of Jerusalem, but only a few were promoted to the rank. I was one of them.'

'Elite killers, I hear.'

Again, Marcus nodded and looked across at the man he had not seen in all the years he was away.

'I hear you are a successful Tirone. First contest won?'

Blasius looked at Marcus and nodded but with a blanched look on his face. 'They ordered the end of the fight as *mortem,* which was unexpected, and I could hardly do it. Very few contests are to the death and my understanding of the bout was a contest to victory not death.' 'What were you fighting as? '

'Thracian. I hear you are to be the same.'

'Apparently; Blasius, I can honestly tell you I don't know the difference, but maybe it comes back to what suits your fighting style.'

Blasius smiled and then laughed 'That remark takes me back to that fight of yours with Britanicus, longer ago than I now care to remember. You did well, but after training in this school for a year, I can assure you he was holding back. The best gladiators are animals, with blood lust instinct, and they are, by far, the strongest and best with the Gladius and each of them have their own fighting styles and tricks.'

Marcus smiled broadly at the memory of the day, in which he took on the giant to pay back a debt to a man he had met only once. 'I will never forget it either.' He replied. 'How did you end up killing your opponent?'

'The sword tip through the neck and he just looked up at me with fear in his eyes. It was not easy to do.'

'You get used to it, Blasius. Let me assure you, it is second nature after a while. When I think of how many I have killed in battle, it makes me wonder how I survived.'

'I hear you almost died.'

Marcus nodded. 'A badly aimed arrow. It was meant for Consul Silva apparently. Pity it did not hit him and miss me, but then if that happened I would not be here. Killing becomes second nature, Blasius.'

'I wonder.' Blasius replied, as he sipped water from a cup provided on the table.

'What happens if there is a command to kill at the end of the battle? Must we comply?'

Blasius looked at him in surprise.' Have you forgotten after such a short time, your *sacramentum gladiatorium,* that our beloved master upstairs got you to sign? Your contract, Marcus makes you subservient to the commands by the Lanista and you did formally speak the *auctoramentum,* did you not?'

Yes, I spoke the oath in front of the physician.'

'Of course, we all did' Blasius said with finality. 'We fight to kill and that is the first order, but in saying that, you should be aware that fights to the death are rare.'

'That is good news, I guess.' Marcus said, as he ladled soup into a wooden bowl

'For a start, the payment back to the Lanista after the killing, is a large sum. The *sponsor* who holds the contest, must pay the Lanista of the school, heavy compensation if they decide on a contest to the death. Thankfully, the amount is enough to persuade most that it is too expensive.'

'How much is a gladiator worth if the host decides on a fight to the death?' Marcus sipped his soup as he waited for the answer.

Blasius shrugged his large shoulders pondering the question. 'Well, to be honest Marco, I don't know, but it would be a large amount and if the gladiator has been successful and draws crowds, then the cost would be far greater. The only figure I heard was around fifty thousand Denarii.'

Marcus whistled softly. 'A fortune for the Lanista. No wonder Aetius looks forward to the contest dates. Our death is his reward.'

'Well, yes and no, Marcus. If Aetius, for example, loses a gladiator he has to find another with promise. The cost of purchasing a slave and then the training is expensive. That is, unless they are dumb heads like you and me, who volunteer.'

'And if we die?' Marcus asked. 'Who pays for the funeral?'

'We all do. There is a fund which is taken out of our pay and it goes towards any funeral expenses and any family.'

'And Aetius? What do you think of him?'

Blasius gave him a stare.' I don't know what you think of our illustrious Lanista, but let me tell you, he is the same as all of them and I have seen most of them around the arena, from time to time.

'That doesn't sound like love.'

Blasius leaned over to Marcus, to emphasize his point. 'They would murder their mothers for a loaf of fresh bread and their whole family, for ten. They are money grubbing mongrels and they act as if they care, but all they complain about is the cost. Aetius is no exception and probably worse than the rest.'

'All he talks about is champions.'

'Well, once the school becomes famous they attract a better class of gladiators and get a far better pick of slaves. Champions pull the crowds and crowds make politicians happy and they then pay for the gladiators from that school at a higher rate. Aetius is desperate for a champion and let me assure you, Marco, he will have all of us killed by better opponents to find the one he wants.'

'How many has the school lost this year?'

'Three, ah, no, four. The last was a horrible fight. He was a strong young'un and pitted against a much more experienced gladiator. I know the opposing man did not mean to kill him, but the boy let his shield drop for a moment and the incoming strike ran him through. You could hear his scream around the stadium. The crowd loved it, but keep in mind, the crowd is never on the arena fighting. They just love the blood.'

'Then how do you know before the contest, whether it is a death match?' Marcus asked as he absently rubbed his shoulder.

'Gladiators are usually informed before the contest but sometimes the nobleman, paying for the contest, change their mind. Nice to have money, eh? The real problem is severe injuries in the arena and they happen, so I strike hard and fast, and then move away. I try to tire my opponent and then look for the weaknesses.'

'I'll keep that in mind.' Marcus replied.

Blasius looked over at the door as Severus walked in. 'Just the two I have been looking for.' He said heading over. 'Marcus, you will be at the senator Sulla's villa next week. There will be five in attendance, from both schools and only two will fight.'

'I am not on the list?' Blasius said with a sly grin. 'No rich and famous women to fuck after the contest? You mean this dumb head here, gets it all?'

'Correct' Dominus wants you rested for Pompeii, which is at the end of Junius.'

'Dominus said there would be more attending, Doctore.' Marcus said with a bemused look on his face. 'Don't listen to him, Marcus. Listen to me. Five only and two of the five will fight. I am not sure about you, but I believe that Caius will fight on the night. Have you spoken to Marcus about the women, Blasius?'

Blasius shook his head as he accepted the news of his upcoming contest.

'Let him know.' Severus said, as he walked away. 'If anyone knows that score it would be you, Blasius.'

Marcus looked at Blasius, with a broad grin on his face. 'Blasius, you dog. Have you been rooting around again?'

Blasius laughed and settled on his stool. He leant over to get Marcus closer to him so he could whisper. 'Do you remember our days, back when we caroused around Rome, chasing young women? Well, when you are a gladiator in the arena they chase us.' Marcus stared at him with a light smile on his face. 'Meaning?'

Meaning, friend, that gladiators are sought after by women of all ages, to the point that they some women are known to drink the spilled blood of gladiators, because they believe it increases their fertility.' Marcus shook his head with a look of distaste 'I heard this and I still can't believe it.'

'Believe it, Marcus; These exhibitions we go to are nothing more than a fight with steel and as many women as you could want afterwards.'

'Noble women?'

'Of course, brother. From my experience, they are the hungriest for gladiator flesh.'

'Why?'

'Well, for a start have a look at your usual plebeian. Fat, flabby and lazy. We are hard and muscular and we fight for honour.'

*

The next morning the training was increased for the upcoming show at the Sulla villa, to celebrate the senator's daughter's wedding. As they were training on the Palus, the day before, Aetius walked out on his balcony above the training ground with a board in his hands. The men stopped their sword and spear work as he hushed them.

'The show will be one week from today, in the eve, at the esteemed senator's villa. The contest has changed and there will now be five, from this school and five from Ludis Maelius, but it is not their top men. This will be a contest for Novicius and Tiro only and these men will be sent. Caius, Cassian, Albus, Drusus and Marcus. Any questions?'

'What style do they fight, Dominus?' Doctore shouted out.

'This is an open contest with steel but no armour except the small Thracian shield. The bouts will not last long but you need to show strength and courage. Two of you will be chosen to fight and this will be made on the night, by our gracious host. I expect you to fight well and honourably and to show the quality, that our school produces. Now get back to work!'

The men returned to their training with grumbling, about who was attending the villa and who should have been included. With their hard bodies glistening from sweat the Doctore moved amongst them, refining and increasing their skill. He stopped them momentarily, listening to their heavy breathing starting to subside.

'Hear me' He said stepping back so they could all see him. 'Strength is not enough. Speed is not enough. Skill is not enough to win. To win, in any contest, you must combine all four of the requirements that make champions. Many of you have heard this before, but they are as follows'

He pointed to the crudely engraved board that hung from the Palus at the end of the ground. Strength, speed, skill and stamina. Do you all understand?' He shouted.

Before him, the men wiped their sweat and nodded.

'The reason why we train you so hard is for stamina. In a bout that might last more than an hour, in the afternoon heat of an arena, against a strong opponent you must have stamina above all else. To survive, you must be able to fight hard and long. There is only one way to survive. Stamina.

Doctore wiped his bald head and walked in front of them collecting his thoughts as he did. 'Do you get it, Gladiators?'

Again, there was a shout of agreement.

'A year ago, at the Pompeii amphitheatre there was a famous contest, between the great Hilarius and a seasoned gladiator of four wins, whose name was not as well-known but remembered after the bout. His name was Priscus. It was late afternoon, in the month of Junius and the hottest time, I can remember. For those of you lucky enough to have watched the great Hilarius, you will know he is the gladiators, gladiator. He is immensely powerful, holds great skill with the sword and shield and has, if my memory serves me correctly, over eleven wins. Have most of you seen him?'

Half the men nodded, while the rest stood listening.

'It was an epic battle and lasted for hours until they called a halt to it. It was called a draw; The only reason I bring this up, is that Priscus survived, not because of his skill and strength but because of his *patientiam*. Say it!'

'Stamina' They repeated in a group. 'I can't hear any of you. Least of all Caius. Say it, again!' The Doctore shouted.

'Stamina' The shout came out.

The Doctore moved across to Caius, who stood sullenly in the back. 'What's the problem, gladiator?'

Caius snarled at him as he approached, and then looked over at Marcus.'
We all have stamina. Why not get back to training?'

Say it!' Doctore shouted at him.

'Stamina' he mumbled.

'Everyone.'

'Stamina!'

'Now get back to work and Caius, for your insolence, another hour on the
Palus this afternoon when everyone else finishes and the person on the
other side will be me. If you want to have a dance, let me know, because
you need a lesson in manners. The other option for you to consider is a
whipping if you keep this up.'

Above them, the voice of Aetius, boomed across the yard. 'Attilius,
Doctore! Get up here.'

Marcus laid his rudis on the stone floor and walked up the stairs,
with Doctore behind him. They entered to find Aetius standing on the
balcony.

'Marcus, I am taking you away from the Novicius position. From this day
on you, will become a Tirone, Gladiator. That means I can set you up for
your first contest which will be at the Pompeii amphitheatre. The contests
are at the end of Junius which some months is away. After your contest
with Albus, you are clearly ready to take on opponents; you agree,
Doctore?'

Severus nodded his agreement. 'What will he fight as?' He asked

Aetius looked up at the ceiling, as he thought briefly about the question.
'I still think Thracian, given your training in the legion. So, from now on,
you use only that dress and armour. Also, we need to work on that arm,
so you will be ready for the contest. However, that is up to the physician
and I will speak to him. I am taking you off the menial duties of Novicus,
and making you a Tiro. The other two Novicus can work the tables.'

Marcus nodded still trying to regain his breath, from the torrid training in
the yard. 'Who do I fight?'

Aetius shrugged. 'I don't know, but the more experienced the opponent,
the more money will ride on the outcome of the contest. Do you fear a

fight?'

'I fear nothing in battle, Dominus.' Marcus said firmly.

Aetius smiled, in that sneer that had become so familiar to Marcus. 'I thought so. Now get back to work and let's make some wealth.'

As they walked down the stairs, the Doctore, looked at him from his position in front. 'Tirone already. By the grace of Mars, Aetius, must have plans in place for you.'

They returned to the dust of the arena below, as the men fought with the shield and dummy. The dummy opponent was suspended from a swinging pole. As the shield held by the dummy was struck by the gladiator's Rudis, it rotated quickly and the attacker needed to move out, or under, the sand bags attached to the dummy arms. Marcus was informed by one of the attendants the apparatus was known as the *congregans hominem,* which literally meant to 'consume man' but the 'rounding man' name held and those who were hit by the rounding man sand bag, attached to one of its arms, remembered it for some time.

Marcus found out the hard way that the bags hurt like a whip lash if they hit on the way back. The Rudis strike had to be hard, to spin the rounding man and the well-oiled apparatus. The top swung quickly to move the bags around to the side of the attacker and many a Novicius, was struck, until they learned how to duck and weave away from the rounding sand bags.

'For those who attend the contest, continue with the rounding man for ten strokes of duck and weave, then change. For the rest of you back to the Palus. I had better see wood chips flying or we will continue after the lunch.'

Severus finished shouting at the sweating men and moved back to the shade, under the arches, that held the upper storey of the barracks. He watched the men as they laboured under the hot midday sun. The Medici walked out from the infirmary with his eyes blinking in the glare.

'Did Aetius speak to you about the left arm of Attilius?'

'No, but I don't see much of an issue. He is strong and extremely flexible, but the arm will cause him pain after training and contests, and there is little we can do about it. I wish a sore arm was the only problems we had out there.' He pointed to the men training on the small arena.

The Doctore nodded, watching Marcus as he pounded the rounding man, with his rudis, and then started to nimbly duck around the sandbags as they flew on the wooden hands of the dummy. 'Aetius is putting a lot of pressure on young Attilius.'

The physician nodded with a hard look. 'He wants a champion, Severus, and from what I have seen of Attilius, he may well have that man.'

'He was trained well in the legion, that is for sure. But I have my doubts on an extended man-to-man contest. It takes a lot of strength and patience and whilst our brother has strength in abundance, I have reservations about his patience. He tries to finish quickly as he was trained, but that does not work against the top gladiators.'

The physician looked at the trainer in agreement. 'Perhaps you need to change his training.' Severus nodded and headed back out to the men.

CHAPTER 43

The afternoon of the contest at the Sulla villa was hot and humid, as the five chosen fighters, sat around the wash area of the barracks. Baths, were a daily ritual after training and eating. Every afternoon the gladiators took a hot bath and then plunged into a similar tub but as cold as it could be, where they stayed until the Doctore told them to leave.

The hot baths were prepared by slaves, who stoked the fire under the hot tub and kept the heat low, to keep the water from getting too hot for the men to endure. At each session, the complaints came quickly from the water holding too much heat to the opposite, where it was too cold.

Many a servant received a hard cuff from a gladiator if the water was not to their liking. Caius complained the most but as Marcus had witnessed over the previous months, he complained about everything.

Once they were shivering from the *fridgridarium*, they were taken back to the hot bath again and then rubbed down with camphor laced olive oil and left on the massage beds to rest. Any small wounds were treated with aloe, applied liberally under a strong bandage.

After they rose, they were taken to the armoury and each man chose a gladius from the array that lay on one of the tables. All of the swords were sharpened that morning and the finely polished steel, glinted on the table.

'Pick the one that feels the best in your hand.' The Doctore said. 'The heavier ones are at the other end of the table, which may suit you Marcus, as they are similar to ones used in the legion.'

Marcus hefted several, until he found the one that felt balanced and picked up a small Thracian shield as he left the armoury, to sit on the outside bench beside the training ground. He felt the pang of loneliness for a moment, as he looked out at the numerous training poles and gantry's holding the rounding men in the yard. He found it hard to believe that the road to Rome, which seemed such a long time before, had led him to the bench he sat on and the life he now led.

In spite of the food, marching and the weather, he missed the legion and the men and he wondered once again about Ovidius and that day so high up on a desolate mountain in Judea. If the arrow had missed and hit governor Silva, what path would his life have taken?

Whilst the barracks held a strong bond of friendship, including the ones he had gained with Blasius and Atticus, any friendliness remained tinged with the understanding that one day they might meet in the arena.

Friendship, became not a comfort, but a distraction and a path to an early death. The only balance, he assumed as he sat there looking out at the practice yard, held an uneasy relationship.

The Doctore walked out and waited for Albus to emerge. 'Lunch, boys and then the trip up to the house. Stay calm and breathe easily. This will be like a training session but with steel.'

They were given a meal of maize porridge, eggs and dates and late that afternoon, they were bundled onto a dray led by four horses, for the long ride to the villa.

They arrived at the estate in the sombre light of late afternoon. In the far distance, heavy clouds with darkened tops moved from the West, with the bottoms of the clouds shining in bright red from the setting sun.

They could feel heaviness in the air. the clouds moved slowly towards the villa and the change in the air, combined with the up-upcoming contests, heightened the tension the group felt as they waited on Severus. The mood amongst the men was jovial and light hearted and tinged with the expectation that at least two of them would be able to release their excited energy.

Marcus and the other four waited beside the dray. He looked around the area as he stood waiting in the approaching darkness. The villa was very different to the Laurentius house, that Marcus had worked on for the months he stayed in Rome. This villa was not as ornate but the grounds more spacious, with wide paths leading to the door of the villa and substantial gardens reaching from the villa to the stone wall, that surrounded it.

Eventually, they were ushered inside and left in a small room with a table adorned with wine and food. From outside the door, they could hear the sounds of the feast.

'Who will fight?' One of them said, as he absently fingered the tip of his sword. 'Hopefully you.' Albus replied. His blond locks fell around his

ears and with one finger, he wiped the sweat forming on his forehead.
'I feel like a large meal, a bellyful of wine and good woman with wide
comfortable hips.'

'And strong legs.' Marcus added laughing. He was joined by the rest with
the others singing out in chorus. 'Strong legs'

Drusus stood up and stretched. 'So what time is the show?' Cassian stood
up a full head height above Drusus, to stretch as well. He yawned while
rotating his sore right arm. 'More importantly, when do we eat?'

'We've eaten, you oaf.' Caius said with a sour face. 'Did you really not
enjoy the maize porridge this afternoon.'

Cassian smiled at Caius. 'There was hardly any left after you got into the
pot. You must shit like a monkey.'

'He likes monkeys with strong legs' Marcus said abruptly. The laughter
broke out until they were half on the ground, unable to breathe and the
tension eased. Caius continued to stare at them without a smile.

Severus entered the room a while later. 'Follow me and when you get in
there keep your eyes on the boys from Ludis Maelius, because you will
be fighting two of them. Don't speak unless you are spoken to first and
don't do anything stupid, which is both a command and a wish because I
know how bloody stupid you idiots can be. Two of you will be chosen to
fight, so I expect you to fight hard and well on behalf of the Ludus
Gallicus'. Severus gave them a steely look, held the door open and the
five filed out in expectation of the coming contest.

In single file, with their large, muscular hands clasped around their
swords and the other one holding the shields, they walked into the *pars
urbana*; the family area, of the large villa. Each of them, wore a short
leather loin cloth and a thin leather strap that wrapped across the back,
over their broad chests and down to their waist. Marcus was the first to
file in, with the rest in line behind him.

The sides of the passageway were adorned with flowers that highlighted
the wall frescos. One in particular, took Marcus's attention, as they filed
past on their way to the large reception room at the front of the family
area. The fresco showed a woman pouring a wine at a table with two
young children. The background of the fresco, reminded him of his farm.
The woman, depicted in the fresco, held a very similar look to his mother
as she prepared and watched them eat their late afternoon meal.

They entered with Marcus, surprised at the number of spectators that lined the outside of the room. He surveyed the long room before him, which held a shallow atrium pool at one end and at the other, a balcony that looked out towards the West, where the faintest hint of magenta lay on the horizon.

The crowd hushed as they entered. Severus lined them up, bowing out of respect to senator Sulla, who moved to the middle of the floor. Sulla acknowledged him and settled his robes with the palm of his hands as he looked around.

He was a large man, with a balding head and a large gut, that extended prominently out of his generous toga. His face was fleshy and his nose reddish. In his hand, he held an ornate Gladius that Marcus guessed had never hit another piece of steel, let alone flesh. His daughter, with her arms entwined with the man she was to marry, stood in the front and middle of the crowd. Around the couple, stood a sea of prosperous and important Roman citizens in colourful clothes. The heavy air held the distinct scent of perfume. The crowd looked rich and excited, Marcus thought to himself, as he looked around the room.

He could see the togas of several senators and the rich clothes of businessmen and their wives. The daughter was indeed a beauty with a wide smile across her face as she held onto the man next to her.

Marcus could not see to the back of the room, so he assumed those of strong social standing got the front position. There was an expectant look on the faces of the onlookers and he glanced at the men standing beside him, as they shuffled their feet and lightly swung their Gladius. Caius looked angry and the rest slightly nervous.

'Friends, as part of our celebrations, I offer a contest tonight between young gladiators from two of our most famous schools. On my left stand the men from the Ludis Gallica and on my right the men from the Ludis Maelius. Since these are amongst the best schools in the Roman empire, I am sure we will have a spectacle that will be talked about for some time to come.' He motioned to his daughter, who stepped out of the crowd.

'Father, thank you from the bottom of my heart, for his gift and since you have asked me to choose the contests, let me have a look.' Slowly, she walked up the row of men from the Ludus Maelius with her eyes keenly inspecting each man. With giggles from the women in the crowd, she ran her hand over their arms and torso. Finally, she stopped to walk across to where Marcus and the others stood and did the same.

As she walked past Marcus she looked up at him with dark brown eyes and then ran her hand over the shoulder of Caius, who stood next to him. 'I have made my decision.' She said and she pointed to the man next to Marcus and then across at the gladiator from the Ludus Maelius. 'These two.' She said finally, returning to the crowd and hugging a woman next to her who smiled at the choice.

Marcus watched as Caius stepped forward, with a man from the other school. Aetius made an appearance from the back and whispered in the senator's ear. He listened intently and moved to the middle of the room.

'So, we have a blond gladiator from the Ludus Gallicus, by the name of Caius and a dark haired, man from Ludus Maelius by the name of Fabiola. Our esteemed referee is Valens and I will leave him to set the contest.'

Marcus felt someone staring and he glanced across to see Cassius Laurentius. He had moved to the front and was staring at him, while listening to another man next to him. He turned, whispered something and both of them laughed as he fixed his stare back to Marcus.

To take his attention off Laurentius, Marcus turned his gaze to the crowd, who were leaning forward in anticipation of the coming contest. They watched as Valens, a tall dark man with a livid scar across his forehead, motioned for the two gladiators to face each other.

'When my arm drops, it will be start of the contest. We expect a robust fight and the contest will finish when the time is up or when one of you are in prone position with no chance of success.'

Valens dropped back and dropped his arm from the front to his side and the contest began. Both men circled, shields up and swords raised. The excitement from the crowd started to rise, as the men got involved with the spectacle before them.

'Move in' A man shouted, loudly as they continued to circle.

'Strike, gladiator. Strike hard.' Another said, as the excitement in the crowd started to rise with the anticipation of the sound of clashing steel and the grunts from the gladiators.

Again, the circling continued until Fabiola feinted to the left and struck up with his sword, only to be fended by Caius who moved his sword to counter the strike. There was an audible gasp from the crowd as the first strike, steel on steel, sounded and the hard noise echoed off the walls.

Again, Fabiola struck and again, it was easily countered. The circling, attack and defense continued, as calls came from the audience for blood. The gladiators were even in skill, Marcus thought to himself as he watched the fight with interest. Caius was nimble and fast but Fabiola was stronger and harder with his sword hand.

They continued to trade blows for some time, as each tried to gain a superior position. Both gladiators were trained to move away and change their body position to counter the other. Fabiola used a sideways strike, then changed, to strike at the legs of Caius but he was too quick and Fabiola had to quickly counter an overhead strike from Caius, each time he tried it. The sound of steel smacking against steel, and the grunts of exertion from each of the men, echoed off the ornate ceilings.

Sweat started to coat the floor as the men circled again. A flash of a sword strike flicked across Fabiola's right shoulder and blood started to seep from the wound. Gasps and clapping could be heard from the audience, as they edged forward to the fight. Sulla's daughter, her face transfixed by the contest, edged forward with her friend until one of the men cautioned her.

Caius moved forward with strike after strike overhead, onto the shield of Fabiola. The sound of the strikes on the small shield amplified the noise, until it took over from the increasing grunts as the contest continued.

'They fight well.' Laurentius said to senator Sulla, as he stood there watching. 'Very evenly matched.' Sulla replied.

Again, Fabiola feinted but this time his opponent was waiting and as his shield position changed, Caius moved in quickly to move his body to a position between the shield and sword of the man before him. Using the handle of his Gladius, he slammed it into the shield watching as it spun out of Fabiola's hand, clattering across the floor and into the legs of the crowd.

There was a loud gasp from some of the women, at the force of the blow and some of the men clapped with shouts to finish the contest.

'Pass the shield back' One man shouted

'No, let them fight it out.' Laurentius said, with a wide smile.

Fabiola looked over at the referee, who in turn looked at Senator Sulla, who looked around the crowd and gave the signal to continue. Fabiola tried to circle back to his shield but Caius blocked his way. He moved to corner his opponent as the spectators moved quickly out of the way.

As they reached the corner, Caius seemed to lose his concentration, looking over at the referee and in a split-second Fabiola moved in with an uppercut with his sword. The steel flashed across the shield and the force of the desperate blow, sent Caius reeling backwards. Fabiola grabbed the flaying shield and pushed Caius heavily to the ground. Within a moment he was over Caius, with his sword tip at his throat and his foot on his chest.

It had happened so quickly Marcus breathed in unison with the audience. Everyone, expectantly, looked directly at the referee who referred to senator Sulla who stood, arms crossed in front of the crowd.

Marcus looked across at Laurentius, who had moved across to Aetius, whispering in his ear. He watched as Aetius nodded, then shook his head and then nodded again. Laurentius snarled and whispered again as Aetius shook his head and then nodded as he pointed to Caius, who lay on the ground breathing heavily, with
the sword point, at his throat.

Finally, Laurentius nodded and walked across to the senator who listened to what he had to say and then nodded as well.

'*Mortem*!' Laurentius said with a shout, watching the audience who gasped as he said it again. '*Mortem* to the loser on the ground.' He moved over to Sulla, who listened nodding and waited for Laurentius to return to the crowd.

The referee looked at the senator who mouthed the word '*Mortem*' with a shrug and with a resigned look on his face, he pointed his hand to Caius, who looked up at Fabiola with a sneer.

'*Mortem*' The referee said to Fabiola who looked down at Caius and shook his head.

Caius looked up at Fabiola with wide eyes. There was no fear in his eyes; only loathing.

Fabiola looked back down at Caius as sweat dripped off his body onto the floor. He took one more look at the referee and quickly pushed his sword point into Caius's throat, until it hit the hard-tiled floor below. He stood up to applause from the crowd. The gurgling from the Gladiator from Ludis Gallica slowed as Caius finally succumbed to the injury and stopped breathing

CHAPTER 44

Marcus took a deep breath, watching as Fabiola returned to the ranks of the Ludus Maelius, with his companions slapping him on the shoulder. Fabiola was not smiling but looking again at the man he had just killed.

He looked over at his companions from the Ludis Gallica, who held the same look on their face. Marcus had witnessed the advent of death in the legion in almost every battle at which he fought, but this was the first time he had encountered death at the command of a private citizen.

He was both shocked and aggravated by what had happened. It surprised him, after the deaths he had created in the battles in Judea. Somehow, this was more personal and yet again, Cassius Laurentius was behind it.

He stared at Aetius who saw his look and averted his attention. He looked around at the blood lust in the crowd, as the body of Caius was removed by servants and the tiled area that held his blood, cleaned until not a trace was left.

The crowd continued to discuss the bout, with the women in awe and the men gesturing sword strikes in discussion of the mistakes Caius had made.

Severus moved over to Marcus and the others and brought them together for a moment. 'Mortem? Marcus questioned. We were told this was not to the death.'

Severus shrugged. 'Apparently, the great Cassius Laurentius said he would pay the cost of the two fights to the death, as long as you, Marcus, became the second contest. Aetius refused the second when Laurentius came to him at the end of the fight but agreed on the first. I suggest that was because the money was enough to make it worthwhile.'

Marcus looked over at Laurentius who smiled grimly back at him with his eyes meeting the stare. 'You mean Aetius was paid to let Caius die?'

'Of course, that is the way it works, Attilius. You at least know that?' Marcus just nodded and looked at the floor.

'Boys, I did not know, but it is not our decision and it is a cost that clearly senator Sulla will pay back to the school. Remember your oath! Be prepared to die and to kill when required. Any questions?' Severus whispered hoarsely, as he wiped his bald head against the heat of the night.

Marcus shook his head and regained his positon in the line-up as senator Sulla moved to the floor again. 'A contest to remember and to gladiator Fabiola for that win.'

He tossed a small leather bag of coins to Fabiola who caught it and returned to the line. 'While the area was being prepared I spoke to one of our gracious friends, Cassius Laurentius, who generously paid for that previous bout. The next one will not be to the death but he has asked for Fabiola to fight again and this time against Marcus Attilius of Ludus Gallicus. Do you agree gladiator Fabiola? There will be another purse for you if you agree.'

The senator turned to his daughter. 'As this is your night, do you agree?'

His daughter moved across the floor to where the gladiators stood and looked briefly at Fabiola and then walked across to where Marcus stood. She ran her hand over his chest and down to the leather strap that fastened at the top of his loin cloth. She looked over at her friends who were giggling as she reached up to run her hand over his shoulder to where the wound lay on his left chest.

'Sword?' She asked. 'A cut for someone so handsome?'

'Arrow.' Marcus looked down at her with a brief smile.

'I want this man.' She said gaily and walked back to her friends and the irritated look from her fiancé. Fabiola nodded as he waited.

'Can the gladiators step forward' The referee shouted out.

Fabiola, with his retrieved shield and new sword walked confidently to the middle. Marcus, with a sideways glance at Laurentius and another look at Aetius, made his way next to Valens, the referee.

'This is the same rules as before and I expect you to fight hard.' Valens dropped his hand and Fabiola started to circle.

Marcus held back, waiting for his opponent to move. Fabiola made his familiar feint to the left and Marcus moved in, dropping his shield to bring it up hard into the open left arm of the man next to him and then brought it down, to sweep Fabiola's leg with his descending shield. Within a moment, Fabiola was airborne and falling to the marble floor below.

Marcus kicked him hard in the side and laid the side of his sword across his neck. As Fabiola tried to move his right arm, Marcus lay his sandaled foot across his wrist and started to draw blood across Fabiola's neck. He could feel anger rise up, as he looked down into Fabiola's eyes.

Fabiola looked up at him in wide-eyed terror and Marcus, who could only hear the sound of blood coursing through his ears, could not hear the gasp from the women or see the nods of the men as they looked at each other.

Senator Sulla moved to the front and gave Valens a nod. Valens raised his hand and declared. 'The contest is over and the win goes to Ludus Gallica.'

Marcus raised himself from his position above Fabiola, when he heard a voice calling out his name and before he turned he put down his hand and pulled Fabiola from the floor.

'You were faster in Judea.' Came the voice, as Marcus dropped his Gladius to his side.

'I must be getting old, Titus.' Marcus said with a tight smile, looking at the man he had seen only three times in his life, as he walked onto the wide tiled floor.

'I know this man.' Came the sound from the back and senator Sulla turned and waited for the son of Vespasian, who was smiling widely, to move to the front of the crowd.

'Titus Flavius Vespasianus, you are welcome to take over as host if you like.' Senator Sulla said in deference to the solidly built man who strode to the front.

'Senator, excuse my indulgence but it is not often you see your saviour. The last time I heard about him was when he lay critically injured at the fort of Masada.' Titus pulled his blue tunic closer to him and walked over to where Marcus was standing. Senator Sulla gave a slight bow and moved away. 'This man saved my life.' Titus said, as he walked over to where Marcus was standing and shook his hand. He waited for the crowd to hush.

'The mount of Olives, Attilius. Do you remember?'

Marcus nodded and grimaced as he remembered the loss of one of his men on the day.

'This man showed magnificent bravery on that day.' Titus said to those in the large room. 'My horse went down under a Jewish spear and they were on me and just at that moment, this man, a solider from the magnificent Fifth legion, took on two men, killed them and pulled me up. Senator Sulla, you have a champion on your midst. Attilius, did you not receive the legion medal on that day?'

'No Sire. That went to a soldier who lost his life that afternoon, after taking a number of men with him.'

'Attilius, Titus is my name. We are brothers, in war, are we not?'

Marcus nodded, looking directly at Laurentius, whose face had deepened considerably in colour.

Titus nodded sombrely as he took the money pouch from Sulla and personally put it in Marcus's hand and embraced him. 'You deserve more and I heard of your injury from the arrow that was meant for governor Silva. I put word through that you were to be taken care of and if you died the physicians would go with you. So, I am pleased to see that they did what was necessary. You have not lost your fighting style.'

Marcus shrugged. 'And you, Titus. The riches of Jerusalem and the sacking of Masada. What is next?'

Titus smiled and slapped Marcus on the shoulder. 'I am happier at war, Gladiator than crowding around the senate house and playing their games. I am pleased to see that you have survived and I will make sure I see you when your next contest comes up.

Suddenly Aetius was at the arm of Vespasian. 'You are welcome, Titus.' He said putting his hand out to shake.

Titus looked at Aetius, sighed and raised his eyebrows at Marcus 'Now I must go back to my host. Good wishes, Attilius and I am sure we will meet again.'

Titus walked off with the disappearing crowd after him, who headed back to the feast and the dancing that would continue into the night.

'You saved Titus?' Aetius said, wide eyed.

'It was a difficult day.' Marcus replied. As Titus left, the other gladiators came over to greet him and in the corner of his eye, he could see Laurentius looking intently at him with a man next to him and together they stared and whispered.

'Who is that man next to Laurentius?' Marcus asked Drusus, who had moved next to him.

'Ah, Bositas, no less. He is the Lanista of Ludis Maelius. One of the true scum of the earth I hear. He makes Aetius look like a lamb. No doubt he and Laurentius have something in common. Wealth transcends all issues of men, Marcus, and of course they all have that common link.'

Marcus looked at him, puzzled for a moment and then returned his stare at Laurentius. 'Why, Vicinius of course. I hear you know him.'

Before Marcus could reply Severus came over and grabbed him by the arm to lead him to the side. 'I was sure the contest with Albus was a fluke but after watching you tonight I now understand. You are blessed by Mercury, Attilius. You can fight better than any I have seen.'

Marcus nodded, placing his shield on the bench waiting for Severus to walk them out. He felt a touch on his arm and he turned to find Cassius Laurentius standing next to him.' 'So, you decided to return did you.' Laurentius stood much shorter than Marcus but he came close to him with his eyes blazing.' You still owe a debt, gladiator, and I intend to collect with interest.' He spat the last words out.

'You will get paid your debt, Cassius and I will pay when I am ready. Would you like to start a fight over it?' Marcus returned his stare until the man backed away. 'If you would like to dance, man to man, Cassius, I have my sword and you can fight me with a sword and shield?' He waited for a response. 'No, I didn't think so.' Marcus said as he watched the man move further from him. 'If you send your men after me I will tear them limb from limb and if you do, tell them they are fighting a Tirarii from the Fifth and see if they go forward. Again, if they do, I will kill them and then I will slit you from your balls up. Understand?'

Laurentius pulled back with a shocked look on his face. 'No one speaks to me like that, you, arrogant piece of shit. What are you? A failed army legionary and a gladiator. We spit on gladiators. They are all stupid, failed men who cannot do anything else. Who else would take death as payment?'

Marcus picked up his Gladius and stood beside him lazily swinging it in the air with his hand so it almost brushed the shoulder of the smaller man next to him.

'I don't work for you Laurentius and I am not one of your slaves, so unless you want to dance right here and now I suggest you leave the room. Otherwise, we can see what a failed legionary can do to the rest of you from your mouth down.' Marcus smiled at him as he waited.

As Laurentius turned he snarled at Marcus. 'This is not the end, Attilius.' The anger smouldered in Marcus as he picked up his gear and walked back to where the others were standing.

As Laurentius reached the other side of the large atrium he turned and looked back at Marcus who was re-joining the group. He stopped and thought for a moment and then looked over to see his wife with a friend tittering and laughing with their attention on the gladiators who stood up, strong and muscular with the women admiring their physiques.

Laurentius he saw the Larisa on his way to the latrine. 'Aetius, my friend, looking forward to the next major contest?'

Aetius stopped and looked at Laurentius with suspicion in his eyes. 'Pompeii, Cassius. I thought you were the *prefect* of the games. The great Hilarius will fight in those two days but betting is hardly worth it, as he has so many victories behind him.'

Laurentius thought briefly on the remark. Hilarius, the peoples champion, the champion gladiator of Rome and the man who was supported and loved by the fallen emperor Nero. Hilarius, the man they all aspired to be; Strong, fearless, skills of a God and the courage of a lion.

'I am the *prefect*, but I was not aware that the great Hilarius was in the contest. I need to speak to you and Boistas later. You are not leaving?'

'Free wine and the party just starting.' Aetius smiled at a young, dark haired servant boy, who walked past with wine on a tray. 'I think not, Cassius.'

Laurentius nodded and smiled grimly as he left the room.

Each of gladiators were surrounded by men and women as they spoke about the fights. When Marcus arrived, the conversation stopped and Fabiola came over.

'You are the fastest I have ever encountered, Attilius. You fight well.'

'And you.' Marcus said with a softer voice. 'And you had already fought one contest. That manoeuvre that brought you down was a favourite of a brother in the legion, by the name of Ovidius. He used it many times in battle and I copied it.'

'I will remember it' Fabiola said as he looked around. 'They are vultures you know. The audience I mean. There is not a brave man amongst them.'

'There is one.' Marcus replied. 'Titus had the respect of the legions and that is rare. Interestingly, no one else seems to like him much.'

Fabiola nodded as he wiped the last of his sweat from his brow. 'Now we are to entertain the women. The best part of the night, I might add.'

Marcus nodded and looked over at the gladiators from both schools who had women and men around them admiring their physiques and engaging in conversation. His eye caught Aetius who walked over. 'A feast and plentiful wine has been laid out in the next room, so ladies and gentlemen, if you will excuse us we must leave.'

A woman came up to Marcus as he handed his Glaidius and shield to an attendant. 'You have so many scars.' she said as she inspected his arms, letting her hand run over his forearm as she looked carefully.

Her mouth was slightly open as she looked up at him. 'A result of hard battles?'
He looked at her, noting her dress made of expensive colourful fabric and eyes that wore heavy makeup. Again, the alluring scent of musk entered his senses.

'Many' he said.

She placed her other hand on his wide forearm lightly fingering one of the scars. 'Do you join the feast?'

'We are to attend in the next room. '

As he replied, he felt a touch on his shoulder and he turned to find Lucia Laurentius standing next to him. 'I told you he was handsome.' She said seductively. 'Since you left me so long ago, Marcus Attilius, the least you could do is have a drink with my friend, Lena and myself later tonight.'

Severus moved into the conversation after getting a hand signal from Aetius to get Marcus and the rest to the waiting feast. 'Excuse my interruption, Mistress Lucia but the men are tired and hungry and the feast awaits.' Severus said deferentially.

'Of course, Doctore. We were just inviting your handsome gladiator to share a wine later tonight, after the feast and dancing finishes.' As Marcus turned to leave, Lucia grabbed him by the forearm. 'How could you leave me like that? If you had asked I would have come with you.' She whispered.

'To Judea?' Marcus said with a light smile. 'You would not have lasted a morning in the sand lands, Lucia.'

She nodded with a hurt look on her face as he finally turned to walk to the dining room. She watched him leave and then called for wine.

Severus nodded and led Marcus away from the women and towards the table at the back of the room, which was being stocked with wine and food. He looked for another seat away from Aetius but it was all that was available. Aetius leaned towards him looking a little drunk but sharp eyed and calculating as always.

'You never cease to amaze me, Attilius. You saved the life of Titus Vespasian and he personally sent orders for you to be tended properly. You are blessed by Zeus. You and I need to speak tomorrow, after training, but you and the boys will be staying here tonight. It is late for the long ride to the school and our gracious host, senator Sulla, has provided accommodation for us all.'

The men of the two schools sat down at a long bench, stocked with food and wine from the feast. The admirers were ushered out of the room so the gladiators could eat and drink and they did without hunger. The events of the evening sat heavily on all of their minds. They reached for wine cups and little food.

'*Per mortem, gladio.*' Marcus said, as he sipped his wine and offered his cup. He spoke across the table to Fabiola 'That was due to Laurentius and you happened to be the victor given the way the fight was heading.'

Fabiola nodded as he listened. 'It could have gone either way but your boy lost his concentration completely and the fight turned. I was so surprised by the order that I almost couldn't do it.'

Bositas who was sitting to the right of Aetius and listening slammed his cup down on the table. 'What shit is this? Fabiola fought courageously, given the fact that he had lost his shield.'

'That is my point, Lanista. If Caius had not stopped at the point of success, he would have won.' Marcus added.

'No, no, gladiator. At our school, we teach our men to fight even when the odds are greatest against them.'

'Did you know about the decree by Laurentius.'

'Of course not, gladiator. Aetius and I were only aware at the time. Do you have a problem with that?'

'Given that none of us knew prior to the contest. I have an issue with that, Lanista.'

'Then your Lanista needs to teach you some subservience. It is not your place to question.'

'I don't agree.'

'Shut up, Attilius.' Aetius said with a curled lip. 'We make the deals and you fight when and where you are told. Remember your oath.' Marcus stared at Bositas until he touched Aetius on the shoulder and they walked off, towards the other room.

'First time?' Cassian asked Fabiola

'What?'

'Mortem.' Cassian replied

Fabiola nodded. He undid the strap that circled his broad chest and he rubbed the top of his shoulder. 'That shit Laurentius. Why did he do it?'

'To get at me, I think.' Marcus replied. 'I owe him a debt and he was out to repay me with steel but it did not work out. We lost a brother and he lost a great deal of money. Not that it might worry him. On top of that, I fucked his wife.'

'Good luck to you, Fabiola. You kept to your oath and followed our code. It was not your decision' Albus said, as he bit into a chicken leg without much enthusiasm. Are you attending the Pompeii games?'

'I heard yesterday. They say that even the great Hilarius will be fighting there on the second day as the final match.'
'You have seen him?' Cassian asked

'Of course. Very few have not. After all he is the champion of Rome. Twice he was offered the ceremonial Rudis by Nero and refused. How many would refuse the sword of freedom unless they were idiots or loved the gladiator's life.'

There were murmurs of assent around the table. 'How many times has he won?' Marcus asked, as he looked around the table. It was apparent that he was the only one who did not know.

'Thirteen, I believe. 'Fabiola said.

'Correct.' Drusus said. 'All our Lanista wants is a champion like that. Hilarius has never lost and if my memory serves me well he has drawn two.'

'I once stood next to him.' Cassian interjected. 'The man was like a mountain of flesh. A lot of fat but the biggest man I have ever seen.'

'So, to be a successful Gladiator you need to be fat?'

Cassian looked at Marcus in mock surprise. 'Are you calling me fat?'

'No' Marcus laughed at the look on his face. 'Maybe a little pudgy.'

Cassius laughed in return. 'Hilarius holds a lot of weight but he moves well for a big man.'

'What does he fight as?' Marcus asked

'Several different types, as far as I have seen.' Cassian replied.

'Hoplomach or Murmillo. He is excellent at both types and he usually wins, because he can outlast anyone.'

'Is he fast?'

'Too big to be very fast but great stamina and very skilled with the sword.'

Skill with the Gladius might be the very least, Marcus thought to himself, given the twelve wreaths that lay around the champions head. The men at the table sat in small talk, eating sparingly and drinking forcefully for several hours before Severus re-entered the room.
'Boys, the guests want to mingle as I have asked them to come in and you know what that means. Attilius, come with me.'

Marcus rose from the table with the good-natured jests coming from the men around the table. He followed the Doctore, until they were out of hearing range.

'There is no doubt Cassius Laurentius has it in for you and he is planning something but I am unable to find out what it is.'

Marcus looked the Doctore with a fixed stare. 'I can handle anything that piece of shit puts forward. If he is not careful, I will take the initiative.'

'Which you cannot' Severus said flatly. 'You are under contract to the Ludis and Aetius is your master whether you like it or not. I came to get you because of a special request. Sit over there on the lounge and wait.'

Marcus could hear the rowdy, drunken behaviour from the room beyond, with the men fraternising with the guests. The gladiators were clearly in high demand and as he lay back on the lounge to try and collect his thoughts he heard a familiar voice.

'Lena wants to see all your scars, Marcus but I am looking for something else' He looked up to find Lena and Lucia naked, save veils that covered their waist and legs and he shifted his position as they stood in front of him.

'You are damaged, I hear' Lucia said softly, as she sat down beside him and ran her hand across his torso to the wide scar on his chest. 'The scars make you even more handsome. Don't you agree, Lena?'

Marcus looked through to the banquet room. All of the gladiators were surrounded by guests as they sat and drank wine. Lucia put her soft hand on his chin and brought his attention back. As she put her lips on his and brought Lena towards them, she whispered, 'I have never forgotten you, Marcus. Never leave me again, gladiator, or by the Gods I will make you pay.'

CHAPTER 45

Cassius Laurentius sat across from Titus, who was smiling at one of the
dancers. She held her pose as the music came to an end in front of the
patrons, who had returned to the banquet room, after the gladiatorial
contest in the main room off the living area.

'How do they move like that? She is a great beauty; is she not?' Titus
said, as he nodded to the dancer who walked out of the room after the
dance had finished.

'Perhaps you share your fathers love of fair haired women?' Laurentius
said with a wide smile. The sinister snarl he had presented to Attilius had
disappeared and his mood had improved.

He had a plan to go forward to rid himself of the gladiator and a man, he
had come to loathe. Lucia was obsessed with him and broken-hearted
when the boy disappeared, which remained a mystery to him. The intense
aggravation he felt would soon dissipate once he rid the world of Marcus
Attilius.

'Only in a professional capacity, Cassius.'

Laurentius smiled again and refilled his cup and offered the flask to Titus
who held out his cup to be filled. 'Quite a celebration tonight and she is a
lucky girl to have such a generous father.'

Laurentius raised his eyebrows at the remark. 'Well, he is a successful
man, Titus, and he has accumulated wealth from his estates. A little too
successful some might say.'

Titus nodded in agreement. 'We are all aware Cassius, that the more
successful you are in Rome the more enemies you make. You have your
fair share do you not?' He said with a stern look.

Laurentius shrugged. 'I do Titus. But then, we all do, don't we?'

Titus nodded slowly. 'Yes, we do.'

'I hear confidentially that Flavian has not been well so I hope he is
feeling better.'

'I trust you will keep that news to yourself, Cassius as it is not knowledge we want out there and that includes the senate. Which reminds me, there was a message from my father that the senatorial promotions are coming up in several months. We have two consuls in Rome this year, and I am sure you know Servilius Vatia Isauricus and Claudius Pulcher well. One of the issues in a senatorial appointment for you, dear Cassius, is you have never been a magistrate which is the straight path to the senate. However, we hope to get around that issue and, I think we have. There is good news for you.'

'I have never seen myself other than a businessman with the best interests of Rome on my mind, but the news is welcome.'

Titus shifted uncomfortably on his lounge. He was staring a cunning animal in the face, who had probably never told the truth. 'Ah, Cassius we all know your concern for our great state and before we arrange the senate seat, you will need to provide the final arrangements for the one, hundred-day games, for the opening of my father's Amphitheatre.'

'Of course, Titus. Your father knows I hold my agreement in business. My interest in the senate is only to further the great name of Rome.'

'And influence?' Titus said with a wry smile.

'Well, that does not hurt business, now does it?'

Titus shrugged. 'I have never been a businessman, Cassius, so I can't comment. So, the senate seat is arranged and in the next week you will meet with my father and I to discuss the one hundred-day games. Correct?'

'Of course, Titus.' Laurentius replied, with a humble look on his face. 'I am more concerned about Flavian, so I hope you will give him my regards.'

'Yes, Cassius. That goes without saying.' Titus replied blandly as he looked towards the crowd at the end of the room, starting to lose their inhibitions as the wine took hold of their senses.

'How far away is the opening of the Flavian Amphitheatre? It seems almost finished.'

'Under a year, at least that is what we have been told and hence the reason for our meeting on the games.' Titus drank heavily from his cup of wine. 'It has taken far too long, but it will be a testament to my father.'

'Of course, of course, Titus. Romans speak about the amphitheatre all the time, so I am happy to hear it is nearly finished.'

'Well, dear Cassius, we must have a schedule for the one hundred days of games, for the opening which you so generously agreed to pay.'

'Well, there were conditions.' Laurentius said quickly.

'Which we will provide, Cassius, including your promotion to the senate. So, we will meet soon and I will get my aide to set up a time, perhaps at my father's office at the Villa.'

'I await your invitation, Titus'

'What my father and I envisage is one hundred days of a range of shows including Bestarii, gladiators, horsemen and perhaps gladiatorix as well. Also, we believe we are best served by having a special match. One that could create a special interest.'

'Such as?' Laurentius asked with interest.

'A contest that creates the title. First Gladiator of Rome.'

'Ah, that is interesting. I will need to spend some time on that, but we can discuss that at our meeting.'

Titus nodded to Aetius as he walked by their couch and Laurentius looked over to see him speaking to Bositas.
'Excuse me Titus, I need to speak to Aetius.'

'About his upcoming champion, Attilius?'

'Exactly, Titus.' Laurentius stood up and shook Titus's hand.

'I hope Aetius takes care of Attilius. He saved my life.'

'But you saved his as well, with special care from the physicians. The debt is settled is it not?

'Perhaps' Titus replied, pleased that Laurentius was leaving the discussion. Like his father he did not trust Laurentius and he did not like him, but even unlikable Romans were useful.

'Gentlemen.' Laurentius said with a wide smile. He walked over to the Lanista's who were standing on the other side of the yellow, ochre room.

Aetius and Bositas, stood slightly drunk, near a window that looked out to the shimmering fires of Rome and the cool night air. Above, the stars shined like distant oil lamps and Aetius looked up at the moon with one eye to keep it in focus. 'What is that globe in the sky?'

'La Luna?' Bositas replied, absently he rubbed his large stomach and took another sip of wine. 'It is the home of the goddess, La Luna, is it not.?'

'Plant on the increasing moon, my grandmother used to say and harvest, on the waning one.' Aetius said with finality.

Bositas turned to find Laurentius standing beside them. 'A good evening is it not, Lanista's? Your boy fought well, Bositas.'

'Attilius fought better.' Bositas said, as he turned to Aetius. 'Don't suppose you would sell him?'

'Aetius laughed out loud.' Not a chance my friend, not a chance. After all, you hold the riches to the territory with Hilarius.'

'Ah, now that is correct, but even Hilarius, who holds every record in Rome, is getting tired and looking to his future. He only has several fights left in him.'

'Well, who could beat him from any of the Ludis gladiator familia we have today in Rome?' Aetius asked. 'Maybe Germanicus? Perhaps not.' He said solemnly.

'Yes, you do hold the riches of the schools, Bositas.' Laurentius commented, as he filled their cups with wine from a silver pitcher. 'Hilarius is the champion gladiator of Rome; Is he not?'

Bositas smiled as he listened. 'Yes, Cassius, he is no doubt the best.'

'Are either of you interested in a wonderful deal?' Laurentius said intently. 'I have an offer for you, that will make you both much richer than you are today.'

Aetius was the first to turn to listen. He sipped his wine in contemplation of the remark. Bositas turned to Laurentius admiring his toga. 'Do tell.' He said quietly.
Laurentius stood up with a finger to his lips and checked quickly around the vicinity. He returned and sat down next to them.

'I have an idea that will make all of us richer and, it will be something Rome will remember for some time to come.'

Aetius nodded expectantly. 'What is the deal'

Laurentius put his wine down and stood straight to emphasize the point. 'Think of it. A promising newcomer takes on the champion of Rome. So, my thought is that we use your new gladiator, Marcus Attilius against one of the greatest gladiators in Rome's history. A man who has taken on the gladiatorial world and won every bout. How many is it, Bositas?'

'Twelve wins, Cassius. Many citizens think it is eleven or thirteen but I assure you it is twelve wins, fourteen bouts and two draws. He has never lost. But Hilarius?' Bositas said quickly. 'Attilius would be severely mismatched.'

'Not necessarily.' Laurentius replied quickly. 'An ex-legionary. A Triarii, no less who fought at Jerusalem and Masada and as a Tirone he fights Rome's champion. By Zeus, we would need to put extra seating in the stadium at Pompeii.'

'Pity the Flavian Amphitheatre is not finished.' Aetius replied, sombrely.

'Here is the deal.' Laurentius said, smiling widely as he sat back down. 'Aetius you agree for Attilius to fight and Bositas you agree with the contest with Hilarius and I will promote it and pay you two thousand Denarii each for the privilege of using your gladiators for the match.'

Aetius cocked his head and looked back up at the moon. 'It sounds like an excellent deal, Cassius, but I cannot see how you win. Bositas?'

'I agree Aetius. Where do you win, Cassius?'

'Twofold. I promote the contest and take a cut of the gate and I will be betting on Hilarius, on the side of course and that will return a handsome profit.'

Aetius rubbed his chin. 'Attilius cannot win.'

Bositas nodded in agreement. 'No, he cannot against Hilarius. Even very experienced gladiators have lost against him and against men at least as big as he is. It would be a sure bet.'
'Exactly.' Laurentius said as he leant in closer. 'There is a great deal of wealth to be made in this deal but there is one thing we must agree on.'

Aetius turned to Bositas.' You agree?'

'I do if you do. You understand your boy will be beaten.'

'So, what must we agree on?' Aetius said turning to Laurentius.

Laurentius held up two fingers. 'The first is secrecy and the second is that the contests are open so there is no holding back from Hilarius or Germanus for that matter against hand-picked Tirones'

Aetius dropped his head. 'I agree to the first but not to the second. Attilius has all the marks of a future champion and I need to encourage that as far as possible. Are you suggesting a contest to the death?'

Laurentius shook his head and then changed his tone, to a more serious and lower whisper 'No, no Aetius, not to the death, but it must be a proper match, don't you think? It will be talked about for ages. We will fill the seats and make a fortune on the way.'

'Hmm' Aetius said as he stroked his chin.

'Three thousand Denarii, to both of you. Do we have a deal.? Aetius, you can buy many future champions with that wealth. I repeat; it must be an open contest.'

'We could bet on the side.' Bositas said as he glanced at Aetius.

Aetius shrugged as he thought momentarily about the match. The payment from Laurentius was more than twelve times the normal fee. Attilius could lose his life from the bout or even mortal wounds and then he would be chasing another champion. But with the funds from the fight, he could purchase the type of slaves that created champions but they were hard to find and very expensive.

Aetius took a quick sip of his wine and studied the look on Laurentius's face realising he was looking at a man who wanted the deal. He reflected on the possible agreement as he quickly tried to balance his decision. Attilius was a future champion. But, he knew that Attilius had attitude and that might create issues as he pushed the man to win in the arena. Also, he needed patrons like the man before him, who waited for an answer, with his eyes flickering between Bositas and himself.

'Four thousand to both of us.' Aetius said abruptly, with a sly look on his face and his lip curled. 'I might lose a future champion and you are going to do very well out of the match. It will be an easy match for Hilarius

---

399

which means that Bositas will win handsomely as well.'

Laurentius looked at Aetius and then at Bositas and paused momentarily to think. 'Four thousand. Are we agreed?'

Instantly, Aetius knew he had offered a price which was below the limit Laurentius had in his mind and he cursed himself for not moving higher.

Bositas winked at Aetius to show his agreement. 'We are agreed.'

'A wise choice and one we will all celebrate in due course. Now I have important matters to discuss with senator Sulla and Titus Vespasian, so *bonum vesperam* friends; a good evening to you' Laurentius turned on his heels to get back to Titus.

'Halt, Cassius.' Aetius said quickly, as Laurentius stopped and turned. 'We did not discuss payment. When do we get paid?'

'On the day before the contest. Agreed?'

Bositas looked at Aetius and nodded. 'Agreed.'

Aetius called out to Lurentius as he strode out of the room. 'Did it occur to you, Cassius, that should Attilius win the contest against the great Hilarius, he would become the champion of Rome.

Laurentius stopped in mid stride and turned with a laugh on his face. 'Are you serious, Aetius? Do you really believe Attilius has a chance against a twelve wreath, champion? Do you?'

Aetius looked at Laurentius regretting the stupidity of his remark. 'No, no chance.' Aetius shook his head and watched Laurentius, clothed in his expensive toga, walk away.

He sipped his wine in quiet contemplation of the deal as Bositas turned to him with a broad smile on his face. 'It is not often one gets an offer like that!' He said excitedly.

'No. Aetius replied, but in the back of his mind a thought formed and became one that placed a thin smile on his face.

Was there the slim chance; of a miraculous redemption from the Gods of Olympus? Was there the possibility of a win by the younger Tirone? If the Gods allowed such a feat, the prospects were endless.

This held the chance of a double win in which Aetius would find himself the possessor of four thousand Denarii and the champion of Rome in his school. He shook his head lightly and took a long draught of wine.

The chances held about the same capability to grow wings and fly to the globe in the night sky. Therefore, he thought to himself, the idea might be to ensure Attilius survived the fight, without too many injuries so he could fight another day. There was only one way to gain that insurance and that was to train Attilius until he could fight at the same level as the great Hilarius.

As Aetius sipped his wine, looking out to that pleasant evening in Rome he knew that Laurentius would heavily back the great Hilarius and increase his wealth. Aetius, deep in thought, looked out at the clearing sky then turned his attention to his companion.

'Bositas, my friend. You are a betting man in the Circus Maximus on chariot races. What odds will the *soribus dividebas* offer on the fights, with Germanus and Hilarius.

Bositas stroked his chin lightly as he thought about the question. 'Aetius, the odds will be long and the gamblers will offer something like twenty to one on the Tirone, Germanus contest.'

'Hilarius?'

'Ah, well, I remember the contest with Hilarius and Tullius, in which Hilarius took apart the best upcoming gladiator in Rome, and that was not more than four months ago. Remember that Tullius was a winner of five fights himself. So, I expect maybe thirty to one; Tirone against Hilarius.

Aetius whistled softly. 'That is high. What will be your bet, Bositas?'

The Lanista pursed his lips as he thought about it. 'Hmm, maybe five thousand Denarii on Hilarius. He is training well and is fitter than I have seen him.'

'Is he holding any injuries?' Aetius asked

Bositas smiled at the Lanista sitting next to him. 'One of the things I enjoy about you, dear Aetius, is that you will try anything. Why would I tell you that?'

'Well, we are friends, Bositas. We can share secrets.'

'And pigs might fly to that beautiful globe in the sky.' Bositas replied as he rose to fill his wine and pointed briefly to La Luna.

CHAPTER 46

'Who amongst you, knows the meaning of fear?' Severus shouted out one morning as he paraded up and down in front of them. 'Well?'

The gladiators shuffled before him. Some standing defiantly, others with hunched shoulders as they looked at him.

'All of you do, brothers. There is no man devoid of fear but the way to rid yourself of that fear is to practice until the motion of your act, be it with a Gladius, a spear, a trident, a net or a shield becomes more natural than the fear that sits on your shoulder. Atticus, do you know fear.'

'Sometimes, Doctore.' Atticus replied with a bland smile.

'There are rules of combat that you must all remember, as you confront your competitor on the brown sands of the *arenam*. The arenam has its rules just like your school. We live and die by the sword and we have rules that bind our profession as strong as old leather on a scabbard. Most of you know the rules but let me state them again.'

Severus looked around at the men who stood there in the early morning sun 'Are you listening, brothers? This is as important as your skills and stamina.

He watched them intently to see if they were concentrating and then continued. 'You are under the oath and you must be prepared to die in the *arenam* at any contest you attend. It may not be a fight to the death but you might receive a mortal blow or be so disabled that the end will happen anyway. Are you prepared to die?' He shouted out.

'Yes, Doctore. We are prepared to die.' Marcus joined in at the last, watching as the men shuffled their feet, in the acknowledgement of their brutal life.

'You are not bakers, nor are you teachers or gardeners or sailors. They do not die in contest, but we do. We are loved and we are hated but above all, brothers, we are respected. Who will take you on in a fight outside the arena, if they know you are a gladiator? No one and nobody of the faint hearted. Do you understand what I tell you this morning, brothers? Respect yourself first because you survive by your strength and skill.

Do you hear me?!' He shouted out. 'Push fear out of your minds and take the sword in your hand as your talisman. Do you!'

'We do, Doctore.' The men pushed their hands into the air as Aetius, who had just walked out onto the balcony, looked on from above.

'You receive a payment for each victory and nothing for a loss. That is, unless you are paid the welcome spectre of death at the sword of your opponent. Then your funeral is paid for by this school. There can be no greater accomplishment by a gladiator than to die bravely under the sword. Who else would do it?'

Severus waited until the cries of agreement quieted. 'If you are the one to defeat your opponent in a mortem fight, custom dictates that if he is able to rise, he will go down on one knee in front of you and he will grasp your thigh. As the final act, you will grab his helmet or hair if the helmet is lost. Your duty is to quickly plunge your sword point into his throat, at the base or cut his throat completely. If you are the defeated one, your adversary will do the same. You must do this quickly so as not to increase the agony of your gladiator brother. Understood?'

The men in front of the Doctore shouted out in unison and arms were raised again.

'You or the man you kill, is not allowed to ask for mercy or utter any sound because if they, or you, do, you will dishonour this school and your family. If you, or your opponent is mortally wounded, you will be carried out and given the hammer on the outside of the arena. The *mallet* is the carrier of a greater life than the one you live today!'

Severus looked up to see Aetius on his balcony, listening to what was said to the gladiators standing in front of the trainer.

'Winners and the defeated exit through different gates. If you are the winner, you exit thought the *Porta Triumphalis* and the defeated through the *Porta Sanavari*. If your opponent, or you, is killed then two attendants who are dressed as *Charon*, our God of death and *Mercury* who is the messengers of the Gods, and they will inspect the body on the arena for death or life. If there is life they will end it, there and then and by the mercy of Mars, as quickly as possible.

Severus paused, took a drink from the ladle and turned his attention back to the men. Again, I tell you men; to take a life is merciful if your opponent is badly injured. You achieve nothing by keeping them alive and they in return. It is your oath to do so.'

'What about Pompeii and the upcoming circus.' Marcus called out. 'Do we fight?'

'All in good time, Attilius. Listen, boys, the arena at Pompeii beckons and your training will be increased. You must learn how to die and then you will understand that the quest for life is underwritten in all that you do in training each day. The harder you train, the fitter you become and the longer you last, in this earthly life below the home of the Gods. Train hard and then you will understand.'

Marcus looked briefly at Blasius who was motioning with his hand that he was bored.

Training continued that day and each day from early as the sun rose and finishing in the early afternoon. As the rains of December had given away to the dryer, but cool months, they rugged up in the early morning. They warmed up by raising their arms with their rudis to move through the sword play exercises, instilled each morning until they could move against each other in strike and parry, without second thought or consequence.

The sword play differed to the army and Marcus could feel the difference. Even as the Doctore pushed and cajoled him to change his style, it was in vain. The techniques he learnt in the legion stayed with him. *Habitum difficile morietu*; the Doctore had told him over and over again. Habits die hard but so do men from the legion, Marcus responded on one particular day. The Doctore had sighed and walked away.

Soon the slightly warmer month of Martius was upon them and as the training moved on, they entered the clear skies and early warmth of Aprilis.

Each day of the week moved into the next with the training constant and the uneasy companion of tiredness sitting with them each afternoon. By late afternoon after their baths most contemplated the meal of barley and vegetables and a hard but comfortable bed. Marcus felt unsure about the training and it was almost as if he was pushed to re-learn, all he had learnt before.

At the Ludis arena, Marcus found the sword play boring and predictable. Advantage was gained by constant small strikes to find the opening between the sword and shield of the opponent. That was unless they fought against a Retarius, where they learnt to handle the weighted net and sharp, three-pointed trident. The Retarius moved stealthily with a long handle that attacked from a distance.

Each of the standards took a different method of attack and retreat. The lightly armed types such as the Thracian, Secutor or Provocator, were fast on their feet with sharp, thrusting swords and skilled at circling. The more heavily armed Mumillione and Hoplomarchus were slower but held power, in the size of their shield and frontal attack ability.

Their daily regime consisted of rising at sunrise, early exercises to strengthen the upper arms and shoulders and sword play, followed by positioning in their contests. The Doctore moved constantly between them, teaching, prodding, berating and monitoring their progress.

They centred Marcus on strength work and the physician watched him most days as he picked up the heavy pole with both hands, to carry it down to the other end of the arena only to drop it heavily onto the ground. He then returned to the other end to await the arrival of the pole on the arms of another gladiator, who dropped it at his feet and so the exercise continued.

'Severus, when you are finished come up.' Aetius called out from the balcony

Severus turned on his heels and walked off in the direction of the stairs that led to the office above the arena. He found Aetius standing near the door of the balcony, looking down at the men as they carried the heavy poles from one end of the arena to the other.

'Doctore, I have received the official contest list from the *officalis arenam* and we have a problem on our hands. For reasons, which are hard to understand they have decided to offer two Tirones, a non-mortem contest, against the number one and two Gladiators of Rome. Namely, Hilarius from Ludis Maelius and Germanus from Ludis Dacicus.'

'Who will fight them?'

'They have decided that Marcus Attilius, from our school, will fight Hilarius and Blasius will fight Germanus. I thought they might pick Cassian that young fighter from Ludis Dacicus but we have been lucky enough to be selected for our two top Tirones.'

'It is a great honour, dominus, but a match that might barely take a short duration. If my memory serves me correctly, Hilarius has twelve wreaths with only two losses, out of fourteen contests and they happened when he was young. He has not lost a fight in eight years.

'What are the chances of Attilius defeating Hilarius?' Aetius said as he scrutinised the face of the trainer. 'If we are honest, Doctore, we know the answer, do we not?

Severus shrugged and sat down heavily in a chair at the table. 'Yes, Dominus. He holds no chance at all. We could sit here and concentrate on the two losses by Hilarius, but he also has a record, twelve wreaths and his last contest was won before the sun barely moved across the sky.'
'Blasius?'

Severus shrugged his shoulders wondering why such an uneven match was agreed. 'None' 'However.' Aetius sighed with his eyes to the ceiling. 'We must be thankful that our school has been chosen with two of our gladiators. They will learn a lot from the bouts.'

'If they are not killed in the contest.' Severus said glumly. 'We are pitting first year men against professional killers. One blow from Hilarius is enough to stop most men in their tracks.'

'My thoughts exactly. But to give Attilius, at the very least, a chance in the contest we need to get him a look at Hilarius training, don't you think? The first step in that is we go and have a look for ourselves.'

'Why would Bositas allow that?'

Aetius smiled widely as he sat down opposite. 'He won't will he? Well, my information is that he is at the slave auctions at Padua for the next several days, so we must move quickly. Order the chariot and let us visit him in his absence this afternoon. Get out of your training gear and get Attilius to do the same and let's go. Make sure Marcus is in a robe with a hood.'

Severus returned to the arena and pulled one of the trainers aside. He gave him strict instructions on the training for the late morning and early afternoon. Shield attacks and rounding man. He returned to the barracks with Marcus as they both changed and met Aetius, who was walking with a cane as they neared the chariot, which had been hurriedly prepared by two stable slaves.

'Where are we going?' Marcus asked

'You have been paired with the great Hilarius at the Pompeii games. We thought a little scrutiny was in order. So, we are going to visit their school to have a look.'

'They will let us do that?' Marcus stood taller than the other two and he looked down with a surprised face.

'No, of course not.' Aetius said with a snarl. 'When we get there, just follow and don't speak. Also, hunch your shoulders when you walk with us, because you look too tall and fit to be a servant.'

The ride to the Ludus Maelius, through the lower part of suburia took little time. They were held up by a downed horse with a broken foreleg on the Via Tiburtina and finally arrived late in the morning. Aetius alighted from the chariot, as a slave took the reins and walked towards the front of the school with a limp.

'You are hurt, Dominus?' Severus said with some concern as he noticed the cane.

'No, you idiot.' Aetius hissed back. 'It is all part of the ploy to get in.'

They entered the school which appeared similar to their own with barracks to one side and the office and kitchens at the far end. A small arena with seating around one side like a small amphitheatre, stood in the middle and the sounds of men training with wooden implements could be heard above the light breeze, that came from the West.

As they neared the office a slave came to greet them. 'Can I help you, sire?'

'I have come to see Bositas. He is expecting me.'

'Ah, sire; the master is away for a while and we do not expect him back for some time.'

'That is odd.' Aetius said, standing with the cane and a grimace on his face. 'Can you get word to him?'

'No sire.' The slave said as he stood there. 'He is too far away for immediate word.'

Aetius looked at the slave for a moment. 'Then we have wasted our time on such a long trip. Perhaps we could sit for a while. My leg hurts and I need to rest.'

'Of course, sire. I will bring refreshments.'

'No need' Aetius said with a flourish of his hands. 'Be on your way girl and we shall rest a while.' The slave bent her head and moved towards the barracks. As she went Aetius turned to Severus and nodded to him. 'Let's go.' They walked quickly to the small arena and rose up the internal stairs to the top. They entered the seating with bright sunshine making them squint as they sat down. The scene below was familiar.

The men stood in formation with the sun at their backs, close to the Palus that rose out of the ground in the middle of the arena. Under the orders of a Doctore on the floor of the arena they struck time and time again with the ludus, they held in their hand. One gladiator each side, feet planted in the brown sand of the arena and the grunts as their rudis hit the impervious sides of the hardened oak to rebound and be struck again.

'Their rudis look heavier than ours.' Aetius said, as he rubbed his left leg.

'Ours are twice the weight of the normal gladius, Dominus as is the custom. I don't think they would be more than that.'

Aetius nodded as he looked for Hilarius, who was not on the arena ground. The training weight of the rudis was increased to double to give the gladiators upper body strength so that the steel sword in battle would feel lighter and easier to use. If this school was using a heavier sword, it was possible it could be an advantage. Aetius thought about the issue for a moment and then pushed it from his mind.

As they sat, whispering about the weight of the swords, Severus nudged Aetius as Hilarius moved onto the arena. 'By the Gods look at the size of him.' Severus said in a loud whisper. 'I had forgotten he was so large. He dwarfs the others.'

Aetius looked over at Marcus who sat hooded and watching intently. 'He is a big man and a head taller than any of the others. What do you think, Marcus?'

There was no answer as Marcus watched the big man amble out to the centre of the arena. He scrutinized the way the man walked, the size of his right striking arm against his left shield arm. There was no noticeable limp or restriction of movement.

'He is big' Marcus said finally, as he thought about the amount of armour the man would carry. 'What will he fight as?'

'I am not sure, Attilius.' Aetius whispered back. 'Probably Murmillo.'

———

409

'That makes sense if you look at his size. That makes me Thraex or Hoplomachus.'

'Which do you prefer?' Severus asked quickly.

'Either but the Thraex might suit my skills better.' Came the reply.

Marcus concentrated on Hilarius, as he threw strike after strike against the Palus. He then moved to the end of the arena to pair off against a smaller man, each with a shield and each with a sword. 'They are using steel.' Marcus said quickly

He watched as Aetius squinted into the harsh sunlight and nodded his head.

The size of Hilarius gave him a height well above his opponent and the force of his large arm and shoulder, brought the blade down onto the shield of the man next to him with such force, that each blow resounded from the wall next to them and around the arena.

Each blow pushed the smaller man back into a weakened positon on his back foot. By the time he had recovered, Hilarius sent another overhead hard onto the shield top. This was a man that won by sheer strength and weight, Marcus thought to himself, as well as admirable skill with the sword.

What Marcus noticed, as he watched the champions movements, was the time it took for the blade to be lifted up by his large arms and brought down, onto the opposing shield. As Marcus watched, Hilarius shifted and brought his shield around to smack into the smaller man which sent him sprawling. Hilarius laughed as the man arose and took his position once again.

'He is very slow and deliberate in his movement.' Marcus whispered to Severus.

'And, very powerful.' Came the reply

After a short while, the men were brought down to the far end of the arena. The Doctore made them run to the other end, pass a cloth to the next man when they arrived who grabbed it and ran back to the opposite side only to pass it to someone else. As they ran, the trainer called out, pushing them to go faster and setting up a competition.

One of the men, barrel chested and bald, took off from one end and ran past his two companions barely breathing when he reached the other end.

'Who is that? Marcus said with his attention returning to Hilarius. Aetius shrugged. 'That is Cassian, one of the rising stars in Rome.'

'He is fast.' Marcus thought to himself, as he watched the young man run to the other end.

'An early end for the man that runs the fastest in the next two turns.' The Doctore could be heard shouting out.

Marcus leant forward as he studied the arena. His hooded countenance could be seen only as a shadow, as he watched the Hilarius run. But he did not run, he trotted, each time he traversed the arena but he was unable to gain a sprint.

The trainer waved him off, which was at the very least special treatment, but with the champion of Rome on the arena with fourteen contests and twelve wreaths to his name there was little room for argument if he wanted to stop.

Once the exercise finished the gladiators were instructed to move back to the Palus, with the exception of Hilarius who walked off the arena ground.

'Do you see any injuries?' Aetius said softly to Severus

Severus shrugged. 'Either he is covering them well which may be the case, because with that many wreaths, comes an even bigger ego and he may not want anyone in the school to see any problems. Or, he doesn't have any, but that is not possible after his time in the arena.'

The strength of the giant's shoulders and arms appeared to be strong and proven by the dents and slices in the shield held by the man he practised with that afternoon.

If there was a weakness, Marcus thought to himself, as he watched Hilarius leave the arena, it was well hidden. His strength and skill in fighting was unquestioned but his ability to move backwards was lacking. He constantly moved forward with his shield held high and his massive shoulders doing the hard work.

'Seen enough?' Aetius whispered from their perch on the highest tier. Marcus nodded as they cautiously made their way out of the school complex and walked to the chariot.

411

Aetius stood, deep in thought as the chariot arrived. He turned to Severus as Marcus took the reins of the fidgeting horses. 'Start him on steel but load the sword with lead weights to make it heavier. Start today, with the same exercises you saw before. Speed and steel will make the difference and when he is exhausted work him harder. Stamina will be his only friend out on the hard sands of Pompeii.'

'Fuck you, Bositas.' Aetius thought out loud as Marcus let the horses slowly trot towards the Ludis Gallicus.

'I need specialist sword trainer, if we are using steel to practise' Marcus said flatly, looking at Aetius who watched the passing houses without interest.

'We have sword trainers, Attilius.'

'Not the one I want.'

'Is he expensive?'

'Probably not, but he will want payment.'

'Severus,' Aetius said with a sour face. 'Hire him anyone he wants.'

Marcus took his time on the road as it was seldom he saw the outside world and as the horses trotted on the paved road, past the looming Flavian Amphitheatre, he started to set a plan in place for the upcoming contest with Hilarius.

'I also want to train differently.'

'Differently to what, gladiator? We have the best training methods in the Roman empire.'

'They don't assist me, Aetius.'

'One needs the patience of the Gods with you, Attilius, is there anything else?' Aetius asked as he turned his attention to view of the hills in the distance.

CHAPTER 47

'Did you lose your entire mind in the hot sun of Judea?' Felix looked at him shaking his head.

'I had little choice, Felix. I have been paired with the champion of Rome and it is not my decision.'

'Feign injury or madness which would be easy for you, you dumbhead, or fall on your sword rather than face that man. He is a killer and I have watched him on a number of occasions and, let me be the first to tell you, he is ruthless. He has never had a bout go beyond one hour on the sundial. Less in most cases. His strength is overwhelming.'

Marcus shrugged his shoulders and looked skyward. 'Then the Gods will need to assist me.'

'You will need more than that. You said you went to watch him train and knowing the way the Ludis keep their men secreted away, I am amazed you got to see him.'

'Aetius has his talents and he is as cunning as a cornered fox.'

'Did you see any impairment or any weakness.'

'I think he has injuries, but he covers them well. He was certainly unable to run the length of the arena and he retired early from the training.'

'That won't help you in a contest with him.' Felix replied sourly.

'Well, he seemed to be favouring his left side when he walked and when he reached the veranda steps, he stepped well with his right foot but the left was slower and did not seem as strong.'

'I watched a contest at Pompeii several years ago. He was in a contest and a trident spike from a Retarius hit him on the left leg. Rumour had it that it got a fever and he was sick for some time. At least several months. So, that may have affected his movement. That means he is weaker on his left side but then, so are you.'

Marcus shook his head as he sat there in the shade of the building with Felix beside him.

'It is almost as strong as my right but it still aches at night.'

'Did you see the great Hilarius using his rudis?'

'He was practising with steel.'

'Gladius! Well, that is interesting. What was his sword technique?'

'Mainly overhead and with great force.'

Felix nodded. 'That technique has been very successful for him over the years and mainly because of his height and size. You are around his height, maybe a little shorter, but he is twice your weight and what we need to work on is how to counter that force.'

'Don't remind me.' Marcus groaned, as he thought about the size of the man and the effect he had on the shield of the younger gladiator, with whom he was practising the previous afternoon. Felix watched intently as Marcus picked up a cup from the bench next to him. Each time Marcus put the cup down and picked it up Felix watched with amazement.

'How long do we have before the contest?'

'Four weeks. The start of Sextilis. I should start praying and adorning the shrine of Fortuna, our goddess of chance and fortune. She owes me after deserting me most nights when I gambled.' Marcus said with a sigh.

'She won't help, Marcus, the only place we will get help is from our work. We need to set a strategy to beat this giant and I already have several ideas.' Felix flashed his wide smile and patted his friend on the shoulder.

'I am glad you are confident.' Marcus looked at Felix smiling in return.

'I didn't say I was confident.' Felix said with a laugh. 'But our goal is to at least keep you alive to fight another day. What choice do we have? You need to win and I need the extra money from this job. You lose and I lose. In the rare chance that you win? Well, only the Gods know how much I can charge after that.'

Marcus took another drink of water with Felix watching him again.

'Then we have much to do and since I am getting paid by your illustrious Lanista for your afternoon sessions, we should start now. This is my siesta time, so if I fall asleep you will know why.'

Marcus stood up, happy to have a friend beside him in training, but he felt a deep foreboding of the contest to come. What were the odds? Miserable, at best, he thought and for the first time he wondered how it was possible that a Tiro, such as himself, could be picked for such a one-sided fight.

Felix stood next to him after placing a gladius on the bench next to where they were sitting. 'Pick up the Gladius the way you might normally pick anything up.' He asked

Marcus looked at him strangely and did as he was asked.

'Now walk over to the other bench, stop and come back.'

'Have you gone mad? Marcus said, as he walked over and returned.

'I never noticed. You are naturally left-handed.'

'Always, Felix, but in the legion, there are no left-handers. You learn with the shield held by the left and the gladius in the right. Any difference is beaten out of you when you start training.'

'Can you use the Gladius with your left?'

Marcus nodded. 'It's my natural hand. Good enough to beat you Felix, you broken-down, sword maker.'

'Well, let us try.' Felix stood up, swinging his sword casually in his hand as he passed the other Glaidius to Marcus, who held it easily in his left hand and the practice started.

'Left handers have a natural advantage, Marco. Gladiators train against right handed opponents and always have and therefore they train sword to right shield side and that is how they learn their trade.'

'So?'

'So, idiot. When they fight against lefties, where the sword arms are opposite, as is the shield side, they don't have the technique to counter it. However, the secret is to ensure your shield is held further to the left of their shield so you take the advantage.'

'Felix, unless you haven't been watching my left arm and shoulder is my weaker side.'

Felix gave him a wide-eyed stare. 'Exactly and now we have to concentrate on building the sword technique from that side, keeping in mind that your stronger right side will hold the shield.'

Marcus nodded as he listened. 'It might work, I guess. Anything would be worth a try.'

'You need to learn how to counter that thunderous overhead strike of Hilarius. The only counter to it is with speed so that the blow sends you backwards and then you move to your left to his open flank.'

'That will also be my open flank.' Marcus said to him with astonishment.

'Correct; you really are a gladiator underneath that handsome facade. That is why speed of that arm is so important and remember, since your weaker side is not holding that heavy shield, you can use that sword to greater effect. So, you must concentrate on speed and moving to the left to avoid the overhead strokes.'

'How does that help?'

Felix stopped the sword play for a moment to catch his breath. 'Grab two shields and let's begin the rehearsal of the fight.'

For the rest of the afternoon, Felix moved him around in practice of the fight with constant barbs at his movement and his habit of moving to the right, to use the shield defensively.

They stood together at the end of the afternoon exhausted and sweating. 'Better, Marco. But you must be able to do this in your sleep. You are naturally left but you have been taught right and that technique is ingrained. From now on, each time you practice in the left position, use this phrase in your mind and regain position.'

'Which is?' Marcus asked, with a wry smile under his sweating brow.

'*Sinistram est optimus*; Felix replied wiping his brow and motioning for them to walk off the arena. As they left the brown sand Felix looked up to see Aetius staring down at them with a slight nod of his head. 'From now on, Marco, everything you do is with your left hand. If you eat, drink, piss or shit it is all with your left and don't worry about the mess.'

Their laughter rebounded off the walls of the barracks as they walked through the door and the hot and cold baths beyond.

*

That night, Marcus lay on his hard bed, listening to the sounds of the night which included the soft moaning of the whores who were brought in most nights, to keep the boys satisfied. The grunts of the coupling gladiators could be heard over the moaning but he smiled as he thought about it. They didn't last long, despite what they told everyone else.

Sinistram est optimus; That was the saying Felix had passed to him, on the brown sand that afternoon. Fighting from the left against one of the greatest Gladiators of Rome held as much fear as fighting from the right. He realised that if he was going to fight from the left he would have to do so convincingly, with power and speed.

Exhaustion overcame him as he drifted off to sleep with the vision of Hilarius uppermost in his mind. If Felix's strategy proved to be correct, he had a chance but if he was wrong, it would end quickly. He knew instinctively, as he lay on the old sheep's pelt, that Hilarius would show no mercy.

He drifted slowly into blackness. The vision of the desolate, long plains of Judea passed through his mind. For a reason, he was unable to understand that evening, he held solace in the memory of that brown land and perhaps because of the legion he missed so dearly. He thought briefly of Ovidius and the arrow through his neck as he went down. He pushed the thought from his mind as darkness overcame his mind.

CHAPTER 48

After some discussion, Marcus finally chose the role of Thraex after speaking to Severus. Felix added that it allowed him speed and protection without the heavy hardware held by the Murmillone, which was the favourite of Hilarius.

The Thracian uniform held the usual loincloth and belt, with his left arm protected by the *Manica*, the bronze arm guard with overlapping metal segments, fastened by leather straps under his arm.

The *parmula* he carried on his right arm was a smaller shield than the long and heavy *scutum,* held by Hilarius. The champions shield was much longer and heavier and a considerable weapon when used by a man of Hilarius' size.

The Thraex uniform held longer leg greaves. wrapped in a thick quilted fabric and unlike the Gladius used by Hilarius, the Thraex used a short sword of similar weight to the Gladius but it was crafted with an angled blade that led to a fine point at the end.

His helmet was distinctive and unlike the Murmillo helmet, that held the casting of a fish, the Thraex helmet was decorated with a tall, solid crest, terminating in the head of a *Griffin*, the companion of Nemesis, the goddess of vengeance.

His bare upper torso, like all gladiators in the arena offered, for all to witness, the gladiator's willingness to die. As if to flaunt death, the most vunerable parts of the body were left exposed, for a well-aimed sword or spear strike, and mortal injury. The bare torso, a flaunting of the vulnerability of the gladiator, offered a symbol of courage and confidence.

'From this point on, you practice only in uniform, Marcus.' The Doctore said as they walked out of the dressing rooms to the practice sand beyond.

Marcus tested the garb and it felt comfortable, except for the helmet which held a lattice front so vision could only be created by movement of the head. Felix turned up for the training, watching him as he worked with the rounding man in full Thraex uniform and constantly moving to avoid the sandbags, that rounded on him after each strike. His speed and power from his left arm had increased and each strike sent the rounding man arms to him, for him to deftly move out of the way. More than an hour passed by the time he finished as finally, Severus moved over to him and gave him instructions.

With effort, he ran the length of the arena, only to return to pick up a pole and carry it down to the other end and then repeat the punishing work. Once he had completed ten laps, Severus allowed him to go to the water barrel for a rest. He dropped his metal helmet to the ground and sat heavily on the stone step.

'Now you are fit.' Felix said, as he sat down next to him.

'This afternoon we are going to practice overhead strikes and there are two manoeuvres I want you to work on. As each strike comes down, I want you to block and take two steps to the left and after the next strike, two steps to the right and then mix them up. If I am correct Hilarius will have to change his tactics to try to get at you and then you can change the tempo up to tire him.'

'I should be that lucky' Marcus grunted as he leant against the step regaining his breath.

'Listen, Marco; this is not a man who is invincible. Everyone, you and I included, have weaknesses. Your job is to find that weakness on the arena. You can't outlast with strength or sword technique. He is too strong and too big. You are strong as well but he has one capability in his favour and you have one in yours.'

'Which is?'

'Experience, Marco! He has entered the stadium many times and he understands the drill. He understands the give and take of the sand, where to hold ground and where to give it up and he understands winning. He is full of confidence and you have none of that.'

'And mine?'

'Youth and speed and don't forget it.'

'Agreed, but I have experience of killing in battle and I know hand-to-hand better than most of these men.' Felix placed his hand on the shoulder of his sweating friend. 'There is a further problem and that is your reputation.'

'My reputation?' Marcus looked at him with an astonished look on his face. 'I don't …'

'I have checked around, Marco.' Felix interrupted. 'You have a reputation for being fast and ruthless and when you put that up against Hilarius, who is the first gladiator of Rome, what is he going to do?'

'Make it difficult, I guess?' Came the reply

Felix shook his head. 'Think about it for a moment, Marco. If you were Hilarius what would you do.'

'Wait for him to tire and then beat the hell out of him.'

'Correct and don't think for one moment that he does not have orders to beat you to a pulp and if you happen to die on the way, well, that is business.'

'Mortem.' Marcus replied bluntly as Felix nodded his head.

'This is not an exhibition match for you, Marco. This is the real thing and you need to keep everything in mind when you walk onto that arena. When do you leave for Pompeii?'

'On the morrow I believe.'

'How long does it take to get there?'

'Six to seven days I believe. There is nothing slower than a dray!'

'Aetius has asked me to accompany you to the arena in Pompeii so it will be an interesting experience. I will appreciate it, that if you don't win against that giant, that you at least stay out of his way.'

'What happens if I win?' Marcus said with a broad grin.

Felix looked at him seriously for a moment and replied. 'Marco, it is unlikely you can win because this is your Tirone year first bout and he is, after all, the champion of Rome. However, if you do win, you will be the toast of Rome and I will be able to boast I taught you everything you know. For what it is worth, Marco I believe you can beat him.'

Marcus nodded 'I hope you are right.'

———

420

'Felix smiled as he rose. 'I have something for you.'
Marcus watched as Felix retrieved a long oil cloth from his bag and
handed it over. Marcus unwrapped it to find a beautifully crafted Thraex
sword with a black bound handle with the head of an eagle and long
tapering blade to a cut point. He hefted it with his left hand.

He whistled softly. This is a truly, beautiful sword.'

'I made it for you, Marco. It has a perfect weight for your hands and
arms. Use it with confidence.'

Marcus placed the sword on the bench and moved over to give Felix a
hug. 'Thankyou friend for your support.'

Felix returned the hug and pointed to the arena. 'Back to training and let's
make this last session one that you will remember. But before you go, I
have been speaking with the Doctore and we have a tactic that we believe
will be in your favour. You must not, under any circumstances, pass this
information to anyone.'

'Which is?'

Felix moved closer to him to whisper in his ear as he looked
around to ensure no one else could be listening.

'But that is not possible, Felix.' Marcus said as he played with the
new sword with his left hand. 'Shields are either left or right handed!'

'Not the one you will be carrying.' Felix replied with a conspiratorial
look on his face.

CHAPTER 49

The long flat road from Rome to Pompeii was as boring as it was monotonous. With the exception of several long hills and a pretty farmer's daughter who smiled at them as the dray trotted past the journey was uneventful.

Marcus shared the back of the dray with Blasius, Felix, Severus and two aides. Aetius had gone ahead, as was his custom, several days earlier to make sure all was in order.

Lush rolling plains drifted past as the dray pulled the men and equipment and the sight and smell of the country made him homesick. It surprised him to think that it had been more than eight years since he had seen his mother and brother.

He made a decision that if he survived the contest with Hilarius, he would make the journey back to the farm and his home.

Each night, they slept in a local inn or on the side of the road, with the attendants fixing a meal and setting up the camp. In the taverns, they created a lot of interest, with most of the patrons watching them warily as they sat to eat and drink and move to the beds in the back of the inn.

On some occasions, they were asked where they were heading. Once it was known, it was to the stadium at Pompeii, the interest increased as did the questions. Marcus did not answer anyone. He left it to Blasius and Severus who could talk all night.

'Your handsome friend does not say much.' A waitress said, at the first inn they visited. Felix simply tapped his head and let his eyes roll back in his head. 'Dumbhead. Nothing more.' With that response Felix, would look over at Marcus with cross-eyes which would start him laughing.

By the middle of the sixth day, they neared the outer buildings of the resort of Pompeii. The city lay on the low lands, on the coast, shining in the sunlight with the massive mountain of Vesuvius, looming above it, in the distance.

The peak of Vesuvius, stood erect above the city below. Sometimes adorned with smoke that issued out of its top and on other days, clouds formed. But on this day, the mountain lay in pristine repose above the city under a blue sky, decorated by one single cloud that drifted lazily above.

The resort town of Pompeii, held refuge for many of Rome's wealthy vacationers, who wanted to bask in the sun and the scenery that Marcus witnessed, on the dray ride down from Rome. As they trotted though the town on that sunny afternoon, they were all astonished by the wealth displayed by the elegant houses and elaborate villas lining the narrow, paved streets.

At one point, they passed through a large square, lined with cafes and bathhouses and in the middle, sat the largest fountain Marcus could remember seeing. A statue of Zeus stood at the top, with his mouth spraying water across the smaller statues below him. To his right, sat a statue of the God, Vulcan, who held fire in his right hand and spear in his left.

The wind pushed fine spray from the fountain over the square and across the dray, as it passed closely by. Marcus shivered momentarily as he pulled his tunic around him and looked up at Vesuvius, standing serenely above the terra cotta rooftops of the town.

Tourists, slaves and townspeople bustled in and out of the small factories and artiste shops that lined the outer streets. The inner streets held taverns, cafes, brothels and bathhouses that seemed endless, as they passed slowly down the main Via Plinio, towards the arena capable of seating twenty thousand spectators.

By early afternoon, the dray finally pulled up at the gates of the barracks. The iron and timber gates sat closed, with an attendant next to it.

'Ludis Gallicus' Severus called out. The attendant nodded lazily as he opened the heavy gates and motioned for the dray to pass through. Tired horses pulled on the heavy cart and trotted down the short road to the entrance.

The large complex known as the Gladiator's Barracks, which comprised the gladiator's training venue and an even larger stadium, was moved to the portico of the large estate, over fifteen years before the visitors of the Ludis Gallicus entered the gates that afternoon.

The barracks offered a kitchen, mess hall, stables and armoury for storing the ceremonial armour and helmets that the gladiators wore in

---

423

processions. Stairs on one side lead to the Lanista's quarters, on the second floor. A room was available for the Lanista of each school attending the games.

A further set of stairs led below the barracks, to the *Ergastulum* which comprised of a slave prison and cells for wild animals. The pungent smell from the slave and animal area was enough to make most visitors wish they had never encountered it.

Inside, the walls were adorned with the rings of slavery, installed to feed the chains, attached to the shackles on the men, when they slept at night.

'These slaves, look hungry. Do they fight?' Marcus asked, as he and Severus made their way through, walking past the cages and the stares of the dirt encrusted slaves, behind the bars. Severus, looked at them briefly as they walked towards the holding pens of the animals. There was a variety, who sat or lay at the back of the cages snarling and growling as they approached.

One black panther; a long, silky black beast, watched Marcus with yellow eyes shining like a beast from the underworld. Its fur shone in the light of the oil lamp carried by Severus.

'Usually and the same as those animals.' Severus said quietly, as he moved towards the far door and the light of day. 'Slaughter'

'Together?'

'Probably. It depends on the *prefect*. You know, the man that pays for the show and in this case, it is Per Laurentius.'

'Of course,' Marcus said flatly. 'Who else would have the money.'

'Many have the money, Marcus, but Laurentius likes blood sports.' Severus replied flatly, as they reached the door to the world beyond the dungeons and stepped through into the sunlight of the arena. 'Death is cheap in Rome' Severus added.

As they felt the warmth of the sunshine, Severus looked over at Marcus who was shaking his head. 'Death is cheap everywhere, Doctore. Even in the army.'

Severus pulled Marcus aside to speak to him as another prisoner was taken forcefully through the door they had just opened. 'Understand, Attilius that what you are about to do, to fight in this arena, is the Roman way of life. Gladiator contests even public executions, allow us to appreciate our moral order by the sacrifice of human victims whether they be slaves, gladiator slaves or those pious Christians. You are a freeman who chose to be a gladiator. Why did you volunteer to fight? You could have returned home to the farm.'

'I almost lost my life and was discarded by the legion so it was this or return to gardening.' He said simply

'Severus shook his head. 'No, Attilius, that is a dishonest answer. You volunteered because the need to fight is in you. You could have chosen ten other paths to take your life but you chose to return to combat. It is your destiny.'

'I ran away.' Marcus nodded with a sad face

'We all run at times, Gladiator. Running just takes us to another place and that place is here and now, for you.'

Marcus looked at the face of his trainer who gestured with his hand towards the large arena before them. It was twenty times the size of their practice arena but oddly, the colour of the sand was the same. 'All those ordinary men and women, who come to watch, are looking for something greater than themselves as they sit up there in judgement of us, who take to the *areanam* to fight and survive.' Severus continued 'They are looking for a champion. Someone to take themselves out of their day-to-day lives. People want a hero and as gladiators we offer that capability. Why? Because so few will take the life and risk that we do.'

Marcus nodded as he moved out towards the arena and to the barracks that were built near the arena gates. 'Romans find comfort in our deaths, Marcus, because it is not them who are being killed. They can watch someone else do it and go back to their homes and lives and talk about it. That is why gladiators are so revered.'

'Not, if you talk to Laurentius.' Marcus quipped, as he looked around.

Severus looked at him sharply. 'Come with me'

The two walked onto the arena and into the middle of the ground. The amphitheatre stretched up on all sides, in a building similar to the ground on which he had fought Britannicus, all that time ago.

Severus picked up a handful of the dry, dusty sand and held it fiercely for a moment letting it fall slowly through his fingers. He watched it mist

425

away in the light breeze that came from the direction of Vesuvius, perched high above the stadium.

'Do you know fear, Gladiator?'

Marcus nodded slowly, sombrely as he looked directly at his trainer. 'Always, I have felt it, but the anger I hold overcomes it and I have learnt not allow it to show. In the legion, we rarely spoke of it but with the brothers there was the need to protect them and that dismissed everything else, in the heat of battle.

Severus gently grabbed Marcus' hand and let the rest of the sand fall onto his. 'This is your life, Attilius. On this sand and with the blood of thousands beneath. There is a knowledge that comes with the spirit of this stadium and of this sand. The life of many a gladiator has ended on this earth beneath our feet. If you fight the way I know you can fight, you have a chance of winning but let me forewarn you for the last time. There are two Attilius in there.' Severus said sternly, as he tapped Marcus on the chest.

'What do you mean?' Marcus questioned

'There is the one that gambles and whores and wants to laugh and there is the one that holds the ability to fight like a champion and the one that wants to win. That is the one you must take to the arena on Sunday morning. That is the one that has a chance of winning. *Intellegite*?'

'*Intellegite*, Doctore. I understand.' Marcus looked at him as he let brown sand with flecks of red fall through his fingers to the ground. As he looked down at the falling sand he saw something on the arena sand near his feet. He stooped to pick it up and look at it. It was the end point of a gladius that lay there, perhaps broken off in a previous contest.

'Understand that Hilarius will not lose easily and more so against a first year Tirone, who he will never expect to lose against. If he did it would be the end of his reputation. But, he knows you are ex-Tirarii and he knows the quality of fighting that comes with that station in the army.'

Marcus nodded as he listened.

'I need to bring your attention to one more distinct issue of this life, Attilius. I mean this life of a gladiator. It holds a paradox.'

'A paradox?'

'Meaning; To fight on the arena, you must conquer fear. But, gladiator, if you conquer all fear, you can never fight successfully.'

Marcus looked at Severus with a slightly bemused look 'Why?'

'Because fear is our uncertain friend.' Severus said, without humour and with a stern face. 'Without it, we lose all foreboding. It is that foreboding that make us practice and hone our skills. Fear accompanies us for a reason. The paradox is that we must respect it and deny it at the same time.'

'And if I lose?' Marcus said, as he walked beside Severus

'If you lose, you have still fought in fear of your life. All great gladiators know fear, but each of them controls it, and respect it, and use it to their advantage. It is the control of fear that matters, Marcus; In order for you to be successful on these sands, you must make fear your servant and not your master.'

Severus looked at the hard body of the Tirone before him with a nod. He stooped to pick up more sand and let it fly away from his hand as he let it fall in the light breeze of the late afternoon. 'And, hence the problem, Gladiator. You are out here all by yourself. Yes, there are spectators and the rich and famous and, of course, the man you are fighting but, in essence, you are all alone to make the decisions in the contest that add up to a win or a loss and a loss can be your life. Those decisions are governed by fear.'

'I would rather be alone than fight with others to protect.'

'Of course, Attilius. We all understand the responsibilities of the legion, but in the *arenam* it is different. You will experience, as we all have, the intense feeling of separation from all other humans in the arena. You must fight, not just to protect yourself, but to win the contest as well.'

'But that is what I am trained for, Doctore.'

'As it is in the legion, but more so as a gladiator. You are now entering a different type of fighting and one that can humble and strike fear, even in the most brutal of men. On these sands, I have seen grown, tough men brought to tears. If you had said that you did not feel fear, then you were either lying or you held the absence of fear.'

'Which is?'

'Recklessness and that can be as dangerous as the opposite.'

'Meaning?' Marcus said as he listened.

'Cowardice, Attilius. That emotion, can rob you of all that you stand for on the sand. It attacks men from within and those that yield to it, lose respect not just of their gladiator *familia* but themselves as well. Understand that fear must be respected but it can never be obeyed. Do you understand?'

Marcus nodded. He waited for the Doctore to start walking again and together they moved from the centre of the arena, to the steps in the distance. 'Then how do you conquer fear?'

Severus stopped again and put his hand on Marcus' shoulder. 'You cannot. You must learn to live with it and watch it carefully. Fear is the most treacherous of companions. It comes close to you when you least want it. When it does, push it away but be aware of its presence. There is one secret you have in your favour, in this fight. Hilarius holds twelve wreaths and that success means he hardly feels any fear and that makes him prone to recklessness. Remember that when you walk on the sand tomorrow.'

'I will do my best.' Marcus said with a last look around as they headed for the steps. After his discussion with Severus he understood, perhaps for the first time, the seriousness of the coming contest. They did not expect him to win with the exception of Severus, who clearly thought he had a chance.

Severus touched Marcus on the arm as they walked together. 'Last word, gladiator; Trust yourself and no other. When you walk on the arena, leave the other man at the door because he will hurt your concentration and let him join you on your return.

Marcus nodded as he thought about it. As they started to walk off the wide arena Marcus could feel trembling beneath his feet. Suddenly, they were thrown to the ground by the force of the brutal current beneath the earth of the stadium. Marcus watched, disbelieving as the barracks started to sway before them and the earth of the arena rippled under his feet and then, just as suddenly, the vibration disappeared.

He looked up to see a white plume rise from the top of Vesuvius in the distance. Several tiles fell heavily from the barracks roof, breaking apart as they hit the ground with a loud crash. He looked around, sensing the eerie silence that fell over the area.

'What message was that from the underworld?' Marcus asked almost to himself rather than the Doctore.

Severus rose up unsteadily, watching as people around the arena started to calm down save the sounds of shouts coming from the slave cells, past the open door near the stadium.

'That was Vulcan having a bad day.' Severus said, as he walked slowly off the arena ground. 'Many say this is his home.'

'Does this happen often? I would hate to feel it if he got angry'

'It happens often I believe but the Gods shine on us and we are still safe. Now *prandium* awaits, as it is almost midday and lunch are my favourite meal. Since it is the hot months, the *merjdiatio* is allowed afterwards, so we can eat and have a well-deserved sleep after that long trip. I saw the *tabula lusoria,* and I am looking forward to the lamb stew they had on that menu. Are you hungry?'

Marcus took a deep breath as they sat down in the kitchen of the barracks and exhaled slowly. 'Not really but given the day after tomorrow I should eat something.'

'Bread, eggs and fish for you for the next two days and tomorrow as many vegetables as you can eat. I will tell the kitchen. One other point for you, Gladiator. On Sunday morning, well before the contest, drink until your belly is full. Understand!'

Marcus nodded, as he looked around as men started to file in until the kitchen started to fill. The tables and benches were filled with gladiators of all sizes and shapes. Blasius joined them as they ate their fill from the range of food which was offered to the familia gladiators and their staff.

'Has anyone seen, Hilarius?'

'He does not arrive until tomorrow morning.' Blasius said with a wry smile.

'No need of practice?'

'He arrives with Germanus, Marco. Apparently, no need of practice to fight us. *Et tamquam agni exultaverunt interfecerunt.'*

'Lambs to the slaughter' Marcus whispered to himself as he tried to quiet the churning of his bowels. 'When do you fight?'

'Tomorrow, after the siesta.'

'You?'

'Sunday morning after the morning Bestarii show. Are they expecting a large crowd?'

'Full, I hear.' Aetius said as he appeared out of nowhere to sit down heavily on the bench. 'Finish your lunch and then practice until mid-afternoon. All eyes of Pompeii will be on you tomorrow, Blasius, so we expect a good result.'

CHAPTER 50

Cassius Laurentius sat regally in his gilded box, surrounded by his family, on the stage designed to be the centre piece of the large arena. Above the stadium a white and black discharge appeared from the top of Vesuvius as it sat, shining and dominant in the distance and above them, the day remained clear and dry.

To the side of Laurentius and his family, sat a number of senators and army hierarchy dressed appropriately. The senators, in their pink-bordered togas sat in a crowd of men, expensively attired with the latest fashion. They walked around the stage area clinking cups of wine and laughing as the spirit of the games started to permeate the arena.

The brothels would have been busy last night, Marcus thought to himself, as he looked out from his standing position, at the bottom of the amphitheatre. Judging by the women all the gladiators slept with the previous night, including himself, they must have brought the whores in by the ship load.

Around the bottom tiers of the amphitheatre, the citizens of Pompeii and those who came to games as tourists, wore a heavy, white woollen toga, the more formal dress of the Roman plebeian complete with sandals of differing colours. It was the required dress if they wanted to sit on the bottom tiers and best seats of the arena.

Marcus looked around the stadium, realising that no matter where one went in the Roman empire, the seating was much the same. Married men sat in one area and bachelors in another, while boys and their teachers resided in yet another.

Women, dressed in their finery, sat alongside the poorest of the citizens relegated to the high seat rows of the stadium. When there was no sitting room, they stood, moving from foot to foot to overcome their tiredness. Several seats below the Laurentius family entourage, sat Priests in black garb and honorary men who held reserved seats at all arenas. It was the congregation of the rich and famous and the very important, Marcus thought to himself as he looked over at the area.

It also mattered where you sat and whom you sat with, in Roman society and the law was clear in that matter, at least. By looking around the stadium that day, Marcus could see society, bluntly on display. He looked briefly up at the bachelor's section, watching as they spent most of their time looking up at the higher tiers, at the women who sat quietly in discussion, looking into the bowl of the arena.

From his position, just inside the open door of the arena entrance, he watched as the patrons settled themselves in the amphitheatre and waited for the show to begin. He stood in full Thraex garb, complete with his shield and Gladius.

Severus called out to him 'Attilius. Over here.'

Marcus made his way to the back of the line and as he passed the men at the front he heard a grunt. He looked to his left to find Hilarius and a man as big as him, who he guessed to be Germanus, looking at him as he passed.

'When the drums begin you follow the procession into the arena and once you have walked around, you are to you stand in the middle of the sand pit, with the other gladiators, in front of the Laurentius box. You are Tirone, so you stand at the back'

From the doors to the arena they could hear the slow beat of bass drums. Finally, Marcus entered the arena at the back of the line watching as the gladiators at the front hit their swords and spears on their shields, in unison with the drum beat. The full stadium joined in with their hands and feet. The sound became deafening, as it echoed off the brown ochre of the arena walls.

They came to a halt near the entrance door and then filed to the middle of the middle of the arena, directly in front of the dignitaries' section. The drums stopped only to be followed by a raucous sound from the trumpeters and the stadium hushed as Cassius Laurentius rose in his resplendent senator's toga, lined at the edges in pink.

'Good citizens and visitors to our famed city of Pompeii. The Gods honour us today and I commend to all, this two days of games, in this majestic stadium. Later this day all patrons will be offered a loaf of fresh bread, baked here in the ovens of Pompeii, and a cup of wine for free.'

Marcus could feel the sweat starting to trickle from the felt cap he held on his head under the heavy helmet he wore as a Thraex. The sound of clapping and stamping of feet filled the stadium and Laurentius raised his hands to subdue the crowd.

'As *prefect* of these games, I welcome our two champions of Rome

today. I present you the great Hilarius, a winner of twelve wreaths and Germanus, who is the proud winner of eight, as well. Gladiators, I welcome your involvement in these games and we all look forward to the contests to come. Don't we, citizens!' He shouted out to the citizens in the amphitheatre around him.

The stamping of feet and hand clapping took over the arena, as the excitement started to rise and again he raised his hands to quell the noise. Marcus looked over the box and there, at the very back, sat Lucia with her hands clasped in front of her, surrounded by other women, who sat in the same repose.

'As a special offer to you, great citizens of Rome, we have a very different contest today and tomorrow and we have selected two of our upcoming and finest Tirone's to battle with Rome's finest gladiators. In these contests the Tiro will be pitted against our champions and I ask you, Romans, if you were a young Tirone, would this not be the chance to show your steel? In the chance to conqueror a champion?'

Laurentius waited for the clapping to subside. 'Those Tirone who have joined us on this day are Marcus Attilius and Blasius Aulus, from the famed Ludis Gallicus and I will ask them to step forward.'

Marcus received a nudge from the side and he looked at Blasius, who motioned to the front. They weaved their way through to stand next to Hilarius and Germanus, with the crowd on their feet clapping. Marcus stood next the considerable size of Hilarius who grunted, as he shifted his feet. As he looked up at the platform that held the dignitaries he saw Lucia, stand up with her hands clasped in front of her.

'This afternoon Blasius and Germanus will pair before the chariot race and the later bouts of Ludis against Ludis. We wish them well and tomorrow Marcus Attilius will contest Hilarius as the final gladiatorial bout. So, good citizens, as a senator and supporter of the great state of Rome, I offer you the best contests in living memory. So, I commend you to come to see the next two days and especially the Tirone's.'

As the crowd shouted out and clapped their hands, Laurentius looked around at the crowd and raised his hands once again. 'Gladiators, leave the arena.' He said with a flourish and they about turned and walked to the drum beats, back to the stadium entrance door in the middle, opposite the Laurentius entourage.

In the hard-packed, dirt area of the bowels of the stadium, the gladiator's quarters lay in semi-darkness and to one side, was a standing area where they could watch the contests on the arena. Marcus had bid Blasius farewell returning his grim smile and forever reliant on custom, Blasius walked behind Germanus, onto the gleaming sands of the arena.

Since Germanus had choice on the gladiatorial form, he chose Murmillo, like Hilarius. Due to his size and speed, Blasius chose Hoplomachus, for his contest with the giant of a man he followed out into the arena that morning.

The Hoplomachus, wore similar armour to the Thraex and handled a circular shield, spear and Gladius. He wore the familiar bronze helmet, a manica on his right arm to protect from sword strikes, *subligaculum*, a leather loin cloth combined with heavy padding on his legs and a pair of high greaves which reached to mid-thigh.

The hoplon, a mid-weight shield, was as much a weapon as it was a tool of defense and Blasius had the option to use the shield to ram Germanus, as the fight started and Marcus knew the tactic was going to be used from the outset.

The discussions both of them held with Severus, on the last day of training, concentrated on how to fight, rather than if they could withstand the force of the men they were paired against.

Severus had been direct in his discussion and savage about the result of concentration lapses. He concentrated on the result if they moved onto the back foot in defense for longer than a moment. As he repeated almost every day in training. The back foot is defensive. The front foot, is the step to glory.

Marcus leant against one of the support pillars in the open area, watching as the formalities were dispensed with and the referee gave instructions. Germanus swung his gladius lightly in his hand as he looked directly at Blasius. He was a head taller and just as wide.

The referee dropped his hand and the circling began. Both men were right handed and Blasius, cautiously, kept his distance in the opening moments. Holding to his instructions from Severus, he saw a sideways movement by Germanus and he moved in quickly using his shield as a ram and with all the strength of his shoulders, he charged Germanus with a loud grunt.

Germanus side stepped the attack and rounded his gladius, handle first into the back of Blasius's neck, which sent him sprawling into the hot sand. Blasius rose quickly, only to watch Germanus walk around with his shield and Gladius in the air, egging the crowd on and listening to the applause.

Finally, he turned on Blasius and charged him with his shield, knocking him over and again throwing his hands in the air to the crowd. Blasius, stunned, got to his feet, shield to the ready to set himself against the man before him.

He raised his sword and started an attack against the gladiator before him with speed and using his shoulder strength to lay strike after strike. Germanus stepped onto his back foot and then went forward with an overhead strike that nearly took Blasius' shield to the ground. Again, he stopped and walked around with his shield and Gladius in the air to listen to the howls from the thousands of spectators who rose to their feet.

Blasius tried to regain his breath, desperately thinking of a way to get through the defences of the giant before him. He could feel the pressure of failure on his mind and a growing fear of the man before him. He had never felt anything like the strength of Germanicus. Despite his own strength, the giant was stronger, heavier and countered every move he tried with ease.

He circled again, as Germanus in an act of arrogance, let his shield and gladius drop to his side as he watched Blasius circle. He motioned for him to come forward. 'Come on, you cowardly pup. Move forward so we can finish this dance. I am hungry and lunch awaits.'

Anger started to overcome Blasius. With shield held high he came in again for another strike and again, Germanus fended the sword strokes easily and smashed his shield against the legs of Blasius sending him sprawling to the ground. Blasius got up immediately and gamely moved in for the attack, throwing overhead strikes against Germanus until the big man moved back and to the side.

'Get up, get up and get away.' Severus shouted, from where the gladiators stood, watching the match. 'How many times did I tell him. Move away and circle.' He said almost to himself.

Marcus felt an irritating tap on his shoulder which he ignored and finally turned around. 'Master, someone wants to see you.'

'Not now.' Marcus replied firmly, with his eyes firmly on the contest

---

which had moved towards the Gladiators door, with the momentum of Germanus pounding his sword into Blasius.

Again, Germanus moved away from Blasius to raise his shield and sword to the crowd as the noise erupted again. As he returned to the fight he raised his Gladius to eye level of the Tirone before him. 'Soon, little pup, the contest will be over.' He snarled. 'Now let us start a proper dance.'

'Master, it is Lucia Laurentius, the wife of Senator Laurentius.' The slave whispered urgently in his ear.

Marcus looked at him in surprise and reluctantly followed the slave into the darkness and a long walk under the seating, to the other side of the stadium. He looked in the faded light to see her standing near to an entrance. He could barely make out her form from the light that invaded the gloom underneath the stadium. She looked anxious and as soon as she saw him she came up to him.

'Marcus,' She said quickly waving the slave away. 'I have come to warn you.'

'Lucia, what are you doing here…'

'You must listen and listen carefully.' She said with her hand on his arm. 'It is Cassius. He is setting this up. He intends to have Hilarius kill you during your contest and that is after he has badly humiliated you in the arena. Hilarius is not a man you can fight and he is being paid by Cassius, to kill you. You must leave, Marcus and don't come back.'

'I left once before, Lucia. My days of running are gone. I will fight tomorrow and take my chances.'

'Please, Marcus.' She implored with her large green eyes looking directly into his. 'You don't understand Cassius. He is determined to get rid of you and he will.'

'Not easily, Lucia. Where did you hear this?'

'I overheard him talking to Vicinius earlier this morning. They are betting heavily against you and Vicinius is placing and receiving the wagers.'

Marcus shook his head slowly. Vicinius; The thought savagely moved through his mind. It was only a matter of time before the son of a jackal entered his life again. 'I have changed my way of fighting and I think I have a chance.'

436

'You will be killed!' She said with horror on her face. 'What makes you think that Cassius does not know this? He clearly must have paid Aetius for this bout. Because, how else could it have been set up? A Tirone against the champion of Rome? It is not heard of in gladiator contests. Bositas and Hilarius would have been paid as well. Hilarius knows what his job is tomorrow. You must run!'

Marcus stiffened and shook his head. ' I am not running. I ran once before and this is my choice. I will meet him in the arena tomorrow.'

From above, the sound of spectators screaming out at the bout between Germanus and Blasius reached down into the bowels of the stadium, where they stood speaking to each other.

'Look at him, he's crawling away.' Came the laugh from above.

'He's done for' Came another shout.

'I must get back.' She said breathlessly. She hugged him closely for a moment and turned. 'Run, Marcus, run away and let me know where you are. Please, Marcus, listen to what I have said.'

Marcus watched her disappear in the gloom. He ran back to the gladiator area to see Blasius crawling away with blood pouring out of his nose and his left arm almost severed. His shield lay on the ground, away from his reach, and with momentous effort he rose unsteadily to his feet with his right arm held up with the sword in his hand.

The hulking form of Germanus came forward and smashed the handle end of his Gladius into his face. He kicked Blasius as he went down. As he attempted to get up Marcus looked over at Felix who had tears running down his cheeks. 'He's done for.' Felix said with a cry. 'Why won't the referee stop the fight.'

Germanus dropped his shield and kicked Blasius again until he fell onto his back and with his left foot on his throat, he raised his sword at the Laurentius box and waited.

Laurentius with a wide smile on his face moved to the front of the box and called out above the shouts and clapping. 'What say you, Romans?'

He looked around at the range of signals coming from the crowd of over twenty thousand and above the shouts and clapping, it was hard to see if there was any direction from the crowd. Laurentius held up his

437

hands to quieten the spectators.

'He has fought bravely so let us leave the decision to Germanus, shall we?'

Again, the roar of the crowd took over as Laurentius signalled to Germanus to make his own decision. Instantly, the crowd hushed as Germanus stood above the bleeding form of Blasius. Deliberately and slowly he pushed the sharp sword point into the base of the Tirone's neck until he gurgled and died.

'No!' Felix called out. He turned to Marcus who had hung his head and leant against the wall for support. 'This was not a fight to *mortem*, was it?'

Marcus put his hand on Felix's shoulder and pulled him from the group. 'Not just this fight but mine tomorrow as well. We have been set up by Laurentius and Aetius. But, I am not sure how much Aetius has to do with it. If he is involved in this death match I will run him through.'

'I'll join you.' Felix replied with sadness in his voice. He looked out at the arena and at Germanus, with his helmet removed, who walked arrogantly around the arena. 'One day I will have my revenge with that gladiator.' Marcus spat as he moved off with Felix in tow.

Two aides, dressed as Mercury the messenger of the Gods, stood above Blasius to witness his death. One of them looked towards the gladiator door and nodded. Moments later the stretched bearers ran onto the arena floor to pick up the fallen gladiator and take him off the sand while another spread sand over the blooded area.

Inside the gloom one of the attendants made a notation on the chalk board near the armoury. A single 'V' was placed against the name of Germanus to note victory. A single 'P' sat beside Blasius's name. 'P' for *Perrit* which
 showed them, as if they didn't know, he had died in the match.

*

Later that afternoon, Marcus and Felix confronted Severus in the corridor of the gladiator area.

'I did not know, Marcus, and even if I did I could not have stopped it. Understand that Laurentius has to pay the school for the death as he organised and supported it.'

'What did Aetius know?'

Severus shrugged his shoulders. 'Again, I don't know and it is not your place to ask him.'

Marcus stood next to him, looking down and glowering. 'One of our brothers was brutally cut and beaten to death in a contest he was told, as was I, that was not to the death! And you don't think it is my place to ask?'

'Ask him what? The slender form of Aetius stood behind them, in the heat and smell of the chamber.

'Did you know that Blasius was to go to his death by Germanus.'

'That is not your place to ask such a question.' Aetius replied haughtily.

Marcus drew the dagger from the belt of his Thraex uniform and grabbed Aetius by the neck and lifted him off the floor. He threw him against a wall and with his foot on his neck he laid the dagger against his chest.

As he did, Felix drew his shining Gladius from its scabbard and placed the point on the chest of Severus who sneered at him. 'You had better put that away boy, unless you decide to use it and if you do we both go to down.'

Felix pushed the blade slightly into this chest. 'If you move forward, Doctore, I will run you through.'

'Shut up, Severus.' Marcus shouted, as he looked down at Aetius

'How does it feel scum.' Marcus said, with vehemence spitting at Aetius. 'Did you know?'

'What?' Aetius looked up at him with surprise in his eyes.

'Did you know that the contest with Blasius was   to the death?'

Aetius looked scared for the first time since Marcus had met him and his eyes darted from side to side. He feebly he shook his head. 'No' He croaked.

'You answer this next question carefully Aetius because if you are lying I will slit your belly here and now. How was I chosen to fight Hilarius?'

'Laurentius.' Aetius croaked. 'I did not know about the Blasius fight to mortem. It was a surprise to me.'

'And more money.' Marcus said slowly. 'You, greedy son of a whore. Did Laurentius pay you for the fight with Hilarius?'

Aetius, his face contorted with agony nodded. 'Yes, but there was no talk, no mention of *mortem*.'

'Is tomorrow a *mortem* contest with Hilarius?'

'I was only paid a stipend for you to fight Hilarius. There was never an agreement regarding the outcome of the bout. I know nothing of any other agreement. Ask Bositas, if you don't believe me.'

'I wouldn't believe him either.' Marcus replied, loosening his foot from the neck of the man beneath him.

Aetius immediately sat up, rubbing the side of his bleeding neck. 'Believe it or not, Attilius, I have your best interests on my side and that is why I took you in to watch Hilarius. Why would I do that, if I was being paid for your death tomorrow? I agree that I took the payment for your contest with Hilarius and you should be aware that those sort of deals, occur all the time between Roman Ludis, but I had no idea that Laurentius might use this as a fight to your death. How did you get this information, anyway?'

'Let's say someone close enough to him to know the truth.

'Why would he arrange a *mortem* fight?'

'For two reasons, Aetius.' Marcus spat at the Lanista who lay on the ground at his feet.' The first is that I am fucking his wife and the second is the obvious fact that he doesn't like it. Look at Blasius! Did he need your permission for that?'

Severus stepped away from the sword. 'The answer to that, Marcus is yes, and no. Yes, he should speak with Dominus first, but in many situations, the crowd takes control of the *prefects* thinking and they go with the crowd as happened. However, Aetius still gets paid.

'Of course. It is always about the Denarii, isn't it?'

'Attilius, think about it.' Aetius said softly, with one eye on his dagger. 'Why would I agree to specialise your training including supporting the change to your left hand which is an advantage on the arena. Understand, Attilius that I believe there is a champion in you and yes, I agreed with Laurentius and his payment, as did Bositas, but there was never a discussion on a fight to the death. Why would I lose a future champion for that amount? It does not make sense.'

Marcus loomed over him in the darkness. 'Does Hilarius know of the change to the left?'

Aetius looked up with a flicker of fear on his face highlighted by the oil lamp on the post next to them. 'I don't think so. There is no way he could have found out unless it came from someone else at the school.'

'Severus?'

The Doctore shook his head. 'Where do I win if that happens?'
'You bet against me, that's how! Marcus said angrily.

'We are family and I would not do that to anyone, including you, Attilius and you can believe it or not. But, believe that I and Dominus, have assisted as best we can to make this a more equal bout.'

Marcus looked at him briefly. Severus, was an indentured slave and at the mercy of Aetius. It was unlikely he had told Laurentius. He looked at Felix who shook his head.

'Then we fight tomorrow as planned and we assume it is a fight to the death. If I survive I want half the payment made to you by Laurentius and I will share it with these two. How much were, you paid?'

Aetius bowed his head under the gaze from the gladiator before him. 'Four thousand Denarii.'

'How much?' Marcus said raising the dagger again.

'Four thousand, five hundred.' Aetius replied.

'Can you ever tell the truth you piece of gutter shit!' Marcus shouted at him.

'Sometimes' Aetius replied with a snarl.

'Who did you bet on?' Marcus said sheathing his dagger

'Neither' Aetius replied as he walked off towards the gladiator's rooms.

'Now, let us prepare for tomorrow. You need baths, food
and rest tonight so let us move on.' 'Blasius' Felix choked, as he returned
his sword to its scabbard. Marcus put his hand on his friend's shoulder
with a quick glance at Severus as he moved off after Aetius.

'I know.' Marcus replied with grief on his face. 'I promise I will
avenge his death on the morrow. There are people who will pay.'

CHAPTER 51

The morning disappeared and the afternoon passed more quickly than
Marcus could have imagined. The tension he felt, increased as the time
approached and the knot in his stomach grew tighter. The sky was blue
and above the arena, Vesuvius smouldered with a dark grey cloud above
its apex in the distance.

He watched the Bestarii fight a large lion and then another took his place
against the sleek, black form of the yellow eyed panther, he saw in the
cages two days before when they arrived at the stadium. The two circled
before the panther snarled and rose up against the Bestarii, sinking its
jaws into the man's arm. The Bestarii shook the beast off and as he pulled
away he thrust his spear into the neck of the giant cat, to the point that he
could not pull the spear out. The shaft broke as he tried.

With startling strength, the large cat rose up again, with the broken spear
trailing and grabbing the leg of the Bestarii with its claws it clamped its
teeth into his lower leg, shaking its head violently until the leg was
severed. As that happened, the Bestarii plunged his short sword into the
neck of the cat, again and again, stabbing furiously until it fell to the
sand, bleeding and lifeless.

The crowd rose to their feet at the spectacle and Laurentius rose to clap as
well. While they watched, attendants came out with a stretcher for the
Bestarii who was rolled onto the timber cart and taken off towards the
gladiator's door. The cat was dragged at the end of a rope to the slave
quarter door, on the other side of the arena where it was finally pulled
inside out of view of the spectators.

The cart passed the standing gladiators inside the door with the attendants
pulling it. The Bestarii passed by them on the car, groaning from the pain
of his leg and blood ebbing from it, onto the slats of the top board and
down onto the dirt floor, below.

'*Malleo*' One said

Felix nodded, as the man passed. 'Off to the hammer and the morgue.' He
said with a detached look on his face. The arena offered constant brutality
and perhaps the hammer, Felix thought to himself, as he looked at the
face of Marcus watching the man pass by, was the only humane offer

of the arena.

Severus moved over to Marcus who was adjusting his dress as he waited. 'Be ready to go soon.' He whispered.

Marcus smiled grimly and nodded. He walked to the back to the latrines and vomited all of his breakfast. He stood up gasping, drank as much water from the pitcher as he could hold and returned to door, to find Hilarius standing in full Murmillone garb and waiting for the order to enter the stadium.

Marcus stood near him in Thraex uniform, holding his shield on his left arm. Severus and Felix had fashioned a double hoop on the back of the shield so it could be switched in a moment to his right arm and his Gladius to his left.

'Let's make it quick, Tirarii. I have fought men like you before and no one can beat the great Hilarius. Go down early, boy, and I will ensure it is an easy passage to the river Styx and you can pay the ferryman with no pain.'

Marcus looked at him through the bronze lattice of his helmet. He realised for the first time that they were not dissimilar in size. Hilarius was fatter and Marcus leaner but their height was near the same and for some reason, he was surprised.

Just as Blasius, had followed Germanus the day before, Marcus took the former position behind Hilarius as they walked out into the arena. Marcus spent the walk studying the gait of the man in front of him and the noticeable limp on the left could be seen in his footprints. They stood together in almost the same spot as the dying panther when it was finally slain. Marcus looked down to see a top dressing of brown sand had been laid across the bloody area.

Marcus came to a stop in the middle of the arena beside Hilarius and directly in front of the Laurentius family box. The spectators rose to their feet as they stood there. This was the last contest and because of what had happened to Blasius the day before, the stadium was full and the interest of the people was on the rise.

Laurentius rose to his feet with his hands in the air and an excited look on his face watching as the crowd started to quieten down. Behind him, Lucia was standing with her hands in front of her and her eyes directly on Marcus as he stood there, sweating in the afternoon sun. He wanted to pull the heavy helmet off his head, but it was impossible with the sword

---

and shield he held.

'So, Pompeiians, Romans and visitors, as promised, I bring you the best for the end of our exciting games. I need not introduce the great Hilarius, who stands before us. The champion of Rome and winner of twelve wreaths and veteran of fourteen major contests. To his left, stands Marcus Attilius, a war veteran in his own right from Judea and the siege of Jerusalem. He is ranked amongst the top Tirone's in Rome today. As you can see, ex-legionnaire Attilius, fights as a Thraex and the great Hilarius as a Murmillone as is his right and we expect an excellent contest. Referee, if you will.' Laurentius raised his arm as a signal to the referee who bowed courteously.

The referee moved behind them, raised his hand and waited for the gladiators to turn to face him. 'Gladiators, the rules are simple. For the sake of the Tirone let me make the rules clear. You start the contest when the rod in my hand drops. If one of you should fall injured or unable to get up, you may use the single index finger upright as a signal of submission, which, I will refer to the *Prefect,* who sits up there.' He pointed to Laurentius who remained standing as the preamble went on.

'Do your duty?'

He waited momentarily and then continued. 'You take three paces apart and on my hand signal, the contest begins.' The referee moved back from the two gladiators and waited until they had taken the required distance apart. He looked up a Laurentius who nodded and dropped his hand. 'Ready to dance, Tirone?' Hilarius snorted in an aggressive voice.

'It will be a slow dance with you.' Marcus replied, just as easily. He noticed that Hilarius had wiped sweat from below his helmet, several times. Marcus felt apprehension, tinged with fear that the Doctore had so painstakingly discussed the day before. He pushed them both to the back of his mind and focused on the man before him. Hilarius' torso was bedecked with scars as was his sword arm below the greave that sat above his wrist.

They donned their helmets and waited for the wooden rod held by the referee to fall. Slowly, it dropped down in his hand.

As they began, many of the crowd stood to get a better view with some behind them telling them to sit. Clapping and feet stamping could be heard around the arena holding the thousands of spectators. The sounds from the crowd felt like thunderclaps, on the arena floor.

Marcus watched Hilarius carefully, mimicking his movements. The overwhelming noise from the stadium and the restricted view from his helmet made him uneasy. He followed the advice the Doctore had given him, just before he walked out onto the arena. He was to follow the movements of the champion before him and then strike when the time was right.

Hilarius, with his shield held low and swinging his Gladius in his hand remained almost motionless and Marcus recognised that Hilarius was used to the fight coming to him, allowing him the advantage. The eyes of the big man watched him closely as Marcus circled for advantage.

Marcus started to turn slowly, in the opposite direction, as he consciously held his shield further to his right to protect his exposed flank and he watched carefully as his opponent did the same. He held back, waiting for Hilarius to move forward which he refused to do. The cat calls and jeers from the arena floated down on them as they stood in their stand-off position.

'Move Forward you coward!'

'You are used to fighting palus logs, not champions.'

'Move forward, loser.' Came a scream from one of the lower seats 'Knee tremblers!'

Finally, Marcus heard Hilarius growl 'What's stopping you boy. Come on and fight.'

Marcus let his Gladius fall slowly to his side as he stood back. 'You are so big, ugly and slow, Hilarius, it is hardly worthwhile to be in this contest. Come forward you fucker and stop standing back like a frightened Jackal pup. You may have a few wreaths but you are too old to fight.'

'Better than none, you, insolent piece of shit.' Hilarius grunted, as he moved into strike position.

Suddenly Marcus leapt up and into Hilarius with a downward strike hitting shield to shield. His curved Thracian sword sliced across the top of shoulder of the champion gladiator. As soon as the attack started, Marcus moved away waiting for another chance. 'You are getting old, you, fat fuck.' Marcus shouted at him, as sweat poured down his face from the soaked felt cap he wore. 'Your fat whore mother would be faster than you.'

Hilarius stared at him. Marcus could feel the anger rising in his opponent as he braced for an attack, which came with such force it almost knocked him senseless. Hilarius moved with surprising agility for a man of his immense size. He led with overhand blows which Marcus could only defend by moving his shield to his left, as the flashing sword of the champion slammed with astonishing force onto the top of his splintering *scutum*. The first strike, almost pulled the shield from his grasp and took a slice from the top of the metal edge.

Barely, beneath the sound that reverberated around the stadium with every strike, Marcus could hear the sound of the big man's breathing. It was not clear and hollow but rasping and hoarse. Each thud of his Gladius sent Marcus backwards and with each step, another massive blow hit his shield.

As he started to pull away his boot slipped on the sand as he desperately tried to reposition it but the sand shifted beneath his foot. He tried to regain his footing but Hilarius moved in quickly, ramming his shield hard into Marcus as he crouched, trying to rise. Using the huge strength from his shoulders, he grabbed the top of the Tirone's shield with his left hand and battered him with his shield until Marcus staggered and fell back. If there was weakness in Hilarius' left side it was not apparent, Marcus reflected briefly, as he scrambled to get out of the way of the charging gladiator.

In a move that appeared only as a blur to Marcus, he felt the edge of Hilarius's shield slam into his sword hand, sending the curved, Thracian handle out of his fingers and across the sand, out of his reach. In a moment, Marcus understood that the giant held two weapons. His sword and his shield. The weight and force of his shield bruised and battered him further, each time it hit him.

'Our brother is fucked' Severus exclaimed, as he put his head momentarily into his hands and then looked at Felix.

Felix watched the contest with horror. Marcus had ignored every piece of advice and training given to him in the past several months. All he could think, as he watched his friend sprawled on the bloodied sand, was his friendly barb he used on him. Dumbhead.

Hilarius was on Marcus in a moment and sensing victory he brought his Gladius up and sent the sword point down into Marcus's exposed left flank where it glanced off his shield and hit his bronze face plate. Marcus instantly saw the tip of the sword penetrate the bronze lattice, but the strength of the helmet stopped it going further.

Marcus tried to get to his feet but under the constant barrage of heavy sword blows combined with the size and strength of the man above him, it forced him harder onto the sand. Marcus let out a shout at the desperation of the moment and tried to regain control of the fight. He finally rose against the barrage to one knee with his shield held high against the onslaught.

Before Hilarius could raise his Gladius again, Marcus, seeing his flank exposed, bunched his hand and slammed his fist into the giant gladiator's side feeling the rib fracture from the force. Then he smacked it as hard as he could again with his knuckled fist. He felt the breath of the big man exhale as he drove yet another heavy punch into his side feeling the ribs give way as the blow landed.

He jumped up as Hilarius pulled back against the blows and decided to move away from him. The big man showed no evidence of pain as he rose, his eyes narrowed and his sword held high. Shakily, but holding his shield firm, Marcus pounced on his sword to pick it up and move back to the fight. He was winded but as his breathing eased, he understood his first lesson of the contest. He needed get at his opponents injured ribs, one way or another.

In the background, Marcus could hear shouts and clapping as the spectators rose with the excitement of the contest.

'Let's see blood!' He heard from one man on the lower tier.

Go, Hilarius. Stick him like a pig!' Shouted another.

He moved his head to rid himself of the sweat from his forehead, that stung his eyes. Momentarily blinded, he moved away from Hilarius as he shook his head to clear the sweat.

'Hilarius, Hilarius. Champion of Rome' Came the chorus from the stadium and in the back of his mind he heard several who called out his name. 'Attilius, win the day.'

'Lie down, boy. It will be easier' Hilarius panted, as he waited for another attack.

During the manoeuvring of the fight they had moved away from the centre towards the area to the left of the gladiator door of the arena and behind him Marcus could hear Felix shouting at him over and over again. *'sinistram est optimus, sinistram est optimus.'*

448

'Not yet' Marcus whispered to himself, as he raised himself up in the air to attack Hilarius with his Gladius aimed at his head. The gladiator moved backwards and this time Marcus started overhead blows against the shield of Hilarius, until the man stopped in mid-stride to hold his ground and exchange strikes.

Held in similar positions, they exchanged blow after blow. The shouts from the stadium increased to the level that could be heard throughout Pompeii. All the spectators rose to their feet as the tension mounted. Screams and shouts poured down into the arena from the stands.

'It does not look good.' Severus said to Felix, who was still shouting out to move to the left.

'This is when Marcus is at his best.' Felix said in return.

'I told him not to trade blows with that man mountain; so why does he keep doing it?' Severus said for anyone who wanted to hear.

The heat of the afternoon sun doused the stadium, as spectators sought more space under the shaded area and those who faced the sun, lay cloth across their head to stop the increasing warmth.

Under the weight of the armour and his shield Marcus could feel sweat pouring off his face and shoulders until his cotton leggings were soaked.

He looked at Hilarius whose torso was drenched with sweat as well and yet the fight went on, blow by blow, changing positions only to strike again. They had been fighting for quite some and the audience became more and more agitated as they looked for an outcome.

Marcus could barely hold against the strength coming from the shoulders of his opponent. For each blow of his Gladius, into the shield of the man before him, he received one in return that almost ripped his shoulder out of its socket from trying to hold his *scutum,* to staunch the power of the glistening blade as it descended onto his shield.

Again, Marcus moved away from close quarter fighting, realising for the first time that Hilarius was breathing hard and much harder than he was. The strikes held a similar force but the man no longer moved with the same speed. He was slowing.

Marcus started to launch himself up and into the gladiator with his Gladius point held at his head and each time he smashed his shield into Hilarius with as much force as he could muster. He retreated and then launched himself again.

Each time, Hilarius stepped back a little from the force of the impact and each time Marcus could hear his breathing increasing and all of a sudden, he saw Hilarius back away to use his sword hand to feel his ribs. He was hurt.

Suddenly, Marcus moved away from where Hilarius was standing and changed his shield to his right hand and then his sword to his left.

'Eh!' Hilarius exclaimed, as he watched Marcus change arms, his sword into his left and his shield to the right. Shield to shield and sword to sword. Immediately, Marcus moved in again, reversing his sword hand as his side and as the shields clashed he slammed the handle of his reversed sword as hard into the point of the man's ribs as brutally as he could muster. Then he moved quickly away. Hilarius grunted and started to bend over, before righting himself again. He was breathing in short breaths and Marcus had seen it many times before. His ribs were broken.

Pulling away again, Marcus tried to regain his breath. How long had they been in contest on the arena? He looked briefly up at the sun that had started its slow descent and he realised it was well over an hour.

He looked up at the box and Laurentius was on his feet with a concerned look on his face and that could only be good news, he thought to himself.

'You, old fuck.' Marcus shouted at him above the crowd. 'My mother could move faster than you, you piece of shit. Champion? Is this the best you can do against a Tirone?'

Finally, the anger in Hilarius took over and he moved hard into Marcus, with blows that resounded off their shields and swords. After the force of each blow, Marcus smashed his shield into Hilarius to stop his advance and moved back again with his left sword arm moving into the open space between Hilarius and his shield, opened flank.

He realised Hilarius was finding it hard to move in any direction. They had moved almost half the space of the arena before Hilarius stopped. He was breathing heavily and he realised that the huge gladiator before him, had difficulty raising his sword arm to meet the blows.

He pulled back to look at Hilarius, who had blood sheeting down his arm from a cut and his right and left ribs held a large, livid bruise from the sword hand strikes. He watched as the giant set himself again and moved forward to attack, moving his shield to his left to protect his broken ribs.

Again, they clashed, and again Marcus moved away but as he pushed back on one leg, Hilarius dropped his sword and sent the point through the side of his shield with enough force to cut through the leggings on Marcus's left leg and open a broad wound on the front. Marcus grunted as he looked down and within a moment, Hilarius was on him.

Using his strength to charge Marcus, their shields smashed together with a thunder that could easily be heard around the stadium. Marcus fell from the force, hitting the ground heavily. With the huge size of Hilarius above him Marcus pulled his shield over him as the blows from the gladiator above, came down with a force he had not experienced in all of his time in Judea. The sound alone was deafening.

For that moment, the world turned in slow motion. Marcus watched as the giant above him pulled his Gladius up for a massive hit and he instantly saw an opening between Hilarius' shield and his right leg and Marcus plunged his sword into the side of Hilarius' knee which sent him backwards with a howl.

As the big man retreated, Marcus moved towards him quickly, starting to circle to the left. As Hilarius send his sword through, Marcus fended with his shield and each time the sword retreated, he stabbed hard towards Hilarius exposed right flank. The grunts and heavy breathing from both men, drowned out by the excited shouts from the amphitheatre, which pulsed down from above.

Finally, the man's flank opened up and Marcus, with a reverse sword hand, smashed the hilt of the sword into his ribs as hard as his tired arm could muster. Again, a loud grunt came from the giant, as he attempted to cover up.

Once again, faintly, in the background Marcus heard the shout from Felix. '*sinistram est optimus!*'

The fight continued with Hilarius moving constantly to his left to defend himself from the curved Thracian sword. Marcus responded by constantly moving to the left, shields clashing as they closed and moved back. Hilarius limping from the bleeding wound on his knee was unable to move quickly. Marcus looked at the man through the haze of swear filled eyes and pulsating tiredness. Whatever happened, he admired him. Hilarius was fighting with broken ribs and a badly, wounded knee.

Suddenly, Marcus felt like he was in the midst of a battle on the plains of Judea as he moved into a familiar pattern of attack. He laid strike after strike against Hilarius and finally, Marcus felt the forgiveness of human

451

flesh. His sword found a position, above the man's right hip and the blade continued through to the hilt until it stopped. He withdrew it only to pull it back again for another strike. The loud shout of pain from Hilarius, echoed off the wall closest to them.

Suddenly, Hilarius started to retreat and finally sank to his knees still holding his shield but his right sword arm loose, shaking and defeated. Pouring blood showed from above his hip where the sword cut had opened the flesh and his right ribs were a single bruise, which reddened as he looked.

Finally, Marcus heard a shout from Hilarius which came out is hoarse whisper as his knees hit the ground.' How... How do you learn to fight like this?' 'By fighting, Rome's enemies.' Marcus panted in return.

The sound of the shouts and barbs from the audience, finally entered his ears as he stepped to Hilarius and lay his sword point on his neck. Despite all the clapping and shouts from the amphitheatre, he could clearly hear the sound of the rasping breaths coming from the big man beneath him.

Marcus stood in front of the fallen champion, with his curved blade point on his neck as he looked over at the referee, who had moved closer to them. Exhausted, Hilarius stayed on one knee, finally falling onto his back with a howl of pain. Blood poured from the wound above his hip and bone showed, protruding from his right knee as his leg lay at a strange angle.

Marcus looked at the referee, who watched Hilarius raise his forefinger to the sky. The act of submission. The referee looked over at Laurentius. He watched scarlet anger spread across Laurentius' face and his wife clapping wildly behind him as did the rest of the inhabitants of the dais.

Marcus stood above Hilarius, his sword point resting on the base of the big man's neck. With body trembling and sweat pouring down his face under his helmet he started to feel his own body for the first time in two hours of brutal combat. His leg ached and finally he dropped to one knee and placed his sword point at the base of the neck of the man beneath him.

He dropped his helmet and felt cap to the ground, followed by his shield and looked at the referee who, in turn looked up at Laurentius who appeared speechless with anger as he peered down from the dais above at the two gladiators. The audience was on their feet, shouting and clapping.

Marcus stood above Hilarius with his black hair cascading down his neck and his body bathed in sweat. The cotton legging on his upper leg was red from seeping blood and exhausted from the fight, he looked down at Hilarius. 'Tell me true, brother. Were you under agreement to end my life.'

Hilarius looked up at him as he pushed his helmet away. He simply nodded.

The stadium erupted as Laurentius raised his hands to quiet them. Around him, Marcus could hear the chant as he finally raised himself shakily to his feet. 'Attilius, Attilius.'

Marcus glanced down at Hilarius, who appeared to be unconscious, due to the loss of blood that still streamed out of his knee and side. For a moment, Marcus felt sympathy for the champion sprawled out on the ground. He fought well and bravely and there was a difference in age and agility. And perhaps, if Hilarius had been younger, the outcome would be different as well.

Marcus looked up at the dais above him as Laurentius raised his hands once again, to stop the shouts. His arms and hands held still as he waited for the clapping to quiet.

'Romans and citizens of Pompeii! By the decree of the Gods, we have before us a new champion of Rome and before you, Marcus Attilius, victor of the contest with Hilarius.'

The crowd around the huge arena in Pompeii cheered again and Laurentius, the richest man in Rome, waited with a snarl, as he looked down at Marcus Attilius. The scene before him was a man standing above a fallen gladiator on the arena with dried blood on his leggings and a dirt streaked face. The muscles on his arms and torso bulged from the exertion of the contest with the man at his feet. In his left hand, the Thracian sword hung from the Gladiators side.

Marcus looked around at the quiet crowd as he watched Laurentius make his plea to the standing spectators. 'So, what say you, Roman citizens. Do we save Hilarius or does he die?' He looked around at the signs made by the thousands who stood around the stadium. Most of the hands were held high with the thumbs up or to the side, as the sign of mercy, whilst others shouted out *'Hilarius occiditis!'*

'Kill Hilarius, kill Hilarius!'

'Mortem?' He questioned, as he listened to the crowd. Most of the spectators held their hands with thumbs up, as they waited.

Laurentius looked around him and finally spread his hands further apart as the crowds quietened down. He had backed Hilarius to punish the young man he hated. Yet, the impossible had happened and the fallen champion of Rome, lay at Attilius' feet with blood seeping out of his leg and his torso black and blue, from the beating the Tirone had given him.

He looked around at the out held hands of the spectators. Most were *pollicem premere*, thumbs up to let the champion gladiator live. There were some who held their thumb turned in the fashion of *pollicem vertere*, to kill but fewer.

To his quick reckoning, he had lost a small fortune. *'Mortem!'* He shouted out. Kill the loser, he thought. How was it possible that this young Gladiator had beaten the champion of Rome? Surely, this was an impossible feat?

Marcus looked up at Laurentius in contempt. He spat blood on the ground from his bleeding mouth and held his gleaming Thracian sword up, point first, towards the man standing on the dais. The audience around the amphitheatre kept clapping and stamping their feet. He turned his attention to the man beneath him on the brown sand and faintly, he heard the man shout.

Marcus held his Thracian sword high in the air and shouted, as hard as his sore body would allow. 'Romans, your *prefect* and your host, Cassius Laurentius, a new senator of Rome, would have you agree to end the life of Hilarius, this great champion, under my sword. I ask you; given the contest you have just witnessed, is this a fair end? I say not!' The crowd hushed as Marcus continued. 'I say not!'

Grasping onto a side beam for support in the Gladiator enclosure, Aetius lay his head against the timber. 'By the Gods, he has done it. He has done it!' He shouted as he grabbed Severus and hugged him. 'Now, he is going to ignore the decision of Cassius Laurentius, in the middle of the arena. The heat has gone to his head!'

Felix, with a broad smile on his face, looked out at his friend, a single figure on the immense arena sand, holding his sword and pointing to the crowd. 'He owns them.' Felix said to Aetius. 'He has them in his palm.' Marcus waited until the thunderous noise calmed down.

'Good citizens of Pompeii; Romans, vote with your feet and if you believe the great Hilarius should survive this contest, stand up and show your opinion.'

Marcus let the Thraex sword fall to his side. Suddenly, his arm felt heavy and unable to lift the curved sword again. He watched as one man, on the lower tier of the massive crowd stood up, with his thumbs up and then another followed him and within moments the whole stadium caught on, as rows and rows of men, women and even children started to stand with their thumbs in the air.

There was hissing at Laurentius, who stood glaring at Marcus and the fallen man beside him. Laurentius, his face scarlet red, gripped the railing until white knuckles showed on his hands.

Marcus walked over to the wall, under the dais and thrust his sword hard into the blood-stained sand and walked back to stand beside Hilarius. 'They are coming to help.' He whispered, as the giant opened his eyes briefly.

In front of the dais and in full view of Laurentius, the shimmering, pitted blade moved barely back and forth as if stuck in a pendulum. He raised his hands to tumultuous applause and walked with his back turned to Laurentius, towards the gladiator door at the other side of the hard, brown sand of the arena.

In the sand, he could still see the mark of his footprints when he walked onto the arena, behind Hilarius, over an hour before.

Behind him a chant began and picked up by the crowd. It worked into a crescendo. *'Taurus, Taurus.'* They shouted and stamped their feet. *'Ortum autem Taurus.* The bull rises! The rise of the bull!'

He entered the gladiator's door marked, *Porta Triumphalis,* the entrance for those who won their contests. When he reached the door, he turned around to see Hilarius, still lying on the sand near the Laurentius dais.

Two attendants appeared, one dressed as Charon, the God of death and one as Mercury, the messenger of the Gods complete with winged heels. They stood over the slumped form of Hilarius and after a signal from the one dressed as Charon, a stretcher came over to pick him up. It took four men to raise the fallen gladiator and finally, he was dumped unceremoniously onto the top of the wooden slats and taken off the arena via the *Porta Sanavari*, the portal for the loser.

455

Aetius stopped him with a hug as he entered the enclosure. 'Not yet, young man, not yet. Go out and raise your hands. The world wants to wallow in your victory.' He pushed Marcus back through the gate.

Marcus nodded, raised his head up and walked back to the standing applause of twenty thousand spectators. He looked over to the other side of the sand and the sword he had thrust out of contempt, into the red-stained sand, held firm, with the afternoon sun reflecting off the polished shaft like a mirror.

FINI

ACKNOWLEDGEMENTS

On publication of this novel there are a number of people that I would like to thank.

My old mate, Joe Lenthen, for his amazing insights into the book. During the initial and later writing of this novel he maintained an extremely positive outlook on the subject matter and the story of Marcus Attilius, as it unfolded. Without his influence I doubt this first novel would have been finished.

The staff at Bobbi Beans, Bulleen, who allowed me to work on the book each day and hardly bothered me except to say hello. Danny and Nick, my thanks and great coffee, as well.

Finally, to my wife, Lee who always allowed me to push off on my own to write this first novel. Her support always proved valuable.

A book of this length requires a large amount of research and there were a number of sources that I used. The internet proved an excellent resource and the second were reference books from the library. Most of the Latin quotes in this novel, First Gladiator of Rome, came from an old text of English to Latin as well as several translation dictionaries, online.

Fortes fortuna iuvat

Robert D Hastings
© 2018

AUTHORS NOTE

For readers who may be interested in history, and in particular the 1st century anno domini, this is a fictional novel of a man who actually lived by the name of Marcus Attilius. Graffiti noting his exploits and probably inscribed by a fan, are there to this day on the Nocerian Gate at the southern end of Pompeii.

Little is known about this Tiro, who beat Hilarius and then another champion by the name of Racius Felix. The feat of defeating two great and very experienced champions might be akin to a novice tennis player beating the world number one and two at a Grand Slam event.

In order to bring the character of Marcus Attilius to the written page it was obviously important to give him the skills to fight Hilarius and his time in Judea with the Fifth legion provided ample experience to achieve that skill and fight the way in which history recorded.

Whilst Marcus Attilius is rated in the 'top ten' of Gladiators, alongside notables such as Spartacus and Spicilus, there is scant information about his life and his exploits, save what is laid on the Pompeii gate. Above all else, he is an interesting character and it is my hope that this novel does him and his extraordinary exploits, justice.

The second book of this series, (The rise of the Bull), offers the final instalment in his life as he continues to train as a gladiator and his match at the finished, Flavian Amphitheatre or Colliseum as it is commonly known.

Made in United States
Troutdale, OR
02/10/2025

28841756R00256